Heartwood

By JoAnn Conner

To Dale –
Enjoy the history!

JoAnn Conner
September 8, 2018

D1707718

Acknowledgments

First and foremost, I give thanks to my mother for her support and encouragement. I regret she did not live to see my first novel published, but I am glad I finished it on what would have been her birthday. I also want to thank Mr. Gary Quistad, my seventh grade teacher, who was the first teacher to tell me I had talent.

Special thanks to Kathi Daley, author in her own right, who generously gave of her time to help me through the writing and publishing process, and for the encouragement of both Ken and Kathi Daley.

Thank you to Dianne Rees for her superb editing, and to Dianne Rees, Mary Oney, and Tamara Wallace for the ratification that the plot was solid. Thank you to Andy Michaud for his help with the cover, and to all my children and grandchildren who give me the inspiration to write.

Preface

This novel is set in post Civil War Bridgeport, California, in the Sierra Nevada Mountains. There are small historical tidbits throughout the novel, such as details about the one dollar gold coin in post Civil War America. Likewise, finding the value of the medicinal plant comfrey and the common treatment for head lice were intriguing.

The story is purely fiction, although some of the characters and incidents in the novel have a basis in historical fact. It was interesting to research how the town of Bridgeport got its name, what business was there after the Civil War, and if they even had a sheriff in 1867. Special thanks to the Mono County Historical Society Newsletter, which I found to be a wealth of information when I wanted to confirm details about Bridgeport in 1867.

Chapter 1

Matthew Raines stood on the porch and finished his last swallow of coffee with satisfaction. He had made a lot of progress on the ranch since he bought it from the widow McKenzie. It had been pretty run down. In fact, the first time he stepped on this very porch, his foot had nearly gone through the rotted wood.

While making his way west after the War Between the States, he had shared camp fires and conversation with trappers and those heading west to find their fortunes in the gold fields. They had told him there was land to be had around the booming mining towns of Bodie and Virginia City. He had come through Virginia City and decided he wanted peace after the war, instead of the rowdy life in a boom town. On his way to Bodie, he had stopped at the general store in Bridgeport to pick up more supplies, and the owners had told him about the widow McKenzie. He decided to ride out to look at the ranch. As soon as the ranch came in sight, Matthew knew it was home. He noted the sagging fence rails and dried up garden, but was excited instead of disappointed. The widow had come out on the porch and watched him approach, shading her eyes. She was a frail woman, with no children and an air of resignation about her. She smiled wanly as Matthew introduced himself and gave her the small package of cakes that Melissa Gruener had sent to her. She told him her few steers had wandered off and her cow had been killed by a mountain lion one night. Her husband had not come back from the war and she had struggled to keep the house maintained alone.

"I'm all done in," she said, looking around her. "We had such dreams…but all I want now is to go back home to what is left of my family." In the end, she gave up and sold out to get just enough money to go back to her family in Ohio. Matthew paid the widow most of the money he had after he and his brother Tim sold their folk's ranch. Maybe he could have gotten it for less, but her sadness and broken spirit touched him deeply. He couldn't help but think of his own parents.

When Matthew came back from the war, he found Ma already gone, and Pa so sick, he had arrived just in time to have a few days with him before he died too. He made sure they were buried under a tree on a knoll above the house, and then wired Tim, who was still up north. They decided it was best to sell the old farm and meet out west to start a new life. Matthew went ahead with half the money and found the ranch. He wired Tim to tell him where he had stopped, and that it had good water, grazing land, and plenty of room for both brothers to build a new life. Matthew had poured months of work into the ranch, rising at dawn and stopping when it got too dark to see what he was doing. Even so, it was not unusual for him to fix a simple supper, and then work on the inside of the house until he fell into bed at night. When Tim arrived, they would build him a house close by and Matthew would be content with the old house. But now, he needed supplies to keep him going.

The day promised to be a hot one, and he knew he had to get started if he was going to make it to town and back before dark. Hanging the cup on a nail outside the door, he stepped to the wagon and checked the small water barrel on the side. "Wouldn't do to lose a wheel and get stuck in this heat without water, now would it Lady?" The Tennessee Walker turned and looked back at him like she understood what he was saying. She felt like family to Matthew, having carried him through some of the worst battles of the Civil War, and they both had the scars to show for it. Come to think of it, she just might be the closest thing to family he had left. Stepping up on the wheel and swinging his six foot frame easily onto the seat of the wagon, he settled his hat on his dark hair, shading his ice blue eyes from the hot sun. His shirt sleeves were already rolled up, revealing well muscled and tan arms. He released the brake and clicked his tongue to signal Lady to step out at a trot, eating up the sixteen miles to the little town of Bridgeport, his nearest neighbors.

He never got tired of the scenery along the way. Matthew remembered the first time he crested the Sierra Nevada Mountains and gazed down at the Walker River Valley. He had been drawn to the area with the stories he had heard of Kit Carson and John Fremont. They followed Jedediah Smith, who was an expert in trapping and leading expeditions. He had spent a full half hour just taking in the rolling green and gold of the valley floor, the rich meadows, and the aspens along the deep stream banks. They were brilliant red and gold, caught the sun, and turned crisp in the September air. Mountains rose on both sides of the valley, some with layers of colors mounting towards the sky as if they were a stack of multicolored flap jacks. Right beside these mountains, you could sometimes see black, porous lava rock, with chunks of heat hardened red, black, or green obsidian littering its slopes. The Piute and Shoshone tribes would carry that obsidian up to trade with their neighbors to the north, the Washoe.

The valleys were lush with green meadows. Evergreens were clustered on some of the hillsides and sprinkled among the aspens in the valleys. Then suddenly, there were washes of brilliantly colored rocks, that looked as if they had been thrown by a giant hand on either side of a sparkling river. It always took his breath away. As a farmer, he had heard of the rich soil and its potential for agricultural success as well as for raising cattle. He and Tim didn't know much about cattle yet, but they knew about farming.

The trip to town gave him time to think about his friends, the Greuner's. Good hearted, old country style German stock that had come to the west to start their dream, they had been his first friends when he came to the area. They had taken him under their wing, with insight in the weather, the country, and the dangers that could come suddenly upon him, especially living alone on the old ranch. It was Melissa who had shown him the leaves of the comfrey plant, and told him of its medicinal value. Tobias, a carpenter before coming to the states, had taught him the art of carefully fitting logs into each other to make a strong, warm home and a solid barn. Matthew had shared his farming background, and Melissa's small kitchen garden was a source of pride for her. She took his advice seriously, and had carrots, potatoes, corn, peas, and beans growing well. This year, she had also planted an apple tree, hoping for future fresh apple pie and then dried apple pie through the winter.

It was close to noon when he crossed the bridge and drove down Main Street. It was actually a good sized town, and the Mono County Courthouse in Bridgeport served as the County Seat. Because of the proximity to the mining camps in Virginia City and Bodie, freight wagons were a common sight, rolling through town. In fact that was how Bridgeport got its name. The freight wagons needed to get over the Walker River, and a bridge was eventually built. Because of the traffic between the mining towns, Bridgeport also boasted the American Hotel, a blacksmith shop, a town doctor, and had the benefit of the Butterfield Stage line that ran through on a pretty regular basis, bringing mail and transporting passengers to other parts of the west. The only business that was not busy was the Sheriff's Office, rarely occupied on a full time basis. The sheriff was also a rancher in the area, and was trying to get a lumber mill started. Since there had never been much need for the law in the small town, it was an arrangement that worked well.

Matthew pulled the wagon up in front of Gruener's General Store, not that it took much effort, as Lady knew the way. She could always expect a treat from the Gruener's, a carrot if they had it, or a little grain. Once, they even gave her a sugar cube, sent by Tobias' family in Germany.

Tobias Gruener was sweeping the walk. Matthew smiled at his big friend as he jumped down and was instantly greeted with a bear hug.

"Matthew! It has been a month since you have been in for supplies!" boomed Tobias. His sandy blond hair was parted down the middle, just as his mustache seemed to part for his big smile, which he was rarely without. "We were beginning to worry that you had fallen from that rotten roof of yours and broken your leg!"

"Hey, she just needs a little work is all!" smiled Matthew, defending his home. The roof did need some work before winter. "I'd ask you to help me fix it, but you might fall right through and make a bigger mess! You're not exactly dainty!" he teased. Tobias roared with laughter.

"I'll leave being 'dainty' to you, my scrawny friend," said Tobias, looking him up and down.

"But I will help you with that roof," he offered. "The good Lord knows you need help with carpentry!" He studied Matthew carefully. "Any word from your brother?" he asked soberly.

"No, not yet," said Matthew, "I can't help but worry at this point." Matthew had wired Tim the other half of the money to scout for small herds for sale to get them started. The last time Matthew heard from Tim, he had found a good deal on a small herd and had found a trail hand, who was fresh from the war himself, to help. Together, they would drive the herd west. He also hinted he had a little surprise for Matthew, but wouldn't tell him what that was all about. That was six months ago; Tim had never made it to the ranch.

Matthew and Tobias walked into the cool interior of the store, laughing at the squeals of little Greta as she ran towards Matthew. The auburn curls of the three year old bounced as she ran and grabbed his legs. Her rosy cheeks and bright smile always touched Matthew's heart.

"Uncle Matt, Uncle Matt, up, up!" she squealed, throwing her hands up to the air. He had been given the honorary status of uncle for the bright eyed girl, who would probably never know her blood uncles. He lifted her high in the air as her mother followed, waiting for her hug. Melissa beamed as her daughter laughed and giggled. Matt threw her up and caught her, enjoying their game.

"Well, I swear, if you get any thinner, we'll just set you in the garden and put a little hay in your shirt to fill you out!" Melissa scolded. "I need a new scare crow!"

Matthew responded by setting Greta down and picking Melissa up, spinning her around before he set her down. "Still strong enough to spin you around!" he laughed. He always felt at home with this family.

Melissa's light brown hair was tied back at the nape of her neck with a yellow ribbon, and she looked thinner and a little tired to Matthew. But she was just as good natured as her husband, and she was always quick to offer a meal or refreshment. "Come on now, let me get some good food in you while I can! Lunch is ready!" She led the way to the back of the store where their living quarters began. The table was set with four places, no surprise for a grinning Matthew. Melissa was a good cook and the stew smelled delicious.

"Looks like the garden is doing well," Matthew commented,"peas, carrots, and potatoes!" The stew looked tantalizing, and he was hungry!

"Thanks to your expert farming advice, we have the best crop ever this year!" she beamed. "Oh, I forgot the pepper," Melissa said as she started to sit down. "We just got a new, smaller grinder and it adds a little bite to the taste."

"I'll get it," Matt said, jumping up.

"It's under the counter," Melissa said.

Stepping into the store area and reaching under the counter for the pepper grinder, movement to his right caught his eye and he turned his head to see a young woman standing near the bins of potatoes and apples. She turned slightly towards him as sunlight, through the window, glistened on the strawberry blond of her hair. Taller than most women, she was slender, and, Matthew thought, a little pale, considering it was summer.

Women in that part of the country were scarce, and this one was young. She hadn't noticed him, and as he was about to offer to help, she turned again and he saw her hand dart into the apple bin and disappear into the pocket of her skirt with two apples!

His boot scraped on the floor as he shifted his weight to get a better look at her. Startled at the sudden noise, she turned suddenly, saw him standing there and jumped, staring at him. It was then he noticed she had a flour bag in her other hand, with goods from the store! She stood frozen for a second, then grabbed a couple of potatoes, threw them into the bag, and backed towards the door.

"Can I help you?" Matthew asked her, stepping forward. Was she afraid of him? Or was she just afraid to get caught stealing! The woman kept backing towards the door, her deep blue eyes wide, and then suddenly turned. Melissa's shawl hung on a peg by the door and as the woman ran to get outside, she paused, and glancing back defiantly at Matthew, yanked the shawl off the peg and ran out the door with that in her arms as well.

"Hey!" Angry at the brazen thievery, Matthew ran after the woman who had just robbed his friends. She was fast, but Matthew had almost caught up with her when she stopped two men coming around the corner and yelled for help.

"That man tried to rob me!" she cried and pointed at Matthew. Stunned, he stopped in his tracks as the two men started towards him, intent on teaching him some manners when it came to women.

"We don't take to men abusing women out here, mister!" said the shorter one as he swung at him, while the other moved around behind him. Dodging the punch and trying to explain, he glanced at the corner just in time to see the woman looking back at him before she disappeared around the building.

The distraction cost him, and he tasted blood as the taller of the two men landed a punch that caught the corner of his mouth, splitting his lip. Matthew stepped into him, grabbed him by the collar, and flipped him over his hip onto the ground. The second man drew back his arm, intending to take advantage of his friend's misfortune. Suddenly, Tobias was there and caught the man's arm in mid-swing, and put it in a vise like grip that made him wince.

"I came to see what was taking you so long to find the pepper, and here you are brawling in the street! What is going on?" demanded the big German store keeper.

"He tried to rob that lady," declared one of the men.

"What lady?" asked Tobias, scanning the street. There was no one else around. The two cowboys looked around in confusion.

"Where'd she go?" asked the taller of the two. He looked at his friend, who shrugged his shoulders.

"Durned if I know," the shorter man replied, "I was too busy with the big feller here to pay attention."

With Tobias in the mix, the two men listened as Matthew explained that he was actually chasing the woman because she had robbed his friends.

"Well, we're sure sorry, mister." The two cowboys apologized and walked away, shaking their heads.

"Come back inside, my friend," said Tobias. "Melissa does not like to see her food get cold. Indeed, she will be more upset over that than the goods stolen from our store."

But Matthew knew his friends were also struggling and the store was barely surviving. The freight companies coming through had stopped some of the miners coming in for supplies and there hadn't been any newcomers for awhile. As he stepped up on the walk, he gave one last glance back to the corner. He was going to do his best to find that woman and demand she pay his friends back for the goods she stole.

Melissa jumped up when Matthew and Tobias came in the room. "Good Lord! What have you two been up to!" She grabbed a clean cloth and dampened it at the sink under the pump. "Sit down," she commanded Matthew, as she drew his chair back from the table a bit. She took the damp cloth and dabbed at his lip, clucking her tongue as Matthew told them about the woman who had robbed them. "I send you for pepper and you go off chasing women!"

"Hey, she was robbing you!" protested Matthew.

"Shhh! You'll break that lip open again and I will not have you bleeding in my stew!" She carried the cloth back to the sink. "Next time I'll get the pepper myself!" she said as she scooted up to the table and started to serve the stew. Matthew and Tobias exchanged a look over her head, hiding their smiles. They knew that was just Melissa's way of saying she worried about them. She dished up hearty servings and passed them to the men, who dug in quickly. Several minutes went by before the silence was broken.

"I haven't seen anyone in town that looks like that," Melissa finally said. "We get lots of miners and cowboys through here, but I would have noticed a pretty young woman new in town, and sooner or later, most everyone comes in our store."

"I haven't seen her either, and no one has mentioned a new family," said Tobias. I'll ask around the town. Doc might know," he said hopefully.

"Well, I hope most people who come into your store come to buy, and not steal!" said Matthew, pulling his chair closer to the table. He knew, as kind as they were, they were struggling themselves. He was determined to find that woman and when he did, there would be a reckoning!

Chapter 2

Matt kept his head down and continued to lash the fencing together with the rawhide strips. The posts were well fitted, but the winter wind could be harsh, and he would rather brace the poles now than deal with a broken corral in the middle of winter.

Only his eyes were raised in the direction of the hills to the north as a lone rider wound his way slowly down the slope towards the ranch. Something was off, and his eyes flicked to his right to reassure him that his rifle was within easy reach. He was relentless in the cleaning and loading of his guns every morning before he walked out of the house. Too many years on the trail and in the war had taught him that could be the difference between life and death. Careless men were dead men.

He carefully scanned the gullies and rocks, but he saw no sign of any hidden guns waiting to ambush him as his attention was fixed on the rider. The rider was a man, but he was coming from the direction where there was ample water and grass, yet he rode as if he could barely sit in his saddle, like a man who had been without food or water for days. He reached over and slipped the dog headed knife back in its sheath on his belt. There was a deep gulley on the north side of the ranch, between the rider and Matt. As soon as the man's head disappeared below the top of the gulley, Matt grabbed his rifle and ran to the other side of the ranch house. Kneeling beside the wall of the house and partially hidden by the water trough in front of the steps, Matt trained his rifle on the gulley and waited. And waited. The man should have come up out of the gulley by now. Fifteen minutes passed, then twenty. He still did not see any sign of any other riders and decided the man must be alone.

Matt faded back into the tree line behind the house and quickly traversed the side of a small hill, putting him above the gulley.

The horse stood still in the bottom of the gulley, trailing his reins. It was a mustang, a beautiful horse, the breed known for being able to go at least three to four days without food or water before they would fail. This one appeared to be a little ragged, but doing better than the man at the end of the reins. The man was crumpled in a heap on the ground, as if he had simply fallen from the horse with no effort the break his own fall. Matthew climbed down the embankment and examined the stranger. One of his hands was still loosely wrapped in the reins. Matthew patted the horse on the muzzle.

"Good boy," he said to the horse. If the horse had continued moving, the man would have been dragged, at least for several yards, before his hand came loose.

The young man looked like he had been at least two days without water. His breathing sounded raspy and his lips were cracked and dry. He was sunburned in spite of his hat, and the effect of the blood loss would be magnified if he was too weak to take water. Again, Matt scanned the surrounding hills for any sign of movement. Nothing else stirred. He listened and heard the chirping of a bird in the tree next to him and saw a prairie dog sitting outside his hole. Reassured, he tried to see how bad the wounds were, but the dried blood caused the shirt to stick to the man's body and Matthew did not want to risk breaking open any clotting that had taken place until he was in a better position to stop the bleeding.

The stranger was dressed simply, but like he knew his way around a trail. His blond hair was matted with more blood that had run down and caked on his face. That wound looked to be a crease in his scalp. The wound that brought him down was in his side, shot clean through just below the rib cage. The blood from another flesh shot at the top of the shoulder ran together with the blood from the side, soaking the left side of his shirt. Matt reached under the man's arms and found that while he himself was a strong man, handling the dead weight of the unconscious man took some effort, and it was several minutes before he had him slung securely over the back of his horse and headed at a walk to the house. This boy needed some work before he lost any more blood, but if they went too fast, the wounds could break open again.

Matt wrestled the unresponsive man into the house as gently as he could and laid him on the extra bed he had built, in preparation for Tim and him to share the house for awhile. He cut the man's shirt off and cleaned his face, while waiting for the water to boil to clean the other wounds. He kept his ears tuned to any sound out of the ordinary. Years of living alone and being in dangerous conditions taught him to pay attention to odd sounds.

He brought a cup of water to the bed and carefully spooned a little into the man's mouth. By then the hot water was ready, and he began the slow process of easing the man's shirt from his body and tending to the wounds. Two hours later, he picked up the wash basin of bloody water, the needle he used to stitch the stranger up, and was about to walk outside to clean up when the man started murmuring in his sleep. Matt set the basin down and walked back to listen. Maybe he could get a clue as to who this young man was and who wanted to kill him. "Boss! Look out!" the young man yelled, trying to sit up, even though he was obviously not conscious. Matt held him down, afraid he would rip the stitches out. For a brief few seconds, the young man's eyes opened and stared at Matt. "Sarah," he gasped, and then collapsed back into unconsciousness.

Matthew stood looking down at the man. From what he said, there had been another man and a woman. Where were they now? And where was the man or men who had shot him? He looked at the young man's six shooter in the holster on the small table beside the bed. There was blood on the holster and the handle of the gun. He stepped over and took the gun out of the holster. Checking the cylinder of the revolver, he found there was only one bullet in the chamber when he took it off the young man. There were several cartridges missing from the loops in the belt. "Sure looks like you put up a fight, young feller," he thought, looking down at the man on the bed. "But who were you fighting and why?" he said aloud. Would they come looking for him? He hoped the young man would recover, but he was badly wounded and had lost a lot of blood. Matt wondered how many days and nights the young man had actually been wandering before he got to the ranch. He would need to be extra vigilant around the ranch until he got some answers.

He cleaned up and checked on the young man again. He was sleeping peacefully for now. Matthew watched him for a few minutes and then turned and went outside. The man's horse was still standing where he left it, and looked mournfully at Matthew as he approached.

"Come on boy, "he said, patting the horse on the muzzle gently. "It's your turn, "he said as he took the reins and led the mustang to the barn. First, he led the horse to water and watched as he drank his fill. Horses didn't over drink, even when they were really thirsty. They knew to pace themselves. Next, he led the horse to a stall and removed the bit and bridle, putting some grain in the bucket in front of the horse. While the horse ate, Matthew removed the saddle and blanket. The horse had not been cared for in days; his mane was matted, the hair under the saddle blanket was stiff and coarse with sweat and dirt, and his tail was sticky with burrs from the brush. Matthew curried and combed and talked to the horse while he worked. It took the better part of an hour, but the horse nuzzled him when he was done, as if to say thank you. Matthew smiled and walked to the door that led to the pasture. Clicking his tongue, he coaxed the horse to the door. The mustang looked out at the horses in the pasture and whinnied, then looked at Matthew before he trotted off to join his new friends.

"You deserve some time off," he said. He stood for a few minutes and watched the horses frolicking in the pasture. They were such beautiful, graceful creatures. Lady was loyal, and had saved his life more than once. He turned and went back to the house after shutting the barn door. It wouldn't hurt to be safe; it wouldn't do to have the stranger wake up and have his horse gone.

Chapter 3

Matt sat in the shade on the porch step and worked the rawhide with his knife to cut strings. He used them prolifically around the ranch to support and tie any number of things together, and he was running short. Any good cowboy also kept a stock in his saddle bags. You never knew when you might have to tie something back together out on the range. He looked out across his ranch with some satisfaction. The fences were mended, the corral was in good shape, and he had enlarged it this past summer. He had extended the corral so it attached to a new opening in the side of the barn; if he had to be away for a few days, the stock could get in the barn for shelter and out for fresh grass and water. He had dug a rock lined ditch from the stream at the back of the property and created a small catch basin at the edge of the corral. The small garden he had planted with corn, potatoes, and carrots was doing well. He had harvested some herbs from down near the creek and had a good supply of dried onion, wild turnips, and some wild mint for winter tea. Best of all, he found a patch of comfrey growing in the sand near the stream. He had harvested as many of the medicinal leaves as he felt was possible without damaging the plants. They were as good as gold in a country where the plant could be used to fight breathing ailments and could be applied directly to a wound to draw out infection.

He turned when he heard the creaking of the door hinge. I could oil that he smiled to himself, but it made for a fine alarm to anyone coming or going through that door. The stranger stood weakly in the doorway, leaning against the jamb.

"Well, good to see you awake and up." Matt greeted as he tied the rawhide strings into bunches of a dozen each. Matt studied the man; he still looked much too pale.

"How long have I been here?" the man asked.

"A week," Matt answered, and put down the knife. "We had best get you sitting down before you fall," he said, looping an arm around the man's waist. "You lost a lot of blood," he said as he lowered him onto the bench just outside the front door. Matt stepped inside to the stove and poured two strong cups of coffee. Coming back out on the porch, he handed one to the young man and sat back down on the step. The man carefully sipped it, his hands still shaky.

"Thanks! I haven't tasted coffee this good in awhile!" He looked at the cup. "At least I don't think I have." He shook his head.

Matthew looked at him curiously, wondering about the head wound. They sat without talking for several minutes, enjoying the coffee and the quiet beauty of the day. Matthew began cutting the piggin strings again, thinking it never hurt to have some extra laid by.

"That's some knife," the young man said, watching Matthew. "I don't think I've ever seen anything like it."

Matthew looked at the knife, running his fingers over the iron dog head that topped the handle. "My father made it," he said. "He made one for me and one for my brother. Only two like it in the world. The head is the image of his favorite dog. Old Buck got between Dad and a rabid coyote. Dad grabbed his rifle and shot the coyote, but it cost Buck his life. The coyote had done too much damage. He died saving Dad's life from that coyote." He returned the knife to its home on his belt, and stood to put a couple bunches of the piggin strings in his saddle bags.

"Got a name?" he asked, as he stepped back out on the porch.

"Paul Warner, sir." he said. "Guess I owe you my life. Thanks."

"I'm Matt," he said, lifting his cup. Paul nodded. His eyes swept the landscape as if they were searching for something. Finally, he looked at Matt.

"Where am I?" asked Paul.

"This is my ranch," answered Matthew, "I named it Heartwood. We are about sixteen miles north of Bridgeport."

"Why did you name it Heartwood?" asked Paul. "I mean, is there a story behind the name?"

"Well," smiled Matt, "it seemed to fit. Heartwood is the dead part of a tree, the core in the middle. But the rest of the tree is still alive and growing. I bought it from a widow who lost her husband in the War Between the States. Seemed like the dream she and her husband had started was like the dead core of the tree, but the ranch still had some life. I've worked hard to grow the ranch into a strong, living thing, just like the outer part of a tree. So, Heartwood." Matthew looked at Paul and smiled. It seemed kind of mushy when he said it out loud, but that was the story.

Paul nodded, and looked like he was thinking. "I like it, he finally said. "Makes a lot of sense." They sat watching the clouds drift over their heads for several more minutes.

"Feel like telling me what happened?" Matthew asked, breaking the silence.

"We were driving a small herd ..." Paul stopped for a minute and rubbed his hands over his face. "I don't know where we came from." His face took on an ashen hue, and he looked panicked for a few moments. "Guess the one that caught me in the head made me a little fuzzy," he said, gingerly touching the bandage around his head. "The boss was scouting out front of the herd and his wife was driving the wagon. I had dropped back a little to catch up a few strays. I saw the men riding up over the hill and tried to warn him, but he couldn't hear me. They shot him. He never had a chance, just shot him in the back, three of them opened up on him. I...can't remember what any of them looked like!"

"Sometimes it takes awhile for everything to come back," said Matthew. "I knew a woman once, the only survivor of an Indian attack on the group of wagons she was on. Near as we could figure, they kept her for days. But she couldn't even remember she was married." Matthew studied Paul.

"Sometimes it comes back and sometimes it doesn't. But, you

do the best you can." Paul sat, staring at the boards of the porch for several minutes. He nodded his head up and down slowly, as if trying to understand.

"I think I remember his wife riding away on a horse. I tried to keep the wagon between her and the men and I started shooting to draw them away from her. Two of them came after me and the third one rode after her. I shot at him first and I think I winged him. God, I hope she got away." He licked his lips and looked at his boots. Matthew let him take his time. "They got a few into me and I fell. I guess they thought I was dead. I came to, but I didn't know how I got there. My horse was standing right there waiting for me. Good horse – came back for me. Then he brought me here." Paul closed his eyes for a few minutes and rested his head on the wall behind him.

Matt thought for a minute that he had fallen asleep sitting up, but after a few minutes, Paul opened his eyes and sat up again. "I just can't remember what she looked like," he said. "I sorta remember what happened, but I can't see any faces." He shook his head, clearly uncertain. "Sorry," he smiled wanly. "I feel so tired!"

"Take your time," said Matt, "you can finish later if you need to rest." Paul shook his head.

"No, I need to tell you everything in case…" he stopped. "I managed to climb up in the saddle and started in the direction I thought I sent the boss' wife, but I couldn't remember which way she went. The herd was gone, I figured they stole them too. The boss was dead. I managed to roll him in a bank and close some dirt over him. Pushed a small rock on top and marked it, in case we ever wanted to go back, we might find him and give him a proper burial. That did me in, and I passed out again. When I woke up, it was morning again and I managed to climb in the saddle. I couldn't remember what to do." He hung his head and rubbed his hands over his face.

"I wanted to track her, but I kept fading in and out. Finally, I just wrapped the reins around my hands and just tried to stay on my horse. First day or two I managed to drink some water and give some to my horse. Lots of grass he picked at, but don't know how long I went without eating. I don't know how many days I wandered out there." He shook his head and searched the surroundings with his eyes. "I hate to think of her out there alone."

"You called out in your sleep for Sarah. Is that the name of the boss' wife?"

Paul looked like he was concentrating for several minutes, starting to speak, then stopping. Finally, he shook his head. "I don't know. I just don't know," he said, looking desperately at Matthew.

"Don't worry about it now. It will come to you when you are ready." But Matthew was not as sure as he sounded. Sometimes people who had been through a terrible experience never did regain their memory of the incident.

They talked awhile longer about the landmarks Paul remembered. Matt had a good idea of the direction he had come from and after awhile, he sat quiet. Paul described the horse she was riding when she ran from the outlaws, but he couldn't remember what the woman looked like. . The way Paul described her, he had respect for her. Could she be the woman in the store? He looked at Paul, and thought about asking him, but the young man was barely able to keep his eyes open.

"Come on, let's get you back to bed before you pass out."

"I'm ok, I need to saddle up and go try to find her." Paul looked helplessly around, turning his head from side to side, with a confused look on his face. Matt looked at him, his hands still shaky and his face pale and drawn. The kid had gumption, that was for sure!

"I'll ride out the way you came tomorrow and see if I can find any sign." You won't do her or me any good if you try to get on a horse now. You're too weak." Paul looked at him and Matt could see a mixture of understanding and frustration on his face. "Someone needs to stay here and check on the stock every couple of days." Matt said, which was true, but it also gave the man an honorable way to postpone the search. "Think you can watch things here?"

"Yes sir," Paul said. Matt wasn't so sure, but if he left the stock fed and the door to the pasture open, they could get in the barn. There was water and grass in the pasture, so they wouldn't need much tending.

"Come on," Matt said, gripping Paul by the good arm and helping him up. "Why don't you take a nap while I fix us something to eat. Let's get some food in you and get you another night's sleep before I leave you on your own for a few days."

Two hours later, Paul managed to sit up to the table and put away a fair amount of stew and some coffee, but Matt could see the young man was barely keeping his eyes open. The nap had not been enough, he was still too weak.

"Why don't you go ahead and hit the bunk," said Matt after dinner. "I'll clean up here."

"If you don't mind…" said Paul, staggering from the table and falling on the bunk. His eyes closed as soon as his head hit the pillow.

Matthew woke up to the sound of Paul crying out in his sleep. He was sweating and feverish again, and Matthew checked his bandages while he slept. He was worried. The wound in his side was inflamed and oozing a yellow pus. He wondered about the wisdom of leaving him alone right now. After hearing Paul's story, he was worried about the woman as well, but he was also concerned about the young man laying there on the bunk. He might very well die if left alone right now, and Matthew might not even find her. If she was still alive.

Matt spent the next two days watching Paul, trying to get beef tea into him, and cleaning his wounds. Paul ran a fever and sweated and tossed, sometimes talking while he was unconscious. It was always about the shooting, crying out the name Sarah a few times, or his boss being ambushed. Matthew cleaned the wounds and changed the bandages several times a day, putting fresh comfrey poultices on the inflamed areas. On the third day, Paul woke up and without fever. He was still very pale, but the wound had stopped oozing and looked less angry. He was upset when Matthew told him he had been out for another two days.

"She could be dead by now!" he said with accusation in his voice.

"And so could you, if I had left." Matthew saw the guilt in Paul's face as soon as he said the words. "I'll leave in the morning, if you are still on the mend," he promised. "She sounds like a strong woman. I'll bet she is fine and maybe even found help by now. She might be looking for you!" He smiled as he spoke to Paul, reassuring the young man. He wished he could believe his own statements.

Chapter 4

Matthew was up before daylight the next morning, packing saddlebags with food and extra ammunition. He didn't plan to be gone more than a couple of days, but in this country, it was best to be prepared. If he did find sign of the woman, he might be gone longer or need more provisions to boost her strength before they could get back to the ranch. Paul had slept well, but Matthew cautioned him about trying to do too much too soon. "The weather is still mild, so the stock should be fine. I've set it up so they can come and go into the barn for shelter. Just keep an eye out for mountain lions and take care of yourself." He walked over to the fire place and took down his old Remington rifle and checked it. He dug some extra cartridges out of a box on the mantle and put them in a small pouch on the table. "Take the rifle outside with you when you sit on the bench, and put the ammunition in your pocket or take the pouch. You can't move fast enough yet to be far away from the rifle. We haven't had any trouble with the Piute for some time, but if you see a mountain lion, just shoot it when you get the chance." He started to walk out the door, then turned back. "Rifle pulls a little to the left."

"Thanks," said Paul. "I'll be alright." He sat on the bench outside the door and watched as Matthew rode away. "Find her, Matt, please!" he yelled as Matt passed the corral. Matt waved and nodded. It was a big country, but he sure was going to try.

As he rode, Matt reminded himself that the Walker River Valley, north of the little town of Bridgeport, was a beautiful stretch of California, dry and hot in the summer, but it could kill quickly in the sudden winter snow that was common in this part of the Sierra Nevada Mountains.

Matthew had listened well to Tobias and trappers he had met in the area. He built a small line shack about eight miles from his ranch, pretty much half way between his ranch and the town. If he had to go to town in the winter, or some other hapless traveler needed it, the shack would be there. Heartwood could be repaired while he lived there, no matter what the weather, but a well stocked line shack could mean the difference between life and death if a cowboy were to get caught in the open too far from the homestead or town. For that reason, Matt had made the shack a first priority and added a stock of cut wood, a few pots, and a store of coffee, jerky, and flour.

He admired the tall mountains that surrounded the valley and paid close attention to the growth of brush and the way the water carved gullies in the landscape. When Tim arrived with the herd, that knowledge of the terrain would be critical in expanding the ranch.

Paul had ridden from the north. If Matthew did not find any sign of the woman before he reached the line shack, he might have to look towards Bishop Creek, the next settlement to the north. Beyond that, lay Genoa, Carson City, Virginia City and the mining camps. Could she have gone that far? If so, they may never find her.

Lady plodded lightly through the high desert sage, fragrant with a smell that reminded Matthew of wild honey. Matthew, trusting Lady's instincts, let his thoughts drift. His mind wandered to the towns to the north, starving for beef. When Tim arrived with the small herd, they could start supplying the camps with cattle. They could build a fine ranch with crops to store for winter, even in the short growing season. They had been farmers before the war, with a small amount of stock, but he knew they could grow. With the water at Heartwood, they could get to where they could sell some of their crops as well. He was worried about Tim, he should have heard something from him by now. If he did not show up in the next few weeks, Matt would go looking to see if he could find any sign of him before it got too far into autumn.

A glint caught his eye and he turned his head to see a sheen of dew dripping and sparkling in the early morning sun. The golden strawberry light brought his thoughts to the woman in the store. His jaw set and he began working on the puzzle of her whereabouts. Was she alone? He had not seen a horse, so how far could she have gone? Neither Tobias nor Melissa had ever seen anyone like her in their store before. Newcomers were noticed, and a pretty young woman would have been the topic of gossip as soon as she got to town. There was no ring on her finger, so she might not be married. What kind of woman wandered the west alone? The answer that came to mind made the bile rise in his throat. But what if it was the woman Paul sought? Could she have a problem with her memory, like Paul? He vowed to find her; she couldn't hide very long and he wanted his friends to get some kind of payment for their goods. Paul needed answers too. He shook his head. Suddenly, his simple life was very complicated. Matthew pressed on through the day, stopping only twice to let Lady drink and nibble a bit of the wild grass. If this woman was out here, she would not last long alone, in spite of what he had told Paul. Paul's description did not speak of many supplies being stored on the extra horse and she would not have had time to prepare. He rode in wide sweeps, looking for any sign of tracks, broken bushes, horse droppings, or anything else that might give him a direction for the missing woman. He was slowly closing the gap between the ranch and the line shack. He began to think about that. What if the men who robbed them were there? Could the woman from the store have found the shack? It would be so easy if the woman was in the shack, but that was too much to hope.

The sun was close to dropping below the horizon when he came up on the ridge above the shack. There was no smoke coming from the chimney, but even from his vantage point near the top of the ridge, Matt could see someone had stacked a fair amount of wood beside the door. It hadn't been there a month ago when he rode this way. Could be some cowpokes way of saying thank you for the shelter, but Paul's story made him more cautious. Even outlaws abided by the creed of survival and being grateful for a shelter provided. Could be a thief had holed up in the line shack, and might still be around. He reined Lady in and backed her down the far side of the hill again. Then, dismounting, he crept to the crest of the hill, keeping low. Someone had been in the line shack. Were they still there? Were they friendly? Could they be the group that attacked Paul, and were they coming back? He thought about all the options, and decided if it was the woman from the wagon or the woman from the store, they might not come in to the shack if his horse was there. If it was the outlaws, and they came back, he would be trapped in the shack. Matthew sighed. "Guess it means a cold night on the ground for us, Lady." He led her over to a couple of boulders strewn closely together, forming a wind break. He picketed Lady close to him, but in a patch of tender grass. He decided he couldn't risk a fire, so he laid out his blankets and then sat in the dark, listening and looking at the stars while he munched on a cold biscuit and a piece of jerky. At least the weather was still fairly mild. It would be chilly tonight, but it wasn't raining or snowing. "At least there is that!" he said to Lady, then wrapped himself in his blanket and tried to sleep.

Chapter 5

Matthew woke early the next morning and crawled to the top of the hill. He lay, stomach down, in the damp grass watching the shack until he decided there was still no one there. Riding quietly around the hill to approach the shack from the back, Matt was alert to any sound or movement that might indicate someone was inside and watching from the window in the back of the small building. Tying Lady to a tree out of sight, he crept up to the back window at an angle, making less of a target to any one bent on an ambush. He listened for several minutes, but still heard nothing. Carefully, he raised his head to peek in the window. No movement. Still, he eased his gun out of his holster and moved carefully to the front of the cabin. He pushed the door of the small shack open slowly. Nothing moved, no sound came from within. It was cold, with no fire in the stove. Certain the shack was empty, he holstered his gun and walked carefully inside. There was not much in the small space, a simple bed frame he had built in the corner near the fireplace, a straw stuffed mattress of sorts, and a few old blankets.

But the blankets were no longer folded at the end of the bed. They were neatly pulled up, like someone had made the bed, like someone was planning to come back soon and sleep the night.

He stepped to the side of the window and surveyed the landscape again for movement. Satisfied he was still alone, he looked around the cabin for a sign that would tell him if this was some lost or weary rider looking for a few days of rest, or if this was someone on the wrong side of the law.

He moved cans on the shelf near the stove, and found a can of peaches and a small bag of sugar someone had contributed to the food stock, but nothing out of the ordinary. No hidden ammunition or anything else that did not belong. Turning, his eye caught something under the bed. Getting down on his knees, he reached under and pulled the small canvas bag out in the open. He opened the bag, careful to move the contents so no one would know they had been inspected.

Stunned, Matthew rocked back on his heels. This was women's clothing! Had the woman from the wagon stayed here? Or, could it be the woman from the store? There was no sign of anything that would indicate a man had been here. Realization overcame him and his mouth set in a hard line. If it were the woman from the wagon, she would have stayed close to the cabin knowing someone would eventually come, or she would have rested and continued on to the town. She would not have left her clothing there. It had to be the woman from the store! Anger threatened to push him to throw her things outside, but that would warn her to stay away, and he wanted badly to catch her and make her pay for what she had done to his friends. Sooner or later, she would come back and he would be waiting. He decided to sleep out on the hill, in case she came back. He didn't want her to see his horse and shy away.

Matthew woke with the sun peaking over the ridge. Stiff from sleeping on the frosted ground for two nights, he turned slowly to look at the cabin. Nothing had changed.

"Damn," he growled to himself. "Where the hell is she?" he knew he couldn't stay another day waiting for her to return. There were chores at the ranch and he had left Paul alone too long. The young man wasn't strong enough to take care of himself and feed the stock every day. He was sure she would have come back by now. He had walked in slow, ever-widening circles around the shack, looking for any sign. There were some blades of grass tromped down a bit off to the north, but a herd of deer had come through, churning up the ground enough that he couldn't find any single set of tracks moving away.

Grumpy from the days of dry camp and cold nights on the ground, he slung the saddle over Lady's back and cinched the belt tight. Rolling his blanket, he tied it behind his saddle and swung into place.

"Might as well go on down and make some hot coffee," he said to Lady. Once inside, he did a more careful survey to check what supplies had been used by random travelers. The wood outside the door had been restocked, and the peaches and sugar would be appreciated. Wandering cowboys tended to share what they could, grateful for what had been left for them. The coffee and flour were low though, and he would need to replenish both of them before winter. Might add some beans too, in case someone got caught here for a few days with no food.

He took his own supplies off the horse and shaved off some bacon in a pan, then mixed up some flour with water and fried that up in the bacon grease for a tastier version of hardtack. He used the coffee he had packed in and left the stock that was at the cabin for the next traveler.

After breakfast, he cleaned up and took one more look around the little shack. Climbing into the saddle, he turned Lady to the east and began to look for tracks or some sign. Where could a woman be out here? Had the outlaws that shot her husband found the woman too? And who was the woman that robbed his friends? Where was she? Was there some new homestead in the area he didn't know about?

He spent the day searching to the north east. He came upon an encampment late in the afternoon, where it appeared several riders had stayed. But he could find no trail that looked like one horse carrying a woman. It felt like trying to find a needle in a haystack, but he could not give up yet. Then there was Paul and his ranch. He had been away too many days. He needed to go back, and then go out again, maybe with some help from the Sheriff. He shook his head. Women were still scarce in this part of the west, and here he was looking for two of them!

He turned Lady back towards the ranch. With luck, he would be home before the moon came up and he could sleep in his own bed tonight, even for a few hours.

Chapter 6

Sarah hated stealing. Even when she told herself she was
keeping a tally and planned to repay everything she took when
she found TC's family, it just didn't sit right with her sense of
honesty. She had never stolen anything in her life until a few
weeks ago. .She was just so afraid of letting anyone see the
gold she had in her saddle bags. Tim told her not to tell anyone
they had it. They had confided in their trail hand after she and
Tim had come up with the idea to hide part of the gold in a
small box on the wagon, and part of it under her clothing in a
pouch so it looked like she was pregnant. Poor sweet Paul, he
was so trusting and naive. He hadn't seemed to notice the lump
under her clothing was getting bigger. They had not told him
yet that they were expecting a baby. But someone, probably the
banker, had told someone else they were carrying gold. Sarah
didn't know where the men were who had killed her husband,
and they could be in this town. What if they saw her? They
must know by now that the gold in the box was not all of it.
They might kill her or little TC. If her husband were here… she
clamped her teeth tight against the tears trying to slip out of her
eyes and down her sun burned cheeks.
"Stop it, Sarah," she scolded herself. "He isn't coming back,
and neither is Paul. It's up to me." She looked over the top of
the ridge at the barn below. Lying on her stomach, she had
watched for over an hour as the sun slowly came over the
mountain. She was sure everyone was still sleeping. Scooting
backwards until she was well below the crest of the hill, she
stood and walked to her Appaloosa. She gazed at the sweet
little boy sleeping soundly in the improvised carrier, wrapped
warmly in the shawl she had stolen from the store in town. TC
had been so excited, waiting to be a father. They hadn't told
anyone before they started west, it was their secret. They
hadn't even told Paul, their hired trail hand. And now her
husband was dead. Well, it was up to her now!

She swung into the saddle and checked the ties that kept little TC junior secured to the papoose board and the side of the horse.

Carefully, she made her way around the hill to the back of the barn. She had to be quick; there was no telling when the hands would wake and start their chores. Swinging down, she looked at little TC again. He was a good baby, and rarely cried. He usually awoke, looked around, and smiled at whatever he saw, waiting patiently for his mother to notice he was awake and tend to his needs. He was still sleeping, but if he awoke and started to cry for any reason, the sound would carry in the clear air. She couldn't risk being caught; she didn't yet know who could be trusted.

Sarah crept up to the big door and listened. There were no sounds, other than the soft snuffle of a horse in the barn. Quickly, she opened the door of the barn just enough to slip through. She stood, letting her eyes adjust to the dim interior. Four horses stood in stalls along the wall to her left. Tack was hung on the wall to the right, and she stepped up and removed a bit and bridle. She hesitated as she looked at the saddles, then quickly decided she did not need another. The mustang looked vaguely familiar, but she quickly discounted the choice. Mustangs could be a little wild and might be too tough for her to handle. The Tennessee Walker was a beautiful horse, but bore scars on its chest and foreleg. Anyone who would keep a horse like that must care deeply. She couldn't take that one. That left the pinto and a paint. The paint could have been a wild horse. Decisively, she picked the pinto and she threw the bridle over its head and adjusted the bit. Slowly, she led him to the door, and swung it open. She led the pinto over to her mount and quickly changed the saddles. Then she led her horse back into the barn to the stall where the mare had been.

"Sorry, old friend," she whispered to her horse, patting her flank and tying the reins in a stall with hay. "I hope to come back for you; you saved my life." Tears came to her eyes as she looked into the big brown eyes of her mare Bandita. The horse had sustained a nasty cut on her front leg while running through some Manzanita as she charged away from the outlaws with Sarah on her back. It was infected and Sarah had no means to treat the wound. "I need a strong horse to protect little TC and me until we can find help." Bandita looked into her eyes and shook her head up and down, like she understood. "I hope the people who live here will take good care of you. I'll come back for you if I can!" She stepped out of the stall and turned to walk back out the rear door of the barn.

"Oh no you don't!" yelled Matthew. "Thief!" He stood in the door of the barn, staring in disbelief. Sarah had not heard him enter the front of the barn through the open door and she froze for a second, then, her mouth set, she slipped through the open back door of barn. Reaching out, she threw a rake leaning against the barn to the ground, then jumped into the saddle of her waiting mount and turned him to run, gripping the reins of the pinto tightly.

Matthew raced out of the barn after the woman and fell head long into the mud just outside the door. "What the...?" He glanced down near his feet and realized he had tripped over a rake lying across the path. He knew he had put that rake against the wall by the door. His head snapped around at the sound of galloping hooves and he saw the woman on his best mare as she rode away!

"Damn you!" he bellowed, picking himself up and trying to brush the mud off his clothes. The woman peered over her shoulder for a minute, and as if it weren't enough that he was coated with mud, she laughed! He ran after her, knowing it was useless, but feeling such rage he had to do something. He stopped and watched her crest the hill, then disappear out of sight over the top. Just before she dropped out of sight, he saw something flutter down to the ground. He turned and loped towards the barn, hastily saddling Old Pepper, knowing Pepper could never catch Willow, but at least he could get him to the top of the hill. The other horses were too far on the other side of the house in the pasture. Maybe there was some clue in what she dropped. He had never been so angry at a woman, and was determined to find her! He wanted his horse back, and he wanted some kind of payment for his friends at their store. He watched the speck on the ground as Pepper slogged up the hill, half hoping she would come back for what she dropped and he could catch her, and half afraid she would come back and take his clue. Finally Pepper got close enough for him to see over the crest of the hill. He could see no sign of her and his mare, and the grass was so dry, it had already sprung back up over her trail. He turned Pepper back to the spot on the ground and leapt out of the saddle to snatch up what looked like a soft wad of yarn. As he unfolded it, he stood staring, dumbfounded. It was a baby bonnet. Why would she have a baby bonnet? What in blue blazes was going on here?

Matthew turned and mounted his horse. Still stunned by the bonnet, he wound his way down the hill. He could see Paul standing outside the barn, rifle over his arm, hand shading his eyes as he looked up the hill at Matthew. Paul was anxious to go looking for Sarah, but he was still weak. He had developed a raging fever from another infection in his wounds and been confined to bed again for several more days.

"Heard the shoutin' and came as quick as I could," he said as Matthew rode up. "Where is she?" His eyes darted around, searching the skyline. "Where did she go?"

"I don't know yet, but I am going to find her and then that little thief will pay!"

"What do you mean, thief?" Paul demanded.

Taken aback by the anger in his voice, Matthew riled quickly. "She stole my best mare, and she stole from my friends at the general store, and I mean to catch her!"

"Why did she leave her horse here and run away, what did you do to her?"

"Her horse…?" Matthew said, stepping around him into the barn. "Well, I'll be!" He walked over to Bandita and patted her neck. He quickly saw the festering wound on her leg. "Paul, get me some hot water and rags. And bring me that linament over by the tack on your way back." Reaching back, he took the knife off his belt and cut the bandages for the horse's foreleg. Matthew and Paul worked on Bandita's leg for the better part of an hour. "She's good stock, I guess I could call it a trade." Matthew mumbled, stepping back and looking at the bandage. "Of course she's good stock, Sarah didn't ride wild stock, this one has great bloodlines."

"What are you talking about?" demanded Matthew.

"Sarah!" said Paul with exasperation, "that's Sarah's horse!" Matthew stood, gaping at Paul. He forgot he had the baby bonnet sticking out of his pocket until Paul gestured toward it. "What's that?" he asked. Matthew held it up and looked at it like he had no idea how it got into his hand.

"It's a baby bonnet, Paul. What do you know about it? Does Sarah have a baby you forgot to mention?"

"Oh. No, she just…" Paul stopped and looked at the ground. "Why would she have a baby bonnet if she doesn't have a baby? Answer me, damn it!"

Paul looked miserable. He shifted from one foot to the other, like he was trying to decide what to do.

"Paul!" Matthew snarled, taking a step closer. "I want to know what is going on and I want to know right now!" Paul finally brought his eyes up to meet Matthew's.

"I guess you got a right to know what I am remembering. Let's go get a cup of coffee and I'll tell you the whole story, at least as much as my mind will let me."

They walked up to the house and Matthew washed the mud off his face and hands while Paul poured the coffee. He swore as he looked at the mud on his clothes. "That woman…!" he growled as he brushed the mud off his clothes and stomped it off his boots. Walking into the house, he saw Paul was already seated at the table, his big hands wrapped around a cup of coffee and his face looking like he was about to have a tooth pulled. Matthew pulled out a chair and sat down, taking a sip of coffee. Matthew stared at Paul until at last he took in a deep breath and pushed it out through his lips.

"Sarah wasn't really pregnant." he said. Matthew stared at him. "Paul…" he began, I don't know how much you've been around farms or women, but there is no 'not really pregnant.' A woman is pregnant or she's not, there is no in between. So, which is it?" He didn't know whether to be angry or feel sorry for Paul.

"Well…what I mean is…there was gold." Paul lowered his voice as he said the last three words.

"Gold?" said Matthew. "What the hell does that have to do with being pregnant or not?"

"Well, see the boss made me promise not to tell anyone. Sarah and the boss had some gold they were bringing to the boss' family. They heard a lot about men in the west that would just rob settlers, so they got the idea to hide some of the gold."

"Was Sarah pregnant or not?" Matthew bit off the words through clenched teeth.

"Well, no," said Paul. "They put some of the gold in a box in the wagon in case they were robbed, but they put the rest in a pouch inside a bundle that Sarah wore under her clothes to make it look like she was pregnant."

Matthew's mouth was open as he gawked at Paul. "That's the craziest thing I ever heard." He said.

"Well, if you think about it, it was pretty smart," Paul was smiling now. "They figured even in the west, men don't usually bother women, and they would bother a woman with child even less. They figured if they put some gold in a box and some under Sarah's clothes, if they were robbed, the bandits would find the gold in the box and think that was all there was. The rest would be safe." Paul was beaming now.

"But what about the bonnet?" Matthew persisted.

"Oh, they had some stuff they were carrying in the wagon to make it look good if anyone got suspicious. You know, like they were collecting stuff for a baby."

Matthew shook his head. He didn't know what to think, but the pieces were coming together. It was clear that Sarah and the thief from the store were one and the same. But, if she had gold, why was she stealing from his friends? He decided not to tell Paul that Sarah had stolen from Tobias and Melissa. At least until he had all the answers.

Chapter 7

Matthew was saddling up, putting coffee and biscuits in his saddlebags when Paul walked from the barn, leading his mustang.

"I'm going with you!" he said, stubbornly setting his jaw. Matthew studied him. Paul was pale, and sweating from the minor exertion of saddling his horse.

"I need you here," Matthew said. "I could be gone for days, and I need someone here to care for the stock."

"I'm going! She was my boss's wife and I owe it to her! Besides," he said, looking into Matt's eyes with defiance, "I'm not sure I like the way you talk about her!" Matt started to snap at Paul, but something in the young man's eyes stopped him. He took a deep breath, then let it out slowly. He faced Paul squarely.

"I've never hurt a woman in my life, and I don't intend to start now," he said softly. "I am angry at her because she stole from my friends, but I won't hurt her." Paul still looked uncertain.

"You're not strong enough yet, Paul," he said. "I can travel faster. I'll find her and bring her back. Then we'll get this sorted out."

"You give me your word?" Paul asked, hanging onto the saddle on his horse.

"You have my word," said Matthew. Irritated as he was that Paul would think he might harm Sarah, he admired the spunk of the young man. "Now, why don't you set a spell and then put your horse away." Paul nodded and slowly mounted the steps to sink onto the bench.

"Just for a bit," Paul said. "Hot today."

Matthew hesitated for a moment, reluctant to leave the young man again. But, at least Paul was in a place with shelter and food. Matthew swung into the saddle and looked at Paul again. He should be alright for a few days. He turned Lady and trotted out of the yard in the direction Sarah had gone. He wasn't sure what to make of it yet, and he figured Paul didn't need to worry anymore right now. He, on the other hand, was worried. A woman alone out here was not a pleasant thought. No matter what she had done, no one deserved to die a hard death of exposure and starvation.

The second day he found tracks. The first tracks he saw were those of his mare. He recognized the tracks of the horse Sarah was riding. He knew the hoof prints of his own mare; the right rear had a little chip in the shoe. The farrier was coming by this week and he had planned to have it replaced, but Sarah had taken her before he could get it done.

The second set of tracks were the ones he had seen at the encampment. Was she being followed? Matthew studied the path ahead of him. Then he urged Lady to the top of the nearest hill and looked out to the east. He saw the three horses riding with purpose several miles ahead. He could not see Sarah, but they were all going in the same direction. There were no towns or settlements in that direction for over seventy miles.

Foreboding sat heavy on his shoulders as he scanned the horizon. He thought about Paul back at the ranch. Then he made a decision. He had to find out if those men were chasing Sarah.

Matthew reached down and drew his Winchester out of the scabbard. He checked the load and replaced it in the leather scabbard on Lady's side. His mouth set in a grim line. He didn't have time to go for help; if they were following her, he would never get back in time to stop whatever they had in mind. Damn it! He didn't have time to chase this woman all over creation! But he also knew himself and he would never rest easy if he could help her and turned away instead. Muttering curses, he gently kicked Lady in the sides and urged her down the hill. Once he got to the bottom, he knew a trail that ran parallel to the one the men were taking. He was out numbered and out gunned and he had to be smarter than them. He had a feeling they did not have good intentions.

Chapter 8

Matthew followed the men for another five miles, keeping in the tree line to avoid being seen. They had slowed their horses to a trot, and seemed to be arguing about which direction they should take. He watched as one of the men got down from his horse and walked in a circle while the other two sat their horses. The man on the ground was pointing to the north, but the men on the horses were gesturing towards the east. Finally, the man on the ground got back on his horse and they started off again towards the east. He watched while they widened the gap and then started forward again. He would do Sarah no good if they got him first.

He had followed them another mile when they dropped over a small hill in front of him. Suddenly, he saw movement in the trees in front of him and reined Lady in to watch. He sat still, searching the trees to find the source of the movement. He was just about to move forward again, when he saw a rider come out of the trees below him, headed back the way they had come. It was his horse; it was Sarah!

"Well I'll be damned!" he said. "She back tracked and gave them the slip!" He watched the hill for a few more minutes to make sure the men did not realize their mistake, and then started Lady back the way they had just come. Sarah slipped in and out of his sight more than once, and he decided he needed to be closer. "If she could give them the slip, I guess she might do it to me too, huh Lady?" he said to the horse. He chuckled. He would have to careful with this one, she was smarter than he had thought. Down on the same level as Sarah, he could see why the men had trouble following her. She would suddenly veer in a different direction, run the horse for about a half mile, then cut off towards her original direction. They lost valuable time trying to figure out what she was doing. She had known then, that she was being followed. Then, she seemed to relax and rode a straight line at a canter. He settled in behind her to see where she was going. If she did have a baby, he wanted to come up on her in a way that would not risk the safety of the baby.

Matthew had been following her trail for two hours when he realized she thought she might be followed again. She was not following a straight trail, and had circled back to check her back trail at least once. He scanned the crest of the hills around him. Was she watching him now? If she was Sarah, why had she robbed his friends? Was she afraid the outlaws were following her? Why didn't she just come into town and ask for help? He shook his head. Too many unanswered questions. The one thing that kept coming to the front of his thoughts was that he had to find her. No woman should be out here alone, especially with the nights turning cold. Thief or not, this time he had to find her. He watched the trail as she veered slightly north, and soon found her reason. A small stream cut along the trail, and she likely stopped to water the horse.

He guided Lady down the embankment to the water and swung down for a drink. At least Sarah had found water; he had found both her boot prints and the tracks of his mare near the shore. Matthew let Lady drink and filled his canteen again. In the west, it was always a good idea to refresh your water supply whenever it was available.

Matthew was just ready to step back into the saddle when the deadly rattle sent a chill down his spine. He saw the snake curled just behind Lady, and moved swiftly to pull his gun and fire. He saw the snake jerk and then lay still, but the firing of the gun and the rattling of the snake frightened Lady, who had reared up trying to fight a snake she could not see. Matthew was knocked off balance and fell backward into the water. A sharp pain made him gasp as something dug into his left shoulder. He lay still for several minutes, unable to move. Gradually, he realized he had fallen on a submerged branch, that had been sharp enough to pierce his clothing and his shoulder, near the collar bone. He tried to sit up, but the pain made him feel light headed. He explored his shoulder carefully, winching at the slight movement. The branch had impaled his shoulder and was wedged tight in his flesh. He clenched his teeth against the pain and lay still for several minutes. He had to get out of the water, it was freezing cold and night fall was only an hour or so away. He tried to sit up again, but the agony was too much. He could not get himself free from the branch. He called Lady, soothing the horse, and trying to get her to come closer. Still a little spooked from the snake, she came to him slowly. It took a few minutes, but he got her to come to his side, and he reached over and grabbed the trailing reins. He braced himself.

"Ok Lady, back up girl, come on," he spoke softly. It was excruciating to feel the branch slowly pull out of his shoulder as Lady helped pull him forward, but he couldn't risk moving too fast. He might lose the reins, and he wasn't sure how much longer he could stay conscious.

Pulling free of the branch, he fell over on the ground, wrapping the reins around his hand as the blackness closed in.

When he came to, it was almost dark. He coaxed Lady to turn so he could grab hold of a stirrup with his good arm. Gritting his teeth, he worked his way up to a standing position. He fought the dizziness and managed to get into the saddle. His mind was racing; he was too far from the ranch. The line shack. If he could get there, at least there would be shelter from the cold.

Matthew urged his horse forward in the moonlight from the fall sky. He knew he had lost too much blood and was feeling light headed. He needed rest and shelter. Fearful of being caught in the rapidly cooling night and unsure of his ability to stay alert, he decided if he could just get to the line cabin for the night, he could move on in the morning. At least he could sleep and replenish his strength. He drifted in and out of consciousness as he gave Lady her head. He pointed her towards the line shack and prayed she would know what to do. The wooziness was almost constant now.

Suddenly, he smelled smoke. Was it Sarah? He scanned the area, but saw no sign of a fire. Nausea washed over him and he realized this was no time to search for friends or enemies. The line cabin was just over the top of that next hill. Riding over the crest, he saw a light in the window of the cabin and smelled the smoke from the fire again. Someone was at the cabin. If it was Sarah, would she help him? He had to take that chance. "Sure hope they're friendly." he said, patting Lady's neck."Not in any shape to go a round with man or beast. Or woman," he smiled wryly. Lady plodded up to the porch and he slid from the saddle. Again, he stood for a few minutes trying to focus his eyes against the flashing lights in his head. Tying Lady near the water trough and a little grass around it, he spoke apologetically."Sorry, girl, I may not be able to do any better than this."

He dragged himself up the steps and stopped for a minute at the door, listening. He heard nothing. Lifting the latch, he eased open the door to find himself facing a rifle pointed right at his midsection.

"You!" he growled, staggering forward, hand outstretched. The effort was too much, and the last thing he recalled was falling into darkness.

When he awoke, the sun was blazing through the window and shining in his eyes. He tried to sit up, but fell back in pain. He explored his shoulder with tender fingers and to his surprise, found a large bandage wrapped around him from his upper arm to his shoulder. He lay still for a minute, trying to remember what had happened. He remembered facing a rifle held by Sarah, but nothing else. He looked slowly around the room, but there was no sign of her, only his shirt lying over the back of the chair beside the bed. His shoulder throbbed with pain, but his stomach was growling. He wasn't sure how long he had been there, but he clearly had not eaten recently. There were some biscuits on a plate on the table and he thought he could smell coffee at the hearth. Matthew tried to sit up, he had to get help. He had to see to Lady. They could both die here if he didn't get up and get back to the ranch. The irony of the situation struck him. He had been trying to save Sarah, and he had gotten hurt in the process. And she had left him to die. Did she take Lady? He tried again to get out of bed, but it was no use. Searing agony forced him back on the bed as a roaring went through his head and the sunlight faded into blackness.

Chapter 9

Sarah rode steadily toward the town. She hated to leave the man back at the shack alone; he was feverish and she was worried his shoulder was already infected. Who was he? He had chased her at the store, she had seen him when she had traded her horse for the mare she was riding, and now he had shown up wounded at the shack. He clearly recognized her, but how did he keep showing up where she was?

 It had taken all her strength to drag him across the floor and get him on the bed. She had done her best to stitch the wound back together to stop the bleeding, but it was deep and ragged. She had tried to dig out bits of wood and dirt from the wound, but whatever had pierced his shoulder had carried the contaminant through the wound, and she did not have the proper supplies to clean it. He had cried out when he was unconscious and she was hurting him as she cleaned the wound, and it frightened her even more. He had even called out her name! She shivered at the thought.

But she had to leave the man. She couldn't help it, her baby came first.

Delivering the baby on her own had taken all her strength and she knew she had never taken the time to fully recover. She only vaguely remembered the two days she lay in the small cave after birthing the baby, waking only to feed the baby and the fire. She had some time to prepare before the baby came, but she had run out of food after eight days. She had gradually become stronger, and finally bundled the baby and rode toward where she thought the town should be. Tim had told her details and direction when they were moving west. He wanted her to know where they were going. His directions had been good, and she had found the town, where she had been able to steal some food. She couldn't risk using the gold, she was too weak to fight and didn't know who she could trust. She still intended to pay them back at the store, but she was still afraid of the men who killed her husband…and maybe Paul too.

It had been terrifying to leave little TC tied to the papoose board on the horse she had slipped in the stable at the hotel. The man from the store had nearly caught her, and then what would have happened to TC! She was so weary, she did not know how much longer she could go on like this.

She stopped the horse and slid out of the saddle. She tried to give TC a little water, and took some for herself. She undid the papoose board and cradled the baby in her arms, wrapping him tighter in the shawl she had taken from the store, and creating a kind of sling for him to be closer to her.

"My poor babe," she said, looking down at the child in her arms. TC was getting weak and seemed feverish himself. He was so young. He needed more to eat, and she did not have enough for him since she did not have enough to eat herself. She hoped the town had a doctor. She had to risk going into the town and asking for help. She carefully climbed back in the saddle, and held one hand on TC this time.

The gold didn't matter to her now, TC was all she really cared about. She couldn't take care of both of them out on the range with winter coming. He had been born early and was small. If the men who killed Tim were in town and stole her gold, she wouldn't be able to take care of the both of them until she found Tim's family. Well, she decided, as long as she had TC, she didn't care. She would find a way.

"Oh, Tim," she cried. "I miss you so. If I could just find your family, we could be safe," she said to the baby. But how. Tim hadn't known where the ranch was yet, he planned to ask around when they got to Bridgeport.

Sarah was so hungry. She had left the last two biscuits and the rest of the coffee in the line shack for the man in case he woke up. After she went to the sheriff, she would tell him to send someone out to the shack. But what if he arrested her for stealing from the store? Had they told him? Had the man described her to the sheriff and told him she stole from the store? She had to take that chance.

She slowed the horse as they came into town and looked at the signs. The Sheriff's Office was small and on the main street. She was not sure she could get on and off the horse again without passing out. She felt so woozy. A man came around the end of a building and walked along the street towards her. "Mister," she called. He stopped and walked over to Sarah. "Can I help you, M'am?" he studied her face, concern in his eyes.

"Would you ask the sheriff to come out for me please?"

"He turned to the office, and then back to Sarah. "Well, I'm sorry M'am, but the sheriff isn't here. He is out on his ranch." Her shoulders slumped and her head drooped. "M'am, are you okay? You look awfully pale."

"Thank you for your help," she smiled weakly. "I'll be fine."

"You sure I can't get you some water or get someone else for you?" asked the man. His eyes were kind, and she almost let him help her. She didn't know what to do. Suddenly, she made up her mind. She would go back to the general store, beg their forgiveness, and ask for help for her baby. They must know the man at the shack, he had come out of the back of the store when he almost caught her. They would send help for him. She couldn't think of any other way. The general store was just up the street. She could make it that far; she had to.

"I thank you for your kindness, sir. I am only going as far as the general store." He nodded.

"The Gruener's are good people. You let them help you, M'am." He tipped his hat and stood watching her as she turned and rode slowly up the street.

Sarah rode as if in a haze, until she gently pulled the reins and stopped in front of the store. Tobias was sweeping the porch again and stopped to watch her approach. Something wasn't right. The woman stopped in front of the store, but she just sat in the saddle, staring at him for several minutes. Then she slowly started to slip out of the saddle, holding tight to the bundle in her arms.

"Melissa!" he shouted as he dropped the broom and jumped off the porch, catching Sarah as her knees gave way.

'What…that's Melissa's shawl!" he growled as he recognized the lump of yarn clutched in her arms. "You…" he began, but froze when the shawl started to move.

"Oh, good Lord," said Melissa in his ear, "Tobias, get her inside. "Please," she said to Sarah, "let me take the baby. You are safe here."

"Baby?" Tobias said, as he swept Sarah up and carried her inside.

"Line shack…west…please!" She grabbed the front of Tobias' shirt. She looked in his eyes and he saw panic. "Help him. You've got to help him," she whispered, and then closed her eyes.

"Bring her in here, Tobias!" Melissa laid the baby in the small tub she kept for collecting herbs and wild turnips, and went to the cot they kept in the back room for Greta's naps. Tobias laid Sarah down carefully, as if he was afraid he would break her. Melissa was already putting water in a basin and coming to the cot to bathe Sarah's face.

"Do you need my help?" asked her husband.

"Yes, first go get Doc and send him here."

"Okay, and then I am going to get Charlie and John together to go check the line shack."

"The line shack?" Melissa asked in surprise.

"Yes, right before she passed out, she said someone at the line shack needed help. The only line shack I know of in these parts in the one Matthew built." His worried face touched Melissa.

"We'll be fine here, Tobias. Greta is baking cookies with Mrs. Phippen and her little girl. Send Doc and then go." She hesitated, looking into her husband's eyes. "Do you think…?" she started.

"I don't know, sweet one," he finished the sentence for her. "If it is Matthew, we will get him back here." Melissa knew he was as worried as she. He rarely called her by endearing names in front of others.

"Be careful," she said. Tobias nodded and walked out the back door, leaving her to tend to the woman and baby.

He was anxious to get to that line shack. Someone needed help, and it could be his friend. Quickly, he saddled his horse and rode over to Doc's. Doc grabbed his bag and ran out the door towards the general store, while Tobias went to the hotel and asked John to come with his buckboard. Charlie at the blacksmith shop listened, then strode over and saddled his horse. By the time Charlie was ready, John had arrived, and the three men headed to the line shack. They rode their horses at a canter until they were outside of town, and then Tobias and Charlie broke into a gallop, leaving John to come along behind with the buckboard. Tobias was anxious to get to the shack and see what needed to be done before they could bring the man in with the buckboard.

While Tobias went out to the line shack, Melissa was helping Doc with the woman and baby.

Doc examined Sarah and the baby extensively while Melissa stood by, ready to help as needed. Finally, he stood, and walked over to the sink to wash his hands. He looked at Melissa.

"Who is she?"

"I don't know," said Melissa. "She rode up to the store, and then almost fell out of her saddle with the baby." Doc looked at the baby, sleeping peacefully in the tub.

"They are both half starved and dehydrated," said Doc. "The baby looks to be about five weeks old. All appearances tell me this woman gave birth without any help, and has been trying to care for the two of them by herself."

"Oh good Lord!" said Melissa. "How on earth did she get here?"

"Judging by the dryness of her skin and the degree of sunburn, I'd say she has been living primarily outside for the past several weeks." He dried his hands. "But how she got here is a mystery." He turned to Melissa. "It won't be easy, but get all the fluids into them you can.

Chapter 10

Tobias and Charlie were still running the horses when they arrived at the line shack. They were good stock and loved to race, for which both men were grateful. Tobias jumped off his horse first and ran to the door of the shack, throwing it open, without any thought someone on the other side might shoot. Charlie came running behind him, gun drawn, protective of his friend.

"Oh mein Gott!" declared Tobias, reverting to his native German in his stress over seeing Matthew lying on the bed, unconscious and looking very much like a corpse. He leaned over and placed his finger on Matt's neck, feeling for a pulse. "Is he...?" asked Charlie softly. Tobias exhaled the breath he had been holding and looked at Charlie.

"No, he has a pulse. But he has lost a lot of blood," he said, looking at the bandages now red with blood and the blood soaked remnants on the floor that looked like they were torn from a woman's petticoat. "We have to get him back to the Doc." He looked at the bandage again. "Charlie, would you get me the bandages out of my saddle bags please. I'm not sure these will stop the blood any longer." Charlie went outside and returned a few minutes later with a bundle of clean, white linen cloth. Tobias smiled as he took them. "Melissa believes in being prepared," he said. "Did you know she was a nurse in the war?" Tobias carefully changed the bandage while Charlie threw out the burned coffee on the hearth and rinsed out the pot for the next visitor. He wrapped the biscuits as an afterthought – people out here did not throw much food away. They both turned towards the door as they heard the rattle of the buckboard pulling up to the shack.

"Is it Matthew?" asked John, coming through the door. He looked past Tobias and found his question answered. "Can he be moved?"

"We have no choice," said Tobias gravely," he needs a doctor." John ran back out and spread a blanket in the back of the buckboard, then came back to help move Matthew. The three men lifted him carefully, with one at his head and shoulder, one in the middle of his body, and one at his legs. They knew the importance of keeping him as steady as possible. They moved him through the door and down the step to the end of the buckboard. Resting his hips on the floor of the buckboard, Charlie jumped in and took his shoulders from Tobias, who jumped in so he could help carry Matthew to the back of the buckboard. They settled Matthew with his head on another blanket and Tobias sitting beside him, cradling his head and shoulders so he would not be jostled too much on the ride to town.

"Charlie, could you close up the shack and then ride ahead to town and tell Doc he has another patient coming and to get ready to do surgery?" asked Tobias.

"Sure," he said, starting up the step. He stopped and turned back to Tobias. "Another patient?"

"I'll explain later," said Tobias as John started the wagon rolling. Moments later, Charlie raced by them on the way to town.

Tobias looked down at his friend. Matthew's face was ashen and the wound had started to bleed again, with the bouncing of the wagon. John was doing his best to avoid every rut and bump he could, but the dirt road was not smooth and Matthew moaned at the pain. Tobias stroked his head, as he would a sick child.

"Matthew, my friend, please don't leave us," he said, his voice breaking. "We need you. Please don't give up." It seemed to take forever to get to town.

They pulled up in front of Doc's to find the doctor and Melissa standing there, waiting. They unloaded Matthew and carried him inside to the waiting table. Tobias shot Melissa a questioning look.

"I'm going to stay and help Doc," she said to Tobias. "Mrs. Phippen brought Greta home just as Charlie arrived. She is at our home with Greta, the woman, and the baby." Tobias nodded and left to go to the store. He was back in minutes, grinning. It was Melissa's turn to arch an eyebrow.

"She is as determined as you, my wife," he said. "She is fixing dinner for us all, has Greta playing with her doll and singing to the baby, and she is making a broth for the lady when she wakes." Melissa smiled as she carried the hot water into the room where Matthew lay. "She would have none of me being there; she said I needed to be with my friend and my wife," he said, turning solemn.

"Good," said Doc, "wash your hands and come in here. I may need you to hold him still while Melissa and I work on him." He looked at Tobias. "I don't want to give him too much chloroform," he said," he is too unstable." Melissa and Tobias exchanged a grim look. They both knew what that meant.

Doc and Melissa worked on Matthew for nearly two hours. Several times, the chloroform was not enough to kill the pain, and while he did not wake up, Matthew jerked and cried out. Tobias held him tight, aching with the agony his friend had to endure.

"There is a lot of debris in the wound. I can tell someone tried to clean it out, but did not have the tools." He pulled out another sliver of wood with the forceps. There was still too much blood. "It would appear he was impaled on some kind of a branch that splintered in the wound as well." Doc was concentrating and peering into the wound. "Ah!" Doc exclaimed. "There it is. Melissa, will you bring me the cauter I put to heat on the stove please."

"I can get it Doc," said Tobias.

"No, I need you to keep him still so I don't lose sight of the area I need to cauterize." Tobias met his eyes and nodded. Melissa returned with the cauter, holding the end with a cloth. "Set it on that metal tray there on the table, Melissa." When she had done so, he turned to her again. "Have you ever helped cauterize a wound?" he asked.

"Yes," she nodded, "many times in the war." Doc nodded approval.

"Then I need you to hold the wound open just as I am so I can get in enough to cauterize the area that is bleeding." She swallowed hard and looked at Tobias, then at Doc. She set her jaw and took over the forceps to hold the wound open. She had done this many times, but never with such a close friend.

"Tobias," said Doc," this is going to hurt him, so I need you to make sure he holds very still." Doc's gray eyes were stern; an expression that was not lost on Tobias. Tobias nodded. Doc looked from one to the other.

"Ready?" They both shook their heads in agreement. Doc picked up the cauter and applied it to the wound. Matthew cried out and tried to buck up on the table. But Tobias had pinned his lower body with his own and had his strong hands firmly clamped just above the elbows on Matthews arms. Finally, it was over. Matthew lay completely still. Doc stepped back and heaved a sigh as Melissa sank into a chair and Tobias leaned against the wall, taking deep breaths. No one moved.

"Well," Doc sighed."If you get any more patients for me, could you try to hold them a day or so? Three in one day is a bit tiring." He smiled, breaking the tension. They all laughed softly, and it felt good. "I will keep him here tonight so I can watch him. Besides, you have a full house," he said to Melissa. "I don't know if the woman has awakened yet, but both she and the baby will need a little care over the next few days. Can you do that?"

"Of course," Melissa said.

"Good. Now, Tobias, can you lift the other end of the stretcher so we can move him off the table to a more comfortable bed?" The two men picked up the poles hanging down on the side of the table and lifted Matthew. They carried him into an adjoining room where there were two beds. "Put him on the one that sits against the wall. I'll put a chair next to the other side so I will hear him if he tries to get up for some reason. Tomorrow, we will move him off the stretcher." He looked at the tired couple. "Why don't you two go get some rest yourselves?" They started to leave, then Tobias turned back. "Thank you, Doc," said Tobias, "Matthew is a good friend," he said, putting his arm around Melissa's shoulders. Doc smiled. Melissa and Tobias opened the door to the smell of a delicious roasted chicken. Jean Phippen was in the kitchen and came to greet them.

"How is he?" she asked.

"He will be fine," Tobias answered. She let out a sigh of relief. "Why don't you two wash up and I will put your dinner on the table."

"Oh, you have done so much already, we can serve ourselves, Jean," said Melissa. "It smells delicious."

"Don't be silly," said Mrs. Phippen. "You are exhausted. My husband brought over the food for dinner and he played with Greta while I cooked. I fed us and Greta, and we tucked her in bed after my Jonas read her a story. He loves children! We sent for Mrs.Lang, who has a young one herself, and she wet nursed the baby. Poor thing was half starved. Mrs. Lang will come back tomorrow as well to see if she is needed. The lady woke briefly and I got her to take some chicken broth before she fell back asleep. Now," she grinned," there's only you two to get fed and then I'll be on my way." Melissa and Tobias enjoyed the roasted chicken, potatoes, and onions, and then were surprised with cherry pie!

"Oh, we don't know how to thank you!"said Melissa.

"I love to cook and Jonas loved playing with Greta. You should have seen him rocking the baby!" she smiled. "Neighbors help each other, and you two have done more than your share today." There was a knock on the door, and Tobias opened it. Jonas walked in and put his arm around his wife's waist.

"Good news?" he inquired. They quickly updated him on Matthew. He was beaming as he looked at his wife. "A fine day's work for all of us then," he said. "I thought you would either need more help or I could walk you home, so I came back."

Tobias clapped him softly on the shoulder. "We thank you, my friend. I think we are all ready for some sleep now."

"Shall we, my dear?" asked Jonas, opening the door for his wife.

"I would love to have you walk me home," she laughed, putting on her shawl and stepping out the door. He tipped his hat as he shut the door.

"What wonderful friends we have in this town," said Melissa.

"Yes," said Tobias. "Now I think we should get some sleep." They checked to see the baby and the woman were sleeping soundly. The baby was now in a large basket on a chair, next to the woman's cot so she would not be alarmed if she woke. Greta was sleeping with a smile on her face as Melissa bent to kiss her daughter. They walked into their room and looked at their bed and both sighed. They quickly climbed into bed and were asleep in minutes.

Chapter 11

Sarah woke to the sound of low voices. She was so tired, she wanted to continue sleeping in this warm, soft, bed. She had nearly drifted back to sleep when TC began to squirm and make little grunting noises. Suddenly, she sat up in the bed, panic overcoming her as she realized TC was not next to her. Then she saw him lying in a cradle next to the bed. How did he get in a cradle? Where were they? The voices had stopped, and she looked up to see a man and a woman staring at her. They both rose at the same time.

"I'm Doc. How are you feeling?" he asked.

"I…," she stopped. "I think… I feel better. Where am I?"

"You are in my home," said Melissa. "You rode up to our store and then collapsed. My husband carried you in, and I carried the wee boy." She reached down and patted the baby on the back and he quickly settled back into sleep. "What is his name?"

"His name is TC," answered Sarah." It was coming back to Sarah now. This had to be the back of the general store and this had to be the woman who owned the shawl she had stolen. Her face flushed at the thought that the woman she had robbed was being so kind to her and the baby.

"Thank you," said Sarah, with tears showing in her eyes. "I am so sorry."

"Don't think about anything right now except getting well," said Melissa. "Are you hungry?" Sarah nodded and Melissa walked over to the counter in the kitchen.

"Young lady, you have been through a tough experience," said Doc. He pulled up a chair and started checking her pulse and respiration. "How did you come to be alone giving birth to this young lad?" he asked, indicating TC. Sarah dropped her head to her chest and took a deep breath.

Doc continued to study her. "How did you manage to give birth alone?"

"My mother was a mid wife. She used to take me with her to birth babies. I was only fourteen when she died of cholera after she delivered a baby. It took the mother, the child, and my mother. But I had helped her birth dozens of babies by then. I knew what to do, it was just...so hard to do it alone. I was worried for my baby." She looked down at her hands in her lap, clasping them tightly together. It was a difficult memory.

"Where is your husband?" he asked softly.

"He's...dead." Her voice broke and she fought to keep from crying.

"How long ago?" asked Doc.

"He was killed by outlaws two months ago," replied Sarah. How much should she tell them? She was so tired of running, so weary of trying to take care of herself and the baby while camping outside and scrounging for food. Melissa came back with a cup of coffee and a slice of bread with butter, which Sarah accepted gratefully. They watched as she ate quickly. She looked again at the sleeping babe.

"Where did you find a cradle?"asked Sarah.

"Tobias, my husband, made it for our little girl before she was born. He had it stored in the rafters and got it down for the little one." She smiled."Would you like some more?" asked Melissa when Sarah had finished.

"Oh no," said Sarah, "I have imposed on you enough." Melissa took the cup and plate.

"It is no imposition. There is plenty, and I will have no guest of mine go hungry. May I bring you more?" she asked again.

"You are clearly in need of more food and drink, "said Doc. "Both you and the baby show signs of near starvation and dehydration."

"Yes, thank you," said Sarah, who still felt her stomach growling. She looked at TC. "Oh! How long have I been asleep! My poor baby!" She reached for him, but Doc gently stopped her.

"You need to build your strength. Nurse him a couple times a day to keep your milk flowing, but we have brought in a wet nurse, who has been feeding him. Eat first, and then you can try to nurse him in a bit. When your body is replenished, you will have more for him," he smiled.

"What about the man at the shack!" Sarah exclaimed, suddenly remembering why she was here. "Did someone go help him? Did they find him in time?"

"Yes, thanks to you, my husband and some friends went and brought him back," Melissa said as she gave Sarah another cup of coffee and another slice of buttered bread. She looked at Sarah with gratefulness in her eyes. "You saved his life, if he had been there much longer..." she bit her lip. "As it was, Doc had quite a time working on him."

"Oh, he is alright then," Sarah said with relief. Sarah ate more slowly this time, and when she finished, she looked at her baby, then at Melissa and Doc. "I need to tell you some things," she said. "I can't run anymore and I can't take care of us trying to live in the outdoors." She twisted her hands in her lap. "I am so sorry. I didn't know where to go or who I could trust." Tears were running down her cheeks. She stood and paced back and forth, wringing her hands.

"Why don't you come and sit here at the table and tell us your story," said Melissa, taking her hands and studying her face. "Maybe we can help."

Doc brought his chair back to the table, and the three of them sat down. Sarah began to tell her story while Doc and Melissa listened intently. They did not interrupt her, knowing it would be easier to just let her tell the story from the beginning and then ask questions. When Sarah finished, she looked at Melissa.

"I feel so awful! I robbed you and now you have been so kind to me! I can pay you now that you know I have gold, but can you ever forgive me?"

Melissa studied her, then looked at Doc. Turning back to Sarah, she took her hand again.

"Sarah, you did what you felt you had to do to keep you and your baby safe and alive. I cannot imagine the courage it has taken for you to hold out so long on your own. It must have been terrible, not knowing where to turn, and being alone. The west is an unforgiving land at times, but…we are not. Of course we forgive you."

"You showed us all the kind of person you are when you first rode up to the store. Your immediate thought was of Matthew and his needs," Doc added. "You could have said nothing, and we would not have known what happened until it was too late." His gray eyes met hers with kindness.

"Matthew is the name of the man from the shack?" asked Sarah.

"Yes. He is a special friend to my family," said Melissa.

"He is the man who chased me out of the store that day I took your shawl," Sarah said softly. She looked at Melissa. "Then I traded my sweet horse Bandita for his mare. My horse was injured. I did not know that was his ranch." Sarah ran her fingers through her hair, her elbows on the table, and her head bent as she gazed blankly at the table top. "This is so confusing. I knew he was following me just before he got hurt. I thought he might be teamed up with the men who had killed my husband." She shrugged her shoulders. "Even if he had been, I couldn't just leave him to die that way." Sighing, she gave Doc and Melissa a weak smile.

"You need to lay back down and get some more sleep,"said Doc. "You are suffering from exhaustion and you need to rest to become stronger."

"Doc is right," Melissa agreed. "Your job right now is to sleep and regain your strength. Mrs. Lang will come several times a day to wet nurse TC as long as she is needed. We will watch him and change him." She grinned. "Mrs. Phippen taught my little Greta a song to sing to the baby. Greta loves to talk to him and sing to him." Just then, Greta came skipping into the room, singing "Oh my darling, oh my darling, come and shine...." Tobias was close on her heels, a big grin on his face.

"I'm not sure she has the words right, but she sure likes to sing!" said Tobias.

"That's the song!" Melissa laughed. "I don't think she has stopped singing it since she got up this morning."

"I think you are correct, my wife!" smiled Tobias. "Ah! I see our guest is awake! I am Tobias," he offered with a small bow. "Welcome to our home."

"My name is Sarah. It is so kind of you to let us stay."

"It is our pleasure," he said. "But you still do not look well; are you going to faint again?" he asked with concern.

"No, but I am afraid I am going to go back to sleep. Please excuse me." Sarah walked back to the bed with effort. She kissed TC on the head, and then lay down again. She was instantly asleep. Even Greta's singing, and the laughter of the three adults, did not keep her awake.

Chapter 12

The pain shot through his chest and woke him with a gasp. Matthew could not move until it subsided. Then, he moved slightly without awareness of his shoulder until he was met with another sharp pain. His eyes flew open and he stared at the whitewashed ceiling. This was not his bedroom, where was he? The door opened and he turned his head.

"I heard you cry out," said Doc. "I can give you a little something to help with the pain, but I would like you to try to take some water and a little food before you go back to sleep."

"How did I get here?' asked Matthew. "I was at the line shack."

"A young woman rode into town with a baby. She was in pretty bad shape herself, but before she passed out, she told Tobias there was a man at the line shack who needed help."

"Sarah," said Matthew. She didn't leave him to die!

"You know her?" Doc asked in surprise.

"Yes. I mean no. Not really." He looked at Doc and saw the confusion on his face."I have been chasing her since I caught her stealing from Melissa and Tobias." Doc nodded.

"Yes, that fits with what she has told us."

"Wait! You said she has a baby?"

"Oh yes. That woman has a lot of courage," said Doc.

"She's a thief!" said Matthew. Doc appraised him for a few minutes before he spoke.

"Have you heard her story?" Doc asked. "She has been through things that would have broken or killed most women." He sighed. "Something to think about," he offered.

"Hello! Doc?" called a voice. Charlie came into the room with a basket over his arm. The smell of food wafted into the room with the basket and Matthew's stomach growled.

"John had his cook at the hotel make up a basket for you two. He figured Doc has been too busy to cook and you need some good food to fill out those bones!" he said, looking at Matthew.

"I can't remember the last time I ate," confessed Matthew. "That sure smells good!"

"Charlie, can you set that down and help me sit Matthew up so he can eat?" Doc turned back to Matthew. "This is going to hurt, but I want you to eat, and that is much harder lying down." The two men arranged themselves on either side of the bed. "Don't try to use either arm, Matthew," warned Doc. He nodded to Charlie and they carefully worked their arms under Matt's back and right shoulder, with Doc maneuvering the injured left side. Slowly, they raised him to a sitting position. Sweat appeared on Matthew's forehead, and he clenched his teeth to keep the groans from escaping his lips.

"Hand me that other pillow, will you, Charlie?" asked Doc, as he slipped the one from the bed behind Matthew. Charlie reached over to the other bed in the room and, snagging the pillow, handed it to Doc. He eased Matthew back a bit on the pillows. Matthew's eyes were closed and he was breathing hard.

Charlie pulled a small table over to the bed and began to unpack the basket. Matthew opened his eyes as the savory smell of the meat pie hit his senses. His mouth started to water; he was ravenous! Charlie took plates out of the basket and dished up three healthy servings of the beef pie with potatoes, and gave the first one to Doc, who arranged it on Matthew's lap. He handed him a fork and then accepted the next plate from Charlie and sat down to eat. Charlie pulled out a big mason jar with a dark liquid in it.

"This is something the new cook made up – calls it sassafras tea. Keeps it in the root cellar, so it is nice and cool." He poured servings into three metal cups and handed those around as well.

"This is delicious," commented Matthew. "Please tell John I said thank you," he said, taking another bite. He ate with care, not wanting to move suddenly and feeling his stomach react to being fed for the first time in days.

"Got a peach cobbler for dessert," Charlie grinned. Some freighters were short on their bill at the restaurant, so they paid in cans of peaches!" The three men ate silently for several minutes, enjoying the good food. Matthew found eating took effort, in his weakened condition, and he could not finish all his food.

"Charlie, that was surely a treat, and nice of John to think of us. Please tell him I said so," Doc commented.

"I will, but he was happy to help," said Charlie. "He was sure worried you weren't going to make it," he continued, looking at Matthew. "You were in bad shape when we found you out at the shack."

"John was there too?" asked Matthew.

"Sure was! He drove the buckboard back after we loaded you up." Seeing Doc setting up bandages, he started packing up the dishes. "Need any help there, Doc?"

"It would be easier if you could give me a hand for a few minutes, Charlie. The wound went all the way through, so I have to lean him forward to get a look at the back. I would appreciate it if you could help support him."

Doc worked swiftly, but carefully, to change the bandages. Matthew grimaced when he took them off, and felt sharp pain as Doc gently examined the wound. He put new compresses on and wrapped Matthew's shoulder again with the bandages. When he was finished, he and Charlie helped Matthew back to a reclining position, leaving a pillow under his head and shoulders.

"Thanks, Charlie," said Doc as the man picked up the basket. Charlie nodded as he walked out the door.

"Do you want something for pain?" asked Doc. "I can give you a little opium for relief, if you want." Matthew was silent for a few minutes, then he shook his head.

"No, thanks Doc. I saw too many men in the war that couldn't stop after they were healed," said Matthew. Doc nodded.

"Shot of whiskey, then? Might take the edge off," he offered. As if on cue, Matthew flinched and clenched his jaw against another stab of pain.

"Yeah, I think I'll take the whiskey," he answered, breathing hard. Doc left the room and returned a few minutes later with a shot glass and a bottle. He poured a shot and handed it to Matthew, who downed it in one gulp.

"Another?" Doc offered. Matthew hesitated, then shook his head yes. He drank this one more slowly, and when he finished, handed the glass back to Doc. He put his head back on the pillow as Doc walked out of the room with the bottle and glass. When Doc returned, Matthew was sound asleep. Doc checked his pulse and checked for fever. Pleased, he looked at the pale man lying in bed.

"You are one lucky man, Matthew Raines," he said to himself. "I've seen men die with lesser wounds."

Chapter 13

Doc stood talking to Melissa and Tobias. They were on the porch of the store, away from both Matthew and Sarah.

"I don't know what to do about this, I hate to ask, but he can't be left alone yet," said Doc. "He still fades in and out of consciousness, but I have to go out and see the Maynards. Their children are both sick and the parents are worried. They can't be moved right now."

"Sarah has no place to go either," Melissa began, " looks like we will have a very full house for a few days." She looked at Tobias. He was smiling at her; they thought so much alike.

"We can put Greta in our room and Sarah and TC can stay in her room," suggested Tobias. "We could put Matthew against the wall in the kitchen, or clear part of the store room for him."

"You are truly good people," Doc smiled.

"We are short a bed, though, and I don't think he should sleep on the floor right now," said Tobias thoughtfully.

"I can help with that," offered Doc, "I can get Charlie and John to bring over one of the beds from my patient room."

"Perfect!" said Melissa and Tobias in unison, laughing at their blended voices.

"It's a lot for you two to do, though," worried Doc.

"We will be fine," said Melissa. "Sarah is feeling better and starting to want to help. She can do little things and it will make her feel better while she lends a hand."

"Hmmm, that could work, but don't let her do too much." Doc thought for a minute. "Mrs. Phippen said she would be happy to help again, but your house is already so full..."

"We'll keep that in mind," said Tobias, but you are right. I don't know if we can put more people in our home!"

"I'll go ask Charlie and John to bring the bed over as soon as possible, said Doc starting to walk away. He turned back. "On second thought, I think I will ask them to come help you move things here first."

"We would appreciate that," said Tobias. "Well, wife, we had better start rearranging our home then," said Tobias as they turned and started back into the store.

Melissa and Tobias were moving supplies out of the small room and stacking them in the store, filling up the shelves as much as possible. They decided to stack some boxes against the kitchen wall and give Matthew the small storage room to himself.

"It does have a window," said Melissa, "and it will be much more quiet than putting him in the kitchen. He still needs a lot of sleep."

"I agree," said Tobias, lifting another box.

"Tobias? Melissa?"called John from the store.

"Back here!" Tobias answered. Charlie and John walked into the kitchen and looked around. "We are moving some boxes out here from the store room and stacking them there against that wall," he pointed. Small stock can go out in the store. We are going to put the bed for Matthew in there so he can have enough quiet to sleep."

"Let's get to work then," said Charlie. They moved boxes and stocked shelves for an hour. Then they moved the cot from the kitchen into the Gruener's bedroom for Greta, and moved Sarah's things and the cradle into Greta's room. When they were finished, they looked around in time to see Melissa coming out of the store room with a bucket.

"It's clean for him now," she smiled. "I even put a curtain on the window."

Tobias walked over and took the bucket from her. He dumped it outside while she rinsed the cloth under the pump in the sink. Charlie and John left to move the bed from Doc's. When they arrived, Doc was getting bandages together for Melissa to use with Matthew while he was gone. Matthew was sleeping fitfully, talking in his sleep from time to time.

"Is he going to be alright?" asked John.

"Yes, but it will take some time. That is why I want to move him to Tobias and Melissa's while I am gone." All three men looked at Matthew. They had never seen him look so wan. They knew him as strong, tanned, and muscular, with a ready smile. The man in the bed was a far cry from the picture they held of their friend.

Charlie and John quickly stripped the second bed of linens, which they carried over to the store. When they came back, they moved the frame of the bed to the store, and set it up in the store room. Melissa was making the bed as they left to go get Matthew.

"We haven't moved the stretcher out from under him," said Doc, "there hasn't been time or need. You can just pick up the poles and we will transfer him over at the store." Doc and Charlie took the poles at the top of the bed, while John took both poles at the foot. Once they cleared the mattress, Charlie took the other top pole from Doc and they started out the door, with Doc supervising and carrying the bandages. Tobias greeted them and took them back to the store room. Doc stopped them in the kitchen.

"Let's get him off the stretcher," he said. They laid him on the table and then the four of them carefully lifted him to the bed. It was a tight squeeze to get them all in the small room, but they managed the transfer with a minimum of outcry from Matthew. As they put him on the bed, his eyes opened.

"Where am I? What are you doing?" he asked hoarsely.

"I have to go out of town for a few days, so we have moved you to the general store," said Doc. Matthew turned his head and saw Tobias standing in the doorway. The big man grinned at his friend.

"Now you will have Melissa hovering over you, my friend," he said. Matthew managed a weak smile, and then closed his eyes as he fell back asleep. Doc shook his head, and motioned the men outside the room. Charlie and John went back to their work, leaving Doc and Tobias in the kitchen. Melissa came in from the store.

"I left a package of bandages for you," Doc said, motioning to the brown wrapped square on top of the boxes against the wall. "I have changed the bandage today, and the wound is no longer seeping. But the bandage will still need to be changed once a day." Melissa nodded. He looked back at Matthew lying on the cot. "He won't take anything but a shot or two of whiskey for the pain. He does not want opium or laudanum, and the pain makes him weak."

"I can offer him whiskey a couple times a day," said Tobias.

"And I will get some beef tea or other food in him as well," said Melissa.

"Well, I better get going out to the Maynards," said Doc. "Those children need me now."

Melissa set about making a soup and some biscuits for dinner. She managed to get some of the soup into both Matthew and Sarah, who was feeling much stronger. After he ate some soup, Matthew sat waiting for Tobias to bring him the shots of whiskey.

"I need to get out to the ranch," said Matthew, as soon as Tobias walked in the little room. "Paul can't manage on his own, he is still too weak."

"And you, my friend, will do him no good," answered Tobias. "You are as weak as a kitten yourself! In fact, I do not think you could sit your horse long enough to make it to the ranch," he said, studying the dark circles under the eyes in the pale face of his friend.

"But the stock have to be fed, and someone needs to check on Paul," began Matthew.

"And it will not be you," said Tobias firmly. Seeing the worry in the face of his friend, he softened. "I know you have poured your soul into that ranch, Matthew. I will ask Charlie to go out tomorrow morning, and if he cannot, I will go myself."

Matthew still looked uncertain. "I promise you, my friend,"

said Tobias, holding a shot of whiskey out to Matthew. Tobias sat and talked with Matthew while he took the shots of whiskey, but Matthew could hardly hold his eyes open long enough to get the whiskey down. Tobias closed the door quietly as he left the room.

Finally, the chores were all done and Melissa and Tobias stood in the middle of the kitchen. Tobias took her by the hand, and led her through the store to the bench on the porch. They sat together, enjoying the coolness of the night and the sharp, clear stars above them. Tobias opened his arms and Melissa fell against his broad chest.

"Well, my wife, our patients and our child are all asleep."

"Yes," Melissa said, "I think we did well for our first day running a hospital!" They both chuckled. "The quiet is nice," she said.

"Yes, it is," he sighed. "Think of all the people who have helped in the past few days," he said. "This is a good town."

"Yes," agreed Melissa. She was quiet for a few minutes. "I wonder if Matthew and Sarah…" she began. Tobias chuckled. "That is something we must not push," he said. "We will have to wait and see if they can work things out."

"Hmmm," she yawned. "I think it our bedtime as well."

Chapter 14

Matthew woke to a slight rustling sound the next morning. He opened his eyes and stared at the ceiling. He caught movement, and turned his head.

"You!" he flashed. "What are you doing here?"

Sarah hesitated, then walked to the bed and set the basin and bandages on the small table that had been set next to the cot. She pulled the chair up close to the bed and reached for the cover over his shoulder.

His other hand shot out and grabbed her wrist. "What are you doing here?" he repeated.

"I'm changing your bandage. Melissa is busy with Greta and asked me to do it."

Of course. He was at Tobias and Melissa's.

"Please let go of me, you're hurting me." Sarah tugged her hand away. The door opened again and Melissa came in, carrying a baby, who was fussing.

"I think he wants his mommy," she laughed, as Sarah stood and took the bundle. Melissa watched Matthew as Sarah left the room.

"She is helping with the chores and we are helping her and the baby for awhile." Melissa explained as she sat down. "Lucky for you she told us where to find you!" Matthew was silent and Melissa looked at him. She gently peeled the bandage away and examined the wound. She cleaned it again and began to wrap it.

"You should be up and around in a couple more days," she said. "It looks better than it did a few days ago."

"How long have I been here?" asked Matthew. He hadn't thought about the time.

"Just three days," she replied. "You were impaled on a branch or some kind of stick. Doc had to cauterize the wound to stop the bleeding." She studied his face. "Doc said if it had been another couple of hours until we found you, it might have been too late."

"Paul!" said Matt, as he tried to get up. "He isn't strong enough to handle the ranch yet himself. I've got to get out there." He struggled to sit up and swing his legs over the side of the bed. He sat gasping and clenching his teeth against the pain. His head was pounding and he felt dizzy.

He was reaching for his pants, hung on the bedpost at the head of the bed, when Melissa stood, with her hands on her hips. "Matthew Raines, get yourself back in that bed before I have Tobias come in here and tie you to the bedpost!" said Melissa, glaring at him. "You know he can and will, if I ask him to!" she said, scowling down at him.

"But Paul…" Matthew began.

"Oh for heaven's sake," she said, fussing with the covers as she gently pushed him back down on the bed. It wasn't difficult; the room was spinning for Matthew. She lifted his legs onto the bed. "Tobias already went out there and helped catch up the chores. I sent him stew for a couple of days too. He is doing better than you! Now stay there until breakfast is ready." She picked up the wash basin and strode out of the room.

Matthew lay still on the soft bed, trying to think things through. Was it just last night Tobias had said he would go out to the ranch? His eyes felt heavy and his shoulder throbbed. When Melissa came to bring him breakfast, she didn't have the heart to wake him. He slept most of the day, but Melissa did manage to get him to eat and take some water. Sarah did not come back into the room that day.

———————————

Matthew sat in a chair at the table the next morning and watched Sarah as she poured him coffee. She brought the coffee, and a single biscuit on a plate. It was late, nearly noon, and he had missed breakfast. A mid day meal was cooking, and it made his stomach growl. Melissa had finally let him get out of bed and take a meal at the table. Sarah's strawberry blond hair framed her face with small wisps as it escaped from the tie at the nape of her neck.

"I guess I should thank you for saving my life." He said as he lifted the coffee to his lips.

"You were hurt. I couldn't just leave you to die," she answered, not meeting his eyes.

"You could have, but you didn't," he said. She just looked at him and shook her head.

"I'm not a monster," she said. "I've only tried to protect my baby. I never wanted anyone to get hurt." She bit her lip. "I just didn't know who to trust."

"How did you get here?"

"On a horse."

Matthew started to snap back at her when Melissa walked into the room and laid the baby in the cradle near Matthew.

"Watch the baby," Melissa smiled at Matthew. "You should be able to handle that," she laughed. "Come Sarah, let's get those diapers hung up before we lose the best sun!"

Matthew leaned over to look at the small boy who lay sleeping in the cradle. He squirmed a bit and Matthew rocked the cradle. Just then, a chill breeze blew through the window and he shivered. Buttoning his vest, he looked down at the baby, then around the room for another blanket for the baby. A canvas bag sat on top of the boxes stacked against the wall, and what looked like a baby blanket stuck out of the top. He stood carefully so as not to bring on the dizziness, and walked over and reached for the blanket. He was pleasantly surprised to find there was no fuzziness in his head, and he moved with less stiffness than yesterday. Gently, he covered the baby. He watched Melissa and Sarah through the window, outside in the sun, hanging up the wash. Melissa looked happy as she and Sarah chatted while they worked.

Tobias came in and grinned at Matthew, absently rocking the cradle as he watched the women. He walked over to Matt and followed his eyes.

"Melissa sure likes having another woman to talk to," he said. "That Sarah has been through a lot." He glanced at Matthew. "She has spunk, that's for sure!"

"She stole from you."

"And she explained that; she was afraid to let anyone know she had gold for fear they would take it and maybe kill her in the process! She paid us back once she felt safe."

"Gold? Where would she get gold?"

"Her husband was carrying some gold to start their life here in the west." Tobias studied Matthew. "You could give her a little kindness, my friend. She was just trying to survive and protect her baby. Alone in a strange land, not knowing who to trust…can you really blame her?"

Matthew considered what his friend said. He looked out the window again at Melissa and Sarah, working together. Sarah was thin, too thin, and at times, when she thought no one was watching, he had seen her wiping away tears.

"Come, my friend, help me move this little man into the next room. I am hungry as a bear and these women have made us a fine Sunday meal!"

Matthew stood up and moved to take one end of the cradle. "Oh no you don't!" Tobias said, "with that arm, you're liable to dump the wee one on the floor!" He leaned over and gently picked up the sleeping baby. With a twinkle in his eye, he pushed the bundle against Matthew's chest. Instinctively, Matthew wrapped his arms around the baby. "Now don't drop him," laughed Tobias as he picked up the cradle.

Matthew stood there as if frozen, staring at Tobias. The baby squirmed in his arms.

"Tobias, please, I don't know how to do this! What if I hurt him?" pleaded Matt.

"You're doing fine! Pretend he's a newborn calf and walk with him into the next room," grinned his friend. Tobias picked the cradle up and walked into the living room area and set the cradle next to a chair.

Matt looked down at the sweet child in his arms and marveled at the perfect little human. The little boy couldn't weigh as much as a new calf, he felt so light. The baby opened his eyes and looked at Matthew, then smiled and wiggled his arms. Surprised, Matthew smiled back.

"Matthew," called Tobias from the next room, "bring the child here."

He walked carefully into the next room after Tobias. While Tobias was getting the cradle into position, the door opened. The women were smiling and talking as they came into the room, but both stopped short as they saw Matthew holding the baby.

"Looks good on you, Matthew," laughed Melissa.

He shifted his gaze to Sarah, who stood staring at him. Suddenly, she walked to him and reached to take the baby. Matthew was afraid to move the baby away from his body for fear he would drop him, so Sarah had to lean in to him and push her hands against his chest to take little TC. Her hair smelled so good, fresh, and like lavender. He felt the softness of her hands as she touched his. Sarah stopped and stood there. Then she smiled at him.

"You can let go now," she said softly, "I have him."

"Are you sure? I don't want to drop him," mumbled Matthew, clearly out of his element.

"Yes. Thank you," said Sarah. That was the first time she had smiled at him. Matt swallowed hard. Her eyes were so beautiful.

"Wash up, gentlemen, Sunday dinner is on the table," said Melissa.

It was a feast, with ham and potatoes and even some greens the women had found down by the creek. They finished with an apple pie and coffee and enjoyed little Greta singing to them for awhile. She was singing when she suddenly smiled at Matt, hopped off her father's lap, and ran over to him.

"I love you, Uncle Matt," she said unexpectedly. Matt was taken totally off guard; she had never done that before. "Do you love me?" asked the sweet girl in total innocence. Matthew felt the color rise in his cheeks as all eyes were on him.

"Yes, I love you too, Greta," he said, leaning down to her. She put her arms around his neck and kissed him on the cheek, then skipped back to Tobias and climbed back in his lap, oblivious to the impact she had on his heart. It wasn't long before she turned against her father's chest and went to sleep.

"She doesn't usually take an afternoon nap, but there has been a lot of excitement around here lately." said Tobias, as he rose to take her to her bed. He came back and sat at the table and they all continued the lazy Sunday afternoon.

Matthew could not remember a more pleasant day. He looked across the table at Sarah and noticed the flush of her cheeks as she and Melissa talked about vegetable gardens and canning.

"Matthew," asked Melissa, turning towards him. "Our apple tree is growing fast; do you think we could do a cherry tree as well here?"Matthew thought for a moment.

"I think if you plant them on that little rise behind the house so the soil drains and doesn't become waterlogged, the roots will do fine," he said. "In fact, I have been thinking of trying pear and apricot trees at my ranch." He saw surprise on Sarah's face.

"Matthew was a farmer before the war," said Melissa to Sarah. "I have followed his advice on my garden and it, as you can see, does very well." Sarah smiled at Melissa, and gave Matthew a second smile.

Maybe Tobias and Melissa were right about her. He listened to the women plan a garden for next year, and what they should plant in the fall. He was trying to follow the conversation, but he felt so tired. He wasn't quite up to full strength yet. Finally, he gave up.

"If you'll excuse me, I think I am going to head off for a nap myself," he said, getting slowly to his feet. "That was a wonderful meal, ladies, thank you."

"I'm glad your appetite is returning and you could do it justice," laughed Tobias. "I thought I was going to have to fight you for that last potato!" They all laughed.

Matthew was still stiff and a little sore. He slipped between the covers and looked out the window at the gently swaying trees. He thought about his ranch and Paul out there alone. He needed to check on him tomorrow. His thoughts drifted back to Sarah. Had he told her about Paul? His thoughts were so fuzzy still, he knew he wasn't as alert as usual. He was thinking of how her touch felt as he drifted off to sleep. It was a pleasant thought.

Chapter 15

Matthew felt much better the next morning and decided he would like to go outside. It was a beautiful morning, just a touch of chill in the air, but the sun was shining and it was pleasant. He and Tobias were sitting at the table, finishing their coffee when he mentioned going out to the ranch to check on Paul. Tobias glared at him.

"Charlie is riding out that way today and will check on him. You, my friend, will not undo all of the work Melissa and Doc have done by being pig headed!" he gave Matthew a look that clearly said he would brook no nonsense."Go sit on the porch and get some fresh air. Whittle something, but get outside and get some sun. You are white as a sheet from lying in bed!"

Tobias nodded his head and Matthew knew it was useless to argue. Matthew also knew it was his friend's way of showing he had been worried. Charlie was a good man, and would make sure all was well.

"Does Paul know we found Sarah," he asked, realizing he had not thought about telling Paul while he himself lay in bed.

"Yes, Charlie told Paul, and Paul is very relieved, " answered Tobias.

"Thank you,"said Matthew. He drew in a sharp breath, a thought striking him. "Tobias, have you seen my knife?" Matthew asked.

"Well, now that you mention it, no," said the big man. "Are you sure it isn't in your room or at Doc's? " He thought for a moment. "I just don't know if you had it at the shack or not," said Tobias, "I was too busy trying to get you some help."

"The last time I remember having it was at the ranch, before I went to look for Sarah," Matthew said, "but I suppose it could be at Doc's. Maybe I will walk over later and ask."

Doc was back, and since Matthew was able to get up and about, he saw no need to move him back into the patient room. Doc didn't need the patient bed right now, for which he was immensely grateful, so they decided he would get Charlie and Tobias to move it back after Matthew went back to his ranch. Sarah came out on the porch and Matthew stood to look at little TC. The little child's face lit up and he squirmed and smiled as soon as he saw Matthew.

"He likes you," said Sarah. Matthew gazed in her eyes, afraid to ask if his mother liked him too.

"He seems bigger in just the past few days," said Matthew, knowing babies grew fast, but how fast, he didn't know.

"I think his cheeks have filled out a little since he has been getting more to eat. I am so grateful to Mrs. Lang for helping when I was not strong," she said, looking at the squirming, smiling little boy. "He is more active than ever!" TC squealed as if in response, and they both laughed. "You are looking better as well," said Sarah, critically appraising Matthew. "Although, your cheeks could still fill out a little too!" she teased.

"If I stay here much longer, the good cooking from you ladies will have me filling out more than my cheeks," he said, patting his slim belly. "No work and too much good food and I will be bursting my buttons!" He smiled at her and she smiled back. The silence between them felt comfortable.

"Well," said Sarah, "we are off to Doc's to let him take a look at TC and make sure he is satisfied with his progress. It is such a beautiful day, I thought I'd get us both out in the fresh air and save Doc the walk." Matthew offered her his hand as she negotiated the steps with the baby, then watched her cross the street and walk leisurely over to Doc's office. She had soft hands.

It did feel good to be outside, to feel the sun on his face. A slight breeze rustled the sage and kept him cool. He watched two young boys throwing a stick for their dog to fetch, laughing when the dog decided to run off with the stick and had the lads chasing him!

A few women came to the store while he sat. One of them was young, with pretty, dark curls and striking green eyes. Her skin was creamy and her full lips smiled at him as she walked across the street and up the steps. He nodded and smiled a greeting in return, tipping his hat as she walked past him and into the store. He sat outside for some time, greeting the townspeople as they walked by, some stopping to inquire as to his recovery. He was content, a feeling he had not had in a long while.

Suddenly, he sat up straight. Three men were riding their horses slowly up the street, looking at everyone they passed, and studying the town itself. They looked somehow familiar to Matthew, and he scrutinized them with care. They were dirtier than the normal trail dust would cause, with greasy spots on their shirts. One had a scraggly blond-brown beard with tobacco stains showing, a filthy blue shirt stretched tight over a pot belly, and a black hat pulled down over his small eyes. His black eyes had a mean look to them as they challenged Matthew from his saddle. The second man was younger, skinny to the point of gaunt. He had coal black hair, and wore his brown hat pushed off his head and hanging by a string around his neck. His shirt was red, with a couple of buttons missing. Matthew studied him carefully, and looked at the two guns tied down on either side. Looked to be Colt 45 revolvers, and they were not new. The third man was dressed in grease stained buckskin. He was older, and had the look of a trail wise trapper. His hair was long, mostly grey, and badly matted. He carried a Remington rifle out and across his saddle. Matthew followed them with his eyes, until they pulled up to the saloon three buildings down and across the street. He watched them go inside. He had a bad feeling about those men; they did not look like they just came to town for a drink. He continued to study their horses after they went inside. He had seen those horses before, but where?

Quick movement pulled his focus back to his right, and he saw
Sarah, holding her dress up and running to the store, clutching
the baby tight with one arm as she ran. Her eyes rose to meet
his as she came up the porch. Her eyes were big and her face
was pale. He could hear her breath coming in sharp gasps. She
looked terrified.

"Sarah, what is it?" asked Matthew, rising to his feet. But she
ran right past him into the store.

He followed her inside. "Is it the baby? What did Doc say?"
She didn't answer him at first, her eyes were darting around the
store like a trapped animal looking for a way out. He walked to
her and put his hands on her shoulders, bending slightly so his
eyes were level with hers. "Sarah!" he said a little sharply. She
stopped and looked at him. Tears started to flow out of her eyes
and down her face.

"They're here." She said, starting to sob. "The men."
Melissa was waiting on the women who had come in before,
and shot Matthew a questioning glance. He shrugged his
shoulders in reply, then turned back to Sarah.

"Come here," Matthew said, placing one hand on the small of
her back and the other gently on her arm, leading her into the
living quarters behind the store. He walked her to a chair at the
table and eased her to a sitting position. The cradle was next to
the chair, and he carefully took the sleeping baby from her and
placed him in the cradle. He sat down beside her and without
thinking, took her hands in his.

"Sarah, you are safe here. Talk to me, tell me what is wrong.
Please." He wanted to take her in his arms and hold her. She
looked so small, so frail, and so frightened. He felt so helpless
as he watched her gasping in air and letting it out in ragged
sobs. She was shaking and twisting her hands together. He
shifted, and gently put his arms around her, pulling her head to
his good shoulder. He had never held a crying woman before
and really was not sure what to do. He stroked her hair, feeling
the silkiness beneath his rough hands. He found himself patting

her on the back and running his hands lightly up and down her back, like he had seen her do with the baby when he was crying.

"It's okay, Sarah," he said to her softly, "you're safe here. We won't let them harm you or the baby." He felt awkward and didn't know what else to do; he still was not sure what exactly had frightened her. Slowly, she calmed and stopped crying. She pulled herself up straighter, wiping her hands across her face. She looked at him.

"The men that killed my husband just rode into town." Her voice was shaking.

"Are you sure?" asked Matthew, with sharpened interest.

"Yes! I hid after they shot my husband, and they rode right by me. They rode right by the window just now, while I was at the doctor. There were three of them together. It was like having the same nightmare twice!"

"One in buckskins, one young one with dark hair, and one with a dirty beard." It was more a statement than a question.

"Yes. Do you know them?" she asked, fear in her eyes again.

"No," he said, "but I saw them." Recognition hit him then. "I think those are the men that were following you the night I got hurt!"

"Are you sure? I didn't see who was following me, I just knew they were there because I saw their dust! I was afraid it was them!"

"Yes, I am sure now," said Matthew, thinking quickly.

Melissa came in the living quarters suddenly, carrying a basket of herbs she had gathered earlier from near the stream. Sarah cried out, jumping to her feet, surprised at the sudden movement. Matthew stood and pulled her into his arms again and held her.

"Sarah, it's ok, they don't know you are here," said Matthew. Melissa looked from Matthew to Sarah, concern on her face. Sarah looked at Melissa, then up at Matthew, and stepped back, blushing.

"I'm sorry, I don't mean to be so weak," she said, looking down at the floor.

"What is wrong?" asked Melissa. "Should I get Tobias? He is out cutting wood in the back."

"I think it would be a good idea, Melissa," said Matthew, "I think we all need to talk. Bring Greta too, we need her close." Melissa looked from one to the other, then with a determined look on her face, she set down the basket of herbs in the corner and stepped out the back door. Sarah walked over to the cradle and looked down at the sleeping boy. Ever so gently, she leaned down and stroked his small head. "He's so little," she said, "I just want to keep him safe." Matthew had a strange feeling in his chest as he watched her, and he did not think it was from his injuries.

"We won't let them hurt either one of you," he said. He set his jaw, determined to keep that promise as long as he had a breath left in his body.

Tobias, Melissa, and Greta came in through the back door. Melissa quickly settled Greta at the table with a book and she and Tobias pulled up chairs. Matthew and Sarah began to explain the problem and Matthew provided a detailed description of the men. Sarah had been afraid to look too closely out the window for fear they would see her, but they had passed right in front of Matthew.

"Do you think they will stay here and look for you?" Tobias asked.

"It won't be hard for them to ask around. I have been helping in the store, so someone is bound to tell them I am here." She gazed at little TC again. "No one in the town knows I have some gold, except the people in this room." She looked at little Greta reading the book and a worried look came over her face. "I should go," she said, almost a whisper. She looked at Melissa with fear in her eyes and shook her head." I cannot put you and Greta in danger even to save my baby."

Melissa looked at Tobias and knew what he would say. She took his hand and a look of understanding passed between them.

"You are not going anywhere," said Tobias firmly. "I will talk to some of the other men in the town. This is our town, and we will not have those dirty back shooters driving away or bringing harm to decent people in our town!" Melissa looked at Sarah and nodded in agreement as her husband spoke.

"We came here to start a new life and raise a family. What kind of life can any of us have if we run before the likes of those swine?" she said quietly. She looked at her daughter, giggling over the pictures in her book. "What kind of life will Greta have if her parents will not stand up to outlaws and murderers?"

Matthew's heart felt like it would burst in his chest. He was so proud of his friends; their courage was what built the west. He looked at Sarah. She was wiping another tear away from her face.

"I don't know what to say," she began, "I will never be able to repay your kindness," she said to Melissa and Tobias. "Thank you," she said, turning to Matt.

"Well," Tobias said, standing up. "you will stay close to the house until we catch these men," he said, looking from Melissa to Sarah. "Melissa..."

"I know how to handle a gun, my husband," she said, walking to the sideboard and opening a cupboard. She reached inside the soup tureen and took out a small Smith and Wesson revolver. She checked the cylinder, and then tucked it neatly in the big pocket of her skirt. She reached up and patted Tobias on the cheek, then settled herself at the table beside Greta and read her the story.

Matthew looked at Sarah, who raised her chin with a determined look. She walked over to the canvas bag she kept on the stack of boxes in the corner. She reached in and took out a modified derringer. She also checked the cylinder to make sure it was loaded, then slipped her gun into her pocket as well. "Nobody is going to hurt my baby as long as I can help it," she said defiantly.

Tobias and Matthew looked at each other and felt a little relieved. These women had backbone!

"I'll take the porch again," said Matthew, picking up his Winchester. His Colt forty-five was strapped to the belt around his waist as he walked out and sat down on the bench by the door.

Tobias paused on his way out to survey the town in front of him. He listened while Matthew gave him a detailed description of the men and pointed out their horses. He nodded. "I'll be back before long. I'm going to go talk to Charlie at the smithy and John at the hotel. They'll pass the word." He studied Matt. "I'll let Doc know too, just in case they come asking about her. They won't get her, Matt. We'll make sure of that." He started down the steps, then turned. "If anything happens, fire three shots in quick succession and I'll come with the calvary!" he smiled at his own joke and walked across the street.

Chapter 16

Matthew sat on the porch at the general store and watched the saloon three doors down. He saw Tobias walking back up the street with John and Charlie, and both were armed. John stopped and sat at the hardware store, watching the saloon as well. When the men reached the porch, Charlie sat on the edge of the walk and Tobias stood on the other side of the door.

"We have spread the word around town," said Tobias. "There are men watching everywhere."

"I see John down at the hardware store, but should he be by himself?" asked Matthew.

"He's not," grinned Tobias. "Look to the second story of the livery stable, next to the saloon." Matthew looked, and was startled to see a rifle barrel at the second story of the barn. "That's Tom McCall, owns the livery stable. Doc is standing by at his place, and Jonas Phippen rode for the sheriff."

"How long before Sheriff Tinkum gets here?" asked Matthew.

"Maybe two hours," replied Tobias. "We are sure Sarah can identify them as the men who killed her husband, correct?"

"Yes. She hid in a small cave behind some brush and the men rode right by her after they killed her husband." As an afterthought, he added, "Paul might remember something too, if he saw them. It might bring his memory back." Tobias studied Matthew.

"You are still looking a little peaked. Why don't you go inside and make sure no one gets through us to the women, or in the back door." Matthew shook his head.

"No, my friend, you are the one with a family. I will be fine here. I can fire a gun sitting down, if I have to." Charlie suddenly got up without speaking, and walked across the street, disappearing around the corner of the sheriff's office. Matthew and Tobias looked at each other and shrugged. Several minutes later, he came back and sat on the edge of the porch again. Without turning to them, he spoke to Tobias and Matthew.

"I went around to the back of the saloon," said Charlie. "I talked to the cook and he said they have ordered food and are drinking. They will be there awhile."

"Good thinking, Charlie!" Tobias clapped him on the shoulder. The men continued their vigil, watching everything, but hesitant to initiate action with the sheriff on the way.

Sheriff Tinkum rode into town in just under two hours after Jonas had ridden to bring him the message. He was a tall man, of average build, but with an air of assumed authority surrounding him. His piercing green eyes were set off by a long beard, and the effect was imposing. He rode up to the porch and sent Charlie out to slowly gather the men to him. Then he nodded to Matthew and Tobias, and rode over to the Sheriff's Office. Since the Sheriff's Office was the opposite direction from the saloon, but still not far from the general store, it was easy to get most of the men in the small office without being observed. Tobias followed the sheriff across the street to his office, but Matthew remained at the general store, refusing to leave the women and children alone.

Sheriff Tinkum listened without speaking as Tobias told the story, giving a condensed version of what had happened to Sarah's husband and why the outlaws were following her. He described the three men and pointed out their horses in front of the saloon. They all took a good look. When Tobias finished, the sheriff stood, and looked at each man.

"Anyone want out?" he asked. No one moved. He then commanded all men in the office to raise their right hands, deputized them, and gave each one a badge.

"There will be no cause to say any of you acted outside the law. Those badges give you the right to act in whatever capacity I so choose." His vivid green eyes scanned each face again. "Alright then, I will go into the saloon and see what is happening. Tom, go back up in the hay loft, and if they draw a weapon or shoot, take them down." Tom nodded. "John, I want you in the alley right beside the hardware store. It is too dangerous to be in front; there is no cover."

"Yes sir," acknowledged John.

"Doc, go back to your office and keep an eye on the front of the store. You can shoot if you have to, but we may need your professional services when this is done. I don't want to risk you getting shot." Doc met his eyes for a moment, and everyone in the room realized the significance of the comment. He nodded, and walked out the back door to his own office.

"Charlie and Jonas, you watch the back of the saloon, in case they run. Tobias, you and Matthew stay at the general store." Tobias shook his head in agreement. The sheriff looked at each man separately. "This stops now. Our women and our families will be safe in this town." All eyes were riveted on the sheriff. "Be careful, men." With that, he racked a shotgun and headed out the door, with the remaining men going their respective directions.

Sheriff Tinkum walked straight to the general store, up the steps and inside. As he passed Matthew, he spoke.

"Inside." It was a simple command, but Matthew rose and followed him just the same. Once inside, Tinkum turned and faced Matthew. "Raise your right hand." Matthew did so without question, and the sheriff issued the oath. As Matthew agreed, he was handed a badge. "Put it on, you are deputized and are acting on my behalf," said the sheriff. Locking eyes, the men knew what the other was thinking. "Your job is to keep the women and children safe, should they get by us."

"If they get by me, I won't know it anymore." Tinkum studied him, then nodded. He understood. Tinkum walked out the door and down the street to the saloon, carrying the shotgun. A few minutes later, he returned, cursing.

"They went out the back while we were meeting! Damn it!" He stood, looking around the town, his eyes examining every shadow and window. "We have to post guards until we find them."

"Their horses are still at the hitching post, so they could not have gone far, said Matthew. "What made them leave?"

"The bartender said they ordered and one of them walked over to watch a card game. He looked out the window and probably saw John sitting across the street with the rifle across his knees. Then it's likely he saw him get up and walk down the street. Bartender thought he might have seen him talk to you two on his way to my office." He took his hat off and wiped his forehead with a handkerchief he took out of his pocket. "After that, he walked over and spoke to the other two at the table, and they just got up and went out the back without finishing their food. The bartender hollered at them to pay, and they threw these at him." He held up two, one dollar gold coins. "Let's go ask Sarah if these look familiar."

The three men went into the general store and walked to the back. Suddenly, Tobias stopped them by holding up a hand. "Melissa," he said, "we are coming in."

"Come ahead," she answered. They walked into the kitchen to see both women standing, facing the door, holding their guns at their sides.

"Ladies," nodded Sheriff Tinkum, tipping his hat. He looked at them with appreciation; they were prepared to protect their own children if need be. Then he stepped to Sarah, and taking off his hat, bowed slightly to her. M'am, I am Sheriff Tinkum."

"Pleased to meet you, sheriff," said Sarah, slightly dipping in a curtsy.

"I hear you have had some trouble and I want you to know I am very sorry about your husband." Sarah dropped her head for a moment, then raised her eyes to his again.

"Thank you, sheriff," she said.

"M'am, I wonder if you could tell me if this looks familiar to you." He put his hand in his pocket and pulled out one of the gold coins.

"It could be," said Sarah, taking the coin and slowly turning it over in her hand. "But I am not sure it is one of the actual coins we carried with us."

"So, you did have dollar gold coins with you?" asked the sheriff. "The description and identification of the men is enough to convict them, but this could be helpful too. There aren't too many of these coins in circulation out here yet." Sarah looked confused. "You brought them from the north, correct?" he continued.

"Yes," she nodded. "But how could that matter? There must be other one dollar gold coins in this area." She looked at the gathering of people in the room, seeking some explanation. Everyone was silent, trying to comprehend what the sheriff was saying.

"Well, actually no, M'am," he said, "not like these." He held out his hand and she gave him the coin back. He held it up for all to see. "You see, M'am, this coin is bigger and thinner than earlier one dollar gold coins, and the mark on it says 1862, minted in Philadelphia. The mints in Charlotte and Dahlonega were closed down in 1861 because of the War Between the States. The only place in the west that minted these coins prior to 1861, is San Francisco."

"I still don't understand," she said, staring at him. "What does that mean?"

"It means," he continued, we don't have many one dollar gold coins in this area at all. We have even less that came from the mint in Philadelphia. Almost all one dollar gold coins in the United States have been minted in Philadelphia since 1861. You brought yours from the north, and they were almost certainly minted in Philadelphia." Tobias and Matthew shared a look of surprise. "That makes it highly likely this is one of the coins you brought west with your husband." He looked at the coin again. "Do you mind if I keep this for awhile, M'am, until we catch them?"

"Of course," she said, then what he had said registered and her face turned pale. "Wait, you haven't caught them yet?" She raised a hand to her throat.

"No M'am, they slipped out the back of the saloon. But we will find them. Just stay inside please, and keep those handy," he said, gesturing at the hand guns. Melissa and Sarah exchanged a worried glance and slipped the guns back in the pockets of their skirts. Melissa looked at Tobias.

"We'll make up a soup and some biscuits for any of the men that are hungry," she said, "just tell them to hail us before they come into the kitchen." She gave him a weak smile.

"I'll do that," said Tobias, giving her a quick kiss on the cheek. "It will be alright, we will catch them soon."

"I am staying right here in front of the store," said Matthew. "If they do get through me, you will have plenty of warning," he said. He met their eyes and saw fear. They knew if the men got that far he would be dead.

"The soup will be ready in about an hour and a half," said Melissa, valiantly trying to distract everyone from their grim thoughts.

"Thank you, Ladies," nodded the sheriff, putting his hat back on. "It is much appreciated." He turned to Tobias and Matthew. "Let's go find those rotten skunks." He walked back out through the store, with Tobias and Matthew behind him.

"We need more men," said Tobias. I saw two of the cowboys from the Hunewill Ranch go in the hotel awhile ago. If we are going to search the town, we could use them."

"Good thinking, "said the sheriff. "Tell the others to meet back at my office in fifteen minutes, and we will form teams to start at each end of the town and make sure everyone knows to be careful." Tobias walked rapidly to the hotel, and returned shortly with the two cowboys.

"Howdy, sheriff, " said the taller of the two, extending his hand to the sheriff. He was young and lean, with dark hair and a horseshoe style mustache. "My name's Ben and this is Azrael," he said, indicating another young man, with a chevron style mustache. Azrael wore a tied down Colt Navy Revolver. It more than made up for the fact he was slightly smaller in stature than his friend. Sheriff Tinkum shook both their hands, noting that Azrael extended his left hand instead of his right. He peered into Azrael's eyes a minute longer than Ben's. "Azrael, Angel of Death and Retribution for wrong doing," the sheriff thought. This was a very dangerous man, and he hoped he was on their side.

"Tobias tells us you need a hand tracking down some men that are hunting a lady," said Ben.

"They killed her husband, robbed him, and now they want to kill her because she can identify them," said the sheriff. "She has a baby too," he added. Ben and Azrael exchanged a glance. "We don't hold with nobody trying to hurt a woman," Ben said, "especially with a baby. If you want our help, you got it." His eyes were deep and steady. Sheriff Tinkum looked at Azrael, who had not said a word. Azrael nodded. Sheriff Tinkum was not a man easily frightened, but there was something in the eyes of Azrael that made his skin tingle. He would not want to meet him alone on a dark road at night.

"Are you willing to be deputized for the duration of this problem?" asked the sheriff. He hadn't asked any of the other men, he had just told them to raise their hands. Again, Ben and Azrael exchanged a glance. They seemed to have an unwritten, unspoken language between them.

"Yes," answered Ben for the both of them.

"Then raise your right hands, please," asked the sheriff. He administered the oath, and handed them both a badge. Azrael did not drop his glance to look at the badge, he just held out his hand, continuing to stare into the eyes of the sheriff. Tinkum watched as both men pinned on the badges. Then he turned and walked to his desk, opened a drawer, and began filling his pockets with cartridges. He placed several boxes of different calibers on the desk. He opened another drawer and took out a box of shotgun shells filled with buckshot, which he emptied into another pocket.

The door to the office opened, and the men of the town began to file in, all except Matthew, who remained at the general store with the women.

"Take a good look at everyone's face and what they are wearing. Most of you know each other, but these two cowpokes are from the Hunewill Ranch." He gestured to Ben and Azrael. I don't want anyone getting shot by mistake." All eyes turned to the two cowboys and, like the sheriff, all felt a chill when they gazed at the medium built, dark eyed cowboy Azrael. No one kept their gaze on him for long.

" Tobias, why don't you describe the three men for everyone again," said the sheriff.

Tobias proceeded to describe every detail he could remember about the three men – height, weight, coloring, eyes, clothes down to the grease spots on their shirts. "They left their horses in front of the saloon, so we don't think they will have changed clothes," Tobias said. "Any questions?" The room remained silent.

"We are going to start at both ends of town at the same time," instructed the sheriff. Two go into a home or business while a third keeps a lookout." He looked around the room."We take them alive if we can, but don't take any chances. They are dangerous men – use your best judgement and remember you all have families or good reasons to live. Don't take chances you don't have to." He scanned their faces, then continued.

"Matthew will stay at the general store, and Tom, I want you back up in that hay loft, watching both directions. You can see a lot from up there." Tom nodded. "Doc, I still want you back at your office to keep an eye on that end of town. You need to stay healthy in case we need you." Doc looked at the men, but did not say anything.

"Where were they last seen?" asked Ben quietly. Sheriff Tinkum turned to him in surprise.

"The saloon, why?" he asked.

"Az is an expert tracker. He spent a lot of time with the Apaches when he was younger," replied Ben. That explained some things to the sheriff.

"Makes sense," said the sheriff, "why don't you two go see what you can find." They started to leave and he added, "be careful." Both men turned, and for the first time, Azrael had a twitch at the side of his mouth. If that was a smile, it had a chilling effect. Neither said a word, but turned back and walked out the back door. No one moved for a few minutes after they left. Tinkum took a deep breath and continued.

"John, Joshua, and Charlie, take the north end of town. Tobias, you and I will be a two man team and start at the south end and work toward the middle. Tell people who we are looking for and explain they are dangerous. If they can't get to their own horses, they may try to steal some. If they can't get to Sarah for the gold, they may try to rob a business or a citizen. It may not be mountain lions around their stock, it might be these skunks, and they need to be aware of the danger. Tell people to stay inside as much as possible, and watch their doors and windows. If they have to be outside, day or night until we catch them, tell them to be armed and pay close attention. Any questions?" No one spoke. "Extra shells and cartridges here on the desk, take 'em if you need 'em," he said. Jonas took a box of cartridges and John took a handful and they each put them in their pockets. Sheriff Tinkum searched every face, then nodded. "Let's go clean up our town." Everyone went in the direction they had been told.

Chapter 17

"How the hell did they know we were here?" asked Jake, spitting tobacco in the dirt. He was almost out of chew and he wanted to get another plug out of his saddlebags.

"Must mean someone knew who we were," said Parker, scratching his matted hair and wondering if he had bugs in it again. Damn it, he'd have to get some vinegar and waste some tobacco to coat his head once more.

"What's that s'posed to mean," asked King. He pulled his hat up by the string and smashed it down on his head. He was hungry, and he left a perfectly good plate of steak and beans to run off into the trees.

"Means the woman must be here, idiot," said Parker. "How else would they know to look for us? We ain't done nothin' wrong here."

"Well, where do you think she is?" asked Jake, grinning and showing tobacco stained and chipped teeth. "I want that extra gold she has, and maybe a little something more for our trouble." He spat a stream of tobacco again, then wiped his mouth with his hand, which he wiped on his filthy blue shirt. "Been a long time since I had me a woman," he said, his mean little eyes gleaming.

"Oh hell, Jake, "said King, "there are too many men with guns here for you to think about poking some woman! We need to just get the gold and run. You can get you a woman in Virginia City with your share of the gold!" He glared at Jake and Jake started to stand, but Parker grabbed him and pulled him back down.

"Get down, you fool!" snapped Parker. "Keep your mind on the business we came for, and that's the gold!" He thought for a moment. "When I was lookin' out that window in the saloon, I seen that man with the rifle sittin' across from the saloon git up and walk down to the general store, where he talked to two more men. Then two of them went down the street and I couldn't see them no more." He smiled. "But the one in front of the general store never left." He nodded his head up and down. "Yep, that's where she is." The three of them sat for a minute, thinking about what Parker said.

"Well, then, let's circle around to that store and see if there is a back way in," said King. "Maybe we can get in and out with the gold before they know where we are." They started to move carefully through the trees in the direction of the general store. They did not see Az and Ben come out the door of the saloon. If they had, they would have seen Az look at the very spot where they had been a few minutes before.

Azrael kept his sharp eyes forward as they stepped out of the door. He quickly scanned to the left, then right, then focused on a point in the woods about a hundred feet away from where they stood. He walked straight to the trees and stopped where the men had been. He could see the crushed grass and the stain where the tobacco spit had hit a downed tree trunk.

He looked towards the general store and he and Ben exchanged a look. They walked through the trees with no sound, coming up on the men as they crept to the back of the general store.

"There's the back of the general store, "said Parker. "Looks like there is a door and a window on the back side, and another window on the side there, between the two buildings." He rubbed his chin, thinking.

"You two take the back door," said Parker. "I'm going around to that window on the side. Maybe we can box 'em in and get that gold before anybody knows we are here."

"What'll we do with her after we get her gold?" leered Jake.

"We hit her on the head or tie her up and we get the hell outta here!" said Parker with a deadly look at Jake. "We got to git back to our horses somehow and run outta town as fast as we can. We ain't got time for you to poke her and if'n we harm her or kill her, there will be a mighty mad posse after us before you can spit a stream of tobacco." He fixed Jake with a scowl. "You get off track on this at all and draw attention to us, and I'll kill you myself."

"I ain't aimin' to dance at no end of a rope," King put in. "I'm with Parker."

"Damn lilly livered…"began Jake.

"Shut it, Jake," snapped Parker. Jake glowered at him, but stopped talking. "Alright, let's git this done and git outta town before dark. Wait for my signal before you rush that door." He looked at the two of them. "We git separated, we meet in Bodie," said Parker. The other two men nodded. They all edged out and crept up to the back of the general store, Parker slipping around the side to the alley. Parker reached the window and slid it up easily. He looked back at Jake and King and motioned them forward, then hoisted himself silently through the window.

Matthew stood up and walked inside the store, where there was shade. He could watch from here, and not have his vision distorted by the setting sun. It wouldn't do to be blinded at a critical moment. He was standing in the general store when he heard a noise he did not like. Slowly, he moved towards the living quarters. He could hear Greta singing and wondered where Sarah and Melissa were with the baby. It sounded like Greta was in the kitchen, near the door to the back of the General Store. Then he heard a board creak, just once. It was off to the side where the bedrooms were. If it were Sarah or Melissa, they would have come walking by him already. He drew his gun and waited.

"Let's git 'er done," said King to Jake and both men rose from their crouch and moved up to the back door. Their guns were drawn and they carefully tried the handle. The door was locked. They were ready to shoulder the door when they heard a voice behind them.

"I don't think you have been invited in, gentlemen," said Ben evenly. "Put your guns down and your hands up. Now."

Jake and King turned their heads and saw two men standing ten feet away. Their guns were in their holsters. Jake and King laughed and brought their guns around to shoot Ben and Azrael down. Suddenly, Ben and Azrael drew so fast Jake and King never saw their hands move. The outlaws fired twice, but failed to hit their targets. The young men walked forward, firing into the two outlaws until they fell to the ground, lifeless. Ben kicked their guns away as Azrael watched. They looked down at the two scoundrels on the ground. There was no need to check for a pulse.

Tobias and Sheriff Tinkum had rounded the corner slowly, just in time to hear Ben's challenge to the outlaws. They reached for their own guns as they noted Azrael and Ben still had their guns in their holsters, and the outlaws were swinging their guns around instead of dropping them. It was over before Tobias or the sheriff put their hands on their gun butts. They stood in disbelief at what they had just seen. Neither of them could have sworn they had seen the young men actually draw their guns, one minute their hands were by their sides, and the next minute, their guns appeared in their hands and they were shooting.

Ben and Azrael looked at Tobias and Sheriff Tinkum, then calmly reloaded their guns and put them in their holsters.

"Where's the third one?" asked Ben. Tobias looked towards the general store and started to run. Two shots rang out. He knew it was not Melissa or Sarah that fired, the caliber he heard was too large. Matthew and someone else had fired.

"Oh, sweet Jesus, let me not be too late!" he prayed. He crashed through the door.

Matthew stood still, listening for the women and watching in front of him. He was pressed against the wall of the short hall between the store and the bedrooms, gun drawn. A man stepped out, clad in filthy buckskin and reeking of sweat, dirt, and something that smelled like a dead animal. He edged around the door frame, intent on the room in front of him. Sarah walked by the door with TC on her shoulder, patting him softly on the back. She caught her breath as she turned and caught sight of the trapper. Matthew could see the horror on her face as she realized she could not reach for her gun with her baby in her arms.

"Don't you scream, missy, or I'll kill you and maybe your baby too," Parker said roughly, leveling his gun at her chest. "If you scream to bring that feller in front, I'll kill him too. Now, where's the gold, "he hissed.

Matthew could not risk taking a step to hit him on the head or try to disarm him, especially with his weakened shoulder. He might pull the trigger if hit, and shoot Sarah and the baby. A volley of shots rang out from outside the door. Parker's head jerked in the direction of the door, and Matthew saw his chance.

"Put the gun down," he commanded. Parker whirled and fired a shot that roared past Matthew's head and lodged in a beam in the ceiling. Matthew fired, hitting the trapper square in the chest. He flew back against the door jamb, then slid to the floor, eyes open, but no longer able to see.

The back door splintered and Tobias, Melissa, and Matthew all found themselves facing each other's guns. They stood motionless for a few seconds, then lowered their guns. Melissa pocketed her gun and ran into Tobias' arms as he put his gun in the holster. Greta jumped up from the floor near the door and ran to her papa, who lifted her in his big arms, and hugged both of those he loved. Matthew looked at Sarah, who still stood rooted to the floor where she had been when she saw the trapper, her eyes looking much too large for her face. TC was crying from the loud noise of the shots.

Matthew turned slightly to holster his gun and realized Azrael and Ben were standing behind him. He had not heard them come up on him. They met his gaze without comment. Sheriff Tinkum walked in the back door and looked at the trapper on the floor. He saw Ben and Azrael, and did a double take over his shoulder, then back at the two young men. He had not seen them come around the building after the men in the back had gone down. He stared at them for a moment, as if he were seeing ghosts.

Ben and Azrael looked at each other, then stepped past Matthew and picked up the trapper. Without a word, they carried him out the front of the store. Charlie, John, and Jonas came around the back. Charlie and John picked up one of the dead men and took him over to the undertaker. Tom McCall walked up and he and Jonas took the other one away. Doc came in the front door with a bottle and a rag and started cleaning up the blood from the trapper. Matthew walked into the kitchen where Sarah still stood and took her in his arms, with TC between them. She shook violently as he whispered to her it was all right now.

Chapter 18

The three outlaws were buried on the edge of the cemetery with only the undertaker and his helper in attendance to dig the graves and lower the bodies. No one read over them from the Book, counting their souls as lost long ago. Their saddlebags and bodies were searched, and found to hold only a few more of the one dollar gold coins. They were returned to Sarah, who offered them to the sheriff and undertaker for services rendered. Azrael and Ben refused any compensation, other than to tip their hat at Sarah in the end.

"Our pleasure, M'am," said Ben, touching his hat and bowing slightly. When she looked to Azrael to thank him, he actually took his hat off and bowed to her. When he rose and looked in her eyes, she was not afraid. She saw only sadness there. They turned and walked away without looking back.

The days after the three men were buried were peaceful. Matthew had been away from the ranch for two weeks now, and knew he was ready to go back home. Besides, Paul needed him. It was his responsibility, his ranch. Doc had examined him and declared he was out of all danger, but should take it easy for awhile and not try to dig any post holes or lift anything heavy for another week or so. He should start back using that shoulder slowly.

He had spent the few extra days with the Gruener's, helping Tobias with a few chores that were more easily done by two men; not heavy lifting, just awkward and bulky. Tobias had likewise promised he would be out to help Matthew with the roof repair before the fall rains began.

Matthew had helped Melissa plant a new cherry tree up on the little rise behind the living quarters, and did some weeding and harvesting in the garden. Sarah worked beside him doing the weeding, and she asked constant questions about farming techniques. He was glad to see she seemed to laugh easier, knowing the men would never come after her again.

Matthew became more comfortable holding TC and felt himself actually growing attached to the little baby, who now smiled when he heard Matthew's voice. The family atmosphere around the dinner table tugged at Matthew's heart, and he caught himself watching Sarah more. Matthew knew it would be his last night at the home of Melissa and Tobias. They had just finished dinner and the dishes were done, except for the coffee cups and the plates for the peach pie they had just enjoyed. Sarah was holding TC in her lap when he spit up, dousing the blanket she had around him.

"Oh no," she said, moving him quickly so he wouldn't get the spit up on his night clothes.

"Matthew, would you mind getting the fresh blanket out of the top drawer in the dresser?" asked Sarah. "I'm afraid TC has soiled this one."

"Be happy to, Sarah," he said, walking into the other room and going to the dresser where Melissa had cleared the top two drawers for her use. He opened the top drawer and blushed at the ladies clothing folded neatly in the drawer. He opened the second drawer and found little TC's things folded. He reached for the freshly laundered baby blanket Jean Phippen had given Sarah for the baby. As he pulled it out of the drawer, something heavy fell out of it and onto the floor. He reached down to pick it up and froze. It was his knife! What was it doing in her drawer? There was only one answer. She may have fooled Tobias and Melissa, but she was still a thief! He was stupid to trust her, and he did not want his friends to get hurt. He tucked the knife in his boot and took the blanket out to Sarah, but did not look at her. Instead, he handed her the blanket and walked outside on the porch to think. He had to talk to his friends. Baby or no baby, this woman was trouble! She had fooled them all.

He stood outside for some time, thinking about what to do. She had seemed so nice, he had let his guard down. How would Melissa and Tobias take the news? They had come to care for her and the baby. By the time he decided what to do, everyone else was asleep. He would tell them in the morning, and then leave to go back to his ranch.

Matthew slept fitfully that night, his dreams filled with images of the baby smiling at him, Sarah laughing with the sun in her hair, framing her face in a halo of red gold. When he woke early the next morning, he was tired and in a grim mood. He got up quietly and went to the livery stable to saddle Lady and pack his belongings on the horse. He brought her back to the front of the general store and tied her to the hitching rail.

He knew when he was done telling them what he had to say, he would not be able to stay around Sarah. Melissa and Tobias could do what they wanted, but he would not stay under the same roof with someone who had betrayed his friends, and betrayed him. He felt angry, and empty. The feelings he had started to develop for Sarah were crushed under the bitter weight of her lie.

He came to the table and ate silently, without pleasure, just to fill his stomach. Melissa shot him a quizzical look, but thought his mood was because he was serious about getting back to his ranch. They had finished breakfast and were talking about the chores of the day when he finally spoke.

"I found my knife, Tobias," he said, looking his friend in the eyes.

"That's wonderful news, my friend, I know how important that knife is to you! Where did you find it?" he asked, a smile on his face.

"Why don't you ask her," he said, glaring at Sarah. Sarah looked at him with surprise.

"What are you talking about?" she said. Matthew pulled the knife out of his boot and laid it on the table.

"What is this about, Matthew?" asked Tobias. "Where did you find your knife, and what does it have to do with Sarah?"

"It was in her drawer," he said, anger flashing in his face. "It fell out when I went to get the blanket for TC last night." His face was hard as he looked at her through narrowed eyes. "Once a thief, always a thief." His words struck her as if he had hit her. Melissa gasped.

"Matthew!" said Tobias.

"I didn't steal it!" said Sarah, tears starting down her face. "Then how else did it get in the drawer of the dresser with TC's clothes?" asked Matthew. His voice was clipped and he was clearly angry. Sarah was sobbing quietly as she looked at him now. It only made him more agitated.

"I felt sorry for you. I was beginning to like you and admire you for the courage you have shown. And all the while, you were playing all of us!"

"Matthew, please," asked Melissa softly, shifting her gaze back and forth between Matthew and Sarah. The shock on Melissa's face hurt Matthew to see, but he didn't seem able to stop. He wanted to protect his friends, and he felt used.

"Melissa and Tobias can do what they wish," he said standing. "I just wanted them to know your true colors." He stepped close to her and when she looked up, his face made her shrink back. "As for me, I think you are a thief and a liar and I never want to see you again."

"Matthew, wait," said Tobias, rising to his feet.

"I'm sorry Tobias, Melissa, but I can't stay under the same roof with her any longer. Thank you for all you have done for me." He looked at both of them, as they were still stunned by what he said. "I will be going now." He strode briskly through the store and out to the hitching rail in front, leaving them all speechless. He undid the reins and jumped into the saddle, turning Lady toward the ranch.

"It's time to go home, Lady. I have been a fool," he said to his equine friend. His clicked his tongue and urged her into a gallop. All he wanted to do right now was get as far away from Sarah as possible. He wanted to go home. If he worked hard enough, maybe he could forget he ever met her. A knot choked his throat as he thought of TC. The thought of the baby smiling at him made his eyes sting. "Come on girl, let's go home," he said, breaking into a full out run. He couldn't get home fast enough.

Chapter 19

Paul came into the barn where Matthew was working on a harness. Matthew looked up at him. He was going to have to tell him about Sarah, but he wanted to choose the time carefully. He had been back at the ranch for two days now, and the thought had been nagging at him. He had no idea how Paul would take all this. Paul had been so relieved when Charlie had told him they found Sarah. Paul had said he wanted to go into town soon and see her, and meet the baby. He hadn't gone yet, but it was only a matter of time, and he had to tell Paul what had happened before he went into town.

"Good to have you back, boss! How is the shoulder?" he asked. He had been in good spirits when Matthew came home. Matthew had tried hard to hide what he was feeling from Paul, and when Paul asked if he was alright, Matthew had just told him he was still feeling a bit weak and tired. The young man seemed to believe him, and didn't question him further.

"Getting better," Matthew smiled, rubbing it a little. He still took a shot of whiskey several times a day for the pain, and he knew he wasn't up to his usual amount of work. "It sure is good to be home, though! Looks like you have done a good job of keeping up the ranch on your own." He smiled at the young man, and Paul beamed under the praise. "I really appreciate the care you gave the horses and the ranch while I was gone." Paul shook his head.

"Well, that's what I do best," said Paul. "Besides, you saved my life, Matt! I will never forget that." He looked at Matthew and his eyes were serious. Then he grinned. "Grub's on, but that is not where I do my best work," he laughed. He was much stronger, and Matthew thought it was good to hear him laugh.

"Be right there," said Matthew, "it's not Melissa's cooking, but it will fill my belly!" he chided Paul. He felt a pang as he thought of the last time he had seen Melissa. Her face still stood out in his mind, looking as crest fallen as Sarah. He was hungry, having only had coffee this morning before coming out to work on the harness. He quickly finished up the harness repair and hung it with the rest of the tack on the wall of the barn. He gave each of the horses some grain, and took time to pat Lady on her white blaze, before he opened the door to the pasture for the horses.

Matthew walked up to the house and washed up before setting down to the table. He looked at Paul serving up the beans and biscuits.

"If you want a job, I sure could use a permanent hand around here," said Matthew.

"Why, that would suit me just fine," said Paul. He smiled as he sat down to the table. Suddenly, he jumped back up and went to the cupboard by the stove. Reaching behind the coffee can, he pulled out an object and brought it to the table.

"Man rode by the other day, said he had been in the line shack. He wanted to say thank you for the warm bed and coffee. He also said he found this in the bed covers and thought someone might be missing it. He said it looked like it was special made, and I told him it was. He liked the story about your father making one for you and your brother," Paul said, as he laid the knife down in front of Matthew. "I knew you would be glad to see it again!"

It was the knife his father had made for him! Matthew stared at the knife in front of him. Was he imagining things? How could this be?

"Then where did Sarah get the knife…" Matthew jumped up and ran to his saddlebags hanging on the hook by the door. He tore into the pouch and felt for it. His hand closed around something cold and hard and he pulled it out. He walked slowly back to the table and laid the knife beside the twin on the table.

"Where did you get the other one?" asked Paul. "I thought you and your brother had the only two in the world, so how could you have two? " He looked at Matthew, waiting for an answer.

But Matthew's eyes were locked on the knives, his face numb with shock.

"Sarah," he said. "She had the other knife. I thought she stole it from me." Matthew shook his head. Suddenly he looked at Paul."You've always talked about your boss, but I never heard you call him by a name. What was his name?"

"I always called him boss or TC," said Paul, thinking. "That's all I ever heard Sarah call him too."

"Describe your boss," said Matthew softly. He listened carefully to every detail, asking a few questions, and growing more disturbed as Paul spoke.

"Didn't you ever see this knife before?" he demanded. "How could you not see his knife?"

"I don't know," said Paul, shaking his head slowly. "I just don't remember ever seeing him use that knife. Maybe he kept it safe for when he got to his new place." He looked at Matthew, puzzled. "Why would TC have your brother's knife?" Realization dawned on his face, and he stood up abruptly. "Was TC your brother?" gasped Paul. He was shaking his head as if he couldn't comprehend what he was seeing.

"I have to go to her." Matthew grabbed his gun and ran for the barn. He saddled his horse quickly, and took off out of the barn at a run. Lady could run for miles, and today was the day she would be tested as well.

How could he be so stupid? Why did he not see it? If he hadn't been so stubborn, he might have realized it sooner. He slowed Lady to a trot. It would do no good to have her exhausted and unable to make it to the town today. What if she didn't want anything to do with him now? He had been severe with her, and said some mean things. He needed her to forgive him. He needed her! He was in love with her! The thought struck him like a blinding flash of lightening in front of his eyes. Abruptly, he reined Lady in and sat in the middle of the trail, his mouth open and his body immobilized as the realization hit him. He

sat for several minutes. This was a new sensation and he wasn't
sure how to move forward. Well, first he had to go back and
get her to listen to him. He urged Lady forward again and made
it to town in record time.

He rode up to the general store at a run and jumped off his
horse. Throwing the reins loosely over the hitching rail, he ran
into the store.

Melissa was stocking the shelves with a new order of canned
goods as he came into the store.

"Where is she?" he panted breathlessly. Melissa turned and
stood looking at him. Sadness showed in her expression.

"She's gone, Matthew," she said, her shoulders slumping as
she spoke. She walked towards him slowly, stopping in front of
him. "I'm afraid you're too late."

"Gone? When? Where?" He looked around the room, as if he
thought she might be hiding. "I have to talk to her!"

"Matthew, you are our friend and we love you. But…you hurt
her. I am sure you thought you were right, but she cried all
night after you left." She hesitated. "Matthew, with all the
things that were going on, none of us realized it, but…" She
looked at him with greater sorrow than he had ever seen on her
face. "Matthew, she didn't steal the knife. It belonged to her
husband." She touched his arm. "We never thought to ask what
TC stood for. The baby is TC, Timothy Charles."

"The Charles is for our father," Matthew said.

"Yes, and it was going to be Matthew Charles, until Tim…"
Matthew looked down at the floor and shook his head.

"I just realized who they were today, Melissa," he said. "I don't
know how I could have been so stupid." He shifted from one
foot to the other and ran one hand over his face. "What have I
done?" he said, as much to himself as to Melissa. Matthew was
miserable. The thought of her lying in bed crying over what he
had said struck him and made him feel like a vile worm.

"Melissa, I was wrong. I see that now. I have to find her and
tell her I am sorry. Please, tell me where she is."

"She left on the stage this morning."

He thought of the Butterfield route. "Towards Carson City?" he asked.

"Yes. She said she was going to go to Virginia City to get the best passage she could find to get to Oregon, and then go home to her sister."

"Where is home, what town or city?"

Melissa shrugged. "I don't know. She didn't say, she thanked us for our help, but said she hated this country. It had been so cruel to her, taking her husband, nearly taking her baby. She said this country had broken her heart too many times, and she wanted to go as far away from here as she could and never come back." She looked away when she said the last, and Matthew felt a pang of regret. "Matthew, she gave us her horse. She said it was for all we had done for her, but she loved that horse." She wiped a tear off her cheek. "I don't think we will ever see her again."

"I have to catch that stage." He turned and walked swiftly to Lady, then climbed quickly into the saddle and started off at a canter towards Carson City. He had to find her.

Hours later, he crested a small hill and saw the stage, sitting off to the side of the road. One side was missing a wheel and the hub was propped up on a log. Swiftly, he rode up to the stage. The driver was sitting on a stump under a tree, on the side of the road. He was smoking a pipe and watching Matthew approach. He had a rifle leaning against the stump, within easy reach.

The horses were unhitched and grazing on the lush grass that bordered the road. Matthew rapidly dismounted and walked to the door of the stage, opening it and looking inside. It was empty.

"Lookin' for sumpthin'?" asked the stage driver, who had picked up the Remington rifle that had rested next to him, and now had it across his knees. He eyed Matthew with suspicion. "We ain't carryin' no gold," he said.

"Easy, old timer," Matthew addressed the seasoned driver, "I mean no harm. I am looking for a woman with a baby. She was supposed to be on this stage."

"You her husband?" The question struck Matthew. He realized it might look strange, pursuing a woman with a baby, when that woman was not his wife.

"No," Matthew said, looking down at the ground.

"Then what you want with her?" The driver lay his pipe on the stump and stood, appraising Matthew more carefully now. He brought the rifle up to chest level, ready to swing in any direction.

"I...she..." Matthew looked at the shrewd old man. "I think she is my brother's widow." It didn't even sound plausible to him, and the driver did not budge. His eyes ran over Matthew's face, as if trying to make a decision.

"You think?" he asked.

"It's a long story," Matthew said impatiently.

"Uh huh." Suddenly, he swung the rifle to point right at Matthew's chest. "Mister, I don't know who you are or what you want with that woman and her baby, but I think your story is as ripe as a four day old dead skunk. His eyes had narrowed to slits. "You ain't goin' nowhere until I find someone who can speak for you. Now, unbuckle that gun belt with your left hand and toss it over here, nice and easy." Matthew did as he was told.

"Look mister, I need to find her. She's getting away."

"Yep. And it seems to me that is exactly what she wanted to do. Now, turn around and get down on your knees." Quicker than Matthew would have thought possible of the old man, his hands were looped and bound with rope. The knots were tight and the rope bit into his wrists.

"Now, we'll just sit here and wait for Larry to bring that wheel back from the Hunewill Ranch and then we'll see if we can get anyone to speak for you." The driver picked up his pipe, then looked at Matthew. Sighing, he heaved himself up again and set down the pipe. He walked over to Matthew. Pointing the rifle at him, he motioned to the side of the stage.

"Maybe your story is rotten and maybe it ain't, but I guess you could at least move on over to sit in the shade of the tree. I ain't a mean man." He chuckled to himself. "Unless of course you make me want to be mean, so don't go getting any ideas."

He watched as Matthew got his feet under him and rose up to walk over by the tree. He sat in the shade, and watched as the old man took Lady by the reins and walked her out on the grass with the other horses. Then, he walked back and sat on the stump again.

"I like horses better than I like people," he grinned, settling himself again on the stump. I don't want your horse suffering because of something you might be tryin' to do." He studied Matthew, then shrugged and went back to smoking his pipe.

"How long before Larry gets back with the wheel?" asked Matthew. He spoke easily, trying to sound at ease, to get the old man to relax and maybe let him go.

"Well, let's see now. I guess they left about an hour ago. A freight wagon can't travel as fast as a horse, so I'm guessing they might be getting to the ranch about now. If the smithy can fix the wheel, and if the Hunewill's will give Larry a buckboard, or bring him back themselves, should be back by late afternoon."

"Late afternoon! But I have to find that woman and her baby before she gets away!"

The seasoned driver studied him carefully. "Well, tell you what, young fella," he smiled. "I got no where to be, and neither do you, until Larry gets back with that wheel. So, why don't you tell me why you are so fired up to find that lady? If your story is good enough, and I believe you, maybe I'll even let you go before Larry gets back," the old man grinned.

Matthew knew it was his only chance to get free to find Sarah. He began to tell the story, choosing his words carefully, attempting to paint the truth with enough softness that the old man would understand he was trying to help Sarah, not do her harm. When he finished, the old driver just stared at him. He didn't smile, he didn't move, he didn't say anything. He just stared at Matthew.

"Damn it!" Matthew snapped. "Can't you see I'm in love with her? You have to let me find her!"

Now, the old man smiled."Please, let me go, I...love her." It felt strange to say it.. He looked at the driver, shock on his face.

"That's what I was waiting to hear," the old man said as he took out his knife and walked towards Matthew. He leaned down in his face and poised the knife to cut the rope."A freight wagon came by after we broke down. The freighters took her and the baby to Virginia City. I don't know any more than that." He clapped his hand on Matthew's shoulder. "Now you go find her, and you make her feel safe." Then he cut the ropes. Matthew jumped up and ran to Lady.

"Thank you, mister!" he yelled as he leapt into the saddle. He had hours to make up. He could only hope Lady could hold to the brutal pace he was setting.

Chapter 20

Sarah sat in the back of the freight wagon, trying to hold the baby still. She leaned against the back of the seat, where the two men sat. They had built a little area for her and TC, and padded it as best they could with extra blankets, but the road was deeply rutted and the ride bounced her without mercy. She was sure she would be bruised when the ride was over, but she had to get away.

She stifled a sob. She was such a fool. She thought she might have another chance at happiness, but Matthew would never let her live down the fact she had stolen once to protect her baby. She had started to have feelings for him and she had grown to have real affection for the Gruener's. They had told her she could stay, but she couldn't stand the thought that Matthew might come to visit them and she would be there. She wiped the tears from her eyes. Well, it didn't matter. She had TC and she had some gold and she would make a life for them. She needed to find a way to get back to her home town. At least her sister was there.

"You okay back there, M'am?" asked one of the drivers. "Do you need to stop for a few minutes?"

Sarah looked at the man and smiled. "You are so kind. That would be nice, just for a few minutes, if it isn't too much trouble." She felt ill. She had not slept well in days, and it had been difficult to eat much, with her stomach churning from all the emotions. She was tired of crying, but she was at a loss to control her tears.

The teamsters pulled the wagon to the side of the road and jumped down. They both came to the back and dropped the gate on the back of the wagon. The younger of the two hopped up in the back of the wagon and helped Sarah to her feet, then handed her and the baby down to the other man. She felt her knees buckle as she tried to stand, and both men grabbed an arm to hold her up.

"I got her, Zack. Get one of those blankets down and lay it out on the ground." Zack jumped into the wagon and got one of the blankets. He walked over to a grouping of boulders and spread the blanket in the shade on the side.

"Ok, Fred, bring her on over here." Zack hurried over to help Fred; he didn't like how pale the lady looked. He had just reached her side when she suddenly thrust the baby at him and then fainted. Fred scooped Sarah up and carried her to the blanket, with Zack close on his heels with the baby. He laid her down gently and awkwardly began to unbutton the neck of her blouse to loosen the clothing around her throat.

"Get me some water, Zack," he said, as he took off his neckerchief and started to wave it in front of Sarah's face. Zack laid the baby down carefully on the blanket fairly close to Sarah, and ran back to the wagon. He grabbed the canteen from under the seat of the wagon and ran back to the blanket. Fred held out his neckerchief.

"Pour some water on it, Zack." Fred dabbed the wet cloth on Sarah's forehead and cheeks, wet it again, and gently patted her neck with the wet cloth until Sarah began to stir.

"Oh, awful!" she said, pushing away Fred's hand. She looked at the dirty red bandana he held. Fred looked at Zack and then sniffed his neckerchief. It reeked of sweat and dirt.

"I'm sure sorry, M'am," said Fred," I didn't have a clean cloth. I'm sorry it smells so bad."

Sarah's eyes fluttered and she tried to sit up. "It would be best if you just laid quiet for a few minutes M'am," said Fred.

"My baby!" Frantically, she tried to sit up.

"Whoa! Whoa, there M'am, here's your baby,"said Fred, as he picked up TC from the other side of the blanket and laid him down next to her. "Now, you just rest for a minute. We'll be right here if you need anything." He stood up and motioned Zack off to one side. They walked over to the edge of the boulders, out of Sarah's hearing.

"What's you thinkin'?" asked Zack.

"I'm thinkin' this lady has seen a lot of trouble and she is not well. I'm not only worried about somethin' happening to her on the way to Virginia City, but I am worried about what happens when she gets there. It is a tough town, and there ain't no good women I know of we could leave her with. Hell, they ain't even got a church there yet."

"What do you think we oughta do then, Fred. We promised her we'd take her to Virginia City."

"I know." He rubbed his chin for a few minutes, then looked at Zack. "She ain't well. What do you say we take her over to Genoa and tell her we'll be back in a week or two and will swing by and pick her up then?"

"Yeah, that might work," said Zack. "There's a little settlement there and some families. She and the little one would be safe there, and there are women that could care for her." The two men looked at Sarah sleeping on the blanket. "I hate to wake her up so soon. Think maybe we could make us something to eat? Maybe she'd be awake and would eat something then."

"That's a good idea! I ain't had a hot meal since yesterday morning. I got the makings for some johnnycakes and bacon – even got a little maple syrup! We could have us a feast!"

"Now I'm really hungry," said Zack. I'll get a fire going and make some coffee and you get the meal going." He looked over at Sarah and TC and chewed on his lip."I think I'll rig up a little more shade for the lady too." Fred nodded his head.

"I sure don't know her story, but she and that little one look like they have been through it and come out the worse for the wear. Such a shame. Pretty little woman like that with a baby and no husband to care for them."

"Sweet, too," agreed Zack. "But, I guess all we can do is try to make this leg of her journey a little nicer." The men stood looking at the two small figures on the blanket, then sighed and walked off to their respective chores. They decided to unhitch the horses and let them nibble on the sparse grass around the stopping point.

Sarah was awake by the time the meal was ready, and they all ate under the shade of the blanket cover Zack had rigged. "This is so good," said Sarah. I haven't had jonny cakes and syrup since…"she hesitated and got a far away look in her eyes for a minute. "Well, since I left home," she finished. "Aww, thank you M'am," said Fred, blushing at her words. Zack grinned at him, and punched him in the shoulder. Zack laughed and so did Sarah, which was a lovely sound to their ears. After they ate, the men cleaned up the dishes and put dirt over the fire, while Sarah fed the baby. They gave the horses water and hitched them up again to the neck yoke and tongue of the wagon. When they were done, they stood looking at each other. Finally, Fred spoke.

"Well, I guess we better go talk to her." He said. Zack nodded in agreement, but they stood for another moment, looking at Sarah, now holding the baby on her shoulder and patting him gently. Sarah smiled as the men walked towards her, but she sensed something was wrong. They sat down on the blanket under the shade and took off their hats.

"M'am," Fred started, then looked at Zack, who nodded encouragement. "We promised to take you to Virginia City, and we will!" he said quickly as her face clouded. "But M'am, you don't seem well and you got the little one to think about." Sarah was very still as she listened. "So, here's what we are thinkin,' and we sure hope you consider it." He looked at Zack again, who was staring at Sarah's face, hoping she wouldn't start to cry. He couldn't stand to see a woman cry.

"Go on," Sarah managed to say.

"Well, we drive this route about every week or so, and we are of the opinion that you aren't strong enough yet to make the drive to such a rowdy place as Virginia City, and then catch a freight wagon like ours up the California Trail to Oregon." "Or catch a stage to San Francisco and take a boat," offered Zack. "Either way, that's a hard trip all by itself," added Zack. "The only family I have left is in Oregon," Sarah said.

"Now M'am, understand we are going to get you to that stage, but," Fred paused, "we think you ought to spend a week or two over in this little settlement we know. There's a man name of John Reese started himself a trading post over in Genoa, just off the trail a bit from the road to Virginia City. He has his wife and kids there, and there are other families there too. They are good people, and we think it would be best if you rested there for a couple weeks with some women folks to help you get strong." Sarah stared at them.

"Then in a week or two, we'll come back and pick you up and take you to that stage line to Virginia City," added Zack. She still hadn't spoken, and the men looked nervously at each other.

"It would give us some time to find someone in Virginia City we could trust to take care of you until you got on the stage," Fred said gently. "It's a rough town, M'am, and we want to make sure someone will watch over you and put you on that stage."

"I don't know what to do," said Sarah.

"You collapsed just getting out of the wagon after riding about ten miles, M'am." Fred looked at TC. "What will happen to your baby if you fall sick in Virginia City?" His brown eyes pleaded with Sarah.

"We give you our word we will come back for you," Zack said. Sarah studied the two men and did not speak for several minutes. She looked down at the sleeping baby in her arms and touched TC's cheek. She raised her head to meet their eyes. "You sure we'll be welcome in Genoa?" she asked. Relief flooded the faces of the two men.

"Oh yes M'am," said Fred, we know John and his family, but," he leaned towards her and touched her arm, "we promise we won't leave you unless you are comfortable there."

"You are such good men," she said. "I will take your advice. I know you are thinking of me and my baby, and I appreciate your help." Fred and Zack jumped to their feet, breathing sighs of relief.

Fred helped Sarah to her feet with the baby and Zack took the shelter apart. He walked over to the wagon, and climbing in the back, he used the branches he had used to build the sun shelter to run from the stacked cargo to the edge of the wagon. He pulled some pigging strings out of his pocket and tied the branches down, then lay the blanket over the top of the limbs to create a sun shade. He tied the corners of the blanket to the branches with more pigging strings, then lay the second blanket in the bottom of the wagon for more padding. He turned to see Sarah smiling at him.

"That should make it a little better for you M'am, some shelter from the hot sun."

"You are so kind, both of you," she said. Both of the men blushed this time. They weren't used to women, and they sure weren't used to thanks and praise. They helped her in the back of the wagon and got her settled, then jumped up on the seat and started the horses.

It was late afternoon when they pulled up in front of the trading post. John Reese himself came out to greet them and listened to the men. He looked at Sarah and TC in the back of the wagon and turned to a young boy playing in front of the store.

"Luke," he called to the red haired boy, "go fetch your mother for me, son." The boy jumped up and ran off to a house standing next to the store. A few minutes later, he returned with a tall, red haired woman. John and his wife spoke for a few minutes, and then they all turned to the wagon.

M'am, my name is John Reese, and this is my wife Martha. We would be pleased to have you stay with us awhile and regain your strength. My wife is an excellent nurse and can help with the baby." The tall, bearded man had an air of kindness about him that put Sarah at ease.

"I don't want to be a burden," said Sarah.

"Oh, no, "Martha spoke, "we would love to have you stay! The children love babies and I would enjoy hearing the news of Bridgeport," said Martha, smiling.

Sarah looked at all of them standing at the end of the wagon. Zack and Fred looked anxious, but the Reese family seemed pleased at the prospect of a guest.

"I would be most grateful," Sarah finally said. Laughter greeted her ears as the freighters and John shook hands.

"Why don't you two spend the night as well," offered John, "we have plenty to share, and it is getting late. You can get a fresh start in the morning." Zack and Fred accepted the offer, and Sarah felt even more relieved. If she did not feel comfortable, she could still leave with them in the morning. Other people from the settlement had come out to greet the visitors, and a young man jumped up in the back of the wagon. He was a clean shaven, dark haired boy of about fourteen. He smiled at her.

"May I take the baby and hand him to my mother while we help you out of the wagon?" he said. Sarah looked at Martha, who was standing at the end of the wagon.

"He's had lots of practice," she laughed, "James is the oldest of my four children," she said. Sarah handed him the baby, and he in turn, passed TC to Martha. Then he offered his hand to Sarah and helped her rise. He jumped down at the end of the wagon and lifted her down. Her knees were still a bit shaky, but she felt at peace here.

"Come," Martha said, "let's get you inside and settled in before dinner." Sarah looked back around to see other men walking the wagon to the side and unhitching the horses. Zack and Fred laughed as they talked to the men. She could relax here, let down her guard. She was safe. She followed Martha inside to a well built, clean house that was very spacious.

Chapter 21

Sarah woke the next morning to the sound of children laughing. She sat up in the comfortable bed and looked at the cradle where TC was sleeping. He had slept through the night, and so had she. She had not slept this well in weeks. She rose and dressed quietly, taking a good look at the cheerful room where Martha had led her last night. Sarah touched the beautiful quilt on the bed and felt a little tug at her heart. She had dreamed of this; a cozy home of her own, with handmade touches and curtains at the windows. She walked to the slightly open window and parted the curtains to look out at the busy little community beneath her room. A group of children were chasing a dog that was running away with a stick in its mouth. They were laughing as they ran, and a few adults stopped their chores to watch them, with smiles on their faces.

A light knock on the door broke through her thoughts and she opened it to see Martha standing there, with a bright smile on her face.

"I heard you walking around and thought I would come and offer breakfast!" she said. "The floors are several years old and they creak a bit when you walk on them," she explained at Sarah's surprised look.

"Oh, thank you! I was afraid I had slept too late and missed it!" She turned as TC stirred. "I think he wants to eat as well!"

"Well, bring him downstairs and we can all eat!" said Martha, turning to go back down the stairs.

Sarah quickly changed TC and descended the stairs. She was met with the smell of fried ham and fresh baked bread. To her surprise, her stomach growled!

"Have a seat right there by the cradle," offered Martha. She laughed at Sarah's puzzled look. "We are a close community and someone always has a baby," she smiled. "We decided to just keep the cradle handy for anyone visiting with a babe."

She set down a plate of ham, bread, and butter for Sarah, with a cup of cold milk. "We have two, as you have noticed, one for guests and the one upstairs in case we need it again," she chuckled.

"Where is the rest of the family?" Sarah asked.

"Oh, they have been fed and out the door for over an hour," Martha said. "This is a break for me, before I need to start other chores." She hesitated, then sat and looked into Sarah's eyes. "Sarah, I know a little about what you have been through, and I want you to know I do have some understanding. I lost a baby coming here; he was born too soon and the journey was too rough." She paused, staring out the window as if in a trance. Then she shook her head and her smile returned as she looked at Sarah. "Do you want to talk about how you came to be here?" she asked, gently. Sarah met her eyes, then slowly nodded her head.

"My husband and I were coming west to meet his brother," said Sarah. "But," she sighed, "my husband was killed and the brother I finally met didn't want us." She bit her lip.

"Didn't want you!" said Martha in surprise. "Why on earth not? You are family, aren't you?" Sarah nodded and a tear rolled out of her eye and down her face. "Oh, I am sorry," said Martha, touching her arm," I didn't mean to make you sad! I only wanted to give you a chance to talk to another woman."

"No, it is alright, I would like that if you have the time," said Sarah. Martha nodded and Sarah picked up TC, settled him at her breast, and began her story. Martha listened to every word, gasping or shaking her head at times, but otherwise did not comment until Sarah was done. When she finished, the two women sat silent, their eyes locked in the understanding that only two women who have seen great tragedy can share. Finally, Martha sighed and looked at little TC asleep in the cradle. When she turned back to Sarah, her eyes were moist. "I wish you had a place, a home for TC and yourself," said Martha.

"That is all I ever wanted, "said Sarah, "Tim and I wanted so badly to start a new life and raise our child here in the west." She touched the cheek of the sleeping boy and gazed at his rhythmic breathing. "I wish I could give something to TC, something for his future."

Martha shifted in her chair and clucked her tongue. She looked out the window, then around her own kitchen. She brought her eyes back to Sarah. "Is there no way to make Tim's brother give you a part of the land for yourself and his own nephew?' asked Martha.

"I do not think so," said Sarah. "Matthew is a very strong willed man."

Chapter 22

Matthew raced Lady towards Virginia City as fast as he dared. He needed to find Sarah, but he couldn't risk losing Lady either. They ate up the miles until they reached Carson City. By the time they reached Eagle Station, Matthew's shoulder was throbbing from the jarring ride, and Lady's sides were heaving with the exertion. He had to stop and find rest for them. He dismounted in front of the station and went inside. A young man was sitting behind the desk on a stool, working at a ledger.

"Got a room for me and a place for my horse?" Matthew asked. He was surprised at how weak he felt; his knees were shaky and he leaned on the counter for support.

"You alright, cowboy," asked the short, brown haired man behind the desk. "You look like you've had a time of it."

"I just need some food for me and my horse, and some sleep." he said.

"Ok," said the clerk, still running his eyes over Matthew's face. I have a room at the top of the stairs and a stable out back. If you want to take your horse out back, I'll have the cook get some grub ready."

Matthew nodded and headed out to walk Lady around to the back of the station. He threw his saddle over the rail of the stall and brushed her down quickly. There was already water in a tub in the stall, and he forked some hay in for her before he patted her on the flank and dragged himself back inside. He carried his saddlebags into the dining room and placed them on the chair next to him.

"Got some food coming right out for you," said the clerk," have a seat anywhere and I'll get coffee." Matthew looked at the empty dining room and chose a table close to the door to the kitchen. He sat down and put his hat on the chair next to him. He rubbed his hands over his face and realized how dirty they were. The clerk came back with his coffee.

"Is there a place to wash up?" asked Matthew.

"Sure," said the young man, "go through that door to the kitchen and right out back there is a tub and pitcher."

"Thanks," said Matthew, rising. He went carefully through the door, in case the cook was headed through it at the same time. Matthew was surprised to see a neat, orderly kitchen and a well built man of about thirty standing at the stove, turning a steak, which he hoped was his.

"Howdy," said the cook, stirring the beans.

"Sorry to get in your way, just need to wash my hands and face before I eat," said Matthew, nodding a greeting. The cook inclined his head in approval and pointed to the open back door. Matthew noted he wore clean clothes and a clean apron. He pegged him as former army.

"Learn to cook in the army?" he asked, coming back into the kitchen. The cook smiled.

"Yes sir! Cooked for the General himself!" he said with pride.

"Which one?" asked Matthew.

"Don't much matter now, does it?" asked the cook, with a twinkle in his eye. Matthew grinned. The cook knew better than to risk a fight with some cowboy who couldn't let go of old grudges.

"Nope," he replied, "it sure don't." He walked on through the door into the dining room and sat down again. The cook came out a few minutes later with a plate of beans half covered by a big steak, with a slab of homemade bread and butter on top. He put the plate in front of Matthew. "Be right back with more coffee," he said.

Matthew ate hungrily, realizing he hadn't eaten since yesterday. He had eaten nearly half the meal when the cook returned with the coffee.

"I guess you were hungry, all right!" said the cook with a smile, as he poured more coffee into Matthew's cup.

"I sure was!" Matthew agreed. "Has the stage already been through?" he asked as he took a another bite of beans and began sawing at his steak again.

"Which one you want to know about?" asked the cook. Matthew's head came up.

"What do you mean, which one?" he asked, a heavy pressure building behind his eyes.

"Well, the Butterfield left about two hours ago and the Wells Fargo left about an hour before that."

"There are two?" Matthew asked. His heart sank.

"Yep," he said. One went to Virginia City and the other to San Francisco." said the cook.

"Which one would go to Oregon? Matthew asked, the food sitting heavily in his stomach now.

"Don't really know for sure," the cook shrugged. "Depends on if you want to catch a freight wagon or join up with settlers going to Oregon, or if you want to go to San Francisco and get on a ship to go up the coast." Matthew stared at him. How could he know which direction she took?

"Did any of the passengers come here to eat?" he asked. Maybe there was someone who had seen a woman with a baby.

"Nope! Not this time. Gent did take a sandwich he said was for a lady though," the cook said as he walked back into the kitchen. Matthew stared at his dinner, suddenly having lost his appetite. How could he find her if he had no idea where she had gone? She had said the only family she had left was in Oregon, but where? She could get a stage, then get a ride on a freight wagon, or go to San Francisco to book passage on a ship. He was overwhelmed with uncertainty and hopelessness. Well, he would go to Virginia City in the morning and try to find someone who had seen her. It was all he could do, but he feared it would not be enough. He stood, placing some coins on the table for his dinner, and walked across the lobby to the stairs. He was bone tired and his shoulder still throbbed. He was glad he had thrown a flask of whiskey in the saddlebags before he left the ranch. He would need it to dull the pain tonight; at least, his physical pain.

He woke late the next morning and rose with effort. His shoulder hurt constantly now, but he managed to saddle Lady and started for Virginia City mid morning. It was past noon when he caught up to the Butterfield stage in Virginia City, but the passengers had all gone their separate ways by the time he arrived. The driver said no woman with a baby had gotten on the stage in Carson City. Matthew described her, but neither the driver or the guard remembered seeing her in Virginia City. He asked at the freight office about wagons leaving for Oregon, but there were none leaving until tomorrow, and no woman had asked for passage. He found another hotel for himself and stable for Lady, getting up before dawn to watch the freighters pull out. Sarah was not with them.

He pushed himself, fighting dizziness and pain, to ride towards San Francisco. He had bought more whiskey in Virginia City, and was drinking it during the day to dull the pain in his shoulder. He stopped several times, sliding out of the saddle and almost falling on the grass or dirt and sleeping for hours in broad daylight. When he finally reached the Wells Fargo offices in San Francisco, there was no record of a woman with a baby having been on the stage.

"Are you sure?" he demanded of the young agent behind the desk. "I've got to find her!"

"I'm sorry, sir," he said, studying Matthew's ashen face. "Our drivers and agents keep very good records, but George is in the back, let me ask him again for you." He stood, then came around the desk. "Why don't you have a seat over there," he said, pointing to a couch set against the wall. Matthew nodded, and walked to the couch. As he sat, he noticed the agent was still standing, watching him, until he was seated. Only then did the agent go into the back room.

A few minutes later, the agent returned with a tall, hard eyed man wearing dusty clothes and a two day stubble of beard. As he walked over to Matthew, he stood to meet him.

"I'm sure sorry, mister, but we didn't have any female passengers from Virginia City," he said, watching Matthew carefully.

"I have to find her!" said Matthew. It was cold here in San Francisco. He shivered and rubbed his pulsing shoulder.

"I wish I could help," said George, "I can see this is important to you." He put a hand on Matthew's arm. "Maybe you should sit back down for a spell," he said.

"I'm okay," he said, "I just need to find Sarah." He looked into George's eyes and knew he was telling the truth. "Thanks," Matthew said, and turned to walk away. George broke his fall, but he was unconscious before he hit the floor.

Chapter 23

Matthew rode slowly up to the ranch, tired and hungry. He had been unsuccessful in finding Sarah. He had been unconscious for two days in the back room of the Wells Fargo offices in San Francisco. When he woke, he was still a little weak, but had spent another day asking around the port and docks about a woman booking passage on one of the ships. No one had seen her.

On the fourth day, he rode out of San Francisco and towards home. He was in no hurry now. He had been obstinate and blind to the signs all around him, and she left because of him. Now, he did not know if he would ever see her again. He had realized too late that he loved her. Maybe he didn't even know what that meant, but whatever his feelings for her, his heart felt dull and sluggish now.

Finally riding onto his own ranch, he smiled without humor. Heartwood. Never had the name seemed so appropriate. Like the dead heart wood in the middle of a tree, his heart felt dead, without feeling. He was alive on the outside and dead in the middle, just like Heartwood. They were a perfect match.

He was sure now that Sarah had been the "surprise" his brother had talked about. She was his brother's widow and TC was his nephew and he had turned them out in the cold when he should have protected them. They were the only family he had left, and now, thanks to his stupid self righteousness, he had lost them forever. He felt he had let his brother down, too. Even if she wasn't in love with him, he should have taken care of them. They were all he had left of family.

He led Lady to the barn and unsaddled her, brushing her down and giving her some grain. Matthew moved mechanically, hanging up the tack and putting the saddle over a rail. When he was done, he leaned against Lady and felt her warmth.

"Well, old girl, at least I have you." He patted her on the flank and then walked out of the barn, latching the door behind him.

His shoulder ached from the long ride and he wondered how long it would take before he didn't feel the pain in his shoulder either. A light was on in the house, and he hoped Paul had dinner ready. He had rarely stopped to fix a meal while searching for Sarah, he was so driven to find her. Then he thought of Paul. How could he tell Paul he had lost her?

He walked across the open space between the barn and the house, mounted the step to his porch and opened the door. He stepped in and hung his hat and holster on the rack just inside the door. He turned and stopped, speechless. Paul sat at the table with his hands in front of him, looking very uncomfortable. And Sarah stood by the table, with her arms crossed.

"Sarah!" exclaimed Matthew, too shocked to move. "You came back!"

"Yes, I came back. This is my husband's ranch too, and I want my half for my son!" Her chin was lifted in defiance as her dark blue eyes seemed to glitter. "I was a fool to think I could have another chance at happiness with you, so just to clear the air, I did not come back to beg. I…we don't need you!"

"Sarah, please, let me…"

"No, let me finish! I have to get this out and I won't let you intimidate me! You will never trust me. I did what I had to do to protect my child – whom I now know is your nephew! I know you don't want us, and we won't stay in this house any longer than we need to. I heard you have been looking for me, and I am sure this is why." She took a pouch out of the pocket of her skirt and tossed it on the table. "I can't give you half of what the outlaws took, but that is your half of the gold I have left, half of what Tim and I were bringing to you to start our new life." She was still standing with her arms crossed over her chest, and her eyes did not waiver. "Well, I can start a life for me and my son with our half of the gold and our half of the ranch!" she said, with determination in her voice. "I have already made arrangements with some of the men in town and

Sheriff Tinkum's lumber mill to bring out some wood and build TC and me a small house."

"Sarah, listen to me," Matthew said, taking a few steps towards her.

"You can't throw us out! TC is your blood, and I insist you give us land for our own house!" Her eyes were flashing, but her chin had started to quiver."I don't need anything from you except our share of the land for TC. I have a horse to go to and from town, and I will plant my own garden for food!" She had her hands on her hips now, and stamped her foot for emphasis. "And I will buy a cow for TC!"

"I don't want to throw you out, I want you to stay," said Matthew softly. He stood a few feet away from her now, looking at her.

"What kind of a trick is this? Do you think you will get all the gold if I stay?"

"I don't want the gold," he said. Her hand went to her throat.

"Why not?" she said, suspicion in her voice.

"I did go looking for you, but not for the gold," he said.

"Then…why?" Her chin was quivering again and he knew she was trying not to cry. He cupped her chin gently in his hand.

"I have been a fool, and I hurt you, I know I did. My own stubbornness and fear kept me from believing you." He stepped even closer to her and stood, very close, looking into her eyes.

"What are you saying?"

"I don't want you to go, Sarah, I want you to stay," he said, searching her face.

"Why?" she whispered.

"I want something else from you." She stiffened.

"What do you want now?"

"I want you to marry me." She stood, without moving, taking shallow breaths. "I love you, Sarah," He said it so softly, she had to strain to be sure she was hearing him correctly. "Please say yes." Tears started out of her eyes as she nodded.

"One more thing," he said.

"What?" she asked, already reeling from the turn of events. "This," he said, slipping his arm around her and pulling her gently to him. He leaned down and met her lips and kissed her. She shivered in his arms. When he pulled back to look at her face, her eyes were wide. He stroked her cheek. They stood, looking into each other's eyes for several minutes, but not breaking the embrace. Finally, a slow smile began on Sarah's face.

"I do think we should build another house though," she said.

"Why?" he asked in surprise.

"Paul will need a bunkhouse. And this house will be too small for him and all our children." She smiled at him. Matthew stared at her for a minute, then threw back his head and laughed.

76826988R00075

Made in the USA
San Bernardino, CA
17 May 2018

Contents

Foreword:
A Necessary Correction

Meral Akkent

When people talk about Turkish women who have migrated, they concentrate on differences, such as the headscarf, and look upon them as beings outside any historical development, as slaves of tradition. When, for example, a 'Turkish girl' is mentioned, everyone knows for a fact that they are 'locked up at home', that they are 'virgins when they marry', and that they cannot attend school because they must look after their younger brothers and sisters. This stereotyping of girls or young women from Turkey means that if they dress differently from the way people expect them to, if they do not wear a headscarf, have blue eyes or an interesting job, they are described as 'not typical' or 'already integrated'. It seems almost impossible for a Turkish woman to define herself in a way that does not correspond to a stereotype.

In *The Science Question in Feminism*, the feminist philosopher Sandra Harding shows that currently although black women are encouraged to speak about their own particular lives, white women still claim the privilege of describing the lives of 'women'. According to Harding, this creates simplifications and ideological distortions.[1]

The same can be said of the way migrant women are described in women's studies. We have seen a growing number of investigations of the lives of migrant women over the past 15 years, but in most of these studies the migrant woman, both in her home country and, for example, in Germany, is defined as 'a victim of circumstances'; signs of resistance are ignored or overlooked, or if they noted, are reduced to a marginal phenomenon.

Sabine Hebenstreit states that feminist ethnocentrism is a defining characteristic of the sociological literature on migrant women;[2] and that as foreign women have been seen as stereotypes, it is generally believed that every member of their society, personally, corresponds to this characterization.

In Germany, research into migrants' lives is usually supported by local councils or private foundations. These projects set out to analyse those factors which are said to inhibit integration, with the aim of developing ways of promoting integration. In many studies the picture is of migrants who are self-evidently a problem, as if it was obvious that integrating them is made difficult by culturally specific differences.[3]

As a result, Turkish migrants have become the object of paternalistic research and practice, and the ethnocentric stereotype has developed since the second half of the 1970s. These studies say little that is relevant to the actual situation of Turkish women; in short they are an expression of the collective Western dream of the Orient.[4]

The result is that to this day the Orient is defined as being fundamentally different from the West – the Occident – with this characterization as 'different' in no way serving as a neutral term, but rather assuming and confirming the West's cultural, economic and social superiority. In this 'Orientalist discussion' Islam is made out to be the dominant ordering principle. The common assumption that Muslim women are especially oppressed by the male members of their families is given a more solid foundation. These standard assumptions are repeated again and again in many studies:

> As today very many Turks are still devout Muslims, who adhere more or less strictly to the articles of faith of the Koran, the roles of the sexes are also largely determined by Islamic traditions. This necessarily means that women have to accept the role prescribed for them by the Koran: i.e. one characterized by inferiority, a lower social position and systematic disadvantages compared with men. (Author's translation)[5]

This study appeared in 1978. As late as 1984 no significant changes in this connection could be found. According to Bernard and Schlaffer the 'Islamic woman' is an oppressed, exploited being, and in contrast the 'Western woman' has at her disposal the achievements of progress and emancipation in every sphere.[6] It is not true, however, that in every European country women's situation has been improved in legal, cultural and economic respects, even aside from the fact that for the majority of women this has not become a social reality.

Up to now, research and discussion in Germany have shown no serious interest in focusing on female subjectivity and female forms of resistance – for example by investigating the active contribution made by Turkish women in Turkey to creating their own lives; by asking how they realize their efforts to achieve autonomy and in which ways they protect themselves against patriarchy, either by an open declaration of resistance, through education and professional training, or by using 'female strategies'. Sociology, with its conceptions of personal identity, is concerned with the dialectic between the individual and society. 'Human beings are the product of social conditions which they, in their turn, react to, preserve, change or form anew' (author's translation).[7]

When this collection was published in Germany in 1991, under the title *Aufstand im Haus der Frauen*, it excited much critical attention with respect to this question. Reactions to the collection fell into two camps. People either felt the need to maintain the prevalent style of discourse about Turkish women, and hence placed it within that tradition; or they saw in it a necessary correction of this presumptuous attitude.

The following quotations from various reviews of the book are typical of the discussion. The German feminist magazine *Emma* contains the following:

> There is hardly a country in which women have to endure as many contradictions as in Turkey. The young feminist movement is threatened by growing Islamic fundamentalism. A group of Turkish women researchers have described what this means for women in their country, for their working conditions, for their sexuality and for the way they look at marriage and the family.[8]

The woman who wrote this review does not seem to have noticed the means women use to combat the forms of repression which she details. She also overlooked the fact that the contributors to the collection saw Islamic fundamentalism as only one factor amongst many others. We know very well from from research into the nature of prejudice that stereotypes are extremely resistant to change, and that selective perception makes it difficult for 'different truths' to be accepted.

Another woman who wrote a review felt the need to reconsider her own position:

> There are very many parallels between the Turkish and the German feminist movements. Anyone reading *Aufstand im Haus der Frauen* will immediately realize this. What actually distinguishes a German women living in a small provincial town from a woman in Anatolia? Both live in a patriarchal society and although they have the same formal rights as men, for decades now they have had to fight for them. Admittedly, 'thanks' to technological progress life is no longer as hard in Germany as it still is for Turkish women in the villages.

The writer of the review regards this collection as an important contribution to international solidarity amongst feminists.

> It prevents us from becoming contemptuous of others. Any woman who still associates 'Turkish woman' with the helpless, backward person wearing a headscarf urgently needs to read this book.[9]

The analyses presented in this collection deviate considerably from the previous standard interpretations of Turkish women living in Germany. Hence, a third review comments: 'This book teaches us something new about the reality of Turkey, its history and the lives that women lead in that country. We are also made aware of the existence of Turkish women who are carrying out feminist research.'[10]

In discussions and private conversations people have often remarked that the questions raised by the book, and its conclusions, have inspired critical reactions and made people rethink their positions. They question researchers' reluctance to question the stereotypical picture of Turkish women and ask who, in the final instance, profits from maintaining it. They also ask how a paradigm change in social work and education might be achieved.

Since 750,000 women from Turkey live in Germany and share public and private facilities with German women (schools, kindergartens, training facilities, workplaces, neighbourhoods, old people's homes, etc.), what has been considered an established fact must now be looked at in a more discriminating way and reconsidered altogether. The controversy which the

collection generated gives us the hope that it will permit us to
move the discourse about Turkish women on to a new plane,
and to reconsider old assumptions. Since our future as women
lies in understanding each other we urgently need – in view of
its political significance – this cooperation.

Notes

1. S. Harding, *The Science Question in Feminism*, New York 1986.
2. S. Hebenstreit, *Frauenräume und weibliche Identität*, Berlin 1986.
3. See Berger 'Arbeitswanderung und Marginalisierung. Kritische Bemer-
kungen zur bundesdeutschen Migrationsforschung', paper given at the
conference at Zif (Centre for Interdisciplinary Research), University of
Bielefeld, September 1987: *Der Beitrag der Wissenschaft zur Konstitution ethnischer
Minderheiten*, Bielefeld 1987, p. 6.
4. See for the discussion of orientalism: Edward Said, *Orientalism*, 1978;
Leyla Ahmed, 'Western ethnocentrism and the perception of the harem',
Feminist Studies 3, Vol. 8, 1982, pp. 521–54; Rana Kabbani, *Europe's Myth of the
Orient: Devide and Rule*, London 1988; Chandra Mohanty, 'Under western
eyes: feminist scholarship and colonial discourses', *Feminist Review* 30, autumn
1988, pp. 61–89; Helma Lutz, 'Orientalische Weiblichkeit', in 'Welten
verbinden. Türkische Mittlerinnen (intermediare) in den Niederlanden und des
Bundesrepublik Deutschland', Dissertation, University of Amsterdam 1990,
pp. 129–51.
5. Karabak Baumgartner et al., *Die verkauften Bräute*, Reinbek 1978.
6. C. Bernard and E. Schlaffer, *Die Grenzen des Geschlechts*, Reinbek 1984.
7. A. Neusel, S. Tekeli, M. Akkent (eds.), *Aufstand im Haus der Frauen.
Frauenforschung aus der Türkei*, Berlin 1991.
8. *Emma*, April 1991, p. 40 (my translation).
9. See U. Droll, *Die Frauenzeitung* 7, 1992, p. 11 (my translation).
10. See M. Bereswill and G. Ehlert, *Schlangenbrut* 8/91, p. 42 (my
translation).

Contributors

Feride Acar teaches at the Middle Eastern Technical University, Ankara.

Yeşim Arat teaches at the Boğaziçi (Bosphorus) University in Istanbul.

Günseli Berik teaches at the New School for Social Research, New York.

Fatmagül Berktay teaches at the University of Istanbul.

Hale Cihan Bolak teaches at Santa Cruz University.

Nilüfer Çağatay teaches at Ramapo College, New Jersey.

F. Yildiz Ecevit teaches at the Middle Eastern Technical University, Ankara.

Yakin Ertürk teaches at the Middle Eastern Technical University, Ankara.

Fatma Gök teaches at the Education Sciences Faculty of Boğaziçi (Bosphorus) University, Istanbul.

Ayşe Günes–Ayata teaches at the Middle Eastern Technical University, Ankara.

Deniz Kandiyoti teaches at Richmond College, London.

Arşalus Kayir teaches clinical psychiatry at the University of Istanbul.

Ferhunde Özbay teaches at Boğaziçi (Bosphorus) University, Istanbul.

Ayşe Saktanber teaches at the Middle Eastern Technical University, Ankara.

Nükhet Sirman teaches at the Boğaziçi (Bosphorus) University, Istanbul.

Yasemin Nuhoglu–Soysal is working on her Ph.D at Stanford University, USA.

Nora Şeni teaches at the Paris VIII University, Paris.

Şirin Tekeli, former university professor, founder of the Women's Library and Information Center Foundation, Istanbul.

Lale Yalçin-Heckmann teaches at the Nürnburg University, Germany.

Şahika Yüksel teaches at the University of Istanbul.

Introduction:
Women in Turkey in the 1980s

Şirin Tekeli

Writing an introduction to an edited book has always entailed difficulties. On the one hand you have to explain the common needs which bring different authors together around the same theme, underline the main ideas uniting them and thus describe the context in which they are written: a task which involves being as objective as possible. On the other hand, as an individual you have your own ideas, and have to balance being sensitive to other individuals' ideas, while yourself trying to formulate a synthesis of the different perspectives.

This book is the outcome of a symposium organized by the Multi-disciplinary Women's Studies Group of the University of Kassel, Germany. In this introduction I first of all describe this symposium. I then go on to outline an analysis of the changing structures and culture in Turkish society during the 1980s which are the common background of all the chapters gathered together in this book. Such an analysis is necessary to understand both the social dynamics of the women's movement which now has an important place in the Turkish political spectrum and the social forces which the women's movement has kindled in Turkish society. I then look briefly to the development of the women's movement in the 1980s which, I believe, is the basic element uniting the different contributions to this book. Finally I outline the book's structure.

My encounter with Ayla

I was invited to the Higher Pedagogical School of the

1

University of Kassel in the spring of 1986 for two 'compact seminars' on women in Turkish society. I met Ayla Neusel in these seminars. She had just been elected deputy rector of the university. Such an extraordinary success by a Turkish woman academic in Germany was both delightful and amazing. Ayla was astonished, on her part, by what I told about the increased feminist consciousness and the women's movement in her native country, as she had been living away from it for thirty years. The idea of organizing a symposium originated from this shared astonishment of two women. What was happening to us? On the one hand, the professional success that a handful of elite women had been achieving in Turkey for many years now seemed to have started to cross national borders. On the other hand, the German audience were most surprised to learn that there was an incipient Turkish women's movement and that Turkish women were fiercely debating every aspect of their feminine identity, as they had known Turkish women only through daily contact with the immigrant community,[1] where most working-class women were deeply submissive to traditional family values. Would it not be interesting to discuss these new developments in a symposium organized in Germany? Thus was born the idea of inviting women academics who had recently done research on different aspects of women's issues.

The symposium organized at the Castle of Hofgeismar near Kassel on 17–21 April 1989 involved the participation of not only Turkish scholars but also German researchers and social workers who worked on Turkish women, as well as many 'second generation' young women who were working in the same field.[2] The symposium got together about fifty women for five days – and even five nights, as lively debate continued until late in the evenings. It was an occasion for Turkish scholars who mainly knew each other through their published work but not personally to get closer, and for old friends who had not seen each other for some time to meet again. It was unforgettable because of many intense, excited and even strained discussions that proved to be enriching for all of us. The symposium was quite unique from the the point of view of organizational ingenuity. Many of the women participants had small babies, and they wanted neither to lose the chance of participating in such an exciting experience, nor separate themselves from their babies for a whole week. This problem, which is disregarded in the usual scientific meetings, can be handled easily if the organizers have a more sensitive, feminist outlook. Ayla, with the sociologist Meral Akkent assisting her in the organization of the symposium, devised a daycare and nightcare centre near the meeting-hall for the young mother–scholars. I would like to thank Professor Ayla Neusel, Dr Meral Akkent and all the sponsors of the symposium for this unique experience.

It was our common belief that the results of the symposium were worth publishing, even before the symposium had ended. While thinking seriously about the project we came to the conclusion that if all the papers presented to the symposium were included, the size of the book would be daunting, so we decided to focus on the papers describing the situation of the women living in Turkey. Thus the important dimension of the symposium which concerned immigrant Turkish women is not dealt with in the book. We published the book first in Turkey, and then in Germany.[3]

Turkish society in the 1980s

What has changed in Turkish society in the last years, that women have begun to question more and more vigorously their gender status, their long-term oppression and their traditional feminine identity? What kind of a society has Turkey become, during the 1980s? This is such a wide question that, although I feel obliged to sketch its main characteristics in a few rough outlines, it would be beyond the aims of this introduction to try to explore its theoretical and empirical sources in depth.

I will now try to underline some of those trends of social and cultural change which more directly affected women's lives. Talking about social change in Turkey is not a novelty, as most social literature has been dealing with this phenomenon since the mid-19th century. Yet the pace of change has been so rapid during the last twenty years that it is not fanciful to advance the hypothesis that the Turkish society is now on the brink of a social mutation. Though it would still be difficult to describe Turkey as a fully 'modern' society, according to classical modernization theories based on the modern/traditional dichotomy, it is quite certain that many traditional elements are now in the process of disintegration. We are now facing a complex and diversified society which impresses observers as a jigsaw of contradictory elements.

It is commonly accepted that cultural values, attitudes and value-oriented behaviours change more slowly than do social structures. But in Turkey we are also witnessing a rapid transformation in this area which can easily be described as a complete reversal. In order to point to some of the most dramatic reversals I will refer to the findings of a 'profile' research based on different attitude studies carried out between 1985 and 1989.[4]

Two of the most striking characteristics of Turkish society are its youth and the existence of distinct cultural groups side by side. The rate of population increase is still very high, though it has tended to decrease slowly over the past few years. As a result of the fact that, although the crude birth rate, which was 51 per thousand in the period 1935–40, had fallen to 31 per thousand in 1985, the crude death rate, which was 35 per thousand in 1935, had fallen still further to 9 per thousand in 1985, Turkey's population had risen to over 51 million by 1985. This rapid population increase, especially as there is a concentration of young age groups, creates heavy pressure on all social institutions.[5]

On the other hand, though there is more than one factor in cultural stratification, we can roughly distinguish three main cultural groups, at least for the sake of analysis. The first can be identified as the traditional rural culture, in which the remnants of a feudal world-view are still effective. In this culture women's social status is generally low, and children are not accorded the right to determine their own future by the family. Social values keep both the family and the individual under strict control. It is clear that the classic patriarchy is the dominant feature of this group.

The second cultural group is made up of the urban, industrialized segments of society, which have more or less internalized modern/Western values. Among these groups, subject to both vertical and lateral social mobility, and motivated by more or less rational decisions, both the family and the individual appear to have more autonomy than the first group. Women are relatively more free, both in the family and as individuals, and they have achieved a more egalitarian status with men.

The third group is what could be labeled as the 'new urban' cultural group, which remains at the intersection of the two other groups. Women and children are surrounded by social and familial pressures that are much more severe than those experienced in the rural culture. Thus the value conflicts, contradictions and violent breaks are more dramatic in this culture.[6]

Some of the most important dynamics of social change leading to the breakdown of traditional society are the growth of capitalism and endless urbanization or migration processes. Until the 1960s migration turned only to cities within Turkey: it was only after the 1960s that a new dimension was added with the mass external migration which started in the early 1950s and has steadily intensified since then. As a result of this process the urban population is growing, and hence the urban cultural group is becoming larger. The urban population, which was not more than 25 per cent of the whole population in 1950, increased to 53 per cent in 1985. Presently Turkey is a society in which about half of the population is living in towns and about a quarter is concentrated in great cities and metropolitan centres. The number of those who are earning their living out of industrial and service activities is about equal to those who are making a living out of agriculture.

The social stratification system has become extremely complex as a result of this process. On the one side small property ownership is still very widespread, though changing its form, and tribal relationships still exist at least in certain regions; on the other side a new stratum similar to the 'yuppies' of post-industrial societies is becoming more and more common in big cities. Low incomes generated by agriculture, the deep inequality of land ownership, and an intensified division of agricultural property as a result of inheritance and increasing mechanization of agriculture all continue to push the rural population to cities. And cities, especially the larger ones, continue to attract new-comers, due to the greater possibilities for earning a living, higher incomes, better services such as education for children – which is still the most powerful means of upward mobility – and the expectation of a relatively free and tolerant social environment.

The hope of a better life prompted a significant number of people to emigrate to industrialized Western societies – until the 1970s, when economic crises affecting those countries cut off a number of possibilities of emigration. Yet many families still undertake incredible adventures with the hope of bypassing strict visa regulations; and there is widespread support for the eventual membership of Turkey in the European Community, with its 'single market' and 'free circulation of labour' from 1993, because of the new possibilities for emigration that this step will open.[7] Research done in 1989 showed that only 30.7 per cent of those interviewed identified Turkey as the country where they desired to live, followed by Germany with 22.9 per cent, indicating that this new hope of a better life is the main motivation for moving.[8]

The 'hope of a better life' is affecting not only the urban cultural group, but also rural culture, as a consequence of increasing mass communication, in which television plays the most dramatic role. Increasing communication services provided by the state (highways, transportation, telephone, etc.) increase the interaction between these two cultures, bringing them closer to each other. One of the most important results of this interaction is seen in the increasing demand for a higher level of consumption. But the Turkish economy developed in such a way that the already existent unequal income distribution was further worsened in the 1980s (Özmucur, 1987); only small higher-income groups could meet rising expectations, and wide segments of middle- and lower-income groups were driven to frustration and disillusionment. If this social and economic polarization has not led the country into crisis, one must find the reason in the effectiveness of key institutions and values. Among these, the most prominent are the family and the widely held belief in fatalism.

The rapid process of change brought into the open the growing uneasiness of the groups keen on maintaining the status quo, and a new radicalism made its appearance in support of declining institutions and values. Extremist fundamentalist Islam had become effective as a counterpart to left-wing radicalism in the 1970s; it continued to consolidate itself in the early 1980s, as the 1980 military coup, far from repressing the fundamentalist religious groups in opposition to left-wing radicalism, gave them some legitimacy by trying to counterbalance the left-wing ideas with religious values. This growing prominence of Islamic radicalism in the 1980s, contradicting the former relative de-islamicization of the society,[9] is one of the most striking features of Turkish society in the 1980s.[10] In fact a return to religious values and radicalism of religious groups was a phenomenon observable in that decade in many parts of the world, including some Western countries. But this trend was most effective in the Middle East, and more particularly in Islamic societies (Iran being the most impressive example). In that sense what was happening in Turkey was neither exceptional nor particularly striking. Yet the government policies pursued during the 1980s in Turkey were such that, in one of the exceptional secular states in the Muslim world, a significant part of the population came to the conclusion that 'the radical Islamic groups were powerful enough to threaten the social order and the secular state' towards the end of the decade.[11]

Despite this anxiety about religious radicalism, another important basic value that social change brought into the fore in the 1980s was the importance attributed to 'reconciliation and consensus', especially in political life. The increasing political polarization and crisis – including terrorism – that Turkish society lived through in the 1970s, ending in the 1980 military coup, had created such a powerful trauma that society as a whole rejected the idea of going back to those years and was ready to pay the price of submitting to military rule. And the fact that the price paid for this relative calm brought about by the military was a loss of democracy meant that 'democratic values' were in the forefront during the 1980s. While we were approaching the end of the decade it appeared that, perhaps for the first time in history, a 'civil society' was coming into existence, made out of divergent groups of conflicting interests which nonetheless formed a common block opposed to the state. Though all of these divergent groups aimed at influencing the state, there was a growing consensus of mutual recognition of their co-existence. Hence interest groups which barely accepted the legitimacy of their counterparts came onto common ground where they valued 'recognition and consensus' and required democratic guarantees from the state. Finally there was a widespread consensus as to the anti-democratic nature of the 1982 Constitution and many other basic laws that the military junta forced upon Turkish society. It is true that the policy of systematic depoliticization pursued by the junta was still quite effective,[12] but when interviewed large segments of society expressed their hope for greater democracy and freedom.[13] Widespread public criticism on issues such as the repression of student organizations or trade unions[14] shows that the relative support given to the anti-democratic constitution of the military rule was rapidly eroding. It was clear that this regime was too narrow and too strict to satisfy the expectations of a changing society.

And yet the political party which governed Turkey during most of the 1980s (the Motherland Party) was far from satisfying the democratic social orientation. Moreover, the 'ultra-liberal' economic policies pursued under the banner of 'restructuring' the old, bottleneck economy by such means as export-oriented production, external competition and privatization came to a dead end after 1986; and chronic inflation which could not be reduced below 70 per cent per annum, changed the generally optimistic outlook of public opinion after 1987.[15] This was reflected in a loss of electoral support for the governing party, which in 1983 came to power with 45 per cent of the vote, but could not maintain this popularity in subsequent elections: 43.2 per cent in the 1984 local elections; 36.3 per cent in the 1987 national assembly elections; 21.7 per cent in the 1989 local elections. The Motherland Party finally lost power in 1991, attaining no more than 24 per cent of votes during the national assembly elections. Mr. Özal, who governed the country as Prime Minister of successive Motherland Party governments until 1990, was, however, still elected President of the Republic – only by the votes of his own party – in spite of growing unpopularity, and this has been a source of strain on the political system since this time.

In the light of these events, one has to conclude that Turkish society has changed dramatically in recent years; the most dramatic change being the fact that the state does not now dominate civil society, as it did for many centuries. Civil society has gained some autonomy and become more powerful, but it is not yet powerful enough to shape the state structure according to its needs, delimiting state powers in order to protect human rights and democracy. But we can be optimistic about the future because, for the first time in Turkish history, the tradition of the powerful centralized state – inherited and restructured anew by the Republic and consolidated three times by military rule, the last being the most radical – has lost its glamour, as have many other traditional values. Citizens have used the electoral power they gained in 1950 to vote for a more democratic, plural regime whenever they have had the chance to express their opinions.

Finally, civil society is defined by a multiplicity of cultural and ideological dimensions. We are far from the Ottoman period's cultural unidimensionality based on religion; we are far from the nationalist unidimensionality of the founding years of the Republic; we are far from the 'tentative realizing of the East–West synthesis' of the 1970s. At present the cultural mosaic of Turkish society is made up of many different value systems: elements of Mediterranean culture, of Islamic culture (including the various Sunnite/Alevi interpretations), of secular Western culture, of atheistic socialism and various regional cultures, are interacting with each other to create an extremely rich and complex whole.

At this point I shall turn to those institutions and values that most directly concern women. The family is the most critical of these institutions. Turkish society differs from Western societies in the stability and power of this institution. The proportion of those who get married to found a family is 91.8 per cent.[16] Though those categorically opposed to divorce are a minority (27.4 per cent), as the acceptable reasons for divorce are cited as 'adultery' (81.3 per cent), wife-battering (65.5 per cent) and alcoholism (59 per cent), it is clear that less dramatic cases of mutual disagreement (incompatibility of personality, etc.) are not viewed as legitimate reasons for divorce.[17] The average age at marriage is low, particularly in rural areas;[18] though a slow increase has been observed recently, this related to the longer period now spent in education, and affects mainly urban women. There are also important differences between rural and urban areas as regards the validity of a civil marriage as against a religious ceremony.[19]

The institution of marriage is shaped by traditional values that organize relations between men and women. The most widespread form of marriage is an arranged marriage based on viewing the bride.[20] Marriage based on a mutual arrangement between the bride and the groom is particular to urban culture and is quite rare (4.8 per cent). In rural areas bride abduction or elopement is the feature this form of marriage takes, in order to avoid the traditional 'bride price' paid by the groom's family.

Intra-family relations remain predominantly patriarchal. In spite of the fact that the nuclear family as opposed to the extended family, is the rule, men (and elders) have authority over women and children. But most people seem to enjoy the family life.[21] And it is clear that this relative satisfaction is ensured by women's submission and silence. Housework is the women's lot;[22] and despite her many sacrifices, the wife does not have a say in important matters. Even in the sphere of consumption, which could be seen as an extension of housework, women ask for a particular item: the person who chooses it and does the actual buying is most of the time the husband, especially for costly consumer durables.[23] The number of desired children does not exceed one or two, but the use of modern means of birth control is rare.[24] But although the nuclear family has become the norm, people tend to include their relatives in social events and leisure activities, as well as display solidarity with them, which shows that the ideal of the extended family is still alive.[25]

The fact that the most traditional institution of Turkish

society has not been affected by the rapid changes that have taken place is quite impressive. But on the other hand, an important dimension of social change is 'relative openness to change'.[26] Among current values, the most critical seems to be that attached to the individual. This new aspiration is most widespread among women and youth, which means that women and young people have become the most prominent agents of social change. Another new aspiration concerns the relations between men and women: here again, it is women who aspire to change these relations into egalitarian ones. For instance, in spite of the fact that in most cases women alone carry out the housework, many women support the 'new' idea of sharing housework among men and women (46.4 per cent). Another striking change is shown by the erosion of support (40 per cent) for the traditional dictum which says that 'women should be busy with their homes and leave the political matters to men'.[27] We must keep in mind that these are attitude changes, mostly among urban culture, but it is not too optimistic to expect that in coming years they will affect actual behaviour among larger segments of society.

But not all values concerning gender relations change as rapidly as the above mentioned. For instance relations between young girls and boys, especially sexual relations, are not easily tolerated, and boys are given more freedom than girls. Having children in a marriage is highly valued by both genders (69.8 per cent); if the right to an abortion is recognized by about half of the population (47.9 per cent), this is not considered to be a 'woman's right', but a family right shared by the husband and wife.[28] People do not seem to be enthusiastic about sex education, and think that if it is included in the curriculum, this should be in high school and not before.[29] A final point worth stressing concerns the headscarf issue which was on the political agenda in the late 1980s as a result of the conflict between radical Muslims and radical Kemalists: most people seem to be rather tolerant on this issue.[30]

Turkish women lived in a society dominated by these structures and values until the end of the 1980s. They not only lived and suffered as a result of the negative aspects; the issue of how they should live was the focal point of intense debate among groups with conflicting political interests. Each group saw the role of women as the critical element in the reproduction of its own value system.[31] This led to a striking phenomenon: despite the enormous complexity of the diversified social structures that I have tried to describe above, most groups uniformly agreed on one thing, and that was the necessary continuation of the patriarchal domination of men over women.

The aim of this book is to analyse how this basic structure is interpreted in different social groups; how it is translated into social interactions; and how women try to control, use to their advantage, or resist these power structures; and finally what type of strategies they develop to cope with them. The end result of these efforts might be the breakdown of one of the last traditional barriers to women's emancipation in Turkish society; hence women will be playing a critical role as agents of social transformation. This last point leads us to look more closely to feminism as a social movement which became visible during the 1980s.

Women's movements and feminism

The 1980s was not the first time that feminism came onto the agenda in Turkey. On the contrary, this was a century-old movement, with its roots in late nineteenth-century Ottoman society (Arat, 1991; Kandiyoti, 1987; Sirman, 1989; Tekeli, 1986, 1989, 1990, 1992). This long history can be analysed in three stages. The first-stage feminist movement attained its apogee during the second constitutional period, after 1908. The movement questioned the status of women in Ottoman society by contesting the traditional role ascribed to women as wives and mothers, and hence tried to loosen women's domestic confinement by defending the right to an education, to work and to participation in public life. Many women's associations were set up and various magazines and journals published. As a result of the transformation of the alphabet as part of the Republican reforms, today's young generations are unable to read this literature, and it is difficult for them to imagine how imaginative and courageous this movement was, and how many similarities it possesses with the present-day movement. The first-stage feminist movement was sensitive, on the one hand, to the aspirations of the modernizing bureaucratic elites of the time; on the other, to the nationalist movement developing in face of the crisis of the declining empire; and finally to the Western feminist movement, which had become visible in many countries with the actions of the suffragettes. But what is most striking to present-day feminists is that the analysis that these well-educated, middle-class Ottoman women developed was based on their own experience.

In the second stage, this grassroots movement disappeared to give way to state feminism. Indeed, some of the demands of the previous period led to some important reforms under the newly created republic, such as the Civil Code reform of 1926 and the suffrage reform of 1934. With these reforms made by the state 'from above', women's status certainly progressed a great deal compared to the Ottoman era. The fact that women had actively participated in the war effort during the War of National Independence had made the recognition of women's demands inevitable. In addition, nationalism, which was the dominant ideology of this period, developed a new role definition for women. Looking for its model to the supposedly more equal gender relations of pre-Ottoman Turks, it wanted to end women's domestic confinement and give them new responsibilities in the development of modern Turkey by opening careers to them like teaching. A corresponding loyalty and devotion to the new secular state was expected from women; once equal suffrage was achieved the state claimed that, 'gender equality being a reality in Turkey', women did not need an organization of their own, banning the Turkish Women's Association, which had formed a bridge between the old feminist movement and the new era. Thus our mothers' generation – both because they got some important rights and were given new opportunities, and because they were forced to do so by repression – identified with Kemalism rather than feminism. In the period between the 1950s and the mid 1970s most women's associations were founded with the aim of protecting the status quo – i.e. women's acquired rights and the secular state which in their view was the only guarantee against going back to old Islamic tradition. Hence they celebrated the important days of the Republic each year, and professed their loyalty and admiration for Atatürk. Consequently the patriarchal nature of the Civil Code, which recognized the husband as head of the family, was never an issue for them, and they tended to ignore the reality of patriarchal relations affecting the daily lives of most women. According to Kemalist women, peasant women were oppressed in Turkey only because they did not have an education and were not aware of their legal rights. They had the illusion that education was the key to everything, and that they were 'emancipated' and beyond patriarchal domination and control.

The 1970s were a period when left-wing ideological groups became effective – more effective than actually powerful – in defining the political agenda of the country by bringing into play new concepts like economic development, imperialism, economic and social injustice, inequality, class exploitation, etc. In this context it was not possible to ignore the fact that women were also exploited and oppressed, despite the official discourse of 'gender equality', and towards the end of the decade a new analysis developed among intellectuals. But this new analysis, which defined the issue as 'the woman question', borrowing concepts from orthodox Marxism, was fundamentally anti-feminist. Peasant women – supposedly the only oppressed group of women of the previous period – were replaced by working-class proletarian women. To end the 'woman question' in Turkey we were invited to fight against class exploitation side by side with socialist men. Thus many young women students, academics who were potential supporters of the new feminist ideology developing in Western countries, became active in small, ultra-leftist groups, fighting each other on many issues – except the 'woman question', where they united on the same sectarian anti-feminist approach. Thus we have lost more than ten years in discovering the new feminism.

Feminism could come to the forefront only after the 1980 military coup, which banned all political activity and crushed the left-wing movements. Some believe that if the movements had not been crushed the women involved in them would anyway have discovered women's specific oppression as Western feminists did. But some women are not as optimistic, and believe that if the movement had not been hit so severely women would never have been able to question the ideological hegemony of the male leaders. Whatever the outcome of this debate, the context in which Turkish feminism made its appearance invited many observers to blame feminism for being a child of the military coup, labelling it a 'Septembrist' ideology (the 1980 coup took place on 12 September). I believe that this is a wrong and unfair definition. Indeed when we look back to the early years of the movement, which started with the formation of the first consciousness-raising groups in Istanbul in 1981–2, we can truthfully say that it was perhaps the first democratic opposition to the military rule. And in many of its specific organizational features the feminist movement remained one of the most democratic avant-garde formations during the 1980s, and contributed to the democratization of Turkish society.

Though it is not possible here to propose a detailed analysis of the new feminist movement, I will mention the following events and actions, which appear to be landmarks of its first ten years. After about a year of intense consciousness-raising activity in small groups, the first public event was a symposium organized in Istanbul in 1982, which is important because 'feminism' as a concept was discussed here for the first time since the turn of the century. In 1983, feminist groups collaborated in the weekly *Somut* with a page in which they shared with the public their new discoveries about women's issues. The most important of these was that daily private life was the real arena of patriarchy. In 1984, Istanbul feminist groups created their first organization, a publishing company called the Women's Circle, and organized many conferences and debates around the book club which it animated. Classics of feminist literature were translated and published. In 1986, Istanbul and Ankara feminist groups together organized a petition campaign in order to ask the government to comply with the UN Convention about the Abolition of All Discrimination Against Women (1979), which was passed by the Turkish parliament a year before. About 7,000 women signed the petition, showing that feminist ideas were gaining legitimacy. In 1987 the first street demonstration after the 1980 military coup was organized by Istanbul feminist groups, in order to protest against wife-beating. For the first time about 3,000 women protested against an injustice that concerned them directly – as opposed to the many demonstrations of the past in which they marched against fascism, to celebrate May Day, etc. The demonstration was the starting point of a campaign launched against violence against women, which would last until the opening of the first shelters for battered wives in Istanbul. This was later continued as a campaign to condemn sexual harassment in the streets, workplaces and home. In 1989 the First Feminist Congress was held in Ankara, ending with a manifesto which summarized ten years of feminist thinking in Turkey. The manifesto claimed that women's oppression is multiple, as all male-dominated social institutions – the family, schools, the state and religion – subjugated women's labour-power, their bodies and their identity. The same year the First Women's Congress, organized by feminists and socialists in Istanbul, ended with an ideological divorce between feminism and socialism: feminist ideology would become independent and not reducible to any other ideology. Through these and many other actions, like 8th March celebrations and innumerable debates, the feminist movement was able to gain legitimacy in public opinion. This was best shown by the public uproar at a decision by the Constitutional Court at the end of 1989 about Article 438 of the Penal Code. This Article provided that, in case of rape, if the woman was a prostitute the penalty of the rapist would be reduced by up to two-thirds. A rape case was brought to the Supreme Court and the court decided that the Article was not contrary to Article 10 of the constitution regulating the equality of sexes as was claimed, as this aimed at protecting the rights only of 'honest women'. The protest campaign initiated by feminist groups with the striking, 'We are all prostitutes' slogan was so effective that most important opinion-makers sided with the feminists, against the court decision. Finally the National Assembly had to abolish this ugly Article. The final stage of the feminist movement in the 1980s was attained by efforts in institution-building. In 1990 two important institutions were opened in Istanbul: the Purple Roof Shelter for battered wives, and the Women's Library and Information Centre.

Some of the striking organizational features of the movement can be summarized as follows: the movement was very careful to remain independent of political parties and chose to be above social classes; each woman who felt herself oppressed could find a place in this autonomous movement. The movement was loosely organized: decentralization was the basic principle and different groups were free to decide on the specific mode of organization and actions; *ad hoc* committees, issue-based campaigns, associations, journals lived side by side and joined forces for events like the protest march against wife-battering of 1987.[32] Ideological pluralism and participatory democracy were thus the rule. With these characteristics, the new feminist movement was perhaps the first authentic example of a democratic movement in Turkey; despite the small number of its activists, the movement was able to mobilize a broad women's movement in society. Political parties, classical women's organizations and the press were among the first to be influenced by the movement and finally the small activist groups were successful in bringing women's issues to the head of the political agenda by the end of the decade.

This success can only be explained if one assumes that feminism proposes a correct analysis of the objective conditions of a particular historical conjuncture: all women were oppressed in Turkey in the 1980s – despite differences of social class, ethnic origin, level of education, profession, etc. – by patriarchal relations which are not only deeply rooted in traditional institutions such as the family, but are also reproduced continually by other so-called 'modern' institutions as well.

The structure of the book

This book, published ten years after a pioneering book about Turkish women (Abadan-Unat, 1981), is an attempt to identify what has or has not changed over that period in the situation of women in a rapidly changing society. The authors represent very well, in my opinion, the diversified and complex society that I have tried to describe above. They are united by two elements: they are young, and they share a feminist outlook. The specificity of the age-group to which most of the contributors belong is that they are all born after the Second World War, at a period in which Turkey made the rapid change from a traditional agricultural society into a modern one, and the authors have all witnessed the transition to a capitalist market economy, urbanization and democratization. Most of them learned about Atatürk from their mothers. This shared experience is the basis of their profound attachment to democratic values. The feminist outlook which the authors share constitutes the specificity of this book, which is the first example of Women's Studies in Turkey. It is true that the contributors do not have exactly the same feminist understanding; some of them even prefer not to call themselves 'feminist'. But what has motivated them all in their academic work is the effort 'to understand how women's condition is determined by the system of power relations that we can call patriarchy in each specific concrete situation and how women try to cope with these pressures' (Nükhet Sirman, in this book).

Aside from these two common aspects, there is an extreme variety among authors. Most of them are academic and social scientists, but they teach in every corner of the world and use different methodologies. This gives to the book its multi-disciplinary nature. There are sociologists, psychologists, psychiatrists, economists, anthropologists, political scientists and historians among them. The themes are also extremely diversified and each article deals with a different group of women – peasants, tribal women, working-class women, urban women, students, politicians, women living in the west and in the east of the country, etc. – hence the mosaic-like nature of the society is reflected quite well in the book.

The articles in the book are grouped in six sections. The title of the first section is 'The Attractions of Tradition', and it deals with the Ottoman past and the revival of Islam. In this section Nora Şeni examines changes in women's clothing at the end of the 19th century through a study of the satirical poems of Istanbul, when clothing was at the centre of the debate about how women should behave. A century later the situation is reversed, with those women who opt for an Islamic way of dress being a minority among the millions in the big cities. Feride Acar reports the results of research conducted on fundamentalist Islamic university students, and finds out that what these women look for in Islam is a protection against the competitive life-conditions that most university graduates expect in their future professional life. Yeşim Arat, too, looks at current fundamentalism in Turkey by analysing Islamic women's journals in order to clarify their message from the perspective of women's emancipation. She discovers that, surprisingly, their impact might not be necessarily against women's emancipation.

The second section, entitled 'Prerequisites of Material Life' contain three articles on the economic problems confronting women in Turkey. Yıldız Ecevit looks at macro-statistical indicators in order to situate urban women wage-earners in the general occupational structure of the Turkish economy. Ferhunde Özbay looks at the problem of housewives, again largely an urban phenomenon, using mainly qualitative data. Günseli Berik deals with women's carpet-weaving activities in rural areas. If participation in the economy is crucial, and the ideology of women's economic independence most attractive, this chapter indicates that women's hopes of autonomy are deeply frustrated by economic and social structures in Turkey.

The third section deals with three critical state institutions which would help women to break with traditional oppressive structures: education, development programs and the mass media. Fatma Gök examines macro-statistics on education as well as suggesting a critical evaluation of a system which falls short of its promises. Yakın Ertürk looks at regional development projects in eastern Anatolia and concludes that women are not better but worse off as a result of these programmes, whose more or less explicit aim is to 'exploit women's labour-power more efficiently'. In the final article of the section Ayşe Saktanber, using rich material, explains how mass-media professionals, including women journalists, reproduce the framework of traditional sexual stereotypes.

The first three sections thus show the dilemmas posed and limits set by existing institutions for women's emancipation in Turkey. The following sections, by contrast, concentrate on the different ways in which women 'resist'.

The fourth section, dealing with private life, begins with an article by Hale Bolak, in which she reports the results of her research on the internal power relations in families where the husband is unemployed and the woman becomes the breadwinner. Nükhet Sirman's article deals with the solidarity networks and power-building processes among young brides in a village of western Anatolia. Lale Yalçın-Heckmann discusses the ways in which Kurdish tribal women in southeastern Anatolia bargain for power.

The fifth section concentrates on the problem of resistance in the public sphere. Ayşe Güneş-Ayata analyses women's political participation and assesses the success of two radically distinct strategies of women politicians: 'womanly' women politicans who act as alter egos for male politicians; and women who try to stand on their own feet. In the second chapter of the section, Fatmagül Berktay critically evaluates the attitude of the Left vis-à-vis the women's movement, on the basis of her experience and of a review of left-wing magazines and journals. In the final chapter of this section, Nilüfer Çağatay and Yasemin Nuhoğlu-Soysal situate the feminist movement in Turkey within a comparative framework, especially with reference to nationalist movements in Third World countries.

The sixth section, called 'Pragmatic Forms of Resistance', reports on two campaigns launched within the feminist movement. Şahika Yüksel looks at the Women's Campaign Against Wife-Battering, and Arşalus Kayır relates the struggle by medical researchers for the sexual liberation of women. The concluding chapter by Deniz Kandiyoti summarizes the plight of Turkish women, resistance and recent struggles, and suggests the different directions which women's studies might – and should – explore in the future.

Notes

1. One of the largest immigrant communities in Germany is Turkish. Of about 3.5 million Turkish workers living abroad, three-quarters are concentrated in Germany.
2. See Günseli Berik (1989).
3. Published as *1980' ler Türkiye' sinde Kadin Bakiş Açisindan Kadinlar*, İletişim Yayınları, Istanbul 1990; and as *Aufstand im Haus der Frauen*, Orlanda Frauenverlag, Berlin 1991.
4. PIAR Marketing Research Co. Ltd, which had done many attitude researches for different purposes during the 1980s, published the main findings in a tabulated form in order to give a global picture of the social change: *Profile Turkey 1989: Values, Attitudes, Behaviors*, PIAR, Istanbul 1989.
5. State Planning Organization, *VI: Plan for Development*, Ankara 1986.
6. Yılmaz Esmer (1991) points to some of these dramatic contradictions: four-fifths of women living in Istanbul believe that there is no difference by birth between the sexes, but three-quarters of them think that the fact of the husband's being the head of the family is a rightful thing, as he should be the breadwinner; and 49% of them believe that the husband might have the right to beat up his wife under certain conditions.
7. In 1988, 69.2% of the population wanted Turkey to become a member of the EC; 59.4% believed that this was a good thing and hoped that it would be a fact in five to ten years. See PIAR, *Profile*, Tables 6.3, 6.7.10.
8. PIAR, *Profile*, Table 6.3.11.
9. Those observing Ramadan were 60.8%; 26.3% prayed regularly in 1985. PIAR, *Profile*, Tables 3.3.17, 18.
10. Believers totalled 94.4% in 1988. See PIAR, *Profile*, Tables 3.3.1, 2, 3, 5.
11. Those who had this anxiety increased from 37.1% in 1987 to 44.7% in 1988. PIAR, *Profile*, Table 5.2.6.
12. In 1988, 55.6% of the population said that they were not interested in politics at all and 35.1% supported a political party. PIAR, *Profile*, Tables 5.1.1, 2.
13. For instance 59.1% of the population said that the constitution must change if political conditions change in 1986 and 45.7% said that some change is necessary to the 1982 Constitution. PIAR, *Profile*, Table 5.1.5.
14. Criticized by 89.1%, PIAR, *Profile*, Table 2.3.15.
15. In 1987 52.4% were optimistic and 36.5% were rather pessimistic, whereas in 1989 these percentages were 20.2% and 73% respectively. PIAR, *Profile*, Table 5.2.14.
16. PIAR, *Profile*, Table 2.1.1. See also, Türk Sosyal Bilimler Derneği (1985).
17. PIAR, Profile, Table 2.2.23.
18. Among women the rate of marriage at ages 19–22 is 56.8%; among men the rate of marriage at 23–29 is 58.2%, PIAR, *Profile*, Table 2.1.2.
19. In 1987, 78.6% of the population required both the civil and religious marriage; 17.6% think that civil marriage is valid alone and 3% think that the religious ceremony is enough. PIAR, *Profile*, Table 2.1.3.
20. 48.1% of couples were married by arranged marriage and bride seeing; 28.4% knew each other through friends or relatives. PIAR, *Profile*, Table 2.1.4.

21. 26.4% of the population said that they were 'very much satisfied' and 52.2% 'quite satisfied' with their family life. PIAR, *Profile*, Table 2.1.18.
22. The housework is done by the women alone in 29.1% of families; by the women with some help from other members of the family in 53.5% of the families; and the housework is shared by the woman and the men in 13.4% of the families. PIAR, *Profile*, Table 2.1.20.
23. 32.5% of women do the daily shopping; for consumer durables, 23% of women decided when they were needed, but only 4% were actually able to shop for such goods. PIAR, *Profile*, Tables 4.3.1, 2, 5, 7.
24. 36.3%; PIAR, *Profile*, Table 2.1.13. See also Hacettepe Nüfus Etüdleri (1989).
25. 32.8% paid regular visits to close relatives; 54.7% visit from time to time; and 45.4% preferred to spend leisure time with family members. See PIAR, *Profile*, Table 2.2.2, 7.
26. Those who are 'very open to change' constitute 22.8%; those 'quite open to change' constitute 22.1%; and those who decide according to circumstances constitute 28.6%; whereas those who are scared by change are a minority (8.6% and 3.3%). PIAR, *Profile*, Table 3.2.1.
27. PIAR, *Profile*, Tables 3.2.5, 6.
28. PIAR, *Profile*, Tables 3.2.8, 9, 10, 41. There is about a 10% difference between boys' tolerance and girls'.
29. 27.5% and 78.4%. PIAR, *Profile*, Table 3.2.13.
30. 58.3% of the population has a tolerant attitude about 'turban'. Those who say that a woman must cover herself constitute 3.3%; and those who are against 'turban' wearing, 7.7%. In 1987 when the 'turban' crises broke for the first time at universities, 33% of the population mentioned this ban as that to which they were most opposed. PIAR, *Profile*, Tables 2.3.15 and 3.3.12.
31. For an interesting analysis of this subject see Nilüfer Göle (1991).
32. Some of these different groups were Association of Women Against Discrimination Against Women (Istanbul), Women's Solidarity (Ankara), Wednesday Group (Ankara), Tünel Women's Group (Istanbul), Purple Roof Foundation (Istanbul); the feminist journals were *Feminist* and *Kaktüs*.

References

Abadan-Unat, Nermin (ed.) (1981). *Women in Turkish Society*, E.J. Brill, Leiden.

Arat, Yeşim (1991). '1980' ler Türkiye' sinde Kadın Hareketi', *Toplum ve Bilim*, No. 53, Spring, pp. 7–21.

Berik, Günseli (1989). 'The social condition of women in Turkey in the eighties and the migration process', *New Perspectives on Turkey*, Vol. 3, No. 1, Fall.

Devlet Planlama Teşkilatı (1986). *Altıncı Beş Yıllık*, Plan, Ankara.

Erder, Türköz (ed.) (1985). *Family in Turkish Society*, Turkish Social Science Association, Ankara.

Esmer, Yılmaz (1991). 'Istanbul Kadınları', *Milliyet*, June.

Göle, Nilüfer (1991). *Modern Mahrem*, Metis, Istanbul.

Hacettepe Nüfus Etüdleri (1989). *1988 Türkiye Nüfus ve Sağlık Araştırması*, Ankara.

Kandiyoti, Deniz (1987). 'Emancipated but unliberated? Reflections on the

Turkish case', *Feminist Studies*, Vol. 3, No. 2, Summer, pp. 317–38.

Özmucur, Süleyman (1987). *Milli Gelirin İc Yıllık Dönemler İtibaryle Tahmini, Dolarla İfadesi ve Gelir Yolu ile Hesaplanması*, Istanbul.

PIAR (1989). *Profile: Turkey (1989): Values, Attitudes, Behaviors*, Istanbul.

Sirman, Nükhet (1989). 'Feminism in Turkey: a short history', *New Perspectives on Turkey*, vol. 3, no. 1, Fall.

Tekeli, Şirin (1986). 'Emergence of the new feminist movement in Turkey', Dahlerup, D. (ed.), *The New Women's Movements*, London, Sage, pp. 179–199.

Tekeli, Şirin (1989). '1980' lerde Türkiye' de Kadınların Kurtuluşu Hareketinin Gelişmesi', *Birikim*, no. 3, July.

Tekeli, Şirin (1990). 'Women in the changing political associations of the 1980s', in *Turkish State, Turkish Society*, ed. Finkel, A. and Sirman, N. Routledge, London.

Tekeli, Şirin (1992). 'Europe, European feminism and women in Turkey', *Women's Studies International Forum*, vol. 15, no. 1, pp. 139–43.

Part I

The Attractions of Tradition

Caricature 7: The Transformation of Men' Clothing

Fashion and Women's Clothing in the Satirical Press of Istanbul at the End of the 19th Century

Nora Şeni

No doubt there are several good reasons that justify the historian's interest in clothing, particularly in women's clothing. Apart from an ethno-anthropological interest and the changes clothing can reveal in social customs and mentality, the topic also has a wealth of information about the Ottoman Turks, especially the Ottomans at the end of the 19th century, as Aliye Hanim's book, 'Contemporary Muslims',[1] published in 1894, testifies.

Aliye Hanim came from the Ottoman elite. She was the daughter of Cevdet Pacha, minister of justice, historian and organiser of common law legislation (*Mecelle*). In her book, she sets the scene with two young Turkish women friends: one, a proponent of Western dress, is opposed to the other, who prefers the comfort of Eastern clothing. The author pronounces in favour of plurality, claiming that sometimes she dresses in Eastern style, sometimes in Western style. Nevertheless, although she refrains from deciding between the two styles, details in her speech crop up like so many confessions of her penchant for European clothing. Thus, she indicates at the outset that her Western-style friend is more cultivated, more sophisticated than the one who still dresses in Turkish style. The latter friend could have, but did not make the efforts 'required for her perfection'.

Aliye Hanim devotes a third of her book to the question of women's clothing and the veil. The other two themes she develops concern the use of slaves in Turkish homes, and polygamy. Women's clothing and veils, slaves and polygamy are all themes that occupied a paradoxical place in the debate on the westernizing of Turkey at the end of the 19th century. These cultural particularities of Turkish life did not fit, or did not fit easily, into the modernizing plans of the pro-Western elites who contemplated Turkey through the gaze of Europeans. But at the same time, it would seem that the Turkish or Ottoman identity lay almost entirely in these cultural traits, as if a great part of Turkish *capital d'être* was tied to these traditional ways. Hence Aliye Hanim's determination to justify herself in the eyes of the West while at the same time tracing the narrow path fraught with ambiguities between the contemporary modernist position and respect for tradition.

As we can easily imagine, this uncomfortable position forced her to break more than once with both the principles she defended and the logic and arguments she developed. This woman, who seems to ground her authority in herself and speaks loudly and clearly in her own name when addressing European public opinion, makes a case for polygamy. While making clear that it would be inconceivable for herself or her friends, she finds it is necessary in the countryside where extra hands are needed to run the households and farms.

There is another, deeper, ambiguity. Aliye Hanım demonstrates very intelligently the exotic picture postcard images fostered in the West with regard to Turkey in general, and Turkish women and their clothing in particular. But when she describes a reception on the terraces of her home on the shores of the Bosphorus, her speech echoes the tone and style of the narrative accounts of travellers – those 'ethnologists' before the term was invented – who were nevertheless champions at evoking ready-made images and somewhat stereotyped attitudes towards the East. She thus makes a special effort to call attention to those aspects of the party that would appear picturesque and typically Turkish in the eyes of a foreigner, but which are self-evident and natural for a Turkish woman unaccustomed to looking at herself through others' eyes. To direct at oneself what one imagines to be the gaze of the West, thereby giving rise to self-denigration is a peculiarity of the Ottoman elite feelings in which Fatma Aliye was steeped.

The question that arises is: how is it that in debating Turkey's accession to contemporary civilization (*çağdaşlaşma*) – as Aliye Hanim does – two-thirds of one's text is devoted to the condition of women and the other third to their clothing?

1. The stakes that crystallized on the issue of the Ottoman women's dress transcend questions of fashion or female morality. The length and form of skirts, the material and the thickness of the veil – this debate on the emancipation of women has served for nearly two centuries as the forum at which societal choices have found expression. In the process of westernizing Turkey, reformists and conservatives expressed themselves exclusively by way of this privileged pretext. It has been used as an emblem or symbol to indicate a position for or against modernization, and to signify a societal choice that goes way beyond the issue of the condition of women.[2]

Serif Mardin has taken the opportunity to describe how, from the 17th century to contemporary times, the conservative current has constantly used the threats weighing upon female morality as a pretext for urban rebellion.[3] The loss of female morality is represented either by *ferece* (a coat) that becomes thinner and makes it possible to guess certain forms of the body, or by an increased, less segregated presence of women in the city, or – as was the case in Konya a few decades ago and which led to an uprising – the wearing of dresses with straps. On the other side of the political spectrum, first the Young Turks, then the Union and Progress Committee and Mustafa Kemal were to make the emancipation of women a *sine qua non* condition of modernity. They would write, speak and militate on the subject. Modernist literature at the end of the 19th century was dominated by two themes: *tessetür-ü nisvan* (covering women), and *teahhüd-ü zevcat* (polygamy). The education of young girls was another theme but it lagged far behind the other two controversies. A writer like Mehmet Tahir, for example, would pay for the printing of a small brochure out of his own pocket in order to explain, without intended irony, that the Balkan war had not been lost because of Turkish women who uncovered themselves and dressed in Western style – indeed, he pointed out, such women had been remarkable for their sacrifices and aid to the Turkish soldiers during the aforesaid war, etc.[4]

2. Broaching the question of women's clothing also makes it possible to note one's political and economic choices, to express therein one's nationalism and concern for promoting and protecting Turkish artisanry and industry in the face of imports.

Aliye Hanım lauds the merits of cottons from Brousse and Damas and argues that these fabrics could very well be used to make European clothes that are just as sophisticated as those made from imported material bought in the Istanbul shops. Mehmet Tahir counted on Turkish women forcing a change on their men thereby helping to bring Turkey into the age of production and industrialization. Tahir recommended austerity to women in matters of clothing and ornamentation.[5]

While the polemic was raging about women's obligation to be covered up and veiled (*mesturiyet*) in public, their clothes changed. Beginning with the *Tanzimat*, city clothes, which seem to have remained the same for centuries, started to change. This stagnation followed by an evolution made possible by the *Tanzimat* raises an important question: what was it in Ottoman culture that maintained the *status quo* in dress and how did the *Tanzimat* allow a transformation of female apparel? The same question can be asked in a different way: can one speak of fashion in the Ottoman city where the state authority issues decrees on female dress? Indeed, we know that the Divine Porte was generous with its *firmans* which, from the 16th to the 20th century, ruled on the colour and the thickness of *ferece*, the length of the veil and of scarves, and the material used for lining women's coats. In so doing, the state confessed that it was, among other things, a question of keeping things the way they had always been. This reference to 'what has always been' is very frequently found in the *firmans*, where concern for preserving established forms sometimes seems to justify the promulgation of the edict – as if things could be or come into being only if and because they had already been from time immemorial. The fact that the state did not delegate the control of female morality to institutions situated between it and the individual, like religion, the ecclesiastical body, the family, the neighbourhood, etc., casts doubt upon the existence, within this social organization, of fashions according to which the accoutrements, dress and bearing of women might change.[6]

Two aspects of the Ottoman state apparatus emerge here: 1. *Its conservatism:* the state's identity as well as that of Ottoman society lay in 'what has always been'; 2. *Its centralism:* its unwillingness to delegate its powers to institutions and channels of civil society could only impede the functioning and diversification of such institutions. But the *Tanzimat* and the process they instigated made a breach in these two particularities: The Ottoman state recognized the necessity for change, though limited to certain areas. Furthermore, the state guaranteed two fundamental principles of a market economy: assuring the security of human life and of private property. But we know it is in the wake of market channels that the institutions of civil society have become autonomous and diversified. Thus, surging through this two-fold breach, fashion – a normative and socializing institution – was to make its appearance and transform, very slowly of course, the clothing of Muslim women in the big cities like Istanbul.

Parallel to the change in male clothing undertaken by the state (for example, by requiring that its functionaries wear the *istanbouline*, that dark jacket with a high collar and buttons down the front), the new dress of the Muslim women of Constantinople would be propagated from the Palace. Indoor as well as outdoor attire would change under the influence of fashion, itself tributary to the westernizing and modernizing currents.

Indoor clothing, a combination of *şalvar* (wide, puffy pants) and *gömlek* (a type of large blouse), gave way to the *entari* (a dress cut somewhat like a nightshirt) and the *hırka* (a woollen jacket). Under Abdülhamit, the *entari* lent itself to the variations of European fashion and the Malakoff style; the tunic and skirts with bustles made their appearance. At the same time the Eastern character of these dresses was preserved by their adornment with embroidery. However far it may have been from the lines and curves of European dresses, the *entari* was the Trojan horse of a practice that revolutionized Turkish women's wear. It enabled the use of the 'corset'. This was a novelty that radically altered the figure of urban Muslim woman. After its introduction, and no matter what clothing was worn, nothing – i.e. the woman's allure – would ever be the same again. While her two friends parade in front of her, one dressed in the European style, the other in the Turkish style, Aliye Hanım concedes that the *entari* is only pleasing to the eye if the person wearing it is girdled by a corset. Indeed, the loose, soft lines evoking the indolence so often reported by travellers were replaced by a firm shape in which the smallness of the waist and the flat belly were enhanced by the generous curve of the hips and an unharnessed, abundant bosom. To a totally reclining posture – on pillows and soft couches – was opposed a different one: erect, tight-waisted, rising to a point accentuated by the use of a parasol. Even if the women of the big cities could not import everything and completely adapt to European fashion, they complied with it by moulding themselves into a shape radically different from the one drawn by the *salvar* and the *gömlek* inside the home and the *ferece – yaşmak – terlik* outside. Indeed, until nearly the end of the 19th century, outdoor apparel was composed of the trio *ferece* (coat), *yaşmak* (veil), *terlik* (slippers). Here is what a traveller, who seems to have a different opinion of the orientalism of the preceding centuries, has to say about it at the time:

> (...) the *yaşmak* that hides the face of the *hanums* prevents one from knowing whether they are young or old, ugly or pretty, and the long case of thick cloth covering them from head to toe makes it impossible to tell how they are shaped or arrayed; they are long, walking packages and one says nothing about them because one wouldn't know what to say.[7]

The trio *ferece – yaşmak – terlik* was to evolve, beginning with footwear.

The only concession the *hanums* have made to European fashion lies in the shoes; old women and women of low condition are practically the only ones who continue to wear yellow slippers; not wishing to look webbed-footed, the others imprison their feet in small, very civilised slippers and even in elegant Parisian ankle-boots with high heels disappearing beneath the soles.[8]

In the next period, following the shoes, it was the coat of the 'web-footed package' that was to change. The *yeldirme*, for example, is a kind of coat worn during summer holidays in the country. With its large collar, it is a European variant of the *ferece*. Covering a small-waisted *entari* with a wide skirt, the varieties of *ferece* worn with a thin veil and a matching parasol confirm the new look of Turkish women. The satire of the 1870s was right on target in drawings of an Eastern woman and a Western woman with noticeably the same shape eyeing each other (see caricature 4). But although its resemblance to the coat made it capable of changing in accordance with European styles, which set the pace during this period, the *ferece* were to give way to the *çarşaf* which comes much closer to Eastern accoutrements. Similar paradoxical phenomena mark the changes in men's clothing. Indeed, just as men's dress was being adapted to

Western fashion under Mahmoud II, the *fez* was imported from
the East. Should this be viewed as a desire to maintain a balance?
In any event, the introduction of the *çarşaf* raises a number of
questions. Until then, the new customs, new ways, and proper
manners had been spreading out into society after being refined
by the Palace. The latest *yaşmak* was first worn in public by the
women of the court. But the *çarşaf* was a completely different
story. Ignored by the Palace, the *çarşaf*, formed by a floor-length
cape gathered at the waist, made it even easier to go about
incognito than the *ferece*. Moreover, at the time of Abdulhamid,
women wearing *çarşaf* were forbidden to enter the Palace, for
fear they might be men in disguise sneaking inside. Thus, the
wearing of this piece of clothing was prohibited in the Beşiktaş
district where the sovereign's dwelling was located. The
caricatures of the time do not fail to associate that fear with the
large and abundant layers of skirts and flounces. The fact that it
hid women's figures even better than the *ferece* no doubt led to
its adoption by the people against the will of the state. But it
would be oversimplifying to see the *çarşaf* as an issue opposing a
modernist State and a conservative population. For, by adapting
to European fashions and being cut in half to become skirt and
cape, this same *çarşaf* would swiftly change and end up as a
Western suit. (It is very much back in style today, but that is
another story.) The history of this piece of clothing in the city of
Istanbul is thus recorded in the change from the *torba çarşaf* (the
'sack' *çarşaf* – potato sack?) to the *tango çarşaf* (the tango çarşaf!).
The *torba çarşaf* – a type of large cape gathered at the waist
covering the woman from head to toe, allowing a short veil
(*peçe*) to be hung across the face – must have been pleasing in the
eyes of the conservators, especially during a period in which the
reign of 'what has always been' seemed compromised. Yet this
piece of clothing was made from fabrics of every colour, striped
or embroidered with gold. Once cut in half at the waist and
separated into skirt and cape, the *çarşaf* would undergo change.
First, the cape was shortened. Naked arms were covered with
long gloves. Then, the hemlines went up. Their fully shortened
form was to be called 'tango'. The veil, too, became thinner.
Made out of fine tulle, it barely hid the face and ran onto the
cape. Later, when even the cape would be abandoned, there
would be nothing left but a scarf to cover the hair. In this
version, the *çarşaf* no longer had any connection to the 'sack to
cover the female shape', but rather became a sign of elegance
and obedience to stylishness. It was a fashion that also required

1. How much trouble she would have had to undo them if she had come out of her mother's womb like that!

carrying a parasol matching the *çarşaf*. The parasol must have been used to hide faces frightened of being recognized beneath increasingly transparent veils.

Hairstyles followed the movement and underwent change as well. Long hair once flowing in multiple braids down the back was swept up into chignons. Women abandoned the old *hotoz*:

> which consisted of a sort of hairdo shaped into a triangle, composed of several *yemeni* – tulle handkerchiefs, bits of lace called *bibile* and ornamented with coins and several dozen diamond and pearl hairpins [*Kayik hotoz*][9]

in favour of a much simpler *hotoz*. This one was formed by a small many-coloured tulle toque set on top of the head at a slight angle. The curling iron was used in Aliye Hanım's home where the young slaves curled their mistresses' hair, swept it forward toward the forehead and decorated it with combs. Just as in the West, the complexity of this hairstyle seems to have made it a favourite target of humorists (see caricature 1).

الباقارينى كوستروك عيب ايمشدر

2. It seems that it is shameful to show one's feet. Seen from Istanbul, the rules of propriety that hide the ankles but allow a very low neckline and expose the women's bosom seem all the more absurd.

3. Above all, be sure that the photo really looks like me.

We can well imagine that the satirical press did not remain a stranger to this issue of clothing which not only reflected a societal choice but, moreover, lent itself so well to laughter. The drawings reverse the bustle of a crinoline and ridicule its use; they exchange the veil for a hat-veil and point out the futility of anxiety over the subject of a veil already made in order to blend with a European custom. These satirical papers occupied an important place in the Turkish press, which expanded enormously during the short period from 1870 to 1877. The experience of political institutions, even of limited representation (in the so-called First Monarchy phase) was accompanied in Turkey by a tremendous development of intellectual and political expression. Until the dissolution of the parliament, this phase was to give birth to the satirical press and a myriad of small humorous papers. One name dominates the press, that of Theodore Kasap. Of Greek origin, he is the one who published the two newspapers, the *Çıngraklı Tatar* and the *Hayal*, in which the caricatures reproduced here first appeared. These papers came after another of Kasap's newspapers: the *Diyojen*. This one was published on an average of twice a week from November 1870 to January 1872. The *Diyojen* contained only two caricatures, whereas every issue of the *Çingirakli Tatar* (April–July, 1873) and the *Hayal* (1873–87) contained one. With naive, simple strokes, these caricatures ridiculed the failures of modernization in the Turkish city, the slow pace of the new means of transport – the tramway, the steamboat and the train. Reflecting the feelings of the people, they would never let a chance go by to sketch the first tremor of fashion and to take a position in the debate on clothing. Many of these drawings concern the behaviour of the Christian or 'Frank' population. The words 'Madame' and 'Monsieur' often appear in the captions beneath these drawings. But these ladies and gentlemen are sketched according to the issue at hand – modernized clothing or locomotion – that was stirring up a cosmopolitan, multilingual city like Istanbul. At times, the caricaturist's eye is that of a Turk making fun of a low European neckline (see caricature 2), at others that of a Christian or Muslim modernist, annoyed by the old-fashioned puritanism of a Muslim woman (see caricature 3). The heterogeneity of this city at the end of the 19th century and the multiplicity of the customs, practices and behaviour found there, made it necessary to face the other, to look at the other, and to look at oneself through the eyes of the other.

4. 'Hanım, do you always go out walking so "closed" in *ferece* and *yaşmak?*'
'Yes, Madame, it is a sin for us to go about as "open" as you.'

The confrontation. Two women face to face. They are looking at each other. They are eyeing each other. One is dressed in the conservative Eastern style, the other has followed the stylish evolution in Turkish dress. This is a frequent context for caricature. But only those that are similar can be measured against each other and compared. The drawings never show bad taste by comparing or confronting a Muslim woman (for whom fashion is first of all a luxury that she cannot afford, or who has very firm religious convictions – two reasons for maintaining the conservative character of her clothing) with another woman, her face uncovered, both her allure and attire in the European style. A European woman and a Turkish woman never look at each other in these drawings, except to reveal the similarity of their accoutrements. Thus, in the caption to caricature 4, there are signs of the incongruity of the reproach made to the Turkish woman (the one veiled by a *yaşmak*) for hiding herself from people's gaze while the European (the one whose face is hidden by a hat-veil) does the same thing out of taste.

'Hanım, do you always go out walking so "closed" in *ferece* and *yaşmak*?'
'Yes, Madame, it is a sin for us to go about as "open" as you.'

It is interesting to note that the term used to designate how far a woman is veiled and covered is 'closed'. 'Open' designates precisely the one who does not cover up, the one who is unconcerned by the *tessetür*. This literal reference to sexual availability, made inoffensive through current, everyday use of the language, takes one by surprise when one begins to translate and hears the sentence word-for-word. Still, the reply of the Turkish woman is all the more amusing as the first woman is every bit as 'closed' as the second. They have an obviously similar bearing in their high-heeled ankle-boots. Perhaps the Turkish one has an advantage in a more deeply arched back, a more clearly drawn waist and a parasol that seems to testify to more studied elegance. The caricaturist pretends, for the occasion, to be unaware of the difference between a hat-veil, worn by choice and for play, and a veil, worn out of an obligation to honour.

In another example of women face to face, the caricaturist gives his preference to the Turkish woman whose clothing has been adapted to European norms. Dressed in an *entari* over a corseted waist, an erect bearing, a wide-collared *ferece* that looks just like a coat, her adversary is a woman in a *şalvar* and puffy blouse, her feet in Turkish slippers (caricature 5).

'Girl, what sort of clothes are those? Have you no shame?' asks the latter woman.
'In this century of progress, you are the one who should be ashamed,' replies the humorist.

Women eyeing each other are not the only ones who stimulate the humorist. He also classifies masculine dress and household furniture according to the signs of modernity and sophistication for which they were chosen. Thus, we read to the right of a caricature split in half by a vertical line: 'the signs of barbarity'. These are represented by a low-lying couch (the *sedir*), a long pipe (the *çubik*) and the *pabuç* (Turkish slippers). On the left, a dress with a fitted-waist and a bustle skirt, a cane and a bowler hat, a table, a grammar book – supposedly to indicate the use of the French language – and the absence of the *sedir*, the caption reads: 'The tools of civilization'. Furthermore, the evolution of

5. 'Girl, what sort of clothes are those? Have you no shame?'
   'In this century of progress, you are the one who should be ashamed!'

6. The tools of civilization / The signs of barbarity.

8. In her bedroom / In the street.

9. There could be anything hidden beneath that!

10. Ten paras, Madame, ten paras.

11. 'Did you put your bustle on backwards in your haste?'
'No, the fashion has changed. This is the way it is worn now!'

12. May the devil take you, Zifos! Why didn't you think about how tight corsets are when you were dreaming about equality!

13. Must men henceforth ride side-saddle like women, in the cause of equality?

women's apparel had as its counterpart the transformation of men's clothing. Caricature 7 retraces the calendar of those transformations. We can read the captions from right to left: '1200' (1784), '1230' (1814), '1260' (1874), '1320' (1904). The turban gives way to the fez, and later to a man with hair and a soft hat; the *istanbouline* and trousers replace the *şalvar* or the *potur* and the long, full jacket worn on top. In 1874, the Turk of Istanbul wore a European suit.

Another duality conveyed by these drawings appears to prefigure advertising today: before–after. It warns against the embellishment of reality that the new clothes permit: before, a woman in her bedroom, wearing a kind of nightgown, and looking flat; after, in the street, fitted waist, back arched, erect, bustled crinoline, moulded hair, and, extending the erect bearing, an open parasol (caricature 8).

During this period, the crinoline that made a bustle at the back of skirts appears to have been called the *pouf*. It fascinated the humorist who devoted more than one caricature to it. The *pouf* lends itself first to poking fun at Hamidian fears: 'There could be anything hidden beneath that!' muses a policeman, caught up by the size of the volume hidden from his view by this cascade of cloth (caricatures 9 and 10). Of course this evokes the fact that it was forbidden to wear the *çarşaf* near the Palace and in the Beşiktaş district.

But the bustle in front instead of at the back was also funny (caricature 11). With a *pouf* on top of her belly, as if she were pregnant, a woman reassures another woman whose skirt bustles where it is supposed to, by telling her that it's the new style. Here we find the usual misogynous tone along with a theme that has endured through the centuries: what those silly women won't do to be fashionable! Decidedly, whether the state issued decrees or not, fashions in clothes flourished in Istanbul at the end of the century.

Feminism and equality of the sexes

It would be a mistake to believe that the Istanbul press of the 1870s was exempt from the modern feminist debate on the equality of the sexes. A certain Dr Zifos appears to have made himself the spokesman and defender of the feminist opinion. I have been unable to establish in which paper and in what terms this doctor expressed himself. Whatever the case may have been, his positions supplied the *Hayal* with material for jokes for

14. If Dr Zifos formed an army like that one, the influence of its rifle butts would no doubt spread throughout the world.

several weeks. The caricatures of the newspaper challenge this Christian-sounding name (was it Greek? Armenian?) to remind him that if there is to be equality, it will not be easy for men. Not for the reasons that are supposed to frighten men in the face of feminism today (e.g. having to compete with women in areas thus far reserved for men) but rather because they must share the bondage of the weaker sex: for example, squeeze their waists into the laces of a corset! Had Zifos thought about this? In the *Hayal* interpretation, it is not the women who become the equals of men, but rather the men who are reduced to the same level as women. And it's dull! What! Must men henceforth ride side-saddle like women? Zifos would do well to reflect first and to think about himself, too, before putting forward such opinions as these!

To show women soldiers, women at arms, means dropping such reservations with respect to the equality of the sexes. The drawing may send out some sort of warning, but the caption is there to poke fun at the bellicose ability of such a battalion, armed by Dr Zifos (caricature 14). In another reading of the

دوقتور ژبقورلك ادما ابلذبري مساوالك دلائلدن اولهرق ٠٠٠٠

15. As proof of the equality upheld by Dr Zifos …

16. 'Monsieur, there must surely be a weight beneath the pan on which you are seated.'

'No, Madame. I can get up and you may sit down, if you wish.'

same drawing, the *Hayal* addresses women in order to display before their eyes the various aspects (frightening? painful? heroic?) of the male condition: killing, making war, etc.

The *Hayal* enjoyed itself to the full with this story about the equality of the sexes. It measured men and women like stallions with a yardstick and weighed them like vulgar merchandise. It purported to demonstrate to women, who tried to cheat in these games of weights and measures or who were simply incredulous, the 'natural inequality' of men and women. One wonders who these incredulous women were in that last quarter-century in Istanbul. (Caricatures 15 and 16).

But along with the story of the equality of the sexes, the *Hayal* also raised for the first and last time the question of women, independently, outside of a societal debate concerning the westernizing, preserving or modernizing of Turkey. Until then, all the caricatures and graphic display of flounces, hat-veils and the like, faithfully reflected the role played by the question of Muslim female clothing within a much larger debate concerning the directions opening up to Turkish society. The opinions stated on women's emancipation and particularly on the subject of women's clothing were also used to publicize choices related to those directions. The cartoons of the period reproduced this typology by maintaining the question of women's apparel in its role of symptom or emblem; but it was done playfully. They played mainly on confrontation, taking advantage of social heterogeneity and ethnic, cultural, religious and linguistic diversity. They were elusive, speaking in the name of some, being surprised through the eyes of others. It was this game that gave caricature in the 1870s its fantastic energy putting an end to false debates and perhaps making it possible to direct our questioning elsewhere!

Notes

The collection of newspapers and slides used here belongs to F. Georgeon. I wish to thank him for making them available to me.

1. Aliye Hanoum, *Les musulmanes contemporaines*, Paris, A. Lemerre, 1894, translated by Nazime Roukié.

2. For more details on this subject, see N. Şeni, 'Ville ottomane et représentation du corps féminin', *Les Temps Modernes*, July–August, 1984.

3. Şerif Mardin, 'Super Westernization in Urban Life in the Ottoman Empire in the Last Quarter of the Nineteenth Century', in *Turkey, Geographical and Social Perspectives* (ed. by P. Benedict, E. Tümertekin, F. Mansur), Leiden, Brill, 1974.

4. Mehmet Tahir, *Çarşaf Meselesi*, Istanbul, 1912.
5. Mehmet Tahir, *Hanimlarimiza Mahremane bir Mektup*, Istanbul, 1911.
6. Cf. Muhaddere Taşçiọğlu, *Türk Osmanli Cemiyetinde Kadının Sosyal Durumu ve Kadin Kiyafetleri*, Ankara, 1958.
7. Emile Julliard, *Femmes d'Orient et femmes européennes*, Paris, Genève, 1896, p. 51.
8. *Op. cit.*, p. 51.
9. Aliye Hanoum, *op. cit.*, p. 140.

2

Women and Islam in Turkey

Feride Acar

Islamist movements have in the recent past been some of the most significant and controversial phenomena on the Turkish social and political agenda. The 1980s were marked not only by the most active and influential presence of Islamist movements since the foundation of the secular republic, but also by the visible presence of women at the forefront of these movements.

This presence is partly due to the fact that, in the 1980s, women started to participate in open political struggle in many segments of society, and the Islamist contingent has been no exception. Also, Islamist movements made deliberate efforts to reach women in contemporary Turkish society and, for reasons discussed in this chapter, the 1980s was the decade when such an appeal struck responsive chords among some women.

A particularly influential medium through which Islamist movements communicated their messages to women was the monthly women's journals. In the latter half of the 1980s, almost all of the religious sects or groups in Turkish society published their own journals of literary, 'scientific', political or general nature, they all allocated specific sections to women's issues and concerns. From time to time some also published monthly journals written and edited by women and aimed at an exclusively female readership. During the same decade the number of Islamist books in general, as well as those aimed towards women readers, also increased significantly. These publications called upon women readers to learn about their faith, to become good Muslim women, to refute their Western or non-Islamic traditional ways and turn to Islam. They promised that Islam would ensure that women ceased to be overworked, oppressed and exploited, that they would become contented, dignified and happy individuals in this world and would attain salvation in the next.

At this time, female university students were demanding changes in the country's laws and the regulations of educational institutions to allow the headscarf in the classroom (as was a requirement of their religious faith), and this came to the forefront of public discussion. Many actions and demonstrations took place in support of these demands, ranging from sending telegrams to public officials to women university students' hunger strikes in the big cities. The result of these and other demonstrations was that women dressed in Islamic garb and engaged in highly visible political activity became almost commonplace. For the first time in the Turkish Republic's history, the conventional view which equated Islam with women's 'imprisonment' at home was being challenged by the appearance of these women demanding an 'Islamic way of life' through open political struggle in which they, very effectively, used the weapons and tactics of modern democracy.

Views on whether this apparent contradiction signified a genuine – though admittedly strange – effort on the part of a group of women to struggle out of the bonds of patriarchy or whether it simply reflected tactical use of women as pawns by the reactionary forces of Islam in their age-old fight with the secular republic, dominated public discussion and political analysis throughout the decade. This chapter is an attempt to shed some light on the issue through an examination of the contents of Islamist women's journals and a series of interviews with a group of women university students who could be identified as followers of the Islamist movement.

The Islamist movement, in trying to present an alternative to the existing sociopolitical system in Turkey, has allocated a significant place on its agenda to the issue of women for two reasons. First, the Islamic religion has from its inception been very sensitive to the question of women's rights and functions in society. Based on the notion that relations between men and women, and the institution of the family, are very important for the establishment and maintenance of a proper Islamic social order, Islam has always emphasized the significance of such issues as the protection of women and the family institution, and education of the young according to Islamic principles.

Second, due to the specific circumstances in Turkey, the conflict between Islam and the secular mentality represented by Kemalist reformism has led to particular confrontation on the issue of women. When values promoting women's equality in social and political spheres – albeit in their formal meaning and for a limited social sector – advanced by republican ideology, confronted the values of Ottoman society and Islamist ideology, the issue of women's position in society turned into a major area of conflict between supporters of secular republicanism and Islamist conservatism (Tekeli, 1979). Thus the issue of women's position in society also acquired a symbolic salience in both ideologies, as reflected in the proportionately large place allocated for women in the political discourses of both (Kandiyoti, 1988).

In contemporary Turkey, the opposing ideologies of Islam representing the traditional and Kemalism the modern have been in confrontation for a long time, the picture has been somewhat blurred. The rhetoric of women's rights which has conventionally been emphasized by secular modernist groups in Ottoman Turkish history and has been the banner of Kemalist republicanism has been turned upside-down by the Islamists, who try to appeal to the dissatisfied and disillusioned women of the republic through promises of emancipation via Islam. For years progressive secularist ideology has argued that the legal rights and social reorganization brought about by secularization and modernization are prerequisites of Turkish women's security and happiness. Recently, Islamist discourse has come to present these two factors of contemporary life – secularism and modernism – as responsible for the humiliation and exploitation of women. Consequently, Islamist ideology has tried to mobilize women to struggle against their inferior status in the present social order and help remedy it via the restoration of the Islamist alternative. Consequently, parallels have sometimes been drawn between the Islamist women's movement, and feminism, which also developed in Turkey in the 1980s (Tekeli, 1986; Sirman-Eralp, 1988; Arat in this volume).

Three Islamist women's magazines

The aim of the following brief review of some of the basic messages of three Islamist women's magazines – *Kadın ve Aile* (Woman and Family), *Bizim Aile* (Our Family), and *Kektup* (Letter) – is to provide background information on the relevant

Islamist discourse of the 1980s and draw attention to some critical points of convergence or divergence among the different Islamist groups' messages.

Kadın ve Aile, first published in April 1985, is the largest Islamist women's magazine (with a reputed circulation of 60,000 in 1988). Commonly known to be the mouthpiece of the most prominent branch of the Nakşibendi sect in İstanbul, it continues to be regularly published.

Bizim Aile, a newcomer to the category of Islamist women's magazines, was a spin-off of another prominent Islamist journal published by a section of the Nurcu order. In the years to follow Bizim Aile's publication was interrupted on several occasions, due to organizational and financial reasons.

Mektup, reputed to be associated with a more radical branch of the Nakşibendi, articulated an activist discourse. Published since 1985 and edited by a woman, the journal's circulation at the time of this study was thought to be in the region of 30,000 copies. Originally published out of Konya, it reflects provincial roots. It has continued regular publication into the 1990s.

In all these magazines women's role as wife, mother and home-maker (that is, her roles in the private sphere) were emphasized above any other role she may possibly fulfil. Yet, for each journal, different dimensions of these private roles were critical and different approaches to these roles observed.

As a measure of the emphasis each of these magazines placed on any specific role category, the quantitative distribution of articles and items dealing with that role were analysed in all three in the period between February 1985 and May 1988. Of the total of 660 items in Kadın ve Aile, 295 dealt, in general, with women's roles in the private sphere. Of these, 54 were concerned with the various aspects of their roles as wives, 85 were on motherhood and 176 dealt with topics such as cooking, decorating, gardening and house-plants, knitting, sewing, home economics and family health – all issues that could be characterized as aspects of the home-maker role.

For Mektup, it was found that of 128 items, 21 were generally related to women's roles at home, of which 19 were concerned with the wife's role and only 2 items with motherhood. There were no articles on women as home-makers.

In Bizim Aile, only four issues of which had been published at the time of analysis, of the total of 34 items, only six were related to family life and consequently to women's private sphere roles. Other items addressed such issues as 'Islamic belief' and 'dress' (17), 'individual freedom in society' and 'education' (11) – all related to women's roles outside the home. Significant differences in the treatment of the same issue were also observed. For instance, in *Kadın ve Aile*, articles on motherhood mostly dealt with topics of a daily, practical nature related to child-rearing – despite the background theme of proper Islamic socialization of the young. In *Mektup*, the few articles on motherhood dealt with Islamic socialization.

From its appearance and the issues it stresses, *Kadın ve Aile* is, at first glance, an Islamist women's journal which parallels the many conservative secular women's magazines worldwide. Its message is directed to urban women for whom family life and home-making is the undisputed centre of life. The appropriateness of this appeal to the lifestyle and values of middle-class and lower-middle-class housewives, who make up the majority of women in small towns and provincial cities of contemporary Turkey, is obvious.

Complementing its emphasis on women's roles at home, *Kadın ve Aile* also featured a strong religious message that particularly stressed the necessity of women leading an 'Islamic way of life' – that is, being obedient wives, good mothers and pious Muslims who conform to Islam's many rules and regulations. These religious messages – presented through the life stories of saintly or martyred Muslim women in history, who are held up as exemplary ideals, or through the extensive, almost interminable, lists of Islam's do's and don'ts to be followed by women of the faith in everyday life in order to earn God's grace – help form a cognitive framework within which not only women's everyday activities and private roles are encompassed and legitimized by divine providence but their entire identity is made subject to the control of a 'community of believers'. This is obviously a powerful, pervasive and effective message to those large sections of the population for whom Islam is still the unchallengeable – though not always well-understood – truth.

In Islamist women's magazines, considerably less space is reserved for such topics as women's education, employment, and their place in social and political life outside of the family, that is, the public sphere – a fact that no doubt indicates the lesser importance attached to these issues in the Islamists' ideological discourse. During the periods in which it was studied, *Kadın ve Aile* (out of a total of 667) published only 16 articles on women's work outside the home and 13 on women's education; a similar distribution was generally observed in the other magazines.

All the magazines were observed to adopt a similar approach, in that they failed to treat women's education and employment as aspects of women's presence in the public sphere. Often making reference to the Prophet's dictum that seeking knowledge is a divine ordinance for all human beings, no Islamist discourse opposes education as such, but, women working outside the home was perceived in totally different light; there was very little tolerance for this in the Islamist contingent. Only when financial difficulty makes it an absolute necessity is women's gainful employment outside accepted. Even then, however, the Islamist view insists that the conditions for such work conform to Islamist principles: men and women must be physically segregated in the work place.

Kadın ve Aile openly encouraged women to stay at home and become good housewives; to make ends meet and use the income earned by their husbands in the most efficient way. It was suggested that if necessary they help the family budget with work that could be done at home. Women's education was, however, treated in a different way. Separate educational institutions for boys and girls were obviously preferred but girls' attendance at secular and coeducational schools was not seriously opposed. Consequently, the Islamic principle of the segregation of sexes and seclusion of women was modified to maintaining adherence to the Islamic dress code. Islamist writers may state their preference for separate education of the sexes but, nevertheless, they advised girls to attend coeducational schools, wearing Islamic dress.

An explanation for such apparent inconsistency is probably to be found in the social and political reality of contemporary Turkey, as well as its recent history. While, obviously, Islam is equally sensitive to the need for segregation of the sexes and seclusion of women in places of work or education, Islamist discourse finds it very difficult to reconcile this attitude with the realities of contemporary life in Turkey. Thus, the magazines reviewed offered a variety of solutions to the problem of how to reconcile Islamic principles with women's roles in the public sphere.

For example, *Mektup*, which had the most radical discourse, put forward an extremist interpretation of the Quranic verse on veiling, arguing that it was necessary for Muslim women to wear the *çarşaf* – the face veil and gloves – instead of simply a long, loose coat and headscarf as advocated by other magazines. Simultaneously, however, the most activist discourse regarding women's public roles can be found in *Mektup*. Among 128 articles, 22 (the second largest batch) were directly concerned with women's roles as active propagators of the faith, which implied that women should pursue open political struggle outside for Islamic Jihad.

Here, instead of the image of submissive women who bore and raised many good Muslim sons and daughters and were passive, obedient, self-sacrificing, pious wives and mothers, the image of activist Muslim women, ready to face every suffering for the sake of their faith, for whom 'propagation of Islam' is their main purpose in life and who defined their identity on criteria above and beyond the confines of home life, was promoted. *Mektup* writers, in quite militant form, called on women to rebel against non-Islamic authorities – including non-believer husbands. They advocated repudiation of the traditional division of labour at home by giving examples from the Prophet's own life. Yet in this magazine too, women's work outside the home was supported only reluctantly and as long as it conformed to Islamic standards of sex segregation.

Anti-Westernism and criticism of women's position in contemporary life also constituted prominent themes of the Islamist message. Despite significant differences in their styles of presentation and language, all three magazines emphasized these values as underlying concerns.

Kadın ve Aile presented a picture of middle-class, urban women situated in a world whose boundaries are drawn by family life. *Mektup* tried to give a fundamentalist Islamist message using a language and style of presentation shaped by Kuranic overtones and as such rather uncommon in press use in modern Turkey. Its message also reflected populist attitudes used to appeal to women in all sections of society but especially to women of lower income groups. *Bizim Aile* used the rhetoric of pluralist democracy, stressing the role of civil society, and could be said to address a relatively more educated segment of the population. Yet, in all three publications, the ideal Muslim woman was opposed to the image of the Westernized woman: the Westernized woman was portrayed as unhappy, overworked, oppressed and exploited; and, they all emphasized that Muslim women who tried to imitate the 'degenerate' and immoral Western women would come to resemble them in these respects. They also would be discontented and be a constant source of mischief and chaos in society. Every issue of *Mektup* featured a column entitled *Vicdan Azabı* (guilty conscience), in which it presented elaborate accounts of sinful women who had left the 'Islamic' life and the dreadful consequences (prostitution, drug addiction, imprisonment) that fell upon these women, who had conformed to the corrupt rules of the secular order and the norms of contemporary society. All three magazines pointed out that resemblance in outward appearance implied resemblance in beliefs. Muslim women were therefore advised to eschew such immoral behaviour as keeping up with fashion, using cosmetics, watching TV or taking seaside holidays, all of which were taken to be indicators of resemblance to Western women.

There were, however, different degrees of anti-Westernism to be observed. For instance, while *Kadın ve Aile* underlined women's role as housewives, published recipes, dress patterns, etc., and included articles on home decoration; *Mektup*, premised on preventing conspicuous consumption, considered cakes, cookies or home decorations to be Western luxuries and discouraged Muslims from such consumption.

Islamist discourse on the notion of gender equality, largely shared by all the women's magazines, refers to equality of men and women before God on Judgement Day. Its perceived reflection in this world is the complementarity of the sexes. Reference was frequently made to the so-called Western concept of equality, which the journals criticized as putting an unfair burden on women. They argued that men and women were naturally different in terms of their body, predispositions and personalities, therefore equality between such different beings was a meaningless concept. In Islam, it was claimed, it is justice which is important, rather than equality. Justice is claimed to protect women better and provide them with broader and more appropriate rights. The Islamic order, it was argued, would bring about true justice and ultimate happiness both to men and women.

An analysis of the content of Islamist magazines also shows that some of the highly controversial issues relating to the role and status of women under Islamic rule are largely ignored. Such rules and practices of Islam as polygamy, a husband's right to physically punish his wife, and two women's testimony being considered equal to one man's in a court of law, rarely appeared in the Islamist women's magazines. Since these are the very issues that are often taken by non-Islamic observers to indicate women's inferior status under Islam, and are reinterpreted or denied to be 'truly Islamic' by revisionist sources, their absence from the agenda of discussion in all the Islamist women's magazines appears conspicuous, if not deliberate.

The views of Islamist women

This section is concerned to provide an account of some findings from a study that was conducted in 1988, with nine women students of the Middle East Technical University (METU) who, from outward appearances could be defined as followers of the Islamist movements; they defined themselves as individuals who 'live Islam'. The interviewees were 'Muslim'[1] students who could be reached in person and agreed to participate in this research project.

Obviously, such a small sample cannot statistically claim to reflect the women university students who responded to the Islamist message in the 1980s. At the time of the study, however, this number constituted close to half of the 'Muslim' women students who had 'come out of the closet' in one of the most prestigious academic institutions in Turkey.[2] Since entrance to METU is extremely competitive on the national level students here have shown high academic achievement and superior intellectual ability. It can therefore be assumed that the characteristics and attitudes of 'Muslim' women students in this institution provide interesting clues as to why Islam may attract educated women in modern Turkey, since they are seemingly 'least likely' cases. The data were collected through long and intensive interviews with the voluntary participants, who were often motivated by a personal need to be 'better understood' by those around them and who willingly provided detailed information, unavailable elsewhere, on a socially controversial subject whch at the time was also politically sensitive. Thus, despite the small sample they constituted a very valuable source of information.

Of the nine students interviewed, two were graduates of İmam-Hatip Lisesi (a public high school of a special kind, where religious subjects are taught alongside regular high school curricula). The others had graduated from high schools that provided secular education only. Seven of the students' families lived in small cities; two had families who at the time of the interviews lived in lower-class neighbourhoods of Ankara (these women had grown up in small towns). Three of the students' fathers had primary school education only; four had continued for another three years into junior high school; one had graduated from the university (it was not possible to determine the educational level of the remaining father). Of the mothers, seven had only primary school education; one was illiterate. Occupation-wise, fathers were mostly workers, independent craftsmen, shopkeepers or low-ranking civil servants; one was a retired judge. All the mothers were housewives.

In general, the students described their families' attitudes towards religion as, 'inclined and respectful towards Islam, but rather ignorant of its true depth'. Only one student said that her father was well-educated and had extensive religious knowledge. With the exception of one student's mother, the mothers did not adhere to the Islamic dress code. In the family where the mother was reported to dress in the approved Islamic manner, there were also other daughters who did not wear headscarfs.

When asked when they adopted the 'Islamic way of life' and started to wear the headscarf, six respondents said this was in their first or second year at the university. Three students had experimented with Islamic dress during their high school years, but they also reported regularly wearing the headscarf only after enrolment at the university. Two of these students were Imam-Hatip Lisesi graduates; the other one was a young women who said she suffered from depression during her high school years and had difficulty in establishing friendships. She said she found comfort in covering herself.

Interviewees said that upon arrival in the big city and at the university they found relations between the sexes very different from what they had previously experienced. The new social environment made them feel uneasy, and most of them expressed negative attitudes towards what they perceived as immoral, sinful behaviour. They often attributed their experience of 'seeing the light' to such observations. For instance:

B: 'I observed a different kind of relationship between girls and boys in METU; in the high school that I went to [Imam-Hatip Lisesi] there was also close friendship between girls and boys but it was different. For instance, there was no physical contact of any kind.'

H: 'Here, the way men look at women disturbs me. They stare, they leer. I always think I must have done something wrong. I blame myself.'

G: 'When I first came to METU, I found the relations between boys and girls very immoral and alienating. I could never adapt myself to such behaviour. One day I decided to cover my hair and turn to Islam. At the beginning I also thought that this was only a reaction, but in time I got used to it.'

Some respondents said that they had always had a God-fearing disposition, which they believed they acquired through their family socialization. These women found the interpersonal relations characteristic of campus life very disturbing. They said they often developed a guilty conscience.

B: 'When I compare myself to others in the METU dormitories, I think I am very conservative and very religious for I believe that God sees me everywhere, doing everything. So I cannot be as comfortable and as free as those others.'

H: 'When I do something wrong, I have a guilty conscience. I feel I have committed a sin against my creator. The relationships here are very artificial. A girl is disturbed by this situation. At the beginning I had some friends. They got used to the way of life here; now they are settled in a shallow happiness, they laugh at stupid things, such as film stars, etc. For a while I was like that too, in my high school years; now, when I look back, I believe that I spent this time in vain. I feel very sorry.'

When talking about their experiences and feelings after they had 'seen the light' and started to 'live Islam', the students said they initially felt very shy, very often afraid – even ashamed – of the consequences of their behaviour. In time, however, these feelings were replaced by self-confidence; the women developed a sense of being generally admired and approved of.

H: 'I initially started to wear the headscarf in the city, as opposed to the campus. At the beginning I was so anxious I could not raise my head, I was terribly embarrassed.'

Z: 'After I started to wear the headscarf, people started offering their places to me in crowded buses.'

All respondents said they had thought they would face negative reactions from society, but that things turned out to be less rough than they had imagined. There had been incidental reactions from some faculty members, but not negative reactions from their friends or families, in fact they had made new friends. All the students said that their families were concerned only about their insistence on wearing the headscarf and dressing in the Islamic way – mainly because of the potential problems with public authorities – and they approved of other aspects of their 'being religious'.

> H: 'My aunts reacted negatively. They are both school-teachers. They said that the headscarf is political. They said I was being marked as a political activist. . . . Since I started to wear the scarf I have been making new friends who also dress in the Islamic manner. Even if I do not know them personally I can easily say hello to them and get to be friends. Of course we feel closer.'

Most of the interviewees agreed that being a university student is an important factor in getting positive reactions from people about choice of dress and lifestyle. In other words, university students' relatively high status in Turkish society brought credibility to their cause.

> Z: 'Usually, people are more polite to me when they learn that I am a university student. For instance, a shopkeeper downtown who ignored me as a customer because of my appearance (he probably thought I was an uneducated peasant woman) changed his attitude after he learned that I was a university student.'

These students all firmly believed that a woman's basic and primary role is to be a mother and wife. None saw their education primarily as a way to acquire and develop a career, as can be seen in the quotations below. They justified their choice of home-making and motherhood on both religious and personal grounds, saying that this is what Islam approves and recommends for women; it is what will make them happy.

> L: 'I am not sure if I would work. I may only think of working in a job that will not disturb my future family order.'

> H: 'My mother said [after I decided to dress in the Islamic manner] "she should not continue with her education if she is going to do this." Because for my mother education means working. . . . In fact, my mother had wanted me to have an

education so that I could be free, not tied to a husband; economically independent and more comfortable. I do not think this way.'

Z: 'I may only work in a job that will not make me uncomfortable.'

N: 'I can work as long as I do not have to make concessions. I have some friends who are working in the private sector [where regulations banning the headscarf do not apply]. But since the man I will marry will share my world view [Islamic], he will know that he is obliged to take care of me. The most important duty of women under Islam is to give birth to children and to raise them properly. I am going to the university in order to be able to educate my children in the best way. I am increasing my knowledge to this end. I have no expectation of earning money.'

With regard to women's roles within the home, many of the respondents shared the basic outline of the views articulated by G, who expects an exceptionally good future for herself in a future Islamic order. She says:

'Women are neither passive nor oppressed [in the Muslim order]. We are already trying to abolish the traditional ways of doing things [that are non-Islamic in origin] and replace them with practices in accordance with Islam. It is true that, today our mothers are oppressed. But the responsibility for this does not lie in Islam. Just the opposite, it is because they did not know Islam well enough that they were oppressed and exploited. In reality, under Islam, women are not obliged to serve their husbands, housework is not their responsibility, men must hire servants. The only obligation for women is to bear children.'

In fact, almost all of the interviewees agreed with Z, who said 'the responsibilities of women under Islam are very few.' They all expressed the belief that the order of Islam is infinitely superior to the present society, particularly as far as women's position is concerned. On a personal level, all expressed a strong conviction that they will be happier in such a social order, where women are not obliged to work at home or outside.

In line with these ideas, all of the students defended the notion that women, by their very nature, are different from men. They believed that women are weaker and more sentimental: Islam's promise to provide justice rather than equality to men and women, they argued, would be protection in line with women's nature. It is on such grounds that many understood the Islamic rule equating the testimony of two women with that of one man.

On the issue of education, most of these women students felt that girls and boys should be educated in single-sex institutions from middle school on:

B: 'Girl–boy relationships may derail the aims of education: the students may lose sight of their educational goals when they are together. Moreover, in coeducational schools certain subjects are not handled in depth, they are left in the dark. Girls can only discuss certain issues with women teachers, otherwise there is a lot of giggling and things like that. Many subjects are not covered well.'

H: 'I believe that to have separate schools is the right thing because I see that men are sexually very weak: for them, there is sex under everything. Men are very vulnerable to sexual provocation: they are weak, and girls are always trying to attract them. This makes coeducation problematic.'

Other students also said that coeducation was detrimental to the very aims of education itself. 'To go to school with boys was a concession I had to make,' said H, who added that she nonetheless wanted to complete her education because otherwise she would always carry the stigma of being 'backward, reactionary'. She said she was making the concession to avoid such labelling.

The following quotation shows how some Muslim-identified women cope and treat their male schoolmates.

S: 'I do not talk with them, unless I have to. I make my answers to their questions short because I am to be secluded. I feel that I belong to my future husband in every way, so I try not to look in their eyes while talking to them. Because, you know, men and women naturally attract each other. There is an attraction even in the glimpse of an eye; this is inevitable.'

Two of the students interviewed, on the other hand, said that they had male friends. A few also stated it is possible for some friendships at school to be like brother–sister relationships.

In the context of marriage, the interviewees were also asked to give their views on polygamy and how they would react to such an event in their own lives. All of them argued that the practice of polygamy as it is defined in Islam (with its insistence on the husband's absolutely equal treatment of his wives) puts too much responsibility on men's shoulders, and is not very practical in real life. Some said that they would be very much disturbed should such a situation befall them. They admitted that on this matter there was a contradiction between their faith in Islam and their personal attitude. Some, who argued that under Islam it is only possible for a man to make a second marriage if his first wife consents, nonetheless found this contingency inherently problematic.

B: 'The man should ask permission from his first wife. I do not know in which hadith or verse this is written, but this rule exists ... However, what is recommended in Islam is that the first wife should accept polygamy if the husband wants it.'

In effect, all the respondents declared that there are valid reasons for polygamy under Islam. They shared the view expressed by H as follows:

'At the end, I must accept this. We should be content with rights given to us by our Creator.'

Similarly B's response reflected the general mood:

'My creator Allah knows how I would be happy better than I do myself. Even if I do not understand everything he has designed, I accept that there is divine wisdom behind certain rules and judgements. I believe in this and I do not question it. Polygamy is just one of those judgements that we should believe has divine wisdom behind it.'

Conclusion

For many in Turkish society in the late 1980s, it was an essentially incomprehensible anomaly that educated young women born and raised in a secular society became followers of Islamist movements. It was very difficult to understand what motivated these women to become active propagators of an **ideology that relegated women to a secondary position in society,** and to struggle against a state system that had for many years officially identified with emancipation of women – particularly in terms of the existing cognitive maps which described the sociopolitical system as a reactionary–progressivist dichotomy.

The foregoing review of Islamist women's journals, and analysis of interviews with Islamist women, may help shed light on some of the less obvious dynamics and latent meanings of Islam's appeal to some women.

Despite differences of social and economic background among the likely readers of Islamist women's journals, none, it is clear, aimed at an upper- or upper-middle-class readership group. Educated women of the higher socioeconomic strata, who by virtue of their class position have benefited the most from the opportunities accorded by republican reforms, were obviously not among those targeted by the Islamist journals. To such women – who often came from families that strongly identified with the reforms and remained devoted to the principles of secularism and women's equality, albeit in the public sphere – the Islamist discourse did not appear to have a particular message.

The targets and recipients of the Islamist message are, on the contrary, mostly girls and women from small towns and provincial cities, of lower-middle-class and recently rural origin, in the metropolitan centres. The latter are often the extensions of the former in contemporary Turkish society (Mardin, 1988: 181).

While it has been pointed out that these groups were still the most conservative in Turkish society, where gender-based discrimination was most often practised and women were more secluded than anywhere else (Kıray, 1979: 359), the effects of social and economic changes were gradually felt here, too. The education system established after the foundation of the republic, and especially the changes which took place in the economy between 1950 and 1980, made it possible for the offspring of small-town, lower-middle-class families to benefit from educational opportunities in unprecedented numbers (Mardin, 1988: 168). Despite gender-based discrimination in favour of boys, girls from these backgrounds also took advantage of the new opportunities provided by the state.

Yet these girls and women also identified with the conservative, patriarchal values of their family and community. Such values, often in harmony with Islam though not necessarily Islamist, grew to be in serious conflict with the modernizing, egalitarian, secular messages received from schools and political authorities. Because the social reality of everyday existence for women in non-privileged population groups was in contradiction to the premises of the official ideology served through the school and media channels, the pressure on these women inevitably grew stronger.

In other words, to the extent that republican ideology could not translate its promises of social and political equality into everyday reality for large numbers of Turkish women, the public promises of official ideology remained meaningless at the level of personal experience, in the private sphere. In these circumstances it was highly likely that women would search for alternative explanations and solutions to their dilemma. And it is hardly surprising that women born and raised in conservative settings, where the legitimacy of religious explanations has always been essentially unquestioned and Islamic values have loomed large in the background, should turn to Islamist recipes for self-esteem and happiness.

The findings of women's studies have shown that women of the social elite who had received a good education have had prestigious and satisfactory careers for a long time now in Turkey (Öncü, 1979). These women were able to free themselves from housework, by employing other women, because their economic means made it possible. They could thus develop strong commitments to their careers. This was approved and supported by their cultural peers and by the political ideology of the state. (Erkut, 1982; Acar, 1983; Kandiyoti, 1988; Durakbaşa, 1988). Yet, research on these women has also indicated that, even for this privileged category, full equality between men and women did not exist in many aspects of working life or in intra-familial relations (Çitçi, 1979; Kandiyoti, 1982; Kuyaş, 1982). It has been shown that even those educated, seemingly liberated women who escaped the home usually undertook extra burdens. The existing situation for professional women was not as unproblematic as might be thought at first glance (Acar, 1983).

Obviously, the republic's promises to women were realized to a much lesser extent for the women who did not belong to the social elite. Since the traditional division of labour in the family and the domination of patriarchal values continued to a still greater extent in the non-elite segments of the population, it is impossible to talk about the physical, financial or psychological emancipation of women from this sector who had to work outside in addition to carrying all the domestic responsibilities (Tekeli, 1986: 189). The women represented in the small study reported here, as well as those addressed by the Islamist journals reviewed, are mainly the products of this social experience.

As far as their family backgrounds and socialization are concerned, these women are worlds apart from educated women of higher socioeconomic backgrounds. Far from the radical secularism of the latter, there is a more probable exposure to and greater identification with Islam in the family backgrounds of these women. Thus, while elite women may have been trying to overcome their conflicts of role through various individual solutions (Acar, 1983), for educated women of a lower socioeconomic background and provincial origins, Islam may provide a more credible, familiar and legitimate alternative.

In this context, it is interesting that both the interviews and the women's journals indicate that the security offered to women by Islam is a very influential force in its attraction. Not only does Islam, by 'justifying traditional sex roles' (Bingöllü, 1979: 389), provide a solution to the conflicting roles experienced by women; it also offers them security through various avenues. The university student who said 'I do not have to work; what is more I need not be embarrassed at wanting to be a housewife and mother. On the contrary, I will be glorified in the Islamic order for doing this' is expressing one critical dimension of the kind of security which Islamist discourse provides to women caught at the crossroads of the traditional pressures of the private sphere and the modern demands of the public sphere. The female writer in *Mektup* who cries 'Ladies, to increase our attractiveness for our husbands at home and to decrease it outside is our fundamental principle', and 'We shall be attractive at home and repulsive outside', is articulating another dimension of the security Islam offers to women. Attempting to minimize competition from other women by insisting on an uncompromising segregation of the sexes and veiling of women, this Islamist discourse offers, to the 'Muslim' woman whose sole provider is her husband, vital protection from the potential threats of modern secular lifestyles and the appeals of Westernized women.

Furthermore, women who have grown up in cultural environments where their sexuality is habitually suppressed are likely, when faced with the option of relatively free relations with men in the more liberal atmosphere of the big city or university campus, to feel guilty and insecure about their sexuality. 'Muslim' students invariably mentioned this, and Islamist women's literature clearly emphasizes the 'Muslim' women's cardinal obligation to protect the social order by restraining her sexual appeal. In this context, the rules of Islamic modesty and requirement of veiling are bound to ease the pressures on these women and protect their sense of self.

Finally, in the literature, participation in a social movement is explained not only by social structural factors, with reference to the movement's ideology or the psychological dispositions of the followers, but also in relation to the concept of 'spatial proximity': the participation of the individual in social movements is also related to the kinds of social movement which are available to them at that time (Snow, Zurcher and Eckland-Olson, 1980). I believe that the attraction of Islamist discourse to university students in Turkey in the 1980s can also be partly explained by its 'spatial proximity'.

Notes

1. Although the Turkish population is almost entirely Muslim, by the late 1980s, the term had come to be used by Islamist groups exclusively to denote their followers, and to distinguish those who opt for an 'Islamic way of life' from the majority who, despite being believers of Islam, try to reconcile their religious identity with secular social and political institutions.

2. Unfortunately, the opportunities for interviewing more women wearing the headscarf were diminished in early 1989, when debates over the issue became very sensitive in Turkish political life. Also, relations between faculty and those women students who insisted on wearing the headscarf were seriously curtailed upon the passing of a constitutional court decision that made wearing of the headscarf in the classroom an offence punishable by the university's disciplinary codes. Thus, although it was originally the aim to interview all the women wearing the headscarf – at the time approximately 20–25 – no more interviews were possible.

References

Acar, Feride (1983). 'Turkish women in academia: roles and careers', *ODTÜ Gelişme Dergisi*, vol. 10.

Acar, Feride (1991). 'Women in the ideology of Islamic revivalism in Turkey: three Islamic women's journals', in *Islam in Turkey: Religion in a Secular State*, ed. Richard Tapper, I.B. Tauris, London.

Bingöllü (Sayari), Binnaz (1979). 'Türk Kadını ve Din', in *Türk Toplumunda Kadın*, ed. N. Abadan Unat, Ankara, Türk Sosyal Bilimler Derneği.

Çitçi, Oya (1979). 'Türk Kamu Yönetiminde Kadın Görevliler', in *Türk Toplumunda Kadın*, ed. N. Abadan Unat, Ankara, Türk Sosyal Bilimler Derneği.

Durakbaşa, Ayşe (1988). 'Cumhuriyet Döneminde Kemalist Kadın Kimliğinin Oluşumu', Tarih ve Toplum, March.

Erkut, Sumru (1982). 'Dualism in values toward education of Turkish women', in Sex Roles, Family and Community in Turkey, ed. Ç. Kağıtçıbaşı, Indiana University Turkish Studies, Bloomington, Ind.

Kandiyoti, Deniz (1982). 'Urban change and women's roles in Turkey: an overview and evaluation', in Sex Roles, Family and Community in Turkey, ed. Ç. Kağıtçıbaşı, Indiana University Turkish Studies, Bloomington, Ind.

Kandiyoti, Deniz (1987). 'Emancipated but unliberated? reflections on the Turkish case', Feminist Studies, vol. 3, Summer.

Kandiyoti, Deniz (1988). 'Women and the Turkish state: political actors or symbolic pawns?', in Women-Nation State, ed. N. Yuval-Davis and A. Anthias, Macmillan, London.

Kıray, Mübeccel (1979). 'Küçük Kasaba Kadınları', in Türk Toplumunda Kadın, ed. N. Abadan Unat, Türk Sosyal Bilimler Derneği, Ankara.

Kuyaş, Nilüfer (1982). 'The effect of female labor on power relations in the urban Turkish family', in Sex Roles, Family and Community in Turkey, ed. Ç. Kağıtçıbaşı, Indiana University Turkish Studies, Bloomington, Ind.

Mardin, Şerif (1988). 'Culture and religion: towards the year 2000', in Turkey in the Year 2000, Türk Siyasi Bilimler Derneği, Ankara.

Öncü, Ayşe (1979). 'Uzman Mesleklerde Türk Kadını', in Türk Toplumunda Kadın, ed. N. Abadan Unat, Türk Sosyal Bilimler Derneği, Ankara.

Sirman-Eralp, Nükhet (1988). 'Turkish feminism: a short history?', paper presented to the Symposium on 'The Plural Meanings of Pluralism' organized by the International Congress of Anthropological and Ethnological Science in Zagreb, July.

Snow, David A., Louis A. Zurcher, Jr and Sheldon Ekland-Olson (1980). 'Social network and social movements: A microstructural approach to differential recruitment', American Sociological Review, vol. 45, October.

Tekeli, Şirin (1979). 'Türkiye'de Kadının Siyasal Hayattaki Yeri', in Türk Toplumunda Kadın, ed. N. Abadan Unat, Türk Sosyal Bilimler Derneği, Ankara.

Tekeli, Şirin (1986). 'Emergence of the feminist movement in Turkey', The New Women's Movement, ed. Drude Dahrelup, Sage Publications, London.

Feminism and Islam: Considerations on the Journal *Kadın ve Aile*[1]

Yeşim Arat

The significance and meaning of Islam and Islamic ideology for women have long been disputed. For many Western observers, Islam was an intrinsically oppressive religion for women (Kandiyoti, 1991). The reality of women's lives in Muslim societies has testified to the fact that Islamic ideology subordinates women. On the other hand, defenders of the faith – men as well as women; sometimes nationalists, or Islamists – have opposed the contention that Islamic ideology oppresses women. They have claimed that men and women are equal in the judgement of God. For the believer, the gender-based division of labour between men and women that Islamic religion has dictated, according to most common interpretations and practices, involves a complementarity, not an inequality, between the sexes.

In this article,[1] I shall assume a feminist perspective, and explore the meaning that Islamic activism might take for women in the secular Turkish polity. For this purpose, I will examine the Islamist journal *Kadın ve Aile* (Woman and Family), in order to develop a hypothesis which explains women's Islamic activism in the 1980s and its implications. In the context of the current controversies concerning the meaning of Islam for women, an attempt will be made to offer an alternative account of the significance of women's Islamic activism. Going beyond the debate as to whether Islam oppresses or 'liberates' women, I will explore the unintended consequences of women's Islamist activities. I develop the hypothesis that women's Islamic activism might in fact open avenues of experience independent of – and in contradiction to – the dictates of Islam which these women preach. Before focusing on the journal, I will sketch the context of Islamic revival in Turkey, and discuss how Islamic ideology is difficult to reconcile with a feminist perspective, developing a framework within which to evaluate women's Islamic activism. Finally I shall return to the journal itself and speculate what women's involvement with it, both as staff members and as readers, might mean for the women concerned.

Islam and women's Islamic activism in Turkey

In Turkey, there has been a tradition of state control over religion (Mardin, 1981, 1971; Sunar and Toprak, 1983; Heper, 1981). Although Islam was the ideology which legitimized Ottoman rule, before the foundation of the Turkish republic in 1923, state institutions extended surveillance over religious ones even during the Ottoman regime. With the advent of the Turkish republic, religious institutions were dismantled and secular institutions gradually increased their hold over the polity. In 1937 the Turkish state was declared constitutionally secular.

The implications of Turkish secularism were crucial for women. Women could be equal to men before law. The 1926 Civil Code which replaced the *sharia* abolished polygamy and recognized women's right to divorce. In 1934, women were granted suffrage. While secular goals dictated that women's opportunities in society be extended, this helped entrench religious opposition to these goals (Tekeli, 1983; Arat, 1989). In this new context, in which the state aimed to be secular as well as democratic, religious groups and opposition were seen as an obstacle to both secularism and democracy. In order to maintain secularism, Islamic groups have been kept under control – at times compromising the dictates of a pluralist democratic order – until after the 1960s.

Gradual liberalization accompanied economic development. Especially after the 1960s, religious groups emerged in the political and social scene in Turkey. Whether in 'response to the life in the metropolis' (Toprak, 1989), or to fill the psychological vacuum left by the secular Kemalist ideology after its attempts to extricate Islam from people's lives (Mardin,

1971), or a postmodern reaction to Turkish modernization (Gülalp, 1992), Islamic groups asserted themselves. The conservative right-wing Motherland Party government that came to power after 1980 used state power to promote religious groups. In the context of the 1982 Constitution, which increased state control over the secular institutions of civil society such as labour unions and associations, the mass media and universities, the ANAP government passed legal amendments to encourage the economic independence of religious groups from the state. At the same time, the state's economic support of these groups was preserved (Öncü, 1989). Islamic financial institutions were established; they flourished and used their profits to open *wakfs* (foundations) which propagated Islamic ideology. Religious courses were made obligatory in secular state educational institutions and the Ministry of National Education helped open Koran study courses. ANAP officials promoted the Islamic world-view not merely with their policies, but also with their way of life. There is today widespread public controversy in Turkey as to whether the concessions offered to religious groups threaten the secular Kemalist tradition.

Women increasingly took an active role in Islamist activities or the Islamic movement that prospered in this context (Göle, 1991). As the number of women who covered themselves according to the dictates of Islam increased, women activists aimed to propagate Islamic ideology in what they said and what they did. Female students in universities, supported or motivated by men, organized protest walks to defend their right to cover their heads in line with Islamic dictates, and took on a political role.

Meanwhile, dissenting groups emerged within the ranks of Islamist women. These women questioned woman's place, both according to Islam and within the Muslim community. Taking a reformist stance, they challenged the patriarchal Muslim heritage and traced women's subjugation in Muslim societies to the operation of male prejudice, as opposed to Islamic ideology (Sirman, 1989). But these dissenting voices soon petered out.

Islam and feminism

Despite the variety of interpretations of Islamic ideology, and the diversity of Muslim practices, it is difficult to reconcile Islamic ideology with a feminist perspective. An egalitarian feminist perspective which argues for male–female equality is at odds with Islamic ideology. Even the most progressive (for most Muslims, revisionist) interpretations of Islam, never actually practised in Muslim societies, cannot consistently argue for male–female equality. For example, Fazlur Rahman claims that socioeconomic context in which the Koran arose is responsible for its unequal treatment of women (Rahman, 1983). In modern times, it would only be consistent with the spirit of the Koran to treat men and women equally. According to this interpretation, it was because women who had lost their husbands needed protection during times of war that polygamy was sanctioned in the Koran. Even then, men who had more than one wife were obliged to treat their wives equally (as women have never had the right to many husbands, the opportunity never arose). Under different circumstances polygamy could be prohibited. Such an interpretation argues that men had a larger share of inheritances, than women, because women received a share of parental possessions when they married. If women's roles and responsibilities changed within a conjugal relationship, this dictate could also be disposed of. Yet other inequalities, such as in cases of adultery, remain. Despite such heroic attempts, it is taxing to account for and dismiss the various inequalities in Islamic law concerning marriage, divorce, inheritance, child custody, court witness, and adultery – let alone to convince other Muslims to practise these egalitarian laws. According to most common interpretations and widely-held practices of Islam, women – whether because they are lustful creatures who need to be controlled lest they undermine the divine order (Mernissi, 1987; Sabbah, 1984), or because they need protection as physically infirm creatures – lack many rights men have. At best, within the Islamic division of labour between men and women, women are not equal, but rather complementary to men.

If we assume a feminist perspective that emphasizes difference rather than equality, the prevalent Islamic stance which upholds a gendered division of labour is still difficult to reconcile with feminist inclinations. The feminist emphasis on difference does not preclude a belief in equality (Scott, 1988). Furthermore, a recognition of women's separate identities and traditional roles as a potential source of power for women does not imply reinforcing or pepetuating those roles as they have always been. Instead, it involves an attempt to undermine the hierarchy that has traditionally devalued women's roles as dependent on male power. An emphasis on difference aims to liberate women from the yoke of the dominant culture by redefining, reassessing and reevaluating traditional roles; and bringing them to public attention.

Finally, it is difficult to reconcile a feminist perspective with Islamic ideology because Holy Law overrides individual choice. In Islam, divine power arbitrates on law, politics, economics – in short, on all aspects of public and private life. Accordingly, God dictates what men as well as women should do. In contrast to a feminist understanding which upholds women's freedom of choice, Sharia law details what women should do or should not do, including what they should wear and where they should wear it (Tabari, 1986). The right to individual choice is inevitably restricted, to allow for coexistence, in a secular polity as well. Secular jurisdiction delimits individual choice as much as divine. Yet secular rules are not as interventionist, nor are they holy: they are open to negotiation and redefinition through human agency. While women might traditionally assume maternal roles, no secular law can dictate that women assume these roles, as Islamic law can.

If Islamic ideology is so difficult to reconcile with a feminist perspective, is women's Islamic activism totally reactionary and threatening to women's interests? Are women merely victims of a mass movement or does their Islamic activism open new avenues of personal experience for them? With these questions in mind, we shall look more closely at the activities of Islamist women and return to the journal *Kadın ve Aile*. To assess women's Islamic activism through this journal, we shall draw on a feminist framework which underlines the importance of extending women's opportunities. This framework should help us to evaluate and speculate on the long-term significance of women's Islamic activism.

Theoretical framework

A feminist perspective that underlines women's difference enriches an egalitarian feminist discourse at the same time as it poses obvious dangers.[2] The obvious danger, as mentioned above, is the risk of reifying traditional roles without changing their public and political status. In other words, without access to new avenues of power, women might fall prey to traditional forms of subjugation. Yet, the 'difference' perspective has its attractions. Women's culture and the strengths women develop in their traditional roles cannot be denied. In order to differentiate themselves from conservative groups which merely want to perpetuate women's traditional roles, feminists who uphold the importance of difference have to develop certain criteria. Mary Fainsod Katzenstein and David Laitin search for a solution to this problem in their article 'Politics, Feminism and the Ethics of Caring' (Katzenstein and Laitin, 1987). They pose the question, 'under what formulations are arguments of moral difference likely to serve progressive ends and when are they likely to fulfil counterprogressive or reactionary purposes?' (Katzenstein and Laitin, 1987: 265). In answer to this question, they develop three criteria, which can be summarized as follows:

1. That the group understands its social and political role in a dynamic, not static manner – i.e., not merely reasserting rights and privileges but assuring expansion of opportunities and enrichment of autonomy;
2. That the group's leaders seek, on the one hand, to nurture and promote diversity across its ranks and, on the other, to remedy differences in mobility prospects among its members;
3. That the political project of the group involves an alliance that is committed to the expansion of opportunities and political power for other disadvantaged classes or groups.

With these criteria, we shall now evaluate the journal *Kadın ve Aile*, not merely with regard to its contents, but rather as a political project in which women staff members, as well as readers, participate. Does the journal *Kadın ve Aile* expand the opportunities of women who work for it or read it?

Kadın ve Aile: an Islamic force

Kadın ve Aile is a monthly women's magazine that addresses women in their traditional roles. First appearing in April 1985, it is published by prominent members of a well-known Islamic sect (the Nakşibendis) who own the weekly *Islam*, and the biweekly *Ilim ve Sanat* (Science and Art). While the magazine is owned by a man, most of those who are involved in the publication process or write for it are women.

Kadın ve Aile is clearly a conservative magazine. The editorial of the first issue addressed the readers of the journal as follows:

You are, in our eyes, hajji mothers and aunts with white, pinked prayer scarves, rosaries in your hands, prayers on your lips; or else serious, merciful, self-sacrificing housewives, loyal to your husbands and homes; or else pretty, clean, twittering, talented little sisters.

We know that it is the female bird that makes the nest and nurtures the ties of love among family members. You are the pillars of the nest and the foundation of society.

You raise the children to be healthy; you provide good breeding and teach manners; you direct them with lullabies, advice and prayers.

Men become happy and successful because of you; when they come home, they forget the exhaustion of the day, the troubles and turmoil of life, and find consolation in you, sleep happily and contented. (*Kadın ve Aile*, April 1985, p. 3).

Kadın ve Aile addresses housewives whose lives are sacrificed to the happiness of their families, children and husbands; their sacrifice sealed with religious benediction. The editorial later reminds its readers of a most popular proverb, derived from a *hadith*: 'Heaven is under the feet of the believing mother'. Within this world-view, women's rights and opportunities are restricted. Autonomy or independence is not even an issue.

We shall be against those who look at you with evil eyes. In the press, there are those with bad intentions who try to alienate the housewife from her nest, her relatives, her principal duties; pull her into the world of fashion, sensuality, pleasure, vulgarity, pornography, alcohol, gambling, flirting and deviant relationships. . . . They try to destroy the family that is the foundation of society and sunder ties between individuals. (April 1985, p. 3)

In the world-view of *Kadın ve Aile*, vices surround the woman's world. In subsequent issues, the journal merely reiterates the vices women should be protected from. This identification of vices is claimed to be based on God's word or the Prophet's preference. Accordingly, although it is a controversial question as to how much Islam prohibits abortion, in an issue focusing on anti-abortion propaganda, the front page of the journal has the caption: 'Murdering Children is Called Abortion' (November 1985). Another issue condemned divorce. Although Islam sanctions divorce, the claim is made that God dislikes it, because divorce means the disintegration of family life and renders children homeless (March 1986, p. 7). To discourage women from working outside the home, an issue was brought out on the problems of working women: an interview with a religious woman gynaecologist underlines how women cannot meet their primary responsibilities to the family when they work outside (June 1984, p. 5). The journal, in another issue, denounces pornography because it threatens family life (January 1986). Fashion, the journal contends, dissuades Turkish women from wearing their traditional costumes and makes them reject their past: unisex clothing denies the need for women's special outerwear that differentiates them from men. Following fashion is succumbing to the cultural imperialism of the West. Perhaps most important, the journal contends, fashion is against religion, because the Prophet asked believers not to wear clothing that infidels wear (February 1986, pp. 8–10).

Kadın ve Aile: new opportunities for women?

Beyond this restrictive ideology, could Kadın ve Aile play 'a dynamic role, expanding opportunities for women and enriching their autonomy', as Katzenstein and Laitin describe? Despite its ideological limits, the journal provides an opportunity for women to look to the outside world, beyond the family.

For those women who work for the magazine, the mere existence of a women's journal where they can be employed, gives access to the outside world. With one or two exceptions, the staff writers and regular contributors are all women. When the journal began publication, three of the editors were married women, mothers who described themselves as housewives; the other two were unmarried university graduates. Working for the journal allowed these women to go beyond family life, extending their personal identities and talents.

The story of one of the assistant editors is revealing. She was a graduate of Atatürk Kız Lisesi (a prominent secular high school for girls in Istanbul) and the Business School of Istanbul University. In her own words, she came from a 'modern' family; however, what did modern mean? In the university, together with some other friends, she began questioning the meaning of modernity and discussed what 'God's path' was. This same group decided they would not be seduced into imitation of the West. They denounced blue jeans and low-cut dresses, and covered themselves up. Their families reacted to their daughters' clothing, but the daughters persisted. After covering herself up, our assistant editor did not want to work outside, despite her high-level education, because she felt she would be harassed as a covered person. This job was perfectly suited to her. She could work for what she believed in. The journal had allowed this assistant editor an opportunity to develop her own life. She had questioned and challenged the readily accepted secular, middle-class values of her family. *Kadın ve Aile* had allowed her to live up to her protest. To borrow a term Macleod develops in a different context, with different references (Macleod, 1992), our assistant editor was accommodating her secular upbringing and education, which expected her to work outside, while protesting against the Western façade of that tradition. The job at *Kadın ve Aile* had allowed her to make her protest more public than would have been possible had she stayed at home. At the same time, despite what the journal preached, she was given the opportunity to become more autonomous by working outside the home. Her questioning, protesting, challenging self might, in time, make her question the restrictive nature of the ideology she was helping to propagate. *Kadın ve Aile*, as an institution, was thus providing the opportunity for women to enter the public sphere by writing articles and working to prepare a magazine for publication.

The journal may have other unintended consequences as well. The observance of Islamic dictates encouraged by the magazine allows women to develop social networks and new skills outside the family. There are recitals where poems celebrating the birth of the Prophet (*Mevluds*) are read; Koran reading sessions; gatherings in the memory of a deceased person; collective attendance at mosques; ceremonies in celebration of religious holidays, weddings and circumcisions. These activities are largely sex-segregated and perpetuate traditional roles, but they might also help women develop organizational skills and managerial capabilities which could be utilized in the public sphere. The journal encourages its readers to learn handicrafts and calligraphy, and organizes competitions and exhibitions so that the women can develop these skills (October, August, December 1985). In this way women learn to express themselves through art and reflect it in the public realm. Finally, the journal encourages women to take political action in defence of their right to cover themselves. These protest activities in defence of headscarves, which the journal calls, 'the most noble women's movement', help politicize women and bring them into the public realm. In the context of a secular polity in which there is no imminent threat of an Islamic order, women's religious activism can open new avenues of power, and vistas beyond the familial realm.

A further opportunity *Kadın ve Aile* offers women is its introduction of the concept of individual rights. The journal defends women's rights to observe their religion as they choose (December 1985, February, June 1987). In practice, this is a defence of women's right to cover their heads in schools and public-sector employment. The journal, in the context of a polity based on secular, liberal principles, resorts to the liberal concept of individual rights in order to defend Islamic dictates. Whether the journal sincerely believes in individual rights or not, the concept is prominent in its discourse. Women who cover their heads because it is God's will discover that it is also their individual right. They find out that there are constitutional articles (Article 24) and laws (Law 3255, Article 175) that provide guarantees for freedom of religion (*Kadın ve Aile*, June 1986, p. 2). In published interviews with women who oppose head-covering, readers find out that even its opponents grant that it is an individual right (*Kadın ve Aile*, December 1985, p. 13). The journal emphasizes that women's votes count, as citizens of the polity. An editorial claims that one day those who govern the country (and oppose headscarves) will ask for votes to strengthen their political power, and then the believers will answer back with their votes (June 1986, p. 2). Consequently, the journal helps heighten the woman reader's consciousness of herself as a citizen with individual rights.

In this context, the protection of minority rights is brought up. Religious women who cover their heads in Turkey are compared to blacks who are discriminated against in the United States (June, 1986: p. 6). One wonders if women readers will make the analogy between discrimination against minorities and that against women themselves. Despite its conservative ideology, *Kadın ve Aile* initiates its readers into ideologies which, in the long run, can help challenge the confines of Islam. Conservative as it is, the journal introduces new avenues of arguments to its workers and readers that may have the effect of empowering them.

Kadın ve Aile: diversity or conformity?

If we were to evaluate the journal according to the second of Katzenstein and Laitin's criteria, we would try to find out if it promotes diversity and helps improve conditions of inequality. The conformity the journal seeks is to Islam. Beyond that, there is an attempt to encourage diversity among Muslim women. Articles on Muslim women from different parts of the world are published frequently. Women from Sri Lanka, Pakistan and Somalia are introduced (June 1985, pp. 24–5; October 1985, pp. 11–13; April 1986, pp. 24–7). Readers are at times invited to help their 'Muslim sisters' – for example, Afghan immigrant women (July 1985, pp. 8–9). An interview with a Surinamese woman who converted to Islam is published condemning the persecution of Muslim children in Surinam (July 1985, p. 24–5). Another interview, with an Iranian woman parliamentarian, acquaints readers with the rights and privileges of Iranian women in the Islamic Republic. Malaysian women explain how they practise Islam without government sanction, more specifically, how they attend state schools with heads covered (August 1985, pp. 24–5).

These attempts to encourage diversity within the Islamic community of women are restricted. An Islamic framework which is quite intolerant of the secular world limits the possibilities of diversity. Solidarity of women of different classes and nationalities is confined to their common Islamic bond. Non-Muslim women of the West are categorically disparaged. Women's movements in the West are rejected, because (the journal claims) they are concerned with the problems of Western women (April 1986). Of Western women, only those who have converted to Islam are taken seriously and interviewed (August 1985, pp. 5–7; June–July 1989, pp. 27–9).

Kadın ve Aile: solidarity for women?

Our third criterion requires that the group concerned enters into an alliance committed to the expansion of opportunities. The journal only supports alliance with other Muslim groups, such as Afghan, Malaysian or Pakistani women. All that these groups share is a conservative Islamic ideology. These alliances, if we can call them that, merely help to reinforce their Islamic ideology.

Conclusion

Kadın ve Aile is a conservative woman's magazine. Independent of its ideology, however, the journal as an institution provides avenues of experience that could help empower women. Women are encouraged to take part in a more active social as well as political life, and they are introduced to the concept of individual rights. This process of opening up could, in the long run, help women question the confines of the Islamic ideology they presently uphold. Consciousness of individual rights could help women challenge Islamic restrictions on their liberties. The experience of politicization could help them claim their rights. In short, women's involvement with Islam need not necessarily oppress or liberate them. In the context of a polity that aims to be democratic as well as secular, it is a step on the road to democratization to recognize Islamist women as they are.

Notes

1. An earlier version of this article was published in *The Muslim World*, January 1990.
2. For a critique of the 'difference' perspective in the study of Middle Eastern women, see Lazreg (1988).

References

Arat, Yeşim (1989). *The Patriarchal Paradox: Women Politicians in Turkey*, Fairleigh Dickinson University Press, NY.

Göle, Nilüfer (1991). *Modern Mahrem*, Metis Yayınları, Istanbul.

Gülalp, Haldun (1992). 'Nationalist versus Islamist politics in Turkey: the social roots of Islamic radicalism', paper prepared for the First Eruopean Conference of Sociology, Vienna, 26–29 August.

Heper, Metin (1981). 'Islam, polity and society in Turkey: a Middle Eastern perspective', *The Middle East Journal*, vol. 35, no. 3.

Kandiyoti, Deniz (1991). *Women, Islam and the State*, Temple University Press, Philadelphia.

Katzenstein, Mary Fainsod, and David Laitin (1987). 'Politics, feminism and the ethics of caring', *Women and Moral Theory*, ed. Eva Feder Kittay and Diana Meyers, Rowman and Littlefield, New Jersey.

Lazreg, Marnia (1988). 'Feminism and difference: the perils of writing as a woman on women in Algeria', *Feminist Studies*, vol. 14, no. 1.

Macleod, Arlene Elowe (1992). 'Hegemonic relations and gender resistance: the new veiling as accommodating protest in Cairo', *Signs: Journal of Women in Culture and Society*, vol. 13, no. 3, Spring.

Mardin, Şerif (1981). 'Religion and secularism in Turkey', in *Atatürk: Founder of a Modern State*, ed. Ali Kazancıgil and Ergun Özbudun, Hurst and Co., London.

Mardin, Şerif (1971). 'Ideology and religion in the Turkish revolution', *International Journal of Middle East Studies*, no. 2.

Mernissi, Fatima (1987). *Beyond the Veil*, Indiana University Press, Indianapolis.

Öncü, Ayşe (1989). 'The interaction of politics, religion and finance: Islamic banking in Turkey', paper presented at the Berlin Institute for Comparative Social Research, Symposium on Muslims, Migrants and Metropolis, June 13–18.

Rahman, Fazlur (1983). 'Status of woman in the Qur'an', in *Women and Revolution in Iran*, ed. Guity Nashat, Westview Press, Colorado.

Sabbah, Fatna (1984). *Women in the Muslim Unconscious*, Pergamon Press, New York.

Scott, Joan (1988). 'Deconstructing equality versus difference or the uses of poststructuralist theory for feminism', *Feminist Studies*, vol. 14, no. 1.

Sirman, Nükhet (1989). 'Feminism in Turkey: a short history', *New Perspectives on Turkey*, vol. 3, no. 1.

Sunar, Ilkay and Binnaz Toprak (1983). 'Islam in politics: the case of Turkey', *Government and Opposition*, vol. 18, no. 4.

Tabari, Azar (1986). 'The woman's movement in Iran: a hopeful prognosis', *Feminist Studies*, vol. 12, no. 2.

Tekeli, Şirin (1982). *Kadınlar ve Siyasal Toplumsal Hayat*, Birikim Yayınları, Istanbul.

Toprak, Binnaz (1989). 'Islam in Turkey: internal and external factors', Berlin, Institute for Comparative Social Research, research paper.

Part II

The Prerequisites of Material Life

4

The Status and Changing Forms of Women's Labour in the Urban Economy

F. Yıldız Ecevit

In Turkey, both urban and rural women do work in addition to their household tasks. In rural areas, more women work, both numerically and proportionally, than in urban areas. In 1985, 85 out of 100 working women did unpaid family labour on agricultural tasks in villages. Statistics, however, indicate a general decline in the number of unpaid family labourers: most are now employed in waged or salaried work.[1] Although wage labour now predominates as a means of subsistence in urban areas, the presence of women in this category is limited. The aim of this chapter is to question why urban women are marginalized in the labour market, as is clear from their limited participation in economic life.

First it is necessary to define my concept of urban women and marginality. Towns in Turkey are defined as settlements with a population of more than 20,000, but here greater attention will be directed to big cities where industry and services have developed, rather than small or medium-sized towns. Due to lack of statistical data on class structures I am unable to provide any analysis of class differentiation among women of working age (12 years and over) living in cities. Nevertheless, I consider that the generalization I make is valid for all urban women, since participation in urban economic activities is an area in which they experience a similar form of marginality.

By marginality I understand the unequal and limited participation of urban women in the organized formal sector, in other words in industry and the service sector,[2] where employment earns monetary returns. The quantitative proportionate indicators of women's participation, and changes between 1960 and 1985, are as follows:

1. The structure of the economically active population in the non-agricultural sectors (industry and services) is extremely unbalanced in terms of sex differentiation:

- In non-agricultural sectors, only 12 per cent of employees were women in 1985, compared to 9 per cent in 1960.
- Of industry employees, 14 per cent were women in 1985. In 1960 this figure was 15 per cent.
- Only 11 per cent of services employees were women in 1985. In 1960 this number was 6 per cent.

2. The proportional distribution of both men and women in industry and service favours the service sector. In other words, more men and women are employed in services than in industry:

- Of women working in the non-agricultural sectors, 68 per cent were employed in services in 1985. In 1960 this figure was 41 per cent.
- Of men working in the non-agricultural sectors, 73 per cent were employed in services in 1985. In 1960 this figure was 65 per cent.

3. Between 1960 and 1985 employment capacity increased by 314 per cent in non-agricultural sectors. This figure breaks down to 232 and 363 per cent in industry and services respectively. Women were able to make use of these capacities at only 13 per cent efficiency. In other words, within a 25-year period women gained entry to 13 new jobs out of 100.

At the beginning of the 1950s the following thesis was put forward in respect of working women in Turkey: waged work outside the household was not women's priority; if women did work they saw it as a temporary activity undertaken out of necessity; home is where they wanted to be and housework and motherhood are their preferred occupations. Women's limited participation in urban economic activities has generally been explained in terms of their family roles and related preferences, and the patriarchal relations in the family. Factors related to the economic structure have been virtually excluded from causal analysis.[3] For the 1950s and 1960s this proposition was not unrealistic. Urban industrial employment then was less prestigious than service sector jobs and was not preferred by women unless they were destitute; however, the service sector was developing fast in this period, providing employment opportunities to both men and women who wanted them. For this reason I believe that the negative effects of patriarchal ideology were stronger than those of the economic structure and this explains why fewer women than men participated in paid employment.

By the second half of the 1970s, however, the number of urban women seeking employment rose and competition began for scarce opportunities as a consequence of the male unemployment rates, urban living conditions and the effects of urban culture. But paradoxically, as women began to demand jobs the potential for the creation of employment opportunities in the industrial sector began to decline after 1978, and particularly after 1980. And although the service sector was still growing, its rate of growth was inadequate in the face of the increasing size of the labour-force.

In the economic situation of the 1980s and 1990s it is no longer adequate to provide traditional answers to the marginality of women in the labour market, even though explanations such as the Islamic disapproval of women's paid work, the obstacles to women's employment created by the patriarchal structure of the family, and women's disinclination to work, are important. Currently, the unequal participation of women's labour and men's labour in economic activities is determined as much by urban economic life itself and its structural characteristics as by traditional factors.

Structural changes in industry and services and women's employment

It cannot be said that since 1978 industry has taken positive steps to provide employment opportunities in Turkey. Western economists maintain that the most successful period in the development of the Turkish industry was between 1964 and 1973 and that this was due to the continual rise in investments.[4] But in the last decade new investments have been severely limited outside a few sub-sectors. While in 1977 industrial investments constituted nearly 30 per cent of total investments, this fell to 28 per cent in 1986, 17 per cent in 1987 and 15.2 per cent in the 1988 programme. The share of manufacturing in constant capital investments has fallen by 40 per cent.[5] Since the adoption of the export-oriented model in 1980 there has been a marked increase in the production of industrial goods. This increase, however, results from increased productive capacity (which was kept below 50 per cent prior to 1978) rather than new investments. In fact industrial growth has resulted from the increase in capacity utilization, and its limits were reached by 1987.[6] Furthermore, a crisis has set in and manufacturing industry began to decline from the second half of 1988.[7] As factories reduced production, due to stagnation in both exports and internal market sales, they began to decrease the number of shifts worked, dismiss workers or send them on leave. Increased dismissals are expected in the coming years as a result of lifting the ban on dismissals that was imposed in the beginning of the 1980s. Economic stagnation has hit small and medium-sized firms hardest, and small and medium-sized subcontracting workshops in textiles and the motor industry have been particularly affected. For example, 80 per cent of the 2,500 workshops in Istanbul are redundant.

Stagnation in industry, and relative decline, obviously have grave consequences for employment prospects. The process leads to small and medium-sized enterprises laying off workers and searching for new solutions, as well as giving rise to a fall in the number of unionized workers and workers covered by social insurance, and a shift from waged labour to the informal sector.

Stagnation and decline in industry have direct consequences for women's employment. These effects are all the more pronounced in the case of industrial sectors with a high concentration of women that are particularly affected by the crisis. For instance, between 1980 and 1985 there was a 20 per cent fall in the number of women employed in the tobacco industry. The demand for female labour in both cigarette factories and tobacco processing plants has decreased as a result of increased imports of cigarettes and a corresponding decrease in domestic production. In addition, dismissals target unskilled workers who are easily replaced, rather than skilled workers and those employed in key positions. As women are generally likely to be of the former group they are more likely to lose their jobs. Furthermore, patriarchal ideology, in the form of belief in the male 'breadwinner', is a further factor in their dismissal.

Further effects of industrial stagnation for the female labour force are related to the increase in subcontracting. In an attempt to reduce costs in order to attract external markets, some industrial establishments encourage their workers to work in their homes by providing them with industrial-style home equipment. Moreover they try to protect themselves against the crisis by seeking new women workers who will work for the factory in their homes. The harmful effects of women's home production with no job security, social insurance and low wages are generally well known.

Finally stagnation and crisis mean that women who seek employment are left without jobs. Under these circumstances many women who need work will look to the service sector. In the last thirty years the service sector has expanded more rapidly than industry in terms of capacity (232 per cent for industry; 363 per cent for services) and has provided more opportunities for women. From 1960 to 1985, over one-and-a-half million women were employed in industry, whereas in services the number of women employed reached a little over half a million. The rate of growth in services was greatest between 1965 and 1975, but this fell from 1975 onwards by 30 per cent for 1975–80, and 28 per cent for 1980–85. After 1980 both the private and the public sector shifted investments from productive sectors towards tourism, communications and municipal services, and growth rates fell below their 1960s level. It is possible to explain the fall in women's employment while employment in general increases, by the proposition that women are not preferred in new investment areas, but there are other explanations. The great majority of service-sector jobs are provided by the state. It is possible to say that centralized state intervention in public services, as opposed to the private sector, is a prominent factor in the declining volume of employment generally.

Thus there was little or no new intake of personnel in the ministries of Transport, Health and Social Services and National Education in the late 1980s. Service sector jobs, aside from unskilled work such as sales or cleaning, require higher levels of training and skill. Compared to the industrial sector, employment opportunities in the service sector usually benefit younger women with higher or secondary education. It could, therefore, be asserted that unequal participation on the basis of gender operates in both sectors although the extent of fluctuation is less in the services than the industrial sector. In 1960, women comprised 6 per cent of service sector employees and in the late 1980s had reached only 11 per cent.

Patriarchal relations in the capitalist market

The limitation in the employment of women resulting from the stagnation of industrial investments and the restricted absorption of appropriately qualified women in the services, despite the overall increase in employment in this sector, shows how changes in the economic structure affect women in waged employment. Obviously, however, these changes in the economic structure are not the single determinant in constituting women's marginality.

It is, therefore, useful to look at some of the ways in which patriarchy in the labour market controls women's labour. The widely prevailing and undeniable power of patriarchal relations exists with equal force both within and outside the family. Patriarchal relations in the labour market function to keep women in the home as unpaid family labourers; and in the workplace, control over women's participation in waged labour is determined by state and patriarchal relations. Although the form and degree of control may change over time, women's marginality is enforced through the following mechanisms:

- The maintenance of a lower level of formal education for women than for men, and a lack of training for skilled work (such as apprenticeship and training courses).
- The exclusion of women from specific jobs and professions (such as in banks, tax offices and local administration).
- The maintenance of a fixed proportion of women in specific jobs and professions (such as in the armed forces, law enforcement and similar organizations).
- Discrimination in recruitment and in the workplace (such as the preference for single rather than married women, differential treatment of women and men as unskilled and skilled workers).
- Sex discrimination in wages (by enforcing wage differentials through changes in job descriptions).
- Dismissal for marriage and for pregnancy.
- Dismissal of women before men in times of crisis, with the help of high compensation.
- Protective legislation preventing women entering certain jobs.
- Trade-union discrimination towards women, and their restricted representation among administrative cadres.

Some of these modes of control over women's labour power take the form of directly visible and strict, regularly enforced rules while others are indirect practices more difficult to detect.[8] Marginalization of women in the labour market results from the actions of biased employers, male-dominated trade unions and, in part, the attitudes of men in the workplaces. The state plays a very important role in this process through rules and practices. Patriarchal relations in the household–family and in working life together constitute the basis of sex discrimination and the marginalization of women's labour power.

Conclusion

As a result of the changes in economic policy in Turkey after 1980 there was only limited expansion in employment opportunities. These limited opportunities have been exploited by men: for every 87 men employed only 13 women found jobs. In recent years the economic crisis has decreased employment, thus raising unemployment levels and reducing real family incomes. The rise in the rate of inflation (75.2 per cent at the end of 1988) has accelerated the rate of decline in wages, salaries and agricultural incomes. Between 1987 and 1988 real wages fell by 28 per cent. Taking 1983 as 100 per cent, public sector wages fell by 46 per cent, while wages in the private sector declined by 23 per cent in the latter half of the 1980s. Between 1980 and 1988, although wages increased to 19 times their 1980 level, and salaries to 23 times, in the same period prices rose by 32 times. As a result, children who were not previously in employment, the unemployed, the old and pensioners began to look for ways to earn extra income. Under these conditions the number of women seeking employment rose. In 1985, the number of women unemployed (which only reflects the statistics) was 662,518. This is as high as 69 per cent of the total numbers of women employed in non-agricultural sectors. According to official statistics, for every 100 women working another 69 are seeking work. This extremely high demand for work led women from the formal to the informal sector due to the pressures and discrimination outlined. There has been a rise in the number of women in cleaning and child minding, and as maids outside the home. Some women have had to accept lower than minimum wages working in the 'black' industries. Others chose to market goods they produced in the home, thus becoming a part of the informal sector.

Today data on women in the informal sector are far from adequate. However, as far as we know from the existing data and observations we can assume that there are a similar number of women working in the informal and the formal sectors. Given the coming effects of inflation, incomes will continue to fall and the rate of impoverishment will accelerate. In this context it can safely be predicted that women's labour power will be utilized increasingly in both domestic and extra-domestic informal activities. In my opinion, women's relationships with informal sector activities in urban areas will no longer be temporary, but are in the process of becoming a permanent, institutional structure. Hence we now need new research into the means of utilizing women's labour power in order to reach new conceptualizations of the subject.

Notes

1. T.C. Başbakanlık Devlet Planlama Teşkilatı. Sosyal Planlama Başkanlığı. *Sosyal Yapı-II Nüfusun Sosyal ve Ekonomik Özellikleri Araştırması* (Social Structure-II Research on Social and Economic Characteristics of the Population), DPT: 2134-SPD:414, Ankara 1988, p. 47.

2. The industrial sector consists of manufacturing, mining and energy. The services sector includes transportation, communication, storage, financial institutions, insurance, real estate, business services, community and personal services.

3. See for this argument: H. Topçuoğlu, *Kadınların Çalışma Saikleri ve Kadın Kazancının Aile Bütçesindeki Rolü*, (Reasons for Women's Work and the Role of Women's Earnings in the Family Budget), Kadının Sosyal Hayatını Tetkik Kurumu Yayınları, Sayı, 4, Ankara 1957; M. Tan, *Kadın: Ekonomik Yaşamı ve Eğitimi* (Woman: Economic Life and Education), Türkiye İş Bankası Kültür Yayınları, No. 204, Ankara 1979; and G. Lewis, 'Career involvement in four professions in Turkey', *The Turkish Journal of Population Studies*, special issue, 1981.

4. T. Bulutay, 'Türkiye'nin 1959–1980 Dönemindeki İktisadi Büyümesi Üzerine Düşünceler' (Considerations on Economic Growth in Turkey between 1950–1980), *Orta Doğu Teknik Üniversitesi, Gelişme Dergisi*, özel sayı, 1981.

5. F. Başkaya, 'Türkiye Ekonomisinin Bazı Yapısal Sorunları Üzerine Bir Deneme' (An Essay On Some Structural Problems of Turkish Economy), *Mülkiyeliler Birliği Dergisi*, Sayı. 102, Aralık 1988.

6. K. Boratov, '1988 Sonuna Doğru Türkiye Ekonomisi Üzerine Gözlemler' (Observations on the Turkish Economy towards the end of 1988), *Mülkiyeliler Birliği Dergisi*, Sayı. 102, Aralik 1988.

7. İstanbul Sanayi Odası, İmalat Sanayinin Durumu (*The Structure of Manufacturing Industry*), Rapor, 1989.

8. Y. Ecevit, 'Gender and Wage Work: A Case Study of Turkish Women in Manufacturing Industry', unpublished Ph.D thesis, University of Kent 1986.

Changes in Women's Activities both Inside and Outside the Home

Ferhunde Özbay

Women are usually the oppressed party in relationships of domination, both within the family and in society. It is important to study the changes in women's activities in order to be able to predict their future participation in these relations of domination. The correlation between women's activities and their status has been investigated in a large number of studies which generally approach the issue by pointing to the inequalities between men and women in their participation in production, in both the extent and the type of work they do. The present study will likewise investigate these inequalities first, while also discussing the changes taking place in women's activities in Turkey.

It is, however, necessary to point out that such an approach is not sufficient to bring out the complex dynamics of relations of domination, since women's activities which are not acknowledged as taking place in the sphere of production are completely left out of the analysis. Moreover, labour statistics generally do not properly reflect the extent of women's participation in production. The categories 'active' and 'inactive' may be appropriate to assess men's activities, since reasons for male 'inactivity' are self-evident. A man who is not working is either sick, old, in prison, has a private income, or is a student: he is either incapable of working or he has enough money to live on. However, most women are economically 'inactive', although they are able to work and have no income. Moreover, they have to perform work as 'housewives' in order to earn their livelihood, and have to pursue this work even when they participate in the sphere of production. It is therefore more enlightening to assess women's activities related to reproduction. The changes in women's activities will be discussed in the second part of this study using such a comprehensive approach.

Two different interpretations have been given to the 'activities in and outside the home' to which the title of this paper refers. All the production and reproduction activities are covered under the first term. The general theory is that, with the expansion of capitalism, production is realized to a large extent through institutions outside the home, while women take up activities of reproduction inside the home. Although this generalization may be broadly true, it is not specific enough when analysing women's activities in Third World countries like Turkey. First of all, there is still a large group of women working in the agricultural sector, whose production and reproduction activities cannot be sharply differentiated as in and outside the home. As well as this, women in the cities increasingly participate in production by working at home as well as performing some of their work outside the home, due to their new responsibilities related to reproduction. This is the second meaning attributed to the title. Oppositions such as active–inactive, inside–outside the home, could be regarded as male-dominated ideologies in advanced industrial societies, appropriate only for defining the economic structure of those societies. One of the objectives of this study is to question continually the existing categories, and to emphasize the need to avoid the dominant ideologies which are reflected even in the scientific language.

The change in women's activities is discussed in relation to the last fifty or sixty years, divided into three sub-periods. The first period extends from the 1920s and the foundation of the republic to the 1950s, when the expansion of capitalism in agriculture started. The main problem here is the dearth of studies based on observations made prior to 1950. The interpretations relating to this period are therefore largely based on a few village monographs and assessments made according to general norms. The second period, covering the thirty-odd years from the 1950s to the end of the 1970s, is a time of drastic social and economic transformations and does not, in fact, have a homogeneous structure. The 1950s are closer to the previous structure, while the 1970s are more like the 1980s. Moreover, the social transformation of the 1980s is considered as important as the 1948–50 period in Turkish history, when capitalism started to expand, and therefore the 1980s have consequently been taken up separately. This division becomes meaningful in view of the objective of this study, which is the detailed investigation of the present situation with an emphasis on the post-1980 period.

The characteristics of the female labour-force

As in almost every society, women's participation in the Turkish labour force is smaller than that of men. In 1985, 32 per cent of the women and 68 per cent of the men aged 12 and above were assessed as the active population.[1] Most of the inactive males were either students (46 per cent) or retired (25 per cent). The large majority of inactive women, however, are housewives (80 per cent) (SIS, 1988).

The proportion and form of female participation in production change rapidly, and this tendency may be expected to continue in the future. Statistics based on population censures show that, with the expansion of capitalism, there has been a shift from the agricultural to the non-agricultural sector, and from unpaid work to paid work (Tables 5.1 and 5.2).

Table 5.1 Distribution of labour force by occupation last week and by sex, 1955 and 1985 (ages 15 +) (%)

	Women		Men	
	1955	1985	1955	1985
Agriculture	94.8	78.0	68.7	30.0
Non-agricultural sectors	5.2	22.0	31.3	70.0
Total	100.00	100.0	100.0	100.0

Note: After 1975 definition of the active population was changed to age 12 and above. Data relating to the recent past have been calculated again on the basis of age 15 and above to enable comparison. Apart from tables, the rates given in the text have been calculated on the basis of age 12 and above.
Source: SIS, 1961, 1988.

Table 5.2 Distribution of active population by work status and
sex, 1955 and 1985 (ages 15+) (%)

	Women		Men	
	1955	1985	1955	1985
Wage-earner	3.8	19.5	22.3	48.3
Employer	0.0	0.1	0.6	3.3
Self-employed	4.7	5.1	47.7	35.0
Family labour	91.5	75.3	29.4	13.4
Total	100.0	100.0	100.0	100.0
Number	5,247.0	4,881.0	6,375.0	11,281.0

Source: SIS, 1961, 1988.

These are not, however, the most striking changes observed
between the 1955 and 1985 statistics. As shown in Table 5.3,
there is a rapid fall in the proportion of female labour in this
period. The participation rate of the female labour force, which
was over 80 per cent prior to 1950 (Kazgan, 1979), decreased to
30 per cent in 1985. There is thus an increase in the difference
between men and women as to their participation in
production. Moreover, most of the active female population
participates in agricultural production as unpaid family
workers. Therefore the female labour force constitutes a less
educated group than the male (Table 5.4).

Table 5.3 Labour force participation rates by sex 1955 and 1985
(ages 15+) (thousands)

	Women			Men			Differ-ence (%)
	Active	Total	% active	Active	Total	% active	
1955	5,262	7,299	72.1	6,944	7,275	95.5	23.3
1965	5,137	9,065	56.5	8,421	9,158	92.0	35.5
1975	5,574	11,750	47.4	10,475	12,267	85.4	38.0
1985	5,221	15,988	32.7	12,444	16,050	77.5	44.8

Source: SIS, 1961, 1968, 1981, 1988.

Table 5.4 Distribution of active population by sex and
education, 1985 (ages 12+) (%)

	Women	Men
Illiterate	28.0	8.9
Literate	8.6	8.1
Primary school	46.4	54.1
Middle school	3.8	11.9
High school or equivalent	9.6	11.5
University or equivalent	3.6	5.5
Total	100.0	100.0
Number	4,881,344	11,281,446

Source: SIS, 1988.

Two main reasons are given for the low female participation
in non-agricultural production: (1) the low level of education;
and (2) scarcity of wage-work opportunities. Indeed, the
proportion of women participating in production and finding
paid work increases as the level of education rises (Table 5.5).
There is a very small number of female employers and
self-employed women, and no significant changes in this
proportion has been recorded in the last thirty years: we cannot
therefore say that education provides great opportunities for
women. On the other hand, although women's opportunities
for wage-work are scarce in Turkey, wages are very low.
Özmucur (1987) draws attention to the fact that, while there is a
decrease in the proportion of paid workers and of the
agricultural sector in the distribution of income, other sources
of income, such as profits, interest and rent, are beginning to
play an increasingly important role. Despite the limitations of
the statistics, it is clear that women are at a disadvantage in their
participation in the labour-force.

Table 5.5 Educational status of housewives, active females and
female wage earners, 1985 (ages 12 +) (%)

	Housewife	Active	Wage earner
Illiterate	32.2	28.0	8.5
Literate	10.2	8.6	3.6
Primary school	47.5	46.4	29.0
Middle school	4.9	3.8	9.0
High school and above	5.2	13.2	49.9
Total	100.0	100.0	100.0
N	9,351.0	5,544.0	951.0

Source: SIS, 1988.

There is limited information about the situation of women
who are engaged in marginal work and are consequently
considered to be housewives in labour force statistics. Local
studies show that there is an increase in the number of women
doing marginal work, especially in metropolitan centers. The
rapidly developing Turkish ready-made clothing industry,
aiming to increase its competitiveness in world markets, tries to
reduce its production costs by paying very little for piecework.
Since such work is organized through informal networks, it is
considered transient work which does not provide security for
the workers. As to the women who do knitting and sell their
products, they consider this to be more a leisure activity than
work. Furthermore, cleaning women prefer to label themselves
as housewives in the censuses, since they consider their work to
be lowly; whereas males who feel inferior because of the kind of
work they engage in declare themselves to be unemployed, and
are therefore recorded as part of the active population. Although
labour statistics reflect a significant difference between active
men and women, it can be stipulated that at least part of this
difference stems from the inferior status of women's work. The
situation of women who are mistakenly listed as housewives in
statistics, in spite of the fact that they do participate in
agricultural production, is due to the erroneous instructions
given to enumerators (Özbay, 1982). The important point here is

that the census authorities entrusted with the preparation of these instructions do not take women's work in agriculture seriously enough.

The most common form of female participation in production is the preparation of foodstuffs in the home. A nationwide study conducted in Turkey in 1986 shows that about 72 per cent of women produce foodstuffs in the home (Table 5.6). The fact that families still ensure their subsistence by preparing foodstuffs at home should be accepted as an indicator of the difficult economic circumstances of the majority within the context of a rapidly urbanizing country in which a shift from agricultural to non-agricultural activities is taking place (Esmer et al., 1986b). As this example shows clearly, instead of postulating that women are the oppressed because they do not participate in production, it would be more correct to say that women's work is not recognized as an economic activity although the majority of them do participate in production. Local studies seem to support this argument. This point may become more concrete with a discussion of women's participation in production in Ereğli in 1982.

Table 5.6 Production of food at home, 1986 (%)

Produce food at home		71.7
Produce most of the food	33.0	
Produce about half the food	15.8	
Produce less than half the food	22.9	
Do not produce food at home		26.7

Note: Percentages are not rounded in the source.
Source: Esmer et al., 1986; Table 2.5, page 9.

Female participation in the labour force in Ereğli

Ereğli, situated on the Black Sea coast, is not a typical Anatolian town: having been a coalmining town since the 19th century, it has a longer history of wage work than many others. Large iron- and steelworks (Erdemir) were established in Ereğli in 1964. This led to immigration of various sectors of the population from other areas and is another reason for the different character of

Ereğli. In a sense, the town is a miniature model of the country. There are factory managers from big cities like Istanbul and Ankara, highly educated people used to metropolitan life who live in Ereğli as if it were a suburb of one of these big cities. On the other hand, there is a group from the villages around Kars who live in Ereğli as if they were still in their villages. One can also find Bulgarian immigrants, as well as migrant workers back from Germany. The natives of Ereğli almost disappear in the midst of this human mosaic.

Mübeccel Kıray turned Ereğli into an interesting social science laboratory. In 1962, Kıray studied the social structure of the town while work was underway preparing for the establishment of the factory. This created an opportunity for observing the changes occurring over a twenty-year period. A small town of 8,000 inhabitants in 1962, Ereğli had a population of 80,000 by 1982. The majority of the male population works today in the mines or in Erdemir. Since both industries employ mostly male labour, and since no auxiliary industry has developed in the town, wage-work opportunities for women are still scarce. There are no female industrial workers except those employed by the small cannery which has been in operation since the 1950s. The number of educated women working in the Erdemir offices, or as teachers, midwives, nurses or in local banks, has significantly increased in the last twenty years – but it should be noted that the most common jobs for women in Turkey, such as teaching or working in banks, pay the lowest wages for an equal level of education (Hamurdan, 1976). There are at most ten women in the liberal professions, working in Ereğli as doctors, pharmacists and lawyers. As there were almost no white-collar women in Ereğli in 1962, it can at least be said that some changes have taken place in this respect in the last twenty years.

Ereğli was called 'green Ereğli' or 'charming Ereğli' before the establishment of the iron- and steelworks. The major agricultural product of the town was strawberries. Today, blocks of concrete have replaced strawberry fields. It is however still possible to see vegetable and fruit gardens as one moves away from the centre of the city. Again, it is the women who work in the fields, as they did in the past. Since mining and related activities, such as transportation, are most important to the town's economy, agriculture has always been considered woman's work. This form of production has changed in accordance with the changing conditions in this developing and growing city. Women in Ereğli are now not only in charge of agricultural production, but also share in the sales of agricultural products. The once-weekly market is a woman's world. Some of these women, in agreement with wholesalers, run stores in the wholesale market. It is even possible to encounter women peddling vegetables and fruit in the streets of the town.

A small survey (of just under four hundred people) conducted in Ereğli has shown that 4.5 per cent of the heads of households are women. None of these female heads of households is married. They are either widowed, divorced or unmarried women, living alone or with their children. Most of them are office workers, while some do not work and subsist on some income from their families or ex-husbands. All these women, however, have a low income. Wives of male heads of households were asked during interviews whether they had a paid job or not. Only 10.8 per cent of the respondents said that they were wage-workers. This is a very small proportion, but it must be remembered that these women do not represent all the married women in town. Any other woman in the household over the age of 15 was also asked whether she worked or not, and 8.8 per cent of these responses were affirmative. It can therefore be said that roughly one in every five women in Ereğli works. Even this proportion is greater than the one obtained from population censuses. According to the 1980 census, the proportion of women aged 12 and above working in provincial and district centres is 11.8 per cent (SIS, 1984).

Inactive women were then asked if they worked occasionally for pay, and 15.3 per cent said that they did. Those who answered the first question affirmatively mostly worked for a wage. Those who answered affirmatively to the second question, however, declared that they worked as farmers and vegetable pedlars, or did lacework, sewing or domestic work. The third question directed at inactive women was whether they helped their husbands in their work: 3.5 per cent of the women in the sample said that they helped regularly, and 7.9 per cent said that they helped occasionally. It thus becomes clear under closer examination that the proportion of women who participate in production is in fact not so small, but stands at around 80 per cent. Those who produce foodstuffs and the like in the home for their own consumption are not included in this figure: the proportion of women who participate in production increases considerably when this group is added, but the women generally do not deem their work worth mentioning.

Social status and social mobility

The fact that women participate in low-status production does not necessarily mean that they do not make an effort to better their social status. On the contrary, when all women's activities are assessed, it can be observed that activities aimed at raising their social status occupy an important place. In Turkey, underdeveloped capitalism on the one hand, and the system of values created by male-dominated ideology on the other, constantly destroy the links which could be made between raising the status of women and their increased participation in production.

Moreover, this process assumes different forms with changing social and economic conditions. Women's economic activity is oriented towards upward social mobility, as is the case with men. Changes in activities are closely related to the conditions which determine social mobility for the majority of the population. It may therefore be meaningful to summarize the opportunities for social mobility and values existing in Turkish society at different times, and to examine the differentiation in women's activities in those periods. I will limit myself to a brief summary of each period, so as to keep to the point, the subject being as interesting as it is large.

The pre-1950 period

The majority of the population (80 per cent) lived in rural areas during this period. In agriculture, small family enterprises using primitive technology produced enough for their own subsistence. Labour, especially male labour, was scarce due to lengthy wars and poor health conditions (Özbay, 1988). Under these circumstances, an order which Kandiyoti (1989) calls 'classical patriarchy' is dominant, in which three generations live together, decisions are made by the elders and fertility is considered important. Serious structural changes are absent due to the lack of accumulation of wealth in agriculture. Even the reforms introduced by the new republic in legislation, education and political life are unable to reach small and isolated villages. In this structure, predetermined patriarchal status-differentiation based on demographic particularities, rather than social mobility, is the order. Individuals gain status with age and according to gender. In other words, relations of domination in the family are shaped in the framework of sex and age. The domination of women by men is considered natural; it is seen as unchanging and remains unquestioned. This situation is not as clear where age is concerned. Individuals are considered to be adults as soon as they get married and have children, even if they are very young; while those who are not married, even if advanced in age, are the losers in the relations of domination. Therefore, almost everyone tries to establish this power relation between family members of the same gender by getting married and having as many children as possible.

Production and reproduction activities in the family are carried out in cooperation, on the basis of division of labour. Women participate in production to a considerable degree, and men also have certain responsibilities in reproduction, especially in the reproduction of male labour and of the family. Production and reproduction activities are not clearly differentiated for either men or women: for example, boys are trained at work. Women consider most of their production activities to be part of their role as housewies.

There is more work and a greater variety of tasks to be performed by women (Berkes, 1942): they are responsible for livestock, if there is any; tilling the fields; taking care of the garden; preparing fuel from dried dung; and producing household goods like food, garments, rugs, bedding, and quilts. In addition to all this, having children and rearing them, caring for the old and the sick, as well as servicing all the daily activities of the family, training daughters and propagating the relations among women required for the reproduction of family life, are also women's responsibilities. In view of this heavy and diversified workload, more detailed rules and levels of exploitation exist in the division of labour among women. Although there is a similar division of labour based on age among men, the relationship of exploitation is usually concentrated in the sphere of production, and on the father–son relationship, due to the less diversified nature of the tasks related to reproduction.

The situation is a little different in cities. Scarcity of male labour in the cities makes the use of female labour necessary. In this period, Kemalist ideology encourages the education of women to the same level as men, and the participation of women in non-agricultural production. A new elite urban class develops, loyal to republican ideologies: intellectuals in general, and bureaucrats in particular, have ensured their acceptance as the elite of the republican period. Intellectuals in Turkey have never enjoyed such a high status.

Women who work as civil servants or teachers have high social status. This is due not to their gender but to their education. It could even be said that society does not consider these white-collar women as 'women'. Kemalist women try to look like men, both in behaviour and in attire (Özbay, 1987). Although an increasing proportion of white- and blue-collar jobs are held by urban women as compared to the Ottoman period, the urban population constitutes only a very small part of the total, and hence emphasis has been placed on rural women in discussing women's activities. It should, however, not be overlooked that there is an obvious status-differentiation between urban and rural, educated and uneducated women during this period.

The period 1950–1980
Capitalism, which started to take off in agriculture during the early 1950s, continued to go through various stages of development until the end of the 1970s. The population increase was accelerated by changes in social and economic structure and the decline in the death rate. All these changes affected women's activities. However, the most important changes during this period were observed in men's activities (see tables 5.1 and 5.2).

The decline in the death rate without a concomitant decrease in the birth rate causes difficulties as households become more crowded. As the need for the labour of all the male members in the family in agricultural production decreases, the workload of the women responsible for tasks related to the daily activities of family members does not increase. Stirling (1955) points out that, towards the end of the 1940s, problems relating to the division of labour increase within the family, and sons leave home without waiting for their father's death. Modernization in agriculture and increased opportunities for non-agricultural work cause serious deterioration of the relations of domination among men. It is no longer possible for a young man to acquire status by continuing his father's work and having many children: he is expected either to enlarge his father's business or to go into some other sphere of business.

After 1950, two factors facilitate social mobility: education and migration. At the beginning of the period even elementary schooling is an important step ahead for the son of a man who never went to school (let alone having a liberal profession as an engineer or a medical doctor), and may be enough for the young man to overtake his father economically, since the level of education of the population at large is very low. It is considered natural for boys – whose responsibilities in the family are relatively reduced and who are in a position to convert the status acquired by education to economic power – to have priority in benefiting from increasing, but still scarce, opportunities for education.

Similarly, migrating from the village to the city and becoming 'urbanized' is an indicator of status by itself. One should mention here the influence of the previous period. The rural migrants are relatively content, even though they have to live in very poor conditions in the city. It must however be immediately added that the first to migrate to the city are not the rural poor. In fact it is those whose families are relatively affluent who have the courage to migrate, as they can overcome part of their problems of subsistence in the city with material support from the village (Özbay, 1988). The transfer of agricultural accumulation out of agriculture first started with these movements of migration, and was then furthered by the merchants. The education and job opportunities provided by the city still gave most of the migrants a possibility of upward mobility. Migration as a means of social mobility acquired a new impetus after the 1960s, as workers started to migrate out of the country.

In a way, young men were liberated from the domination of their fathers through education and migration, although this was not an easy process. Kıray (1964), who observed the father–son conflict within the family in Ereğli in 1962, points out that it was mainly women who suffered from this rupture. According to Kıray, the mother acted as a buffer in the clash between father and son, the break thus becoming less tragic for both parties. The mother was on the son's side in this struggle, as she tried to help him become independent and shape his own life. While the fathers are defeated in this power-struggle among the males of the family, there is a decrease in the responsibilities the father is expected to have, like bringing up the boy to maintain this relation of domination and perform reproductive activities. The mother, on the other hand, starts to take more responsibility than the father, by cooperating with educational institutions in preparing the son for a profession. Women in this period start to participate more in decision-making concerning children's marriages also, and the activities required in this connection. In short, the mother's responsibilities in reproduction and related matters have increased. Differing status-levels are gained by the young people of different social classes through education and migration: the responsibilities of mothers differ accordingly. Reference is made here to middle-class families, as it is they who determine the direction of change. Have education and migration played a status-increasing role for women as well since the 1950s? Studies conducted during this period show that educated women, compared to uneducated ones, and women in urban areas rather than rural women, live in better conditions (Özbay, 1979). However, the proportion of educated women is smaller than that of men, and there is gender inequality for the same level of education (SPO, 1988). Women acquired higher status by means of migration from the village; but this was realized, not by shifting from the agricultural to the non-agricultural sector as was the case for men, but rather because there was no longer a need for women's participation in production. The abundance of male labour and the scarcity of non-agricultural work opportunities are the main reasons for the ideological disappearance of women's participation in production; coupled with the relatively high value of paid labour, financial support from the village and the problem of women participating in production without neglecting their reproductive activities, which produce a decrease of this obligation at the family level. A true bourgeois class starts to take shape in the cities during this period, while the intellectuals begin to lose their relative importance (Öncü, 1992). Non-participation in production starts to be an indicator of status among women. Becoming 'an urban housewife' is the dream of young village girls, who wish to escape from the heavy workload of the rural areas and the authority of the older woman in the family, and become 'the mistress of one's own home'. Women working in the cities also prefer the position of housewife. Çitçi (1979) points out that women in the public sector do not enjoy working, because of their double workload. A nationwide survey conducted in 1973 shows that the majority of married women of childbearing age indicated that they were not glad to be working.

During this period, mothers in villages want their daughters to become teachers, midwives or nurses, or to migrate to the city. A survey of rural Turkey conducted in 1975 shows that mothers want their daughters, rather than their sons, to settle in towns. This is partly due to the image created in the pre-1950 period of Kemalist intellectual women. In spite of this maternal attitude, girls in the villages are still not sent regularly to primary school. Their school attendance is irregular, due to the volume of housework; besides going to school, daughters are expected to help with housework and childcare (Özbay and Balamir, 1978). The education of girls is even more problematic after they are through primary school. Since there are no high schools in the villages, girls would have to leave their families to go to school in town. This cost of education is considered a waste, since girls will not bring material benefit to the family in the future. However, the older girls' contribution to housework increases as they approach 'the age of marriage'. Marriage is regarded as more important than education to the girls' future status, since women cannot exist by themselves outside the family, even if they are educated. Moreover, a high level of education decreases their chances of finding an adequate husband: efforts are made to keep the level of girls' education below that of potential bridegrooms, so as not to increase the risk of their becoming old maids.

Elementary education becomes valuable when it assists in finding a husband in the city, and therefore makes migration possible. In a word, social mobility for rural women in this period is made possible mainly through marriage. The significance of marriage is higher than in the previous period. Women obtain a stronger position among the other females in the family through their status as married women, as well as a better position in the relations of domination which are becoming evident between the classes. An important observation here is that the social mobility of women through the dependence of marriage is a way of hinging the classical patriarchal system onto capitalism. In this way, the relations of domination between men and women have been able to adapt to new conditions without too much change.

The 1980s

Education and migration were seen as the most important components of social mobility for the majority until the 1980s. In the 1980s, however, the change of status through education and migration becomes more uncertain than previously, although expectations still exist in some groups. As a result of inflation, newcomers to the cities have to face worse conditions than was the case before, and similar deterrents exist where education is concerned. Post-1980 economic policies have not fostered the development of paid labour which was the basic aim of education and migration. On the contrary, priority is given to trade, especially foreign trade, and tourism. The dominance of trade, as compared to industry and public services, has increased the importance of money. Thus affluence has become the main element of social mobility in this last period, and the man with money is respected within relations of domination in society. The commercial knowledge required in business is not taught at school. Indeed, there is a tendency to consider that long years spent in school to get a diploma are a useless investment. There is, however, no decrease in the number of students because there is still a very small proportion of people with higher education in Turkey. A large number of students both work and attend school in this period, and a shift to studies related to trade can be observed. Disciplines like sociology, history, education, philosophy, physics, chemistry and biology have largely lost their appeal.

The change in the values relating to social mobility is also reflected in the activities and choices of individuals. It is well known that the educated young women compete with uneducated older men in the labour market. However, since the proportion of educated women is still very small, they would not constitute an important threat for old men, even if all of them started working (Hamurdan, 1976). However, as paid labour loses its value educated men go into business, and relinquish the positions they previously acquired with difficulty to educated women. Women thus frequently accede to important positions which have lost their prestige. In the universities, for example, the salaries were so low that some professors resigned and sought jobs in the private sector. They were mostly men. Moreover, applications by women to new positions in the universities were more and better than applications by men, when there were any.

Rising inflation has caused downward social mobility for some families, and obliged them to work more than before just to keep their existing place. The change in social mobility in both directions is a fairly recent phenomenon in Turkey. This increase in downward mobility has imbued money with a value above all else. Esmer et al. (1987) studied the direction of mobility of males by profession over a five-year period. The results were as expected. While the majority of traders, industrialists and members of the liberal professions declare that they enjoyed a better life in the last five years, all the other professions show the opposite trend: the position of the majority has worsened.

Compared to the previous period, there is a decrease in the status and appeal of being a housewife, as well as in the complaints concerning the double workload of working women. Participating in production to earn money has become compulsory for very many women, despite the problems of the double workload. The results of research by Esmer et al., in contradiction to the official sources, show that unemployment has increased and that 64.3 per cent of unemployed are women. In this study, the unemployment in this period is regarded as a 'women's phenomenon' (1986: p. 33).

In a comparison of the findings of the nationwide study conducted in 1973 by Hacettepe University and of the research conducted in Ereğli in 1982, the changes in women's attitude towards work are quite striking (Table 5.7). Interviews conducted separately from the Ereğli survey with women of various sectors have shown that they engaged in various activities to earn money of their own. The main activity in this context is the lottery parties they organize among themselves. These parties, called 'silver day' or 'golden day', became very popular in the 1980s. The women meet not more than once a month in one of their homes, collect from amongst themselves a predetermined sum of money (according to the value of silver or gold on that day) and draw lots to determine the winner. As each woman gets to win in turn, these paying parties are somewhat different from gambling, and may even be considered as an indirect way of saving money. It is important to observe here the change whereby women who get together for a chat focus on money as the main topic of interest.

Table 5.7 Attitudes of working women towards work, Turkey 1973 and Ereğli 1982 (per cent)

Like to work	1982 Ereğli	Turkey	Big city	1973 City	Village
Yes	82.1	36.3	43.4	39.8	27.8
No	17.9	63.7	56.6	60.3	72.2

Source: The 1973 Hacettepe Survey Woman Questionnaire; The 1982 Ereğli Survey Woman Questionnaire.

This change appears as a growing tendency for gambling among women of higher classes. As was the case in the preceding period, women still cannot ensure upward social mobility with money alone. Marriage to someone earning money is still considered the only possibility of gaining social status. Thus, in the process of rapid social transformation in Turkey, women are not motivated to request social status for themselves. Since higher status is possible only in conjunction with a rise in status of the whole family, women are obliged to concentrate their efforts on the other members of the family.

Men, on the other hand, are increasingly inclined to neglect their family responsibilities, as the race to earn money becomes more and more frantic after 1980, resulting in an increase of women's responsibilities in this respect. For example, we see more and more women taking the place of men in daily shopping since the 1980s. Again, we may compare the findings of the 1968 and 1973 nationwide surveys with those of the 1982 Ereğli study. In spite of the methodological problems arising from the fact that the latter is a local study only, it is still possible to get some clues as to the nature of the change that is taking place. As can be seen in Table 5.8, whereas daily

Table 5.8 Distribution of responsibility for family expenditure 1968 and 1973 Turkey and 1982 Ereğli (%)

| | Person responsible for daily expenditure | | | | |
	Older	Husband	Wife	Both	Total
1968[a]	20.7	40.7	24.8	14.6	100.0
1973[b]	17.1	38.3	21.3	23.3	100.0
1982[c]	1.4	23.6	52.0	23.0	100.0
	Person responsible for large expenditures				
1968[a]	20.0	44.8	11.9	23.3	100.0
1973[b]	16.3	43.9	8.8	31.1	100.0
1982[c]	2.5	52.8	4.1	40.6	100.0

Sources: [a] Timur, 1972 p. 106; [b] 1973 Population Survey, Female Questionnaire; [c] 1982 Ereğli Survey Woman Questionnaire.

shopping activities seem to shift from family elders to husband and wife between 1968 and 1973, it is mainly woman's work by 1982. Such a trend has, however, not been observed where the acquisition of consumer durables is concerned. Durable goods are usually purchased by the head of the family alone, or sometimes together with his wife.

Another field of increasing activity for women after 1980 is children's education. It has already been mentioned that, after 1950, women start to play an increasing role in this respect. The specific characteristic of the post-1980 period is especially related to the changes occurring in the educational system. In this last period, government policy is to pay low wages and limit investment in education, thus encouraging the private sector to provide better quality education. Students failing the entrance examination for private schools on the basis of the central examination system have less chance with each passing year of succeeding at university entrance examinations. It becomes necessary to have a private tutor, or to attend special courses, to be coached for examinations at all levels. All these activities are especially important for middle-class families to prevent the younger generations from going into downward social mobility. Although education has lost its relative influence on upward mobility in this period, it retains its importance, as its absence would accelerate downward mobility. Consequently, all the activities of middle-class women to prepare their children for examinations and establish contact with the schools take precedence over all other business. As has already been pointed out at the beginning of this chapter, in the post-1980 period, even women who do not work outside the home have to spend more time outside their home than in the past, both for daily shopping and to take care of the problems connected with their children's education.

Very important changes are likewise observed in repro-ductive activities within the home. Increased home facilities, as well as the development of technology for household appliances, has influenced the division of labour among women at home. For example, whereas clothes used to be washed by beating them with stones at the village fountain or in the stream, running water in the home and the development of detergents first facilitated hand washing. Although in 1986 machine washing was still limited in villages (11 per cent), washing machines start being used extensively in the urban sector (50 per cent), especially in large cities like Istanbul (75 per cent), Ankara (71

per cent) and İzmir (55 per cent) (Esmer et al., 1986). Of the
homes in Ereğli, 69 per cent have a washing machine in 1982. It
is not possible to give a definite figure for the users of automatic
washing machines, as their use has spread only in the last two or
three years. However, the status of clothes washing has risen
with mechanization. Consequently, the custom of paying for a
woman to come in and do the washing disappeared, as doing
the washing became a task that could be assumed by
higher-status individuals within the family. A similar change,
although not yet as extensive, can be observed in relation to the
use of the dishwasher. The facilitation of domestic chores and
childcare has however not decreased women's workload as
much as one would think, as women have now to undertake
more managerial activities.

Another activity which is mostly left to women is the
management of familial relations. Women have increasingly
begun to assume duties connected with the marriage problems
of the younger generation, in sectors in which paying bride
money is no longer the custom. The choice of a spouse,
arrangements between the families, exchange of visits and
presents, preparations for the marriage ceremony and
furnishing the home of the newlyweds are all activities in which
women play a role both at the decision-making and
implementation levels. Furthermore, the woman has to keep a
good, warm relationship with relatives in accordance with her
husband's work and leisure-time requirements. Indeed,
relationships with relatives constitute the prime security in
times of social and economic difficulties, and their reproduction
is therefore important. Women consider these relations
important because they provide support for the family in case of
need, as well as help when the woman has problems connected
with her role as a housewife. As for men, apart from economic
issues like business and inheritance, they increasingly tend to
play a more passive role in family relations. This is due in a
sense to the disappearance of the relations of domination among
men in the family.

Relations of domination among women, though weaker,
have not essentially changed. This can be seen in Ereğli, in the
tension and conflicts among related women. The most typical
example is the mother-in-law/daughter-in-law quarrel. Similar
problems also occur very frequently between mother and adult
daughter; separate homes reduce these tensions. It is observed
that relations of domination exist, though at standard level, in

the case of cohabitation. In answer to the question, 'Who should be responsible for housework if there is more than one woman in the house?' 65 per cent of women in Ereğli said the mother-in-law when she cohabits with her married son, and 87 per cent the mother when mother and daughter live together. Rather than reflecting the real situation, these answers show that the change in standards was not yet clearly defined in the 1980s. Cooperation and division of labour among women, even if they live in separate homes, is still strong. The main field of cooperation is the care of children. The fact that elderly women help in caring for the children does not mean that they are beginning to lose in the power relations among women. Childcare is a prerequisite for the establishment of relations of domination with the younger women. The care of children is consequently a tool used in the pursuance of these relations among women, even if they do not live as large families. In short, the increase in the number of activities undertaken by women in the management of family relations ensures that relations of domination among women are constantly reproduced – which, in turn, delays the attainment by women of a status equal to that of men.

Conclusion

The fact that women acquire identity through the family is more clearly defined with the expansion of capitalism. As women shoulder additional responsibilities connected with the social status of the family in 1980s Turkey, they appear to take over from men the capacity to act as family representative. Even government policies relating to the family, and especially to children, are addressed to women, as they begin to be considered the family representative. The contradiction here resides in the fact that the man is the legal head of the family. If a man does not legally recognize his family, his children are not granted citizenship because they are classed as children of unclear parentage: they cannot obtain a birth certificate, go to school, get a job or even be legally married. In a sense, the woman assumes increasing responsibilities in family affairs through the man's delegation of authority.

The relations of sovereignty in the framework of gender in the family and in society are so deep that the changes observed in the activities and status of women can only take place within this framework. As women identify their social status with that of the family, the rise or fall in status of any member of the family confers new status on them, and gives the impression of social mobility. They consequently direct their activities toward increasing the status of the family, especially that of its male members. This delusion is the reason why women complain little about their low status in production or failing to receive just compensation for their labour, and why they do not unite to fight for their rights.

Note

1. The unemployment rate for both is about 12% (SIS, 1988).

References

Berkes, Niyazi (1942). *Bazı Ankara Köyleri Üzerine Bir Araştırma*, Ankara Üniversitesi, DTCF Yayını, Ankara.

Çitçi, Oya (1979). 'Türk Kamu Yönetiminde Kadın Görevliler', in *Türk Toplumunda Kadın*, ed. Nermin Abadan-Unat, Türk Sosyal Bilimler Derneği, Ankara (second edition, 1982).

Esmer, Yılmaz, Hamit Fışek and Ersin Kalaycıoğlu (1986). *Sosyolojik ve Demografik Yapı ile İlgili Bulgular, Metodoloji ve Uygulama*, Cilt I, Türkiye' de Sosyo-Ekonomik Öncelikler, Hane gelirleri, Harcamaları ve Sosyo-Ekonomik İhtiyaçlar Üzerine Araştırma Dizisi. TÜSIAD, Istanbul.

Esmer, Yılmaz, Hamit Fışek and Ersin Kalaycioğlu (1986a). *Sosyolojik ve Demografik Yapi ilf İlgili Bulgular, Metodoloji ve Uygulama*. Cilt I. Turkiye' de Sosyo-Ekonomik Öncelikler. Hane gelirleri, Harcamaları ve Sosyo-Ekonomik İhtiyaçlar Uzerine Araştirma Oizisi. TÜSIAD: Istanbul.

Esmer, Yılmaz, Hamit Fışek and Ersin Kalaycioğlu (1986b). *Turkiye' de Hane Geliri. Hane Halki Harcamalari Ve Hayat Standardi*. Tilt İt. Türkiye' de Sosyo-Ekonomik Oncelikler, Hane gelirleri, Harcamalari ve Sosyo-Ekonomik İhtiyaçlar Üzerine Araştirma Oizisi. TÜSIAD, Istanbul.

Esmer, Yılmaz, Hamit Fışek and Ersin Kalaycioğlu (1987). *Türk Hanesinde Sosyo-Ekonomik Beklentiler ve Değişme*, Cilt III, Türkiye' de Sosyo-Ekonomik Öncelikler, Hane gelirleri, Harcamaları ve Sosyo-Ekonomik İhtiyaclar Üzerine Araştırma Dizisi. TÜSIAD, Istanbul.

Hamurdan, Yusuf Ö. (1976). *Türkiye' de İstihdamın Yapısı ve Yönlendirilmesi*, SPO, Ankara.

Kandiyoti, Deniz (1988). 'Bargaining with patriarchy', *Gender & Society*, vol. 2, no. 3.

Kazgan, Gülten (1979), 'Labor-force participation, occupational distribution, educational level and socioeconomic status of women in Turkish economy', in *Women in Turkish Society*, ed. Nermin Abadan-Unat, E.J. Brill, Leiden.

Kıray, Mübeccel B. (1964). *Ereğli – Ağır Sanayiden Önce Bir Sahil Kasabası*, SPO, Ankara (second edition 1982, İletişim Yayınları, Istanbul).

Öncü, Ayşe (1992). 'The transformation of the bases of social standing in contemporary society', in *Changing Turkish Society*, ed. Mübecel B. Kıray,

Indiana University Press: Bloomington, Indiana.

Özbay, Ferhunde (1979). 'The impact of education on women in rural and urban Turkey', in *Women in Turkish Society*, ed. Nermin Abadan-Unat, E.J. Brill, Leiden.

Özbay, Ferhunde (1982). 'Evkadınları', *Ekonomik Yaklaşım*, vol. 3, no. 7.

Özbay, Ferhunde (1985). 'The impact of social and economic transformations to the functions of the family in rural Turkey', in *Changes in Family in Turkey*, ed. T. Erder, Turkish Social Science Association, Ankara.

Özbay, Ferhunde (1987). 'Frauenleben', in *Turkei*, ed. Ömer Seven, VSA Verlag, Hamburg.

Özbay, Ferhunde (1988). 'Long-term demographic trends as factors contributing to the persistence of small producers in agriculture: the case of Turkey', paper presented at the Seventh World Congress of Rural Sociology, 25 June–2 July, Bologna.

Özbay, Ferhunde and Nefise Balamir (Bazoğlu) (1978). 'School attendance and its correlates in Turkish villages, 1975', unpublished project report, Hacettepe University, Ankara.

SIS (State Institute of Statistics) (1961). *1955 Turkish Population Census*, Ankara.

SIS (State Institute of Statistics) (1967). *1965 Turkish Population Census*, Ankara.

SIS (State Institute of Statistics) (1981). *1975 Turkish Population Census*, Ankara.

SIS (State Institute of Statistics) (1984). *1980 Turkish Population Census*, Ankara.

SIS (State Institute of Statistics) (1988). *1985 Turkish Population Census*, Ankara.

SPO (State Planning Organization) (1988). 'Türkiye' de Kadınlara İlişkin Veriler ve Çalışmalar', unpublished report, Ankara.

Stirling, Paul 1965. *Turkish Villages*, John Wiley & Sons, Inc., New York.

Timur, Serim 1972. *Türkiye' de Aile Yapısı*, Hacettepe University, Ankara.

Towards an Understanding of Gender Hierarchy in Turkey: A Comparative Analysis of Carpet-Weaving Villages

Günseli Berik

Introduction

Recent research on rural women in Turkey has begun to challenge the enduring images of rural women prevalent in Turkish literature, popular media and academic writing. Contrary to early portrayals of rural women as passive and oppressed, new representations show how they exercise power in shaping and improving the conditions of their lives (Sirman, Yalcin-Heckmann, this volume). Documentation of the multitude of gender arrangements in different parts of Turkey still remains to be done. An additional task, which I consider has not yet been adequately recognized as a research project in gender studies, is to identify the sources of the differing representations of rural Turkish women. One possible source (see Sirman, this volume) is researchers' use of different conceptual frameworks that are likely to lead to differing understandings of the gender systems in rural Turkey. This, however, may not be the only source of variation; variation may be manifested in tangible and striking gender arrangements that are discernible to a single researcher using the same conceptual framework in her/his research in each village. If so, then the typical response is to view these differing gender arranagements as simply 'cultural differences', i.e. as idiosyncratic and not susceptible to explanation. In my view, a further task is to determine whether or not there exists some general patterns within the diversity and if there is some systematic basis to the variation observed. This project requires an accumulation of case studies and comparative analyses.

My entry point into this project is my research on rural carpet-weavers,[1] during which I observed a regional diversity in the nature of gender inequalities and their transformational possibilities, over and above the general patterns across villages. Regional variations existed in the extent of men's control over women's labour power and weaving income, and the degree of gender inequalities in workload, consumption possibilities and access to schooling. Besides variations in measurable dimensions, there were also differences in the quality of relations between men and women (amicability, terseness or hostility and hierarchy between spouses). This exploratory examination provides a comparative discussion of the gender systems in four carpet-weaving villages, with the object of presenting a primarily synchronic picture of variation in their gender inequalities/arrangements and to relate them to the variation in the nature of agrarian transformation, the predominant forms of weaving organization and household organization. Specifically examined are the connections between different types of economic activity women engage in and the types of household structure they are a part of in order to identify the conditions under which the workload inequality between the sexes is greater and men exert greater control over women's labour power and income.

In examining gender inequalities/arrangements, I focus upon and isolate a few variables for anlysis. Given the scope of the paper, discussion is necessarily lean in detail, abstract and sketchy. The focus is not on marital/conjugal negotiations, women's strategies and action but rather to understand the structures and constraints that define women's work activities, relative workload, and decision-making power. Clearly, a comprehensive analysis of the gender systems requires an examination of gender dynamics, the actions of men and women and the structures that limit open/up possibilities for those actions. I consider these differing approaches in gender analysis as complementary.

This chapter first describes social relations under the three forms of production in carpet-weaving and their mutually reinforcing relationships with agrarian structures and forms of household organization. This will show that each form of carpet-weaving organization has different implications for weavers' workload and control over their labour power, and that each form of production flourishes in the midst of particular agrarian and household structures. Secondly, the nature of gender inequalities in workload and women's control over their labour power and income in four villages representative of different articulations of carpet-weaving forms, agrarian structure and household organization are discussed. Finally, some patterns across case studies are highlighted and the likely future directions for change in gender inequalities assessed. The conditional generalizations reached are intended as hypotheses to be explored in further research.

Carpet-weaving, agrarian structure and gender inequalities

The implications for gender inequalities of women's participation in carpet-weaving or of rural transformations in Turkey have not been extensively studied. However, the few available studies reveal that the nature of agrarian transformation is an important source of variation in women's living and working conditions. Kandiyoti (1984) argues that the extension of labour-intensive, cash-crop agriculture brings about an intensification of women's agricultural workload, while specialization in mechanized grain-production implies their retreat from agricultural labour. Ozbay's study (1982) reveals that heavy reliance on women's labour in agriculture stifles their chances for schooling. With regard to control over income, Ayata's case study of carpet-weaving in Kayseri (1987) mentions that weavers enjoy considerable bargaining power in spending weaving income, despite the fact that engaging in weaving does not alter the terms of their (limited) relationship to the world outside the home.

A more bleak yet fairly uniform picture with regard to gender relations in the household emerges from studies on carpet-weaving and other rural handicraft production in the Middle East and India (Afshar, 1985; Anti-Slavery Society, 1978; Mies, 1982). Based on her Iranian village case study, Afshar (1985) argues that as women became year-round carpet-weavers and their weaving brought in substantial cash incomes, men's grip over women tightened; they began to pressure women to work longer hours to complete carpets earlier, and daughters were deprived of schooling. Moreover, women's mediated relationship to the cash economy has continued, since carpets were sold and yarn was bought by men. In a similar vein, the Anti-Slavery Society (ASS) (1978) identifies an alarming increase in the use of child labour (from the age of 5) in Moroccan carpet workshops and factories as export demand grew in the 1970s. The ASS Report notes that families who are dependent on their childrens' meagre earnings are eager for them to work long hours under strict discipline, unhealthy conditions, and even without pay during a lengthy apprenticeship period. Finally, Mies' (1982) study shows that growth of lace production for export was accompanied by growing inequality between men and women. Impoverished peasant men either began to lead a parasitic existence on the basis of women's lacemaking or became traders marketing the lace produced by their wives. These studies show that, regardless of whether they engage in paid work at home or in factories and live in rural or urban areas, there is an increase in men's control over women's and children's labour power and product and an intensification of women's labour effort.

Carpet-weaving in rural Turkey

Since the early 1960s women's employment and income-earning possibilities in handwoven carpet production in rural Turkey have expanded parallel to the rapid process of industrialization and growth in the Turkish economy. The same period has also witnessed the expansion of labour-intensive agricultural cash-crop production, especially in coastal regions, while the central Anatolian plateau has specialized in mechanized grain-production. In rural areas, increased carpet-weaving has meant that in some regions, carpets traditionally woven for personal use became commodities, and in other regions, commodity production was introduced together with the initiation of weaving. Despite spreading towards Eastern Turkey in recent years, carpet-weaving today is still concentrated in the Western and Central regions of Turkey.

Currently, weaving is undertaken under three forms of production: petty-commodity; the putting-out system; and workshop production.[2] The key commonality of these three forms, which is relevant to the evaluation of the regional variation and changes in gender relations, is the fusion of kinship and work relations. Under all three forms, weaving does not introduce weavers to a new set of social relations, but represents a continuity of the social relations of which they are already a part. At home or in workshops, these women weave with their sisters, mothers and daughters, and at most with co-residents of the same village community. Moreover, the weaver's relationship to the last link in the chain of intermediaries, from the urban merchant-exporter down to the village level, is often not direct but through her male kin. In most cases, carpets or the woman's labour power are sold by her father, husband or father-in-law. Quite commonly, the local carpet dealer or the workshop owner is also a relative.

In spite of the common characteristic of kinship-based work relations in the three forms of production, the location of weaving makes a difference to a woman's control over her labour power. While the home weaver has control over the allocation of her labour time among various tasks during the working day, the workshop weaver's day is rigidly divided between weaving and various household-based activities. Moreover, the location of weaving affects how weavers are perceived by others, particularly by men in the household. Even if they maintain regular weaving schedules, home weavers are regarded as weaving in their 'spare time', while workshop weavers are perceived as 'cash-generators'. The separation of home and workplace seems to lead to overt pressures on workshop weavers to intensify their effort and to increase the time spent on weaving.

The form of organization of weaving has implications for both household and agrarian structure most compatible with weaving. There is a correspondence between forms of weaving and household structure: there is a higher incidence of nuclear household organization in regions of home weaving; and a higher incidence of extended households where workshop weaving is predominant. The division of labour among women in the household underlies this outcome. Workshop weaving is more compatible with the existence of larger or extended families that comprise a greater number of adult women. Where workshop weaving is predominant, the conflict between weaving work and weavers' reproductive responsibilities (childcare, domestic tasks) is minimized through adjustments in the division of labour among women in the household and even in the community. This resolution reinforces the extended or large family arrangement, protects the sexual division of labour in reproduction from challenges, and preserves gender inequalities in workload. It also result in a more rigid pattern of household division of labour compared to home-weaving, whereby young women specialize in weaving and old women in other (especially, reproductive) tasks.

As for the correspondence between forms of weaving and agrarian structure, it should be noted that the majority of carpet weaving households (79%) are agriculturalists who mostly cultivate their own land. Beyond this, however, it is difficult to make generalizations about the type of agrarian structures that characterize weaving villages. Weaving commonly co-exists with labour-intensive, diversified cash-crop agriculture with its year-round labour demands, as well as mechanized grain-agriculture, where labour demands are limited to at most a few months per year, and agricultural production is insufficient to support smallholders.[3] While agrarian structure does not affect the incidence of carpet-weaving, it does affect the form likely to be established and to dominate in a given region, and thus the volume of annual weaving output. Where the agricultural season is short or agriculture creates no demand for women's labour, weaving output and earnings are likely to be greater (given household needs for cash income and the sexual division of labour whereby weaving is women's work). In regions or mechanized agriculture there is a higher incidence of landlessness and greater dependence of rural populations on non-agricultural incomes. Thus, workshop production is most suited to villages practising mechanized agriculture, as merchants and intermediaries are guaranteed a year-round supply of labour for weaving and find it is profitable to establish workshops.

In contrast, for smallholder households that engage in diversified farming both the time allocated to weaving and the need for non-agricultural incomes will be more limited. Thus, home-weaving is particularly well-suited to villages practising diversified agriculture, where women engage in weaving during the brief, non-agricultural season.

Based on the foregoing analysis, two patterns can be identified: (1) workshop weaving prevails in regions where there exists a high incidence of extended family households and mechanized agriculture with its unequal land distribution; (2) home-weaving prevails in smallholder, nuclear households which also engage in diversified, labour-intensive cash-crop agriculture. In both patterns, conflicting demands for reproductive tasks are resolved. However, the former pattern maximizes, while the latter minimizes annual carpet output. In my study, as well as villages that are representative of these two patterns there are also villages that exemplify two different articulations of weaving organization, agrarian structure and household organization. The following case studies examine these four patterns and draw the implications of each for the state of gender inequalities (see Table 6.1).

Case studies

The four different articulations of carpet weaving forms, agrarian structure and household organization yield distinct opportunities and limitations for women who live in their midst. Each articulation, represented by a case study village, has clear implications for women's living and working conditions.

In each case study gender relations and inequalities in the context of 'production' and 'consumption' activities are evaluated. The sexual division of labour as the basic concept, and the associated concepts of control over women's labour power and women's workload relative to men form the focus for production. Control over labour power refers to the relative independence of women weavers from men and older women (especially mothers-in-law) in the household with respect to the use of their labour power. For gender inequalities in consumption the focus is on women's control over income and household expenditures, as well as gender differences in the nature of consumption.

Case 1: Konya, represents an articulation of workshop weaving with mechanized grain-agriculture and extended family-households. Characteristic of this articulation is the maximization of men's and old women's control over young women's labour power and the volume of annual carpet output.

In Konya the introduction of commodity production in carpets in the late 1950s coincided with the process of agricultural mechanization, which resulted in the elimination of labour-intensive harvesting tasks undertaken by men and women under subsistence grain-farming. These changes led to the emergence of a rigid sexual division of labour whereby men and women specialize in different non-agricultural activities: all young women are carpet-weavers; men engage in wage work in mining and seasonal construction or in petty trade. Only a few

Table 6.1 Typology of Carpet-Weaving Villages

Agrarian Structure

Form of production in	Crop	Land Ownership	Labour use	Household organization
Case 1: Konya				
Workshop	Grains	High proportion of landless	Unpaid family labour	High incidence of extended family households
Case 2: Milas				
Petty commodity production (home)	Diversified cash-crop	Smallholder	Unpaid family labour	Nuclear
Case 3: Isparta				
Workshop	Diversified cash-crop	Smallholder	Unpaid family labour	Relatively high incidence of extended families
Case 4: Nigde-2				
Petty commodity production (home)	Limited grains	High proportion of landless	Very limited unpaid family labour	Nuclear

men farm on behalf of small landowners.

The high incidence of extended family households (50% of sample households) and the associated age hierarchy among women maintain discipline in workshops and also resolve the contradiction between weaving and reproductive work. Workshop relations are an extension of kinship relations, which recreate the age hierarchies that effectively police young women's behaviour at work. The weaving days, which extend from sunrise to sunset, are regulated by the morning and evening prayers. This means that, excluding lunch breaks, the summer weaving day is 13–14 hours and the winter weaving day is eight hours. On the longest days weavers must still attend to household chores at the end of the day, and the fact that their weaving hours start at dawn does not excuse them from staying up as late as other household members: men can sleep late, but women must adjust to shorter sleeping hours.

In addition to their heavy workload, weavers have no control over decisions related to weaving work (such as, when to start weaving, when to take a break or retire from weaving, choice of workshop). For example, the system of advanced wage payments results in rigid work schedules. When the weavers' male kin are paid large sums in return for weavers' future labour, this ties the workers' labour for long periods of time and eliminates the flexibility of taking a day off. Moreover, certain practices combine to raise the intensity of work and extend the time devoted to weaving; for example, weavers compete with each other to complete carpets earlier. These competitions, which are supported by family members, appeal to weavers because they help alleviate the boredom associated with the work. There is also a practice, known as 'pocket money carpet', recently instituted by workshop owners in agreement with weavers' male kin as a way of increasing the labour time devoted to weaving. According to this practice, weavers who continue weaving during their seven to ten days break between each completed carpet can control the resulting earnings. Finally, other practices, which indicate tight control over women's labour power, such as village endogamy, are reinforced.

As for women's control over weaving income, participation in decision-making over household expenditures and consumption level, striking age and gender inequalities were observed in this village. Weavers exercise control over part of their income, but this does not exceed one-sixth of annual weaving income and is under the weaver's control only if she devotes extra time to weaving.[5] This income can be used only to purchase small items, such as clothing or goods for the weavers' dowry. The main part of weaving income is spent on subsistence goods, consumer durables and construction or repair of houses. In addition, household elders' pilgrimage trips to Mecca, educational expenses for brothers, and conspicuus consumption by men are among the main categories of spending out of weaving earnings. Consumption patterns in this village are marked by inequalities. For example, a father whose three daughters weave undertook six pilgrimage trips on the basis of weaving income. Or a husband whose wife weaves for 14 hours in the summer heat in a cramped workshop went on a vacation with his friends to the seaside.

In sum, we observe that as a result of the expansion of weaving in this village, men's control over women's labour power, their workload, and gender inequality in workload has increased. Weaving allows early separation of young couples from the extended family household and thereby alleviates age-based supervision of young women, but it also strengthens the extended family household because of the conflict between workshop weaving and care of young children. While weavers' control over a portion of their earnings is a positive development, it is important not to overlook the limited nature of this control.[6]

Case 2: Milas, represents a fairly typical configuration of smallholder, diversified, labour-intensive, cash-crop agriculture with petty commodity production in carpet-weaving and nuclear household organization. There are three other examples of this type of configuration in my study, and in all four cases weaving is a secondary source of village income, even though for the small proportion of landless or for young families, it is critical for subsistence.

In Milas, a longstanding weaving tradition was revived in the early 1960s when weaving became the primary source of cash income. In the late 1960s, however, the relative importance of weaving income and the intensity of carpet-weaving declined following the introduction of tobacco farming. Today, tobacco and olive oil are the main sources of income for most households and weaving is carried out in a four-month period between the cultivation and harvesting of these two crops. Both men and women engage in all the sub-activities comprising fieldwork, with a task division within each sub-activity (e.g. in tobacco planting men prepare the soil, women plant the individual seedlings). Since each weaver weaves at home and is not subject to her mother-in-law's supervision, she controls the allocation of her time and has flexibility in carrying out her daily tasks. Moreover, the flexible sexual division of labour in agriculture is associated with a flexible sexual division of labour in weaving: a few young men weave along with their mothers or wives. In short, as a result of the predominance of smallholder agriculture in the village and the diversification of economic activities over time, the workload of both men and women has increased, but both sexes share this increasaed workload through a flexible sexual division of labour.

In this village, gender inequalities in consumption and control over income are not striking. Weavers have considerable say in spending both the weaving and other household income. Weaving earnings are spent on daily consumption items, consumer durables and agricultural inputs, and also on the schooling expenses of girls as well as boys. What is striking in Milas is that daughters commonly continue their schooling (albeit usually for fewer years than boys) beyond elementary school.

Case 3: Isparta, represents an articulation of workshop production with diversified, labour-intensive, cash-crop agriculture, and the predominance of nuclear households (70% of the village sample). Agriculture is based on such crops as opium poppies, sugar-beets, potatoes, onions, sesame, and roses, all of which entail labour-intensive production processes and rely on unpaid family labour. Both men and women engage in agricultural field work, with considerable flexibility of sexual division of labour, whereby specialization is at the level of sub-activities of field work (e.g. men engage in planting, women in weeding).

Carpet-weaving was introduced in the village in the early 1950s, both under the putting-out system and in workshops. While agricultural diversification since the late 1960s and 1970s increased the demands for women's labour in agriculture, it has not displaced carpet-weaving. Instead, it led to the institutionalization of flexible weaving schedules in the growing number of workshops, and to adjustments in the age division of labour among women in the household. The fact that workshop weaving is not as rigidly structured and disciplined as in Konya can be attributed to the greater agricultural workload of women in Isparta and the consequent difficulty of maintaining weaving schedules in the summer months. The payment system in Isparta workshops is based on a daily accounting of each weaver's output, in order to make intermittent attendance possible. The daily work hours are fixed but shorter than in Konya – ten hours in summer, eight in winter. In addition, workshop weaving co-exists with home-weaving (under the putting-out system), which provides a more flexible work schedule than a workshop. Since, in order to concentrate on a broader range of work responsibilities, women withdraw from weaving at an earlier age than those in Konya, workshop weavers tend to be younger and belong to the same age group. Partly as a result of the narrower age range of weavers less supervision by kin is built into the daily operation of workshops, and consequently relations among workshop weavers are more harmonious compared to Konya weavers.

As in Milas, ` so in Isparta, gender inequalities in consumption are not striking. As a result of the weekly payment method, weaving earnings are used only for daily consumption expenditures and weavers have considerable say in this spending.

Case 4: Nigde-2, represents a combination of petty commodity production in carpet-weaving with mechanized grain-agriculture and a high incidence of landlessness and nuclear household organization. What distinguishes this case from others is the virtual absence of agricultural production due to the soil's infertility and acute landlessness. These characteristics render this village a quintessential context for the growth of rural home industries. As in Konya, mechanized grain-farming on a limited scale is carried out by a few sharecropper farmers on behalf of small landholders. There are no seasonal or permanent wage employment possibilities in the village.

The population has remained constant for several years now because of outmigration. Were it not for the revival of a longstanding weaving tradition since the 1960s, the village's lack of economic viability would have resulted in its being abandoned. Most households eke out an existence based on non-agricultural income sources: carpet-weaving; animal husbandry; men's seasonable migrant labour and other activities, such as trucking, which they are able to undertake by pooling two or three households' savings. However, most young men have no work and depend on their wives' weaving earnings. Similar to home weavers elsewhere, relative to workshop weavers these women have more flexibility in combining reproductive work with weaving. Since many husbands are away for most of the year and nuclear households are the norm in the village, these women have greater autonomy in their daily lives.

Due to the virtual absence of agricultural production and the fact that weaving income is directed to investment, consumption levels are very low. Even at this limited level, gender inequality in consumption is evident. Men's expenditures on tea, coffee and cigarettes – considered by both sexes in other villages to be their entitlement – are the main items in the household budget. We should also note that women have no property rights in the trucks that are bought by pooling their earnings.

Discussion and conclusions

These four case studies have identified variations in the extent of men's and older women's control over weavers' labour power and income as well as gender inequalities in workload and consumption, and have attempted to explain these differences in terms of the form of organization in weaving, agrarian structure and household organization. Below, some tentative conclusions are presented as hypotheses to be explored in further research.

Gender inequalities in workload (and in consumption) are more acute and the sexual division of labour is more rigid where mechanized grain-agriculture prevails or where agriculture is not a viable economic activity (Cases 1 and 4), in comparison with villages of diversified agriculture (Cases 2 and 3). In the former cases, where agriculture does not provide subsistence for the majority of households, women become full-time carpet-weavers. The fact that women weave does not reduce their non-weaving workload, and may even reduce men's workload in cases where they remain unemployed and can afford not to migrate to urban areas. Here, it should be noted that the overall workload of weavers (as distinct from gender inequality in workload) in villages of diversified smallholder agriculture (Cases 2 and 3) may be greater than that of weavers in villages of mechanized grain-farming (Cases 1 and 4). Without full consideration of working conditions and hours, however, this conclusion is tentative.

With respect to control over labour power, this research has shown that weaving in a workshop is associated with women having less control over their labour power compared to home-weaving. This conclusion is based not only on the observation that women who weave at home have greater flexibility in allocating their time but also the fact that workshop weavers have little or no say in making a wider range of decisions that arise in workshop weaving. Moreover, once women become wage workers outside the home and a sharp division between weaving and other tasks is established, there is greater occasion to intensify pressures on weavers for them to generate as much output as possible during the time set aside for weaving.[7] However, there are regional differences in the extent to which workshop weaving becomes compulsive. Differences in conditions of work in workshops between Isparta and Konya regions are attributable to differences in agrarian structure. A narrower range of economic alternatives in the Konya region sustains more rigid work schedules and is associated with greater control over women by men and older women in the household. In the Isparta region, on the other hand, diversified cash-crop agriculture that offers a wider range of economic alternatives is associated with less pressure on weavers.

Comparing Cases 1 and 2 that lie at either end of the spectrum in terms of annual carpet output, we reach the following conclusion: petty commodity producer carpet-weavers located in predominantly smallholder agricultural households (Case 2) have more control over their labour power and income, and bear a relatively equal share of the household productive workload in comparison with workshop weavers in regions of mechanized grain-agriculture where a relatively unequal land distribution exists (Case 1). This means that, where the relative importance of weaving income is the highest (and agriculture inadequate for subsistence of the household) women are worse off relative to men in terms of the criteria identified.

Finally, let us briefly speculate on the possibilities for transformation of gender inequalities in Case 1 and Case 2. This exploration is based on an assessment of the possible dynamic associated with carpet-weaving and the agrarian structure. In this regard, the Konya village is the interesting case. While the gender inequalities are sharper than elsewhere, due to the dynamic attributable to carpet-weaving, there is also greater transformative potential than elsewhere. In Konya, where workshop organization is an extension of kinship relations and embodies age hierarchies among women, participating in collective labour outside the home does not offer better prospects for women to challenge gender hierarchy than does carpet-weaving in the home. To the contrary, the spread of workshop weaving increases the economic value of women and hence leads to increased controls over them by men and older women in the household. However, this outcome might be seen as a short-term conservative effect on gender relations, since workshop weaving generates high earnings that allow earlier separation of young couples from extended family households. Thus, it can be expected that the decline of extended family households will erode age, and possibly, also gender hierarchies (albeit while intensifying the work burden of women in nuclear households). However, the declining incidence of extended family households occurs in a context where there is greater demand for higher knot-density and large carpets, hence an impetus for expanding workshop production. In order to expand production, carpet merchant-manufacturers will look for villages where agricultural incomes are low and hierarchical age and gender relations exist, and thereby create new Konyas. This implies that the transformative possibilities in the gender and age hierarchies in villages such as Konya will be checked by the mobility of capital.

By contrast, the Milas village (Case 2) represents a more static structure in comparison to Konya. In such villages the role of carpet-weaving in shaping gender relations is not significant. Here the dynamism derives from the main economic activity – agricultural production – and future changes in gender relations are likely to derive from changes in the agrarian structure, such as increasing landlessness.

Notes

1. The empirical evidence in this chapter comes from my research in 1983 in ten villages in Western and Central Turkey. The villages were selected on the basis of their representativeness in terms of the relations of production in both carpet-weaving and agriculture in rural Turkey. The quantitative data pertaining to weavers and their households is from structured interviews with 133 weavers. For a summary of the results of this study, see Berik (1987).

2. Petty commodity producers weave at home using looms and tools owned by the household, and purchase or prepare the yarn used. Upon completion, the carpet is sold, usually by the male head of household in regional or local markets. Under the putting-out system, weavers weave at home using the yarn, and sometimes the looms and tools, supplied by the carpet merchants' agents, who collect the completed carpets.

3. While Ayata (1987) considers labour-intensive, diversified cash-crop agriculture to be an unlikely setting for rural industrial activities, my study shows that the dependence of smallholders on non-agricultural incomes to meet a range of needs from basic consumption items to inputs for cash-crop agriculture explains the widespread participation in weaving activity in such contexts (Berik, 1987).

4. The association of extended family organization with a high proportion of landlessness in this study contrasts with findings of earlier studies for Turkey (Timur, 1981; Kandiyoti, 1984), and suggests that formation or longevity of extended households could be the outcome not only of household prosperity

but also of the inability to secure subsistence based on landholdings.

5. Ayata (1987: 79–80) discusses the existence of a similar practice in the Kayseri region, where a two-part wage exists and weavers control between 10% and 20% of weaving income. However, in contrast to the Konya case, the Kayseri weavers gain control over this small portion of their income without having to put in additional hours.

6. For a detailed analysis of the transformation of gender relations in this village with women's participation in wage labour, see Berik (1989).

7. It should be emphasized, however, that the conclusions regarding workshop production versus home production are based on the kind of relations prevalent in carpet workshops and cannot be generalized to all paid work outside the home.

Part III

Women in Public

7

Women and Education in Turkey

Fatma Gök

The relationship between women and education can be studied in two dimensions. The first dimension is the analysis of women's underrepresentation compared to men at all levels of the educational system. For example, the number of women educated in Turkey since the establishment of the republic is much smaller than that of men (I provide the relevant statistical data as an appendix to the chapter). The Turkish educational system has expanded and developed markedly since the formation of the republic in the 1920s. In a developing country an obvious inequality of women vis-à-vis men in every sphere of social and economic life is not unexpected. Certainly, it is important to document and analyse the undereducation of women, the history of women's education and the status of women's schooling (the number of females educated, the literacy rate, and the level of educational attainment).

However this is only the first dimension of inquiry about women and education. Another important way of studying the relationship between women and education is to focus on the educational process, including both formal and hidden curricula, the content of that education and the structural barriers to women's participation in the educational process. This second area of study addresses the social functions of education in the context of the sex–gender system which places women in subordination to men.

In this chapter I first of all examine the social functions of education and then go on to question whether education functions in the same way for women as for men. My attempt here is to contribute to the continuing discussion about the educational inequality of women in the context of Turkey. I believe that it is important to deal with both dimensions.

The social function of education

The process of education reproduces the dominant ideology of the society in which it takes part. This process takes place in conjunction with the realization of the other functions that the economic base demands of an educational system for its reproduction. The social functions of education can be summarized as follows:

1. The educational system supplies the necessary labour-power by selecting and training people for various positions. This training process is realized in such a way that it meets the demands of the existing social structure. Thus the educational process helps to maintain the already established system of social stratification, and to render the existing social division of labour legitimate, natural and inevitable for each successive generation.
2. The transmission of the cultural and political values of a given society through education achieves the socialization of the individual. Individuals' internalization of a society's values solidifies the definition and expectations of proper citizenship.
3. As the educational system undertakes the above functions, it inevitably reproduces a social system based on the opposition of social classes and gender.

Let me try to formulate the social functions of education, as outlined, from the perspective of women. During the educational process, as the dominant male ideology is reproduced in various ways, women are oriented towards a lower level of economic opportunity, and jobs and positions with less social prestige. Women are therefore driven into work which is a continuation and derivation of their family role, rather than choosing jobs which are directly concerned with production. For this reason we must question the generally held belief that education, and experience in particular formal education, is the most important factor in women's liberation.

Certainly, education has a liberating potential, but the limitations set by social structure must not be overlooked.

While education reproduces given social power structures, it also establishes the view that only the individual's personality and capabilities determine his or her social position. Education transmits the requisite skills and behaviour demanded by the economy to the young generation. This is accompanied by an internalization of an ideology which naturalizes the discrimination taking place along class and gender lines. The outcome of schooling is a process of legitimization. Rich or poor, boy or girl, the children finish school having been prepared for their social roles.

The quantity and quality of education women in Turkey have enjoyed since the foundation of the Turkish republic is still far from changing their social position. Men still hold the major decisionmaking power in Turkish society. Although most of the teachers at all levels of the educational system are female, almost all principals and supervisors are male. It is even thought odd when a women undertakes the decisionmaking role which is considered to be the male domain. The role that seems natural is for a woman to get married and struggle with the daily routine of intensive labour and wear herself out. Those who disregard these terms and go on to succeed in their chosen professions experience an unconventional life and usually prefer not to marry, or if they do, choose not to have any children.

In studying women's relationship to the educational system, documentation of the inequality and sexist practices behind the official statistics is insufficient. It becomes important to analyse the content of this relationship from the women's perspective. For instance, when we study women's role in maintaining the labour-force for economic production, it is not sufficient to understand this in terms of women's relation to the educational process, if we do not take into account women's predetermined role in the family. A more positive approach would analyse the educational process as the interaction of parallel spheres: the private sphere of family, child, etc.; and the public sphere of social and economic functions.[1] I emphasize the role of education as an interaction of public and private spheres for the following reason: the relation between achievement level at school and in life after school varies greatly between men and women. In other words, the relation between success in school and one's place in society is shaped by the sex–gender system. For example, in the USA girls achieve higher grades than boys in high school. About an equal number of male and female students graduate from high school, and more women enroll in higher education, but men graduating from college outnumber women.[2] Before higher education, girls' achievement level is better than boys'; they lose their advantageous position before they join the workforce. This simple fact, demonstrated by many studies in various parts of the world, proves that increasing the representation of women in schooling does not automatically yield women's equal participation in social and economic life. As well as examining women's participation in schooling we must consider the effect of education as part of the wider sex–gender systems which dictates women's future lives. Education as a social institution possesses only limited authority, being affected by wide-reaching social, economic and cultural dynamics. In addition to a number of other factors (class, ethnicity, race, geography) which influence the educational process, the sexist social structure shapes the outcome of women's education. Thus the issue of women's inequality and discrimination against women goes beyond the availability of educational opportunities to issues like the content of education and the sexist character of educational ideology. Furthermore, we must also look at whether legal and institutional guarantees exist in order to ensure the use of those skills and abilities which women have gained in the educational system.

Other significant matters influence the relationship between women and education, prominent among which are the special characteristics of the Third World countries like Turkey which influence women's level of consciousness. For example, the sensitivity of rural or urban areas towards educational equality is open to family, social, cultural and regional variables. In rural areas, increasing educational opportunities are mostly utilized by young boys, whereas the education of young girls is tolerated only up to a certain age. The level of women's consciousness, and whether women question those socially prescribed roles might become significant factors in explaining their post-school positions.

The situation in Turkey

What faces us in Turkey, in terms of the social function of education and its effects on institutions as well as on women, is far from satisfactory. The various gender-based discriminations which women experience throughout their educational lives serve to perpetuate those values which society attributes to women.

In formal education, compulsory primary-school education is universal. It therefore has the potential to provide equal further access, and shake sexist values by giving girls the chance to develop their capacities, in order to break free from male dominance. Unfortunately, schools, which are inevitably a part of sexist society, make no effort to change the traditional female role, and children are made to abide by cultural norms. This normalization process is accomplished through a number of factors, primarily by textbooks, which are written from the perspective of the dominant male ideology and indeed are mostly written by men.[3] As we humorously notice in the Turkish textbooks, Ali plays ball and Suna plays with dolls; fathers earn a living while mothers go shopping and prepare dinner. The quotation below from a first-grade primary-school book shows us the drastic situation:

Made-up dolls, sparkling balls, kittens, dogs, miniature pianos. . . . There is a kitchenette. Inside it there are shiny plates, pots. A tap is fixed on to the kitchen wall, when it is turned on water runs out. . . .

Defne was happy when she saw all this. 'What lovely toys,' she said. There were some dwarfs beside the toys. They were smiling at her.

'Which one do you like most? We will give it to you,' said one of the dwarfs.

'The kitchenette,' replied Defne.

Then they showed her a clock which played a pleasant tune when they wound it up. Defne said,

'Give me this too, so that I can take it to my brother. He is ill in bed. He could listen to the tune and enjoy it.'

'No,' replied the dwarf, 'You may only choose one of them, the kitchenette or the clock.'

'Then I shall take the clock and leave the kitchenette,' said Defne.

Defne had given up her own choice for her brother. Her behaviour pleased the dwarfs, so they gave her the kitchenette as well. Defne gave out a cry of joy and woke up to realize it was all a dream.[4]

The majority of the teachers who work at these conventional

institutions implement a rigid national curriculum which fosters the dominant ideology.

In general, while male and female identities are developed in the middle school, the situation becomes more striking in the vocational–technical schools. Boys and girls are placed in schools which put them into totally different environments: while girls are led into fields which are consistent with their female roles, boys are led towards productive fields, such as carpentry, pottery and applied electrical work. The fields where women predominate are less prestigious, have lower earning capacities, are more labour-intensive, and require less intellectual development. We can clearly see that the state organizes and supports this discriminatory system in the vocational–technical schools. Although differences according to students' class backgrounds exist, we can more or less come to a general conclusion. While women in Turkish society are in theory encouraged to be producers rather than consumers and to participate in economic life, in practice they are expected to undertake a narrow range of jobs which society sees fit for them – such as tailoring, nursing, teaching, and secretarial work – which develop neither creative nor intellectual powers. Another important development with regard to women is that religious functionary schools have become widespread over the past thirty years in Turkey, becoming one of the mainstays of the educational system and a back-up for religious politics. The enormous expansion of these schools has become a matter of concern for many sectors of Turkish society. The over-expansion of these schools gives us important clues as to the extent to which state educational policies are formulated against women's interests.

In higher educational institutions, male–female inequality reaches a more dramatic level. Women are handicapped by this since it is here that the production of knowledge and the training of the necessary labour for higher skills takes place. The number of women who attend a higher educational institution is less than half the number of men, especially in those schools which prepare students for highly valued and economically better positioned jobs. The structure of higher educational institutions benefits certain groups and classes, and this discrimination is deeply felt among women. As the income of families becomes more scarce, the possibility of girls being sent to colleges in order to further their education becomes difficult.

Conclusion

In order to understand fully the relationship between women and education one must see more than simple discrimination in terms of quantity, but must develop an approach that deals with the social functions of education from women's perspective. Important issues such as sensitivity towards the condition of women, the quality and content of education, the ways of transmitting this content, and the structure of educational institutions could be examined with this kind of approach.

Although schools exist within a male-dominated society, they have a certain degree of autonomy. They are crucial because they can play an important role in the process of social transformation. While generally they reproduce inequality along class, sex and race lines, these are distinct from the major social institutions, such as workplaces, in that they are inherently much less hierarchical and much more participative. Whether among students or teachers, the female–male ratio tends to be more equal than in other social institutions.

Because schools transmit and produce knowledge, they can be autonomous from the economic process, and have the potential of promoting critical hearts and minds. What we need is to bring to light the potential power of education, without expecting it to transform the whole of society.

Appendix

Some Selected Indicators of the Inequality of the Female–Male Ratio in the Turkish Educational System

Table 7.1 Ratio of Female to Male Students in Primary and Secondary Education in Turkey, 1986–87 (%)

	Female	Male
Primary school	47	53
Middle school	35	65
Vocational–technical middle school	32	68
High school	43	57
Vocational–technical high school	28	72

Source: State Institute of Statistics, *Ministry of Education Statistics 1986–1987, Formal Education*, Ankara, 1988.

Table 7.2 Literacy Rate According to Gender (%)

Year	Male	Female	Total
1935	29.35	9.81	19.25
1940	36.20	12.92	24.55
1945	43.67	16.84	30.22
1950	45.34	19.35	32.37
1955	55.79	25.52	40.87
1960	53.59	24.83	39.49
1965	64.04	32.83	48.72
1970	70.31	41.80	56.21
1975	76.02	50.47	63.62
1980	79.94	54.65	67.45
1985	86.35	68.02	77.29

Source: State Institute of Statistics, *Social and Economic Characteristics of Population, 1985 Population Census.*

Table 7.3 Secondary School Enrolment Rate (%)

Year	Male	Female	Total
1946	11.9	12.7	12.1
1951	18.9	13.1	17.2
1956	36.8	25.3	33.2
1961	42.0	25.0	36.4
1966	46.5	28.5	40.1
1971	51.3	29.5	42.7
1976	49.8	30.4	41.6
1980	50.3	33.0	42.0
1987	58.4	39.0	49.5

Source: Numbers are calculated from Ministry of Education, *Turkish Education at the 50th Anniversary of the Republic*, Istanbul, 1973; State Institute of Statistics, *Annual Statistics, 1976–1978*; State Institute of Statistics, *Secondary School Statistics, 1980–1981.*

Table 7.4 Rate of Schooling at High-School Level (%)

Year	Male	Female	Total
1935	2.7	0.8	1.8
1945	2.9	0.7	1.8
1950	1.9	0.5	1.2
1955	2.6	1.0	1.9
1960	6.5	2.4	4.6
1965	7.8	2.9	5.4
1970	14.2	5.7	9.9
1975	14.1	6.2	10.7
1980	15.2	9.1	12.3
1985	15.6	11.6	13.6

Source: Numbers are calculated from Ministry of Education, *Turkish Education at the 50th Anniversary of the Republic*, Istanbul, 1973; State Institute of Statistics, *1975–1980, 1985 Population Census, Social and Economic Characteristics of Population*, Ankara.

Table 7.5 Female Students at the Higher Educational Level (%)

Year	Female students
1927	11
1930	13
1935	15
1940	20
1945	19
1950	17
1960	20
1965	21
1970	21
1975	22
1980	26
1985	32

Note: The rate of increase in 1980 and 1985 is somewhat misleading. When we look at women graduating from higher educational institutions we have somewhat different rates which are 28%, 23%, 23% and 22% for the years of 1975, 1979, 1980 and 1985.

Source: Percentages are calculated from the following resources: Ministry of Education, *Turkish Education at the 50th Anniversary of Turkish Republic 1973*; State Institute of Statistics, *Annual Statistics 1987*, Ankara, 1987.

Notes

1. Gail P. Kelly and Carolyn M. Eliot, eds, *Women's Education in the Third World: Comparative Perspectives*, State University of New York Press, Albany 1982, p. 4.

2. J.H. Ballantine, *The Sociology of Education: A Systematic Analysis*, Prentice-Hall, Englewood Cliffs, NJ 1983, pp. 82, 83.

3. All the textbooks except one, which my son had in his first grade, were written by men. This can be interpreted as a cause and the result of the sexist system.

4. Beşir Göğüş, *Turkish for Primary Schools*, Ankara 1987.

Rural Women and Modernization in Southeastern Anatolia

Yakın Ertürk

The status of women in Turkey, both political and academic, has long been viewed within the context of the degree to which rights granted to women under the Atatürk reforms have expanded to various regions and sectors of society, and the level of women's representation in the public sphere.[1] Although it is well acknowledged in all circles that the reforms have not gained universal acceptance and practice, it has however been noted that the success achieved so far surpasses comparable developments, even in Western societies which are assumed to be more advanced in the field of women's emancipation. For example, figures show that only 3 per cent of lawyers and 6 per cent of doctors in the United States are women, whereas in Turkey the figures are 18.7 per cent and 15 per cent respectively (Öncü, 1981: 184).

Observable achievements in women's rights came to be understood as an inevitable component, or even a criterion, of Turkey's aspirations and struggle towards Westernization and contemporary values. As such, the 'woman issue' came to be interpreted as the need to spread modernizing processes to the masses.'[2] Eastern Turkey was thus regarded as being at the very bottom rung of the modernization process.

In the 1980s, the radical policies of economic liberalization further reinforced this understanding of modernization. However, at the same time the fact that economic and political determinants are gender biased, often operating to the disadvantage of women, became increasingly recognized. It is emphasized in many of the contributions to this volume that women are extensively put to work in Turkey, irrespective of whether in the east or west, countryside or city, agriculture or industry. Yet women are systematically excluded from the decisionmaking processes in all sectors. Politics, no doubt, is the most manifest institution in this regard.[3] Women's exclusion from active politics has the following implications:

1. A neglect of gender-related structures and issues in policy formulation, or leaving the matter to men on behalf of women.
2. A gap between the sphere of political struggle towards establishing democratic principles and institutions, and the sphere of everyday life in which the basic values of the society are reproduced.

As a result women who, in accordance with Kemalist reforms and understanding, have achieved significant positions in various occupational structures, have not been able to show a parallel participation in processes of policy formulation and decisionmaking. In cases where women have taken part in the latter, they have done so according to rules of a professional world which inherently reflects male experience. In other words, institutionalized politics at local, national, and international levels is, more or less, a male domain which is cut off from the processes of everyday life. Women who go back and forth between the two worlds often face the dilemma of having to pursue a split life, which may contain conflicting demands and role models. The process, of course, is not free of contradictions. Women in the course of daily affairs unavoidably impose alternative gender roles, at home and at work, thus challenging conventional modes of conduct.

Traditional forms of social order, on the other hand, are based on some degree of complementarity between male and female activity, and therefore there is no clear division of society into two separate domains of everyday life and politics (or decisionmaking). This is not to overlook the widespread crude oppression of women under traditional patriarchal power-relations, but rather to emphasize the fact that traditional structures and their reproductive mechanisms comprise more of an integrated, interlinked entity. Women as part of such a totality have greater access to the means through which they can exert control over the conditions of their life. Modernization, on the other hand, superimposes modern/secular structures on to the traditional order without necessarily fully integrating women, thus limiting or destroying their ability to exercise control. The most contradictory and striking examples of this phenomenon have been observed in southeastern Turkey. The specificity of the region can be attributed to (1) its historically autonomous status vis-à-vis central institutions; and (2) its internal structures of kinship, class and ethnicity.

This chapter will attempt to discuss the experience of southeastern Anatolia within the diverse patterns of change in Turkey and will focus on how rural women are affected by and cope with the rapid social transformations.

The modernization process

Particularly in the last three decades the process of modernization – with expanding market mechanisms, state institutions and, more recently, state-initiated development projects – has accelerated the formation of new linkages between rural communities and the outside world (both national and international).

The totality of these processes, which can be called rural transformation, encompasses a wide range of changes, such as the spread of rules of citizenship, secular civil codes, formal education, rural infrastructure, agricultural mechanization, rural migration, commodification of agricultural production and consumption, restructuring of intra-household relations and more symbolic changes in meaning and identity-construction, among others. These transformations have advanced somewhat later in the eastern regions compared to other parts of the country, and the outcome has been perhaps the most contradictory. Nomadic pastoralism, small-scale subsistence farming, petty commodity-production, landlordism and large-scale commercial agriculture coexist side by side. In addition to such diversities, the region is also characterized by strong ethnic and kinship relations.

The process of modernization, with all its diversities, is in fact a manifestation of national integration. Impact of these changes on the lives of rural women will be examined under two headings: institutional integration, and rural development projects. The latter, no doubt, is but a tool of the former. However, such projects are undertaken in order to control the direction of the process of development, and therefore need to be examined separately.

Institutional integration

The term institutional integration is used here in the most general sense, to describe a process of incorporation of the eastern regions into the market economy and their subjugation to the state through economic, social, political and cultural institutions.[4] This has not, however, been a technical process proceeding in a unidirectional manner, but rather one in which local traditional structures have responded and restructured themselves under the pressures of encroaching socioeconomic forces. At the very basic level of survival, structural adjustments have been possible through a restructuring of household relations and division of labour which has had direct consequences for the use of female labour in domestic and market production, as well as for women's ability to exercise control over their own activities and the wider processes in which they function. Rural women's role in agricultural production, although limited in the eastern regions (Aydın, 1986; Ertürk, 1980; 1988; Yalçın-Heckmann, 1991) has been central to research and discussions for the past ten to fifteen years (Özbay 1979; Sirman 1980, Balamir 1984; Kandiyoti 1990). Yet the implications of legal and cultural change for women's daily existence have not yet been systematically studied. It is this aspect of the socio-economic integration of south-eastern Turkey, particularly with respect to Kurdish women, which is most noteworthy. The contradictions of integration have, at times, put women in totally alien situations in which their conventional methods of survival have become ineffective. Many of the women over 30 years of age in the region do not speak Turkish, the official language; many are married by religious law, which is not recognized under the modern, secular legal system; many are not even registered with the central population bureau, thus they do not officially exist.[5] Therefore the consequence of institutional integration or modernization is for these women an increasing marginalization and vulnerability within the requirements of the new and unfamiliar institutional order. This leaves women totally dependent upon local power structures in reproducing their daily existence. Hence the dependence of women on men, and of men on more powerful men, is reinforced as they try to cope with the demands of modern secular institutions.

The following incident, which was reported in the daily *Cumhuriyet* on 27 September 1987, is all too revealing of the contradictions women may confront. The report concerns Ayşe Ulaç, a woman in her forties who has lived all her life in her native Belliban subsettlement (*mezra*) of Uğurca village in Adıyaman province. Ayşe is the mother of eight; she has no schooling and does not speak Turkish. Her problems start when she applies to Adıyaman population bureau to legalize her religious marriage. It turns out that Ayşe does not have a record with the population bureau, and therefore cannot document her citizenship. She is instructed to apply to the security office, where she is given a document permitting her temporary residence just like a foreigner. In accordance with the 'foreigner' status, Ayşe cannot work without a special permit or gain legal custody of her children, and worst of all, she has a six-month residency permit which is subject to renewal. Failure to extend the permit in time may result in deportation! She receives the following response to her appeal from the Ministry of the Interior (Min. of Interior, Gn. Dir. of Population and Citizenship Affairs, Correspondence no. 38 217–236.117): 'The procedure followed by Adıyaman Security Directorate is in order. The document given to Ayşe Ulaç, who has no record with the population bureau and does not speak Turkish, by the Adıyaman Security Directorate is consistent with the law. Therefore, the complaint is rejected.' Although, the above incident may be considered an exceptional case, and perhaps motivated by factors which are not obvious, it is nevertheless significant in showing how vulnerable women can get when local and modern legal practices clash.

Research shows that, in villages which have remained relatively isolated from market forces and state institutions, women have remained more effective in exerting control over resource management and daily activity. Studies carried out in different parts of eastern Anatolia (Ertürk, 1976; 1987; 1988) reveal that, despite much variation, the conditions most conducive to women's participation (production, resource-management, decisionmaking) are found in villages where modernization is least institutionalized, characterized by small-producer households rather than large-scale agriculture, and mountain villages as opposed to plain villages. Since the groups within these categories rely more or less directly on household division of labour for their sustenance, women maintain an active role in household economy. This provides them with greater opportunities for negotiating their place in the relational network both at home and within the village community. It must be emphasized, however, that it is also women in this category who become a target of greater patriarchal control as their households become more intensely involved in the market and external institutions.

When modernization is considered from the viewpoint of basic infrastructural services the situation is reversed with regard to women. Since the less modernized villages lack sufficient roads, water, electricity, sewerage, labour-saving domestic technology and the like, the burden of underdevelopment falls immediately on women. For example, in one village in Erzurum, women walk two hours to obtain water. Depending upon the household's water needs and number of women available the trip to the water source may have to be repeated several times a day, and fetching water is but a small portion of women's overall responsibilities. There is no doubt that modernization does reduce the drudgery, particularly of domestic production. However, in the long run, an improved rural infrastructure necessarily leads to gender and class biased processes, as it stimulates the diffusion of market forces and state mechanisms (Yotopoulos and Mergos, 1986).

Can this process be reversed in favour of women (as well as small producers, the landless and other marginal rural groups) through the contemporary tool of modernization, namely rural development projects? Such projects are in theory adapted to eradicate poverty, low levels of productivity and inequalities in the Third World. Practice, in this regard, has not fared so well. The next section discusses Turkey's experience in rural development projects with a focus on rural women.

Rural development projects

Rural development projects in Turkey are directly linked to the regional policies which aim to reduce regional disparities between eastern and western regions. Concern for the underdevelopment of the eastern provinces has gained greater recognition in the 1980s, with the intensification of separatist armed conflicts.

To redress the existing regional disparities, a planned rural development approach was adapted to supplement the free market economy model. Accordingly, in 1971 the Department for Less Developed Regions (DLDR) was established within the State Planning Organization (SPO). The DLDR declared twenty-eight provinces[6] less developed (LD) regions, to be given priority in development through planned project intervention. Most of the LD provinces are located in eastern and southeastern Turkey. Several projects of varying scope and size have been designed and implemented since the late 1970s.[7] Among these, some of the major ones are Çorum-Çankırı (1976–82); Erzurum (1982–89); Bingöl-Muş (1989 and since); and Yozgat Rural Development Project (YRDP), which became effective in 1991. In addition to these, there are numerous small-scale sectoral projects.[8]

Rural development experience, in Turkey, with regard to women, can be examined within the context of four models:[9]

1. Projects without a gender orientation.
2. Projects with a women component.
3. Special women's projects.
4. Integrated rural development projects.

The bulk of the projects implemented or underway have been of the first and second type. Those of the second type – i.e. projects with a women component – almost without exception emphasize conventional women's tasks, such as handicrafts and home economics, and totally exclude women from extension and training activities of agricultural and livestock production. A beekeeping project in Giresun provides the only example of a production-oriented women's project. YRDP is an example of the first type of integrated project. It has been designed to achieve community participation by supporting village-level organi-zations with related external networks (governmental organi-zations, NGOs, financial credit, extension, market, etc.) and provide the organizational context in which target groups – men and women alike – participate in identifying and planning project interventions. If the project is implemented as designed, YRDP would set a model for a participatory development approach which aims to integrate rather than marginalize women within the modernization process.

By and large, however, project interventions have been far from satisfactory in reversing the gender bias of development.[10] Most projects are prepared by a team of technical experts[11] who concentrate on devising techniques to increase agricultural productivity and household income-levels. Since rural house-holds are conceptualized as autonomous commercial farming systems – internally unified and altruistic – the differential status of gender- and age-groups are overlooked. Furthermore, a culturally specific protectiveness over women in the southeast is taken for granted by the technical experts, who interpret the varying degrees of sex-segregation as immutable patterns which act as inherent obstacles for development agents – who are mainly men – to deliver development packages to women producers. Hence, a major bias is introduced from the outset, often resulting in avoidance of the issue rather than challenging it. As a result, modernization promotes the segregation of women, with status attached to women's domesticity.

Conclusion

The objective of the foregoing discussion was to provide an overview of how rural women in southeastern Anatolia have experienced modernization, as it is manifested in the process of national integration, through the mechanisms of formal state institutions and planned development projects. This endeavour does not claim to exhaust the wide range of existing situations, but merely to outline the most commonly observed patterns which I have identified through research and project activities in the region since 1976.

It has been argued that the most developed villages are those in which women's dependence, seclusion and marginalization are the greatest. Conditions for women's effective control over the forces governing their life are most promising among small producers and in peripheral villages where women's domesticity has not yet become fully institutionalized. Paradoxically, women from these households and villages are the most constrained by time due to their heavy workloads.

Overcoming the drawbacks of modernization for women in southeastern Turkey appears to be directly linked to the process of pluralist democracy, which would enable grassroots participation in determining the direction and method of change. This objective challenges and even contradicts the modes of behaviour so commonly promoted within current political trends. No doubt a major concern in this regard is the ethnic conflict in which Kurdish women are drawn, more and more, into nationalistic aspirations which tend to override gender contradictions. The ethnic issue, however, is not the focus of the current discussion. However, reference should here be made to two other political trends: (1) Fundamentalist movements, which define the role of women within the context of a patriarchal Islamic ideology, pose an alternative model. This trend does not contradict but rather complements and supports the nationalist ideologies mentioned above. (2) Government policies which systematically favour non-secular, conservative notions of women, family and morality, and as a result infringe upon efforts to reverse gender-biased perspectives and practices.

Given these trends, the desired objectives may not be so easy to reach within government-initiated programmes. However, despite the official approach, the choice of experts and planners, in promoting one set of principles over others, can either reinforce the subordination of women or produce new contradictions and alternatives to facilitate far-reaching and fundamental change. The latter alternative requires strong NGO involvement, not only in acting as advocacy groups, but also in producing alternative models supportive of grassroots initiatives. This poses a challenge for the women's movement and organizations, which are currently largely urban-based and middle-class-oriented. Addressing issues which tackle the diversity of women's experiences would not only contribute to the advancement of women's organizations but would also enable them to gain an effective voice in the political arena.

Notes

1. Efforts to 'modernize' women's status is not restricted to the republican period. During the early 1800s, Ottoman intellectuals attempted to reconcile their Islamic identity with Western values. Some concrete measures taken in this direction were the teacher training school for girls opened in 1863; the American girls' college which was initially opened in 1871 for Christians and which later admitted Muslim women as well. In addition, there was the publication of a women's magazine in 1895 and, finally, the first women's university, established in 1915 (Abadan-Unat 1981; Jayawardena 1986).

2. The concept of modernization referred to here is based on the principles of the Western development model, and assumes that modernization can be achieved through diffusion of modern values and technology to underveloped sectors, regions or countries.

3. While during the 1935–39 period there were eighteen female representatives in parliament (4.5% of the total), this figure went down to four (0.9%) for the 1977–80 period, and in the 1983 elections only six women entered parliament.

4. In the process of national integration, the state relies on military and political institutions, both of which are predominantly male-dominated. Since other local organizations of the central bureaucracy – such as education, health,

credit, extension, etc. – also tend to be supportive of a male-dominated society, the expansion of the state has created a public sphere of men and a private sphere of women. In other words, state business came to be seen as men's business.

5. Although there may be men who share similar status, by and large men are more integrated into the institutional nexus. For reasons of schooling, military service and employment, male children are registered at birth or shortly thereafter. Military service, in particular, has always been the main vehicle through which Kurdish men learned Turkish and got socialized into the ways of mainstream society.

6. These twenty-eight provinces are divided into two categories. First priority provinces are Adıyaman, Ağrı, Bingöl, Muş, Bitlis, Diyarbakır, Gümüşhane, Bayburt, Hakkari, Kars, Mardin, Siirt, Tuneeli, Van; second priority provinces are Amasya, Artvin, Çankırı, Çorum, Elazığ, Erzincan, Erzurum, Kastamonu, Malatya, K. Maraş, Sinop, Sivas, Tokat, Ş. Urfa, Yozgat.

7. The Southeastern Anatolian Project (GAP) is the largest regional development project taking place in the east. It comprises thirteen major subprojects, mainly for irrigation and power generation, and covers an area of 73,863 km².

8. These projects are carried out under the auspices of the Ministry of Agriculture and Rural Affairs (MARA), with technical assistance and loans from international organizations, such as the World Bank, FAO (Food and Agriculture Organization), IFAD (International Fund for Agricultural Development), among others. There are also projects initiated by NGOs, the major one being TKV (Turkish Development Foundation).

9. These models have been discussed elsewhere (Ertürk, 1990). For the purposes of the current discussion brief descriptions will have to suffice here. Projects of the first type are based on economic growth models and assume a trickle-down (and trickle-across) effect. The second type is more equity-oriented. Women are defined within their domestic and reproductive roles and are perceived as one of the special groups whose welfare needs must be considered. The third type is designed specially for women, to provide support for long-neglected problems. Finally, the fourth type sees women as part and parcel of the rural community, and therefore considers them in the initial stages of project design. Integrated rural development projects offer the greatest potential for long-term and sustainable participation of women in mainstream currents.

10. The first comprehensive discussion at the governmental level on women and development took place at a conference in September 1987, held in Erzurum, which was sponsored by FAO and MARA in conjunction with FAO-financed research on the role of women in agricultural production in Erzurum villages (Ertürk, 1988). This research was carried out during the final stages of Erzurum Rural Development Project, and so the findings were of no consequence to the project.

11. YRDP was the first to have a rural sociologist/women in development specialist on the team of experts in all project identification, preparation and appraisal missions.

References

Abadan-Unat, Nermin, ed. (1981). *Women in Turkish Society*, E.J. Brill, Leiden.

Aydın, Zülküf (1986). *Underdevelopment and Rural Structures in Southeastern Turkey: The Household Economy in Gisgis and Kalhana*, Ithaca Press, London.

Balachandran, Chandra S., Peter F. Fisher and Michael A. Stanley (1989). 'An expert system approach to rural development: a prototype (TIHSO)', *The Journal of Developing Areas*, no. 23, January, pp. 259–70.

Balamir, Nefise (1984). 'Restructuring of the household division of labour, as a process contributing to the persistence of small commodity producers', paper presented at the Middle Eastern Studies Annual Meeting, *UCLA*, no. 29.

Beck, Lois and Keddie, Nikki, eds. (1978). *Women in the Muslim World*, Massachusetts: Harvard University Press.

Beneria, Lourdes, ed. (1982). *Women and Development*, Praeger Special Studies, New York.

Charlton, Sue Ellen M. (1984), *Women in Third World Development*, Westview Press, Boulder, Co.

Dauber, Roslyn and Melinda L. Cain, eds. (1981). *Women and Technological Change in Developing Countries*, Westview Press, Boulder, Co.

Ertürk, Yakın 1980. 'Rural change in southeastern Anatolia: an analysis of rural poverty and power structure as a reflection of centre–periphery relations in Turkey,' unpublished PhD dissertation, Cornell University.

Ertürk, Yakın (1987). 'The impact of national integration rural households in southeastern Turkey', in *Journal of Human Sciences*, 1, pp. 81–97.

Ertürk, Yakın (1988a). 'Appraisal of the conceptual and social implications of the Muş-Bingöl Rural Development Project', consultancy mission report submitted to IFAD.

Ertürk, Yakın (1988b). *Women's Participation in Agricultural Production in the Province of Erzurum*, FAO, United Nations, Ankara.

Ertürk, Yakın (1990). 'The women dimension in rural development projects implemented in Turkey', *Status of Rural Women in Turkey: Problems and Proposals for Action*, ILO-DFT Consultative Meeting Report, Ankara.

Jayawarden, Kumari (1986). *Feminism and Nationalism in the Third World*, Zed Books, London.

Kandiyoti, Deniz (1990). 'Women and Household Production: the Impact of Rural Transformation in Turkey', in Glavaris, K. (ed.), *The Rural Middle East*, Zed Books, London.

Leahy, Margaret E. (1986). *Development and the Status of Women*, Lynne Rienner Publishers, Inc., Boulder, Co.

Oncü, Ayşe (1981). 'Turkish Women in the Professions: Why So Many?' in Nermin Abadan-Unat, (ed.), *Women in Turkish Society*, E.J. Brill, leiden, pp. 181–92.

Özbay, Ferhunde (1979). 'Kırsal Yörlerde Kadının Statüsü, Işgücüne Katılımı ve Eğitim Durumu' (Women's Status, Labor Force Participation and Education in Rural Areas), AITIA *Yönetim Bilimleri Dergisi*, no. 1, 201–224.

Poats, Susan V., M. Schmink, A. Spring, eds. (1988). *Gender Issues in Farming System Research and Extension*. Westview Press, Boulder, Co.

Sirman, Nükhet (1980). 'Women in production in western Turkey: a case of commoditisation in agriculture', paper presented at the Women and Development seminar at the Institute of Development Studies, University of Sussex, 13 February.

Stoeckel, John and N.L. Srisena (1988). 'Gender-specific socio-economic impacts of development programs in Sri Lanka', *The Journal of Developing Areas*, no. 23, October, pp. 31–42.

Tekeli, Şirin (1981). 'Women in Turkish politics', in Nermin Abadan-Unat, ed., *Women in Turkish Society*, E.J. Brill, Leiden, pp. 293–310.

Yalçın-Heckmann, Lale (1991). *Tribe and Kinship Among the Kurds*, Frankfort am Main; Peter Lang, U.K.

Yotopoulos, Pan A. and G.J. Mergos (1986). 'Family labor allocation in the agricultural household', *Food Research Institute Studies*, vol. 20, no. 1.

Women in the Media in Turkey: the Free, Available Woman or the Good Wife and Selfless Mother

Ayşe Saktanber

During the 1980s it became increasingly common to speak about women in the mass media.* A marked increase in the number of monthly publications for men and women has been observed over the decade and for the first time there are special women's programmes on television.[1] This decade has at the same time been a period of important developments in mass communications. Colour television has been introduced, two new channels have been set up and total broadcasting time has been greatly increased.[2] The increasing activity in the daily press and publication of new dailies are accompanied by the appearance for the first time in years of news weeklies.[3] As in many parts of the world, colourful tabloids aim to increase their circulation by publishing colour pictures of nudes, while some of the news weeklies try to boost their sales by using women and their sexuality as a metaphor.[4] Advertising, too, a semiotic practice specific to the media, begins to occupy an important place, especially through television advertising, making its

* I would like to thank Gül Özyeğin and Nükhet Sirman for their valuable assistance in preparing this paper. I would also like to take this opportunity to thank the organizers and participants of the Kassel University symposium on 'Women in Turkey in the 1980s and in Migration.'

mark on social memory and fantasies by constructing its messages on the basis of cultural codes relating to women and their sexuality.

This increase in verbal and visual discourses on women, however, does not contribute to the establishment of values and norms that would alter the subordinate position of women in society. To the extent that an increasing visibility in any discursive field does not necessarily indicate a removal of social pressures in that field, the greater visibility of women has to be evaluated similarly, as this discourse does not include women's views and opinions. The best proof of this is that women are present in these discourses mainly as the 'devoted mother' or the 'faithful, good wife', if not through their sexuality, and a male-defined sexuality at that. In fact, it has to be noted that this increasing discursivity around women is mainly centred on sexuality. Even more important is the fact that the female identities constructed through the media are increasingly defined in terms of a patriarchal discourse on sexuality. This discourse transforms women into passive, easily possessed and dominated objects of sexual pleasure, fragmented for various uses. Consequently, as women watch themselves being gazed at in different media, they are shown the 'ideal' womanhood demanded of them and are told to love themselves, 'as I love you' and be 'as I want you to be'.[5] This discourse, which many women working in the media have helped construct, has been widely accepted and indeed, having been adopted by women wishing to remain desirable, has become firmly entrenched.

The press does, however, attempt to give a place to female identities that remain outside the dominant male discourse. Two developments in the political process are responsible for this: one is the place accorded from time to time to views by activists of the feminist movement that has been gaining ground since the 1980s,[6] the other is the increasing preoccupation with women of the left, the social democrats, and to a certain extent, of the liberal right – as well as a certain section of the press itself – in reaction to the Islamic movements that developed in the 1980s.[7] In spite of this, it is still too early to know whether or not women's identities defined outside patriarchal discourses will secure a lasting and determining place in Turkey's media. Under the present conditions the patriarchal perspective dominates the way women are portrayed in the media. Thus, they are valued mainly in terms of sexuality but are unable to make their sexuality, as they define it, a part of their identity.

The techniques and forms of representation used to portray women in the Turkish media are no different from those used in the West. On the contrary, in radio and television programmes, in men's and women's magazines, images of women are constructed entirely in line with Western-dominated media codes, which are universal.

Nevertheless, as female identities constructed in the media, and images of women produced in accordance with these identities, acquire their meaning in the framework of a specific culture, it is necessary to understand the forms and codes according to which women's identities are defined in discourses of the popular media in Turkey. It is also necessary to understand the nature of the relationship to women the media constructs for itself. This will require an analysis of the position of women in society's media culture, a position that enables certain ways of seeing women.

Two kinds of women

For women in Turkey, living under the tutelage of men is both a legal and a social norm.[8] Therefore, adjectives like 'free' or 'independent' indicate that a woman is not under the protective mantle of a man or that she has violated the authority of the man under whose tutelage she legally exists. In this context, the sexuality of the 'free', 'easy' woman is open to any gaze and usage, unlike the protected woman, whose sexuality can only be discussed through inference and allusion. Thus, according to their position in this framework, women in Turkish society can be divided, at least at the representational level, into those almost totally devoid of sexuality and those who are nothing but sexuality. The possibility for any legitimate sexuality on the part of those women represented in the media as asexual can exist only within carefully drawn boundaries; that is, within the confines of their own bedrooms. And yet, to the extent that any woman's image in the media turns into a sign open to everyone's gaze, it can be submitted to all kinds of sexual investigation and harassment, even when sexually it is not overtly mentioned.

Nevertheless, the distinction mentioned above continues to operate in the ways the media constructs its relations to women. That is, specific women's spaces exist in the media in which elements evoking sexuality are not openly mentioned, as well as others wherein sexuality, either specific to women or not, is intensively used. In women's programmes broadcast on television and on the radio, which is a state monopoly in Turkey, women are treated as 'gracious ladies', 'respectable housewives' or 'revered mothers'. The first women's programmes on the radio started in 1939 and, bearing such names as 'The Home Hour' and 'Home', allowed women no other identity than that of 'mother of the home'. These programmes continued until the 1970s and were composed of childcare and education; health and family relations. Between 1974 and 1980, programmes such as 'Woman's World' and 'Women and the Family' began to be broadcast. The regulations that define the goals of these programmes describe women as 'one of the fundamental elements ensuring a happy future for society'. Apart from her identity as 'mother and wife within the family', woman is also defined in these guidelines as 'a human being in the world, a citizen in society'. In these programmes, however, women have no other identity than the one framed by the family. From the 1980s onwards, programmes that 'address adults generally' replaced those targeting the family through women's identities. These programmes with such titles as 'Good Morning', 'During Daytime', 'Noontime', and 'Afternoon', are especially timed to accord with women's housework schedules. As well as containing information on social security, housing, rules regulating social life, the protection of young people, old age and retirement, and national interests, these programmes cover a wide range of home-related subjects, including practical tips, home economics, childcare and health, nutrition, the benefits of healthy family relationships, as well as measures to be taken against social degradation, and to promote good neighbourly relations, harmony within the family, and conditions for happiness. These latter themes particularly target women, being prepared with an understanding that such concerns are the responsibility of women. In sum, these programmes are made with the view that 'the family is the core and indispensable element of Turkish society' and that women's place in society is squarely within the family.[9]

Although television programmes aimed at the family and women in the family have been broadcast since 1968, a daily programme entitled 'For You Ladies' prepared especially for women was broadcast for the first time in 1984. Initially a bi-weekly broadcast, this programme has become an intrinsic part of daily morning television programmes.[10] In terms of structure and content 'For You Ladies' is similar to newspaper magazine supplements targeted at women, which are also both producers and carriers of a specific notion of womanhood. In the same way that supplements provide information and ideas on home decoration, ways of facilitating housework, recipes, current fashions, tips on make-up, and gynaecological information, the same themes are from time to time taken up by television programmes, relying usually on the authority of an expert. Horoscopes, lonely-hearts columns and, of course, sensational reporting on love, marriage and crime, as well as the latest developments in the private lives of film stars, singers and models are not included in TV programmes, but receive wide coverage in newspaper supplements.[11] When actors and singers appear on TV shows and interviews, they are always presented as model ladies and gentlemen. Photo-novellas, the most popular items in the magazine press, are replaced on TV by Latin American soap-operas (tele-novellas). These melodramatic tele-novellas constantly deal with love and emotions, and thereby valorize housework and homelife, which are traditionally devalued for not producing surplus-value, by investing them with love and emotion. In this way, the bonds linking women to housework, marriage and the family are strengthened. In the context of these serials, love and sexuality defined in terms of marriage are associated with a sacred, almost divine emotion that is linked to fate and able to transcend all social boundaries.[12]

The result is that women's (ladies') television programmes depict women as 'good' mothers, 'accommodating' wives and professional women who prioritize their own womanhood above all else, and whose sexuality is not evoked other than in their beauty, elegance and carefully arranged appearance. Newspaper supplements add to this construct the image of the 'free' or 'bold' woman exhibiting an exaggerated sexuality. These latter 'inviting women', whose sexual attractiveness is displayed by their cleavage, are generally movie stars, singers or fashion models who do not criticize marriage, but complain, nevertheless, that art and marriage do not always go together. The implicit invitation extended to men has the effect of showing women what 'sexual allure' is supposed to be. At the same time, the cost of this sexual attractiveness constructed through the exhibition of a daring nudity and/or flashy clothing and meaningful looks is also shown. Hearts are ever-lonely, the sadness of breaking up with the latest lover is great, social pressures have taken their toll. The other side of fame and wealth is thus depicted through reports of 'fallen' women who, having succumbed to such temptations, are betrayed and lose their homes, honour and even their lives.

Whereas televised women's programmes invoke sexuality only in the context of health/ill health and therefore through a medical and gynaecological discourse, it is present in tele-novellas as a verbal and visual undercurrent whose boundaries are delimited by ties of sacred love and marriage. These limits are somewhat transgressed on evening television by imported serials and advertisements. Still, as imported serials are 'foreign', and advertisements are commercial, the official ideology of womanhood and sexuality is not challenged. Moreover, as officials constantly point out, programmes that may offend national sentiments and Turkish traditions and customs (in general, bedroom and kissing scenes) are never broadcast without censorship.

Working women, apart from those who market titillation (and sometimes even including them), are considered 'successful' only if they are businesswomen who are at the same time perfect housewives and mothers. Whether working or not, the woman who is approved of and intended as a model is the affectionate, soft, understanding good wife and devoted mother who has not strayed from the dictates of womanhood and who, to top it all, has perfectly adapted to the requirements of modern life. Not surprisingly, therefore, newspaper supplements often include columns that have legal, medical, educational, sociological and even sexological references and are intended to help women overcome the problems they face at home or at work. Rather than posing the questions from an individual woman's point of view, the discourse developed in these pages addresses women as a sector of the population who must exercise commonsense and moderation in all things. Needless to say, the same approach governs both television and radio broadcasting.

Apart from magazines that specialize in particular subjects such as fashion, knitting, embroidery or cooking, women's magazines primarily address the 'modern woman' constructed in the bourgeois liberal discourse. In spite of the fact that this modern woman can appear in many guises, including the simple housewife, the accent is on the 'independent, successful, dynamic, intellectual woman who has earned a place for herself in society at large. These magazines point to goals for women beside caring for home and children.

Among the many magazines of this type (*Kadın* (Woman),

Kadınca (Womanly), *Elele* (Hand in Hand), *Rapsodi, Marie Claire, Vizon* (Mink)), is one – Kadınca – which has supported a feminist discourse ever since it began publication in 1978, and thus occupies a special place.

To be a *Kadınca* woman

Kadınca is a rare example in the popular media in that it is trying to define womanhood in Turkey outside male discourse. This magazine establishes a discourse that calls on women to be daring and aggressively energetic, exhorting them to discover themselves, especially their feelings, capabilities and sexuality. It denounces the social constraints women face and at the same time exposes women's own role in reproducing these constraints.

The attitude on sexuality continually espoused by Kadınca is that it is a normal and valuable part of women's identity and that women must get to know their own sexuality and acknowledge it as part of their very existence. And yet this feminine sexuality, or heterosexuality, that is promoted and praised in articles, ironical questionnaires, humorous reports calling on medical doctors, psychologists and psychiatrists for expert support, is constantly subverted by the full-page advertisements that comprise about a quarter of the magazine and reflect a patriarchally defined femininity.[13]

Furthermore, the magazine's cover often resorts to pornography's voyeuristic codes.[14] A cover story on women's orgasm, for example, is hailed by a cover photograph of a symbolic woman whose bare neck and shoulders are meant to indicate that she is having an orgasm. The same story announces the '3K' formula which is supposed to define the three basic elements of orgasm: the clitoris (*klitoris*), the head (*kafa*), and the husband (*koca*) (January 1987). The term 'husband' is further explained somewhere in the text: husband (that is, man)! In other words, even Kadınca cannot ignore the dominant view in Turkey that allows women a legitimate sexuality only within marriage.

What Kadınca hopes to achieve is to open a space for women in a basically male world. Since its targeted readership is the urban middle-class woman, the magazine can make space only for women in this urban, middle-class world.

Kadınca targets the 'modern' woman who, as she learns about herself and her sexuality, knows how to manage her husband/man with minimum concessions, a woman who is decisive, aware of her rights, able to stand on her own and possessing self-respect. But she is also a woman who can lay a Western-style dining table, who cares for her hair, face and body using various cosmetics, diets and exercise, one who follows current fashions and is informed on home decoration.[15] Economic independence is stressed, but women are encouraged to pursue a career not so much with this aim in mind but as a means to acquire a particular persona. Although housewives are not denigrated, their lifestyle is not consistent with the desired persona which women are exhorted to develop and rebuked for not pursuing with zeal.

In its language *Kadınca* distinguishes itself from women, thereby denying that all women, including its staff, may be facing similar situations. Instead of using the pronoun 'we' when taking up women's problems, the pronoun 'you' is used, saying, 'you must put your foot down, you must not let yourself be oppressed, you must unite!' This distancing is made possible by the stamp put upon the magazine by its young editor, a popular public figure whose image is that of an independent, liberated individual.[16] Consequently, the message is, 'If I can do it, so can you!' This is the most important stance that separates the magazine's discourse from that of feminism, which by calling on all women (us) does not construct an 'other' woman.

In a stocktaking statement released as the magazine celebrated its ninth birthday, *Kadınca* drew attention to the support it extended to feminist debates in Turkey with messages such as 'Put An End to Gender-Based Discrimination', 'Battering of Women Must Stop', 'Women Must become District Governors,'[17] 'Fight For Your Sexuality', 'Equal Rights in Marriage', 'We Denounce Fundamentalism', 'A Ministry of Women's Affairs Must Be Established'.[18] The magazine increasingly supports a feminist line today, turning the spotlight on those in the press who denigrate women, while it praises those that adopt a pro-woman stance.[19] The editor may often ask her editorial colleagues to refrain from writing disparagingly about women: 'I plead with my colleagues, please do not do that. Does the press lack material to the point where it has to squeeze the juice out of women?' (October 1986).

No to the free woman: freedom to use women

The common characteristics of papers which rely on sensational news-making and publish pictures of nude women with fabricated captions in order to increase their circulation, is that they aim to ensure their survival by exploiting women. In Turkey, the use of women's sexuality as a metaphor has increased parallel to the development of the weekly news magazine press. The most important of these is *Nokta*, launched in 1984, which has since managed to give a new identity to the Turkish weekly news magazine industry by setting its own agenda of weekly news, keeping an ironic distance from political ideologies, and refusing to be delimited in the issues it takes up. And yet, the use of women's bodies and sexuality as the constitutive element of cover pictures has also become one of the most important parts of this new imagery projected by the media.

Nokta itself argues that they deal with love and sexuality because they attribute to it as much importance as politics, culture and the economy, and that furthermore they are breaking the monopoly of primitive morality, conservatism and degenerate taste on sexuality. It points out that it does not want to adopt a cold, academic approach to sexuality that completely excludes eroticism.[20] However, taking into consideration the fact that the magazine's covers at least once a month use women's bodies and sexuality in a manner that is completely gratuitous and may or may not bear any relevance to the issue at hand, it can be seen that in order to break the monopoly of primitive morality and conservatism on sexuality the manufacture of multitudes of meanings through women's bodies and the use of the female body after fragmenting it and turning it into a medium of marketing techniques seems to be necessary. It seems then, to liberate sexuality, one must sacrifice women's bodies and sexuality.

The 24 January 1988 issue of *Nokta* featuring a cover story entitled 'İncirlik: A Sensitive Spot' is a blatant example of its approach to sexuality and to women's sexuality. The story is about the political sensitivity of the İncirlik Air Base, one of the American military installations in Turkey, as a result of developments in international politics. The cover features a woman's reclining naked body from waist to knees, constructed as a symbol of the air base. The female sexual organ of this bisected body, covered by a fig-leaf, is the airstrip from which a fighter plane is about to take off. Thus, military weaponry, the most aggressive symbol of power, is identified with male sexuality and transforms female sexuality into the passive, easily appropriated medium of this power. At the same time, reference is also made to the rights held by the state/the ruling power over women and their bodies by identifying the female body with a strategically important military air base over which the state exercises sovereignty. Thus, ruling power is once again masculinized and women's bodies and sexuality not only are translated into a field over which the ruling power holds rights of appropriation, but made to symbolize all other fields over which such rights are claimed.

As in the above example, the view that almost any subject can be explicated by means of a woman's naked body, which makes women's sexuality the focal point of any discussion of sexuality itself, is not only sexist, but deprives women of any identity other than a sexuality defined by the male gaze. Women are deprived of identity in such a construction not only because they are reduced to a mere body, but because they are packaged into guises through which an infinite number of meanings can be adduced. And to the extent that these meanings continually indicate sexuality, no identity outside of sexuality is accorded to women.[21]

Women, their bodies appropriated and made into signifiers of various magazine cover scenarios, become, in advertisements, identified with the properties of the commodity in question, becoming the means of conveying the message that, like a woman, the product is available to be possessed. With the properties grafted onto them in advertising, women, the ever-flexible raw material to which can be attributed any meaning, describe the product or service marketed: devoted mothers in margarine ads, meticulous housewives in detergent ads, smiling bank clerks in bank ads, modern, capable women in ads for home appliances, a fiery and yet flowing creature in ads for motor oils, femininity enthralled by the masculine attraction of the vehicle in automobile ads. From now on, acquired with every purchase will be the properties symbolized through women. These women, however, are 'other' women constructed at the symbolic level. In other words, rather than creating a realistic effect, these ads define a symbolic womanhood, impossible to attain, yet constituting its very essence.

But when women become the subject of factual newspaper

reports, they, in line with the nature of the discourse of news media, instead signify the reality of women. They are no longer reflections of the essence of womanhood, becoming instead the parts of the reality that constitutes that essence. In this context, women feature as news items in relation to issues such as social morality, virtue and honour, and are newsworthy in so far as they adhere to, or more frequently violate, such norms. Thus women appear mostly in news items dealing with law cases, such as adultery, infidelity, abduction/elopement, love affairs, family homicides, or wife battering. Motherhood is another issue which makes women newsworthy: either the mother who sacrifices herself for her children or the mother who, in a 'fit of madness', harms her children. Additionally, a woman will also figure as the visual material, to make a piece more striking, in the report of hold-ups, burglaries, political scandals, business malpractice, or confidence tricks, whether she herself is involved or is mistress or lover of the man involved. Even those 'well-behaved' women under strict surveillance whose sexuality remains concealed cannot escape the form of sexual harassment described above. Sometimes a careless sitting posture catches the eye of the 'objective' camera; often the very presence of a woman suffices to provoke meaningful innuendo. Whatever the content of the news, Turkish dailies have made the use of women as visual material their almost traditional practice. This is a clear indication of their exploitative attitudes towards women.[22]

The way the media depict women is directly related to the way in which women are socially defined. The various types of women that appear in the media, such as housewives, professional women, stars of screen and stage, peasant or shantytown women, Islamist veiled women and others, are represented in a way that belies the apparent plurality. This is a definition of womanhood constituted by the common denominator of its different states. At this point, Henri Lefebvre's views on the limits of pluralism become relevant to the state of womanhood in Turkish society. According to this view, liberal pluralism will, for example, accept different moral codes, but will continue to require a specific morality; or it will accept different religions, but require specific religious attitudes.[23] It can likewise be said that although various types of women are accepted in Turkish society, only one specific womanhood is acceptable, one which has been best described as 'a lady in the drawing-room, a cook in the kitchen and a whore in bed.' Women who do not accord with this conduct are 'free, available' women.

Women who transgress these acceptable limits and produce their own definitions of femininity are subject to social harassment. For example, women who consider their sexuality to be a normal part of their identity are considered guilty of bringing their bedroom identity into their everyday lives, thus escaping social control, and disrupting social order. When these women are depicted in the media, if they are not artists, garrulous feminists, or topless tourists, they are, more often than not, 'intellectual' women 'living alone with their love affairs, sexuality and problems', a newly emerging type which has recently become the subject of magazine covers.[24]

Do laws have the last word?

The end of the 1980s in Turkey has been witness to events that clearly demonstrate a dichotomy in the definition of womanhood. A decision of the Constitutional Court − the product of an understanding that divides women into the protected and the unprotected; those whose sexuality is covered and those who have no other identity outside their sexuality − has endorsed and furthered this division. In a case that was debated extensively in the press, a local court applied to the Constitutional Court for the repeal of Article 438 of the Turkish Penal Code, which stipulates that 'sentences for the rape or abduction of a professional prostitute could be reduced by two-thirds.' The Constitutional Court rejected the application by seven votes against four, thus perpetuating the distinction between 'virtuous' and 'unvirtuous' women. The court decision explained that 'the resistance shown by a prostitute may rightly not be taken as seriously by the offender', adding that there existed a difference between the dignity of a virtuous woman and that of a prostitute.[25] This decision was greeted with great indignation, not only by feminists and various public organizations but also by opinion-maker newspaper columnists and cartoonists, most of whom are men.

These latter criticized the law only to the extent that it was interpreted as being a breach of human rights and demonstrated once more the refusal of the state to side with the oppressed.[26] Moreover, there appeared in the press protests that were strange to say the least. One columnist questioned the value of victimizing those who were already victims, especially when there were so many other women whose virtue was dubious.[27] Thus women's virtue became once more the object of scrutiny, this time in articles and cartoons that ranged from efforts to uncover the historical origins of prostitution as a sacred institution, to others that discussed the difficulties of determining who is virtuous. In a society that equates sexuality with nudity, cartoonists' drawings symbolizing prostitutes (that is, women whose rape is less costly) as women with mini-skirts, bare breasts and lots of flashy jewellery, have, in effect, managed to epitomize what unvirtuous women look like. This has enabled women to learn what they should not look like if they do not want to be branded unvirtuous. In short, thanks to this law which transmits messages not only for one type of woman but for all women, men's right to decide a woman's virtue has been further strengthened.

In the end, it was only feminists who questioned the messages this law produced for all women, despite the attention the issue received in the press. Feminists denounced the law for 'demeaning women by drawing a distinction between virtuous and unvirtuous women, and for inciting rape by implying that there were women who could be raped and that, in cases of rape, there could be attenuating circumstances' and bought advertising space in newspapers to announce that they 'rejected the virtue obtained through Article 438'.[28] Nevertheless, all these actions have to this day not succeeded in shifting the focus of debate to the notion of womanhood informing the court's decision. The press, which has not to date included women's own point of view in the discourse on women it has established, is also responsible for this failure.

The state of affairs which I have outlined in this chapter – the fact that the media's relationship to women, far from being pro-women, treats women within the dichotomous framework evidenced in this constitutional decision, shows that, in spite of all its good intentions the press still deals with women with an approach that is far from satisfactory. It therefore appears that women in Turkey must engage in a serious struggle in order to form and appropriate their own identities. In this sense, it looks as if the media is becoming a new arena of conflict for women in Turkey.

Notes

1. It was in the 1980s that liberal economic policies were introduced, a move which also led to a search by the printed press for new markets. Over the 1980s

women's monthly magazines such as *Kadınca, Kadın, Elele, Kapris, Rapsodi, Marie Claire* and men's magazines such as *Erkekçe, Bravo, Playboy, Playman, Men* begin to be published. And in 1984, television begins to broadcast a programme called *For You Ladies* prepared specially for women.

2. Television in Turkey began to broadcast from a single channel in 1968; colour TV became available in 1984. This channel (TV1) is at present broadcasting 115 hours a week. In 1986 a second channel (TV2) and in 1989 a third channel (TV3) were added, bringing the total broadcasting hours to 70.28 per week, and GAP TV, broadcasting only in the southeast, adds another 25 hours a week.

3. *Nokta*, one of the leading news weeklies, began publication in 1982 as a magazine journal and switched to cover news stories in 1983. *Yeni Gündem*, a left-leaning weekly that folded in 1983, was published over the same period. In 1987 *Tempo*, another general interest news weekly, and *2000'e Doğru*, a politics-oriented left-wing weekly, added even more diversity to the publishing scene. A number of monthly and weekly youth, children's, art, culture and political magazines appeared in Turkey in the 1980s. But the above mentioned are the ones that have had the most impact on the popular media.

4. *Yeni Gündem*, a news weekly that appeals mostly to an intellectual left and democrat readership, talks, in the editorial entitled 'Last Kitchen' published in its ninety-sixth and final issue, about the difficulties of surviving in the market without featuring women on its cover.

5. There is an extensive feminist literature dealing with the ways in which the popular media and advertising interpret and define women. See especially Janice Winship, 'Sexuality for sale', in Stuart Hall et al., eds., *Culture, Media, Language*, Hutchinson, London, 1980, pp. 217-23, and Rosalind Coward, *Female Desire*, Paladin, London, 1984.

6. It could very well be said that the press began to include the feminist movement in its news reporting after the 17 May 1987 march against the battering of women. Interest in the movement by the press increased in the wake of the First Women's Caucus held in Istanbul two years later, and features explaining feminism began to appear in dailies. To the extent that it fitted the sensationalism of the press, other feminist activism – such as the purple needle campaign in which women sold purple needles to protest against the sexual harassment women experienced on the street, and their storming of coffeehouses and bars, traditional male spaces, as a way of claiming public space for women – was also widely reported.

7. Women have become the main target of discussions of Islamic revivalism, as a result of the fact that Islamists have made the right of women to remain veiled in schools and government offices the symbol of their movements. Such action had been prohibited by statute, if not law, in a country that took pride in its secularism. Thus, that section of the press that supports secularism has begun to create venues where the position of women in Turkish society can be discussed. For example, *Hürriyet*, a right–liberal daily with the highest circulation figures in Turkey, took an open stance against Islamist movements and, in its reporting of these movements, gives veiled women a lot of coverage as symbols of backwardness. *Cumhuriyet*, a daily that is considered to be the most serious newspaper in the country, opened up a discussion page in October 1989, inviting readers to contribute 'on the woman question', an invitation that

has proven quite successful, with at least one letter appearing on women's issues daily. It should also be mentioned that one of the factors that have led to so much discussion on women is also the 25% quota accorded to them by the Social Democratic Populist Party of Turkey.

8. For a discussion that would illuminate the specificity of the Turkish case, see Şirin Tekeli, 'Do women want equality or liberty? Thoughts on discussions over the civil code' (in Turkish), in Şirin Tekeli, *Kadınlar İçin*, Alan Publications, Istanbul, 1988, pp. 338–45.

9. See 'Radio and television broadcasting since their inception' (in Turkish), in *Türk Aile Yapisi*, State Planning Organisation Publication No. DPT:2165–ÖIK:338, Ankara 1989, pp. 72–3.

10. Ibid., p. 74.

11. *Sabah*, the daily with the highest circulation, started in 1989 to publish a magazine supplement called *Melodi*, subtitled 'A Quality Women's Newspaper'. This supplement, designated directly as a woman's supplement, has, in addition to the usual horoscopes, a section on its inner page entitled 'What Will Happen To You Today'. In this section, under rubrics such as 'Awake Your Hidden Powers' and 'Strange Happenings', the doors of 'unknown' and 'mysterious' worlds are opened to women and a 'German Professor' Günter Wolf interprets women's dreams. In contrast to television, which represents official positivism, this supplement does not fail to put to use the 'mystic' aspect of womanhood!

12. For an attempt to conceptualize the definitions of womanhood, love and sexuality in tele-romances, see Michèle Mattelart, 'Women and the Cultural Industries', in Richard Collins et al., eds., *Media, Culture and Society*, Sage, London 1989, pp. 63–81.

13. Advertisements for the cosmetics that have been developed for almost all parts of a woman's body (shampoos, hair colourants, deodorants, anti-wrinkle creams, eyeliners, depilatories, nail varnish and so on) turn every inch of a woman's body into a marketable field, as well as telling women how to apply care and attention to all these parts in order to become attractive for men. See Rosalind Coward, 'Sexual liberation and the family', *m/f*, no. 1, 1978, pp. 7–24.

14. On the voyeuristic codes of pornography and the ways in which these codes are used in pornography to construct reality effects, see Susanne Kappeler, *The Pornography of Representation*, Polity, Cambridge, 1986 and Annette Kuhn, *The Power of the Image, Essays on Representation and Sexuality*, Routledge and Kegan Paul, London 1985.

15. Fashion, beauty, slimming, decorating and cooking are headings that are never absent from any issue of the magazine. Thus these are turned into indispensable parts of women's lives and womanhood is rendered unimaginable without them.

16. Duygu Asena, the editor of *Kadınca*, is the author of a book that has in the past few years earned bestseller status in Turkey. The book, a much-discussed and read quasi-autobiographical 'confession' and 'critique', has also been made into a feature film starring an actress who publicly defines herself as feminist. Asena, who has become the symbol of the liberated, free modern women in Turkey, has a full-page editorial in every issue entitled 'First Word' (*Ilk Söz*) in which she addresses women using an intimate discourse through which she is able to set the agenda of the issue as well as secure her

authority over her readers.

17. In spite of the lack of legal impediments, women graduating from the appropriate schools have not been appointed as district governors, a refusal which became the focus of feminist protest, with a number of women applying for the post as a way of drawing attention to the issue.

18. See *Kadınca*, December 1987, pp. 19-20.

19. The magazine has a page entitled '*Kadınca*'s Choice', the top half of which lists, under the logo of a photo of lips, 'the ones to be kissed', those in the media who support male–female equality and who say positive things about women. The bottom half of the page lists the names of those who have demeaned women, this time under the logo of lips and the words 'the ones who need pepper', referring to a popular form of punishment meted out to children who speak rude words.

20. *Nokta*, 5th anniversary special supplement, 1989, p. 28.

21. In an article entitled 'The Exploitation of Women In Magazine Covers', the magazine *2000'e Doğru* has taken issue with the use made of women's bodies on magazine covers, taking its cue from feminist concerns. It featured feminists' protest, giving examples from the covers of *Nokta* and *Tempo* (28 February–5 March 1988).

22. For example, in the survey of *Hürriyet* that I carried out between December 1989 and January 1990, I calculated that women constituted 70% of the visual material.

23. H. Lefebvre, *Le Manifeste Differentialiste*, Paris: Gallimard, quoted by Mattelart, 'Women and the Cultural Industries', p. 76.

24. This topic became the cover story of *Nokta*'s 2 November 1988 issue. The cover bears the photograph of Duygu Asena, the editor of *Kadınca* magazine, a photograph that alludes to the final scene of the film based on Asena's novel (see note 16 above), in which the female protagonist sits down naked on the floor in front of her typewriter to write, having resolved to shed all her past and live alone and stand on her own two feet. The cover photo shows Asena sitting in front of her typewriter on the floor in a dress that leaves bare her shoulders, arms and legs. The magazine report, which is basically a commentary interspersed with interviews with women who choose to live alone, is entitled 'Alone Every Day' (pp. 66-73). According to the magazine, the common characteristic of women who choose to live alone (including divorcées) rather than get married and have children, is that they are professionals: well educated, good earners and between the ages of 25 and 45. What remains unsaid in the report is that all the women interviewed live in Istanbul, one of the largest metropolises of the world. The questions that receive most attention in the report are the women's sexual lives, whether or not they fear loneliness once they get old and lose their attractiveness, whether their female neighbours are afraid that their husbands might be allured by them, and whether their emotional and sexual lives are fulfilling. The piece goes on to assess the psychology of women living alone and concludes that, 'women who start out to become free and independent individuals learn from experience that this has a very high cost. The reality that they are all aware of is that a deep relationship with one or more people (to love a man or children) means a return to dependence. Because they know that love can only exist and develop through an intense and sustained relationship. When such a

relationship cannot be ventured into, what remains is fragmented relations, fragmented passions and sexualities, and, finally, a fragmented individuality.' Thus the article downplays the contentment experienced by single women, and completely negates women's choice of independence.

25. *Cumhuriyet*, 11 January 1990.

26. For example, Ismail Gülgeç, a well-known cartoonist, drew cartoons identifying prostitutes with Turkish democracy and equated their plight with that of pensioners and workers on short-term contracts (*Cumhuriyet*, 14 January 1990 and 19 January 1990). Another of his cartoons depicts a vampish woman with bare hips, legs and bust, her eyes blackened with a censor's ink, holding in her hand the scales of justice. Next to her lies a discarded book of justice and the cartoon, captioned 'Our New Approach to Justice', thus identifies prostitution and perhaps the lack of virtue with this new kind of justice. Tan, another cartoonist of *Cumhuriyet*, in his cartoon on prostitutes, drew a woman in a mini-skirt and halterneck blouse who has in her hand a sign that reads 'officially-approved special reductions for those who wish to rape'. But what is striking about this cartoon is that the woman, in a pose that denotes her shame, has her eyes lowered and head bent so that the viewer cannot see her face. These cartoons commonly show women immodestly dressed: in all probability unintentionally, women who are accused of having loose morals are always depicted as wearing flimsy clothing, and the boundaries which are not to be transgressed if one wishes to appear virtuous are thereby shown.

27. Yılmaz Çetiner, 'Hit the Whore', *Milliyet*, 15 January 1990.

28. See *Cumhuriyet*, 14–15 January 1990. For an article that heeds feminist arguments and makes a point that is rather different from the ones mentioned above, see Melih Cevdet Anday, 'More Than Shameful', *Cumhuriyet*, 19 January 1990.

Part IV

Private Lives

10

Towards a Conceptualization of Marital Power Dynamics: Women Breadwinners and Working-class Households in Turkey

Hale Cihan Bolak

This chapter addresses the patterns of marital negotiation in urban working-class marriage in which the wife is the major breadwinner. Focusing on the ways women engage with male authority in mostly nuclear households, I locate these negotiations in the intersection of economic, cultural and affective layers of marital dynamics, looking for continuities and discontinuities with traditional patterns. Using my own research, I argue for a framework that addresses the reciprocal interactions between gender divisions and intergenerational relationships on the one hand and the new responsibilities assumed by men and women inside and outside the household on the other.

The primary concern of researchers who have studied the Turkish family in the last two decades has been the effects of social change and urbanization on the structure and dynamics of family relationships. Considerable attention has been focused on the enduring role of the 'functionally extended family' in buffering the impact of social change, with one example being the continuing importance of women's role as mediators between fathers and sons. The loosening of the relationships of support and authority between different generations of men, and the increased dependence on daughters rather than sons, have been identified as some of the dimensions of change (Duben, 1982; Kağıtcıbaşı, 1984; Kandiyoti, 1984; Kıray, 1976, 1982, 1984). For example, Kağıtcıbaşı (1984) proposes looking at family change in terms of changes in the system of mutual dependency relationships, noting that while intergenerational relationships may no longer involve *economic* dependency, they still involve *emotional* dependency.

The emphasis on the continuity of emotional dependency and discontinuity of economic dependency raises questions about gender. For example, the implications of a strained father-son relationship, and the loosening of patrilineal kinship ties when a young man sets up a social life in the city, on 'household strategies' and marital power dynamics; and the effect of mother–daughter relationships on marital relations in the urban context, have been the less explored dimensions of social change. Similarly, relatively little empirical research has focused on examining the realities of economic survival for rural migrants to the cities, especially with respect to the responsibilities assumed by men and women in the household in different sociohistorical time periods. Kıray (1984) has observed astutely that while urban living has burdened the wife with additional responsibilities, the husband may be able to shrug off his share of what is considered to be the most classic male responsibility, economic maintenance of the household; concluding that women's employment has had little positive impact on women's classic responsibilities inside the household. Similarly, Özbay (1994) has drawn attention to Turkish women's efforts towards raising or maintaining the status of their families, which take different forms in concert with the changing opportunities for social mobility and associated values. As making money became, more than ever, the prime concern of low-income families in the 1980s, resulting in men's increasing marginality to the life of the household, the valorization of domesticity among women seems to have declined, while their involvement in the productive and reproductive responsibilities of their households increased.

Close ethnographic studies of households and families in urban Turkey are still rare. The project on which this chapter was based was carried out in 1986–7 in Istanbul, and had the goal of taking a close look at relationship dynamics in the working-class urban households in which the wife's income is indispensable to the maintenance of the family's livelihood. Given the small numbers of married women in the urban labour force and the prevalence of the patriarchal family ideology, this particular situation represents a culturally non-sanctioned form of sexual division of labour and provides a vantage-point for studying the mechanisms for coping with possible disjunctions between the cultural ideology of the patriarchal family and the realities of economic survival.

Discussion in this chapter will be limited to the following questions: How are the power dynamics constructed and negotiated in the marital relationship? Through which mechanisms are these dynamics maintained, reinforced or challenged? What are the patterns by which women engage with culturally sanctioned male authority? How does the experience of these processes vary as a function of relationships within the extended family?

Problematizing marital power

Without going into a lengthy discussion of the literature on power in intimate relationships, suffice it to say that research in this area is plagued by at least two major problems. First, informed mainly by the decisionmaking approach, operation-alization of power as the outcome of decisionmaking processes has been surprisingly one-dimensional. This approach has prevailed despite the various theoretical and methodological criticisms (Glenn, 1989; McDonald, 1980). Secondly, how power is interwoven with other aspects of marital and kinship relations – which assume a particularly critical role in Turkey – has not been a major concern.

Some recent feminist social science research departs from convention in its insistence on relational models, which not only shift the focus away from decisionmaking outcomes but also challenge and transcend Western culture's dichotomy of power and intimacy. For example, Meyer (1991) has argued the need for incorporating the dilemmas involved in the 'love–power dichotomy' in a model that emphasizes the mutual and differential interest of parties in a dynamic relational context, including an analysis of structural aspects (p. 33). Meyer's and Komter's (1989, 1991) work has been influenced by Lukes's (1974) relational theory of power, which focuses on the actual content of relationships as defined by the participants. This is a three-dimensional, process-oriented framework, which addresses both the ideological and the structural aspects of power.[1]

Komter (1989, 1991) conceptualizes power in terms of its exercise in direct, observable conflict (manifest power); in terms of covert conflict and the mobilization of power or ideological values towards the prevention of issues being raised (invisible power); and finally as the discrepancy of interests of those exercising power and those subject to this power (latent power), which can be uncovered by identifying the parties' subjective preferences under hypothetical conditions of autonomy. Applying this model to an understanding of power in different domains of marital life, she directs our attention to five elements of power processes: 'desires for (or attempts at) change; structural or psychological impediments; the partner's reaction to change; strategies to realize or prevent change; and conflicts that may arise in the process of change' (Komter, 1991: 59).

I take a similar relational approach and foreground the dynamics which mediate power negotiations. Marital negotiations take place within a social-psychological landscape involving dynamics which may or may not inscribe power. While these dynamics are often acknowledged as important mediating factors, they tend to fall by the wayside in the search for causal relationships. Even research which points to the dynamic nature of marital relations and emphasizes the ongoing negotiation of the rules governing these relations often suffers from a common tendency to look for a causal relationship between an independent and a dependent variable. Beneria and Roldan's (1987) research on industrial home-workers in Mexico City is an example of compromising such mediation, in a final analysis which argues for the determining effect of the relative contribution of women to the household budget on the allocation of resources.[2]

In some empirical studies of marital power in Turkey there has been a concern with establishing a relationship between the employment status of the wife and power outcomes. Different researchers have made various observations about this relationship (Kuyaş, 1982; Ecevit, 1986). Drawing on my data, I shall argue the need for nuanced articulations of the mediations between breadwinner status and marital negotiations. There is no simple link between women's wage-work, their use of employment as a leverage to gain more power, and the renegotiation of gender relations in the household. The conditions for the sustenance or transformation of power relations are shaped by the interactive and mutually reinforcing effects of cultural, economic and emotional dynamics, best captured in a multidimensional and process-oriented approach that is sensitive to the complexity and interrelatedness of the multiple layers of marital interactions. I start my discussion of the data by arguing for the relevance of the cultural construction of gender for power relationships in the households of women wage-earners, followed by a discussion of women's expectations and how they relate to negotiations around finances, division of labour and marital intimacy. Then I situate negotiations at the household level within changes occurring in the broader cultural context, and use illustrative case-studies to flesh out the different patterns by which women engage with male authority.

Field research

In this project, I studied 41 households in which married women factory workers had been making a substantial contribution to the family income in the recent past. In order to determine eligibility for this study, I conducted initial screening interviews with 140 women. The selection of 41 households was partly based on my initial rapport with the women and the willingness of the husbands to co-operate. Given the conspicuous absence of couples data in Turkey, interviewing as many husbands as possible was a major goal.[3] Separate and often group tape-recorded interviews with 41 women and 27 men constituted the main source of information from the participants. The interviews were semi-structured and followed a life-history format.

The sample represents that sector of the urban low-income population in which men are not fully accountable in their most traditional responsibilities, namely, providing for the household. Wives worked full-time, five or six days a week. Since most did shift-work, their evenings were spent at work at least every other week. Wives were the major breadwinners in 58 per cent of the households, and the only stable breadwinners in 68 per cent of the households.[4] In 60 per cent of the households, husbands were either unemployed or did shift work/had flexible hours. Families were predominantly nuclear and relatively young. Except for one couple who were only recently married, all the couples had children.

Women respondents' ages ranged from 22 to 38, with a mean of 31. Their average residence in Istanbul was 19 years, and the mean age at arrival in Istanbul was 12. Six women were born in Istanbul, and most of the others had arrived there before the age of 18. As such, most women's secondary socialization occurred in the city. About half of the women had an elementary school diploma. At all levels of schooling, there were fewer drop-outs and more graduates among the men. The mean age of entry into wage-work was 17, and the average time in employment was 13 years. The men were slightly older and in general had more education than their wives.

The role of cultural mediation in marital negotiations

Women's expectations and marital realities
Whether or not women assume an assertive stance in marital negotiations is closely related to whether they see their employment as a resource, a source of leverage for power. This brings up the issue of the differential constructions of female employment by women and men. Elsewhere (Bolak, 1990; 1992), I have argued that the cultural context and particularly the construction of gender inform the internal negotiation of the dominant gender ideology by the women wage-earners and their husbands, and account for their differential positioning vis-à-vis the 'male provider' discourse. Women and men differ in how they construct female employment. Analysis reveals that women are not as threatened psychologically as are men by the disruption of such normative patterns as the ideal of the male provider.

Women's contextualization of their experience begins with the family. They see their employment as 'what is best for the family', and their overall evaluation of their husbands as 'responsible' or 'irresponsible' to the family (rather than to them) is an important determinant of their expectations from them. For women, more than for men, familial concerns are more important than gender conflict in marital negotiations. And thus, for women, the strong familialism characterizing the culture 'buffers', to some extent, the potential gender-conflict based on men not working and women working, or women earning more than men.

Almost all the women appreciate the relative independence that comes with their monthly pay-cheques. However, whether their breadwinner status empowers them in marital negotiations, and what stance they take to male authority, varies. Limitations posed by culturally sanctioned norms about male authority, including violence and the lack of alternatives to marriage, notwithstanding, individual women's life-experiences and how they make sense of them, the circumstances surrounding the marriage, the relative mesh between marriage expectations and current realities, and how they evaluate their husbands in terms of 'responsibility' and 'respect', mediate and inform marital negotiations as well. Most women's notions of manhood centre on the man's potential for responsible behaviour, rather than on his current ability to provide for his family. So, even women who have entered marriage with the expectation that their husbands would maintain the livelihood of the household refrain from flaunting their employment if, contrary to their expectations, they find themselves as the sole breadwinner, as long as they do not see their husbands as 'irresponsible'.

The prediction of previous research (Erkut, 1982) that role-sharing may not be viable for women in Turkey is not borne out for the large majority of women in this study. Women do expect their husbands to participate in domestic tasks, especially those associated with parenting, and unmet expectations result in more conflict than previous research suggested. It is true that having witnessed their hardworking mothers taking on both the domestic and breadwinning obligations, women feel less reliant on men whom they generally see as incompetent and peripheral to the running of the household. But they always make upward comparisons, comparing their husbands with men they hear about 'who are more helpful at home'. The conflict ensuing from these comparisons, however, is heightened when the husband defaults on both domestic and economic grounds.

The traditional women with longer rural backgrounds whose gender ideals were frustrated in their marriages, and younger, more urbanized women who are more assertive in their demands on their husbands, are the most dissatisfied with the absence of male participation, because they do not see their 'sacrifice' reciprocated. The most serious confrontations occur in households in which the husbands are unable to ask their wives to stop working for pay, and where the women are able to use their income as a source of leverage for power. These households are mostly in the category 'open power struggle', which is discussed below. Although women's economic superiority increases their expectations, and to some extent their husband's participation, it is only when their employment is constructed by their husbands as a 'contribution' and not a 'cost', and when the couple agree that the 'breadwinning' responsibility is a joint one, that male participation becomes somewhat predictable (Bolak, 1992a).

The typical understanding in the few households with the man as stable provider is an agreement that the woman works for a specific goal, whether it is to save money for a house or for retirement. Although they might both agree that they would not be able to own a home without her earnings, they hold on to the notion that she will work only as long as she can manage the 'double shift' (Hochschild, 1989), which, combined with the husband's job stability, serves to undermine any potential leverage she might have because of her breadwinner status. This ideological justification of inequality, like the specific excuses couples construct to sustain gendered parenting and housework, are excellent examples of invisible power dynamics. Women who end up taking the major responsibility for children's discipline or grocery shopping trace their husbands' lack of involvement to their lack of exposure to appropriate role models while growing up. For the women, the construction of the men as 'orphans' (literally or figuratively) or victims of unfortunate circumstances provides a gender-specific excuse and justification for their husbands' inadequate involvement in family work. Again, the locus of explanation for men's irresponsible behaviour shifts quickly from gender to the family, revealing the greater weight placed on the latter in the culture.

The relationship between women's breadwinner status and control over financial resources is also a mediated one. It is true that those women whose financial autonomy is not challenged by their husbands are all primary breadwinners. Similarly, if men are unemployed, they have to consult with their wives over any major expenditure. It is also the case, however, that as long as men do bring home some money, it is very difficult for women to veto a major decision such as buying property. Finally, how women use their leverage is again intimately related to their marital expectations and the nature of marital relations. For example, in the case where the man has shrugged off all his responsibilities and the wife has assumed the primary provider role over a long period of time, she also has full control over the finances and hands him a fixed allowance. But in most other cases, the decision as to who will manage the finances is a type of control which rests with the man. For example, it is not uncommon for women to be appointed as 'financial managers' by their husbands in households where resources are limited. Knowing that they can stretch the money a little further, women end up assuming an extra burden.

In households where the traditional basis of male authority is still relatively secure, women with financial superiority often help maintain the status quo and corroborate their husbands' 'masculinity' by handing over their pay-cheques to the men, even if they end up being the financial managers themselves. A woman with considerable control over the finances may nevertheless want to hand over this control to her husband, and may expect him to have a say in where she goes and who she sees in her spare time. Where male authority is not so secure, women's negotiating power and the strategies they can use are a joint function of the significance of her income for the family budget, marital history, whether there is a threat of violence, and the nature of the extended family relationships. For example, while one woman who is having to maintain the household on her own despite her husband's stronger income quits her job as a way of inviting her husband to assume some responsibility, another woman who is in a better financial position manages to bring herself over the years to a situation where she is able to use her whole pay-cheque to make monthly instalments on a flat in her name.

Although it is generally difficult for women to admit to using their employment as leverage to gain power in the household, the nature of the everyday interactions in which they are embedded inform their reference-groups, which in turn influence their self-perceptions and the stance they take with their husbands. A traditional woman, whose work exposes her to only one other woman (also from her own village) and an occasional interaction with the foreman, and whose social life outside work is restricted to obligatory visits to her husband's relatives, has a quite limited repertoire to draw upon when compared to a woman who works with six hundred men and women on the same floor and socializes with them after work. In the first instance, the husband feels much more in control and is less threatened by the woman's employment; in the second csae, the intense socializing that goes on at work has a radicalizing influence on the woman, increasing her sensitivity to inequality at home and thus making her husband feel more threatened by the solidarity among women at work.

Men's jealousy about woman-to-woman relationships and their attempts to control their wives' movements stem from the threat they feel from the solidarity that women forge with other women, and their feelings of being left out! Kıray (1984) identifies communication problems as a major source of incompatibility that arises after the move from the rural context, in which extended family relationships and sex segregation prevail, to the big city, where on the one hand couples are relatively isolated, and on the other hand, they are exposed to the urban culture of 'sharing'. It is because of this 'residual isolation' that young couples especially experience this alienation as problematic. Much as women complain about their husbands' lack of understanding and appreciation they mostly take a patient yet nonchalant attitude towards their husbands, while urban life makes men more dependent on their wives' attention and understanding. In fact, for most men the wife is still the confidante and the person closest to them, whereas women seem to gain more options. Although women's maternalism leads them at times to overlook their husbands' expensive hobbies, it often does not make them emotionally dependent on men. It appears that female employment leaves men's needs for 'mothering' unmet at the critical time when they also lack the support of the extended family.

Relationships with the extended family and community
Marital power relationships are embedded in the context of extended family, kin and other community relationships. For example, the nature of a woman's relationship with her family of origin, particularly with her mother, has a major influence on her negotiating power in marriage. Women with the most leverage in marital negotiations have mothers who, like themselves, are strong, and support their decisions to keep working while making a point of not getting involved in their marital problems. Women with the least leverage, on the other hand, are more traditional women who are isolated from their families of origin.

Even within the limits of this small-scale study, the observations of family scholars concerning the growing reliance on daughters rather than sons for old-age security finds some support. It is in this context that the relationships with the wife's family gains significance. Women who have come out of their short periods of separation from their husbands with an increased confidence in their abilities to support themselves and their children can more easily envision the prospect of divorce if they can count on their families, especially their brothers, to be supportive. Those women who lack this support find it harder to make this decision, and are more vulnerable vis-à-vis their husbands' control.

With the erosion of the economic basis of the patriarchal relationships between different generations of men, the relationships of support and control are also weakening. This shift in men's connection with their families of origin has implications for their relationships with their wives, contributing to a more negotiable state of affairs in the household. After their relatively sheltered lives in the village, men find themselves on their own in the city with a lot of responsibilities that they feel unprepared to deal with. For example, quite a few of the men I talked to regretted as being premature their decision to get married. Confronted with the challenges of urban living and feeling overwhelmed by the economic responsibilities which they feel inadequate to fulfil, it is common for men to compensate by using other means to maintain their sense of manhood in the community, such as entertaining their friends and lending money. This behaviour makes them the target for their wives' accusation that 'he wants to show off even though he is poor'.

Indeed, an asymmetrical situation emerges in several households, with the wives having to be extra thrifty at home to compensate for their husbands' tendency to be spendthrift outside the home. In other words, men's generosity outside the home necessitates women's thriftiness inside the home. Spending prerogatives and priorities appear to be gendered, too, with men more interested in ostentatious spending and women more realistic and pragmatic in their priorities. In several households men do not collaborate with women towards ensuring the welfare of their households; instead, by competing for scarce economic and emotional resources, recapitulating in their own relationships with their sons their unfulfilling relationships with their fathers. Consequently, not only the wives, but also the children are compromised in this pursuit of manhood (Bolak, 1990; 1992).

Men's relationships with their agnates and fellow villagers are uneasy ones in the urban context of economic insecurity, where high expectations of financial help and assistance with finding jobs make disappointment almost inevitable. Afraid of rejection and of further injury to their sense of pride, the men may avoid going to their kin for help. When the men are broke, no longer able to maintain their ostentatious spending and hence their status in the community, they become totally dependent on their wives for support. It is when the woman's economic advantage coincides in this way with the man's loss of community supports that her leverage increases and he becomes relatively defenceless. This painful process often results in a paradoxical situation with the woman burdened by a disproportionate amount of responsibility on the one hand, and an increased leverage, on the other.

With time, the woman is also able to have a greater influence on her husband's relationship with his family and friends. It is when the man is economically vulnerable and disillusioned by the lack of support from his own community that he finally starts to take his wife more seriously. Hence, especially in those areas where he was vulnerable to the influence of his kin in the earlier days of marriage, she gains an increased negotiating power, bolstered by her economic advantage. For example, she is able to assert herself more in her husband's work-related decisions, having relatively greater success in discouraging him from getting into questionable business partnerships with his brothers or other kin. Likewise, she becomes less vulnerable to violence by her husband stemming from problems with her in-laws.

A woman's increased assertiveness with her in-laws and especially her brother-in-law is a sign of what I see as a more negotiable set of authority relations developing in the households of women providers. One concrete example of the weakening nature of patriarchal relationships is a woman's ability to avoid visiting her in-laws even when she has no financial autonomy. Resistance to socializing with kin is often the only recourse a woman has and which she can easily legitimate by reminding her husband that she is a 'working woman'. The fact that two-thirds of the women preferred 'being able to do certain things without having to consult their husbands' over 'having a husband take full responsibility for maintaining his household' suggests the importance of autonomy for these breadwinners.

In what follows, I illustrate with examples how marital negotiations are not simply a function of how much money each spouse makes, and how different dimensions work in concert to determine the tone of these negotiations.

Patterns of negotiations at the household level

In her argument for deconstructing the notion of patriarchy, Kandiyoti (1988) contends that 'systematic analyses of women's strategies and coping mechanisms can help to capture the nature of patriarchal systems in their class specific and temporal concreteness and reveal how men and women resist, accommodate, adapt, and conflict with each other over resources, rights and responsibilities' (p. 285). How the cultural ideology about gender is negotiated at the *household* level by working women and their husbands is an empirical question which is the prime concern of this study. A close scrutiny of the sample reveals a complexity which I hope to illustrate by presenting concrete case-studies representing different interactions of the various levels of determination.

Open power struggle
Most intense negotiations take place in the households of younger and more urbanized women with longer schooling, employment prior to marriage, apparent lack of conservatism, and childcare needs. These women consider their husbands to be unappreciative of them and insensitive to their needs, and engage with them in a power struggle which often has the appearance of a 'tug of war'. They choose their female co-workers as their reference-group and compare their husbands with men who 'help more'; they seem to experience the least conflict resulting from the disjuncture between the girlhood dream of being perfect caterers for their husbands and the modern ideal of 'role sharing' to which they are exposed on the shop floor. Family life is characterized by conflicts over expenditure, women's access to money, and physical violence. The women are engaged in an open power struggle with their husbands and strategize to maximize their control. The men perceive their prerogatives threatened by the seeming autonomy and assertiveness of their wives, and employ different means to curb their autonomy. Their perception of their wives as having overstepped their limits as 'disrespectful women' makes them overly defensive and prone to using 'manifest power'.

Kadir and Hatice Koşan have both been employed in different factory jobs. Hatice Koşan stayed in her first job after they got married for two-and-a-half years, during which time the factory her husband was working in closed down and he was left idle for seven months. She left her job to get severance pay to use towards the down-payment for a place of their own. If she had stayed in her job, she would now have been the primary breadwinner. She was at home for two years, worked in another job for one-and-a-half years until that factory closed down. She took another job, but left after two years to go into shift-work, which she has been doing for the last two years. During the two years she worked at her previous job, her husband lost his factory job again and was unemployed for a year-and-a-half. He has been in his current job for three years, but he wants to leave and return to the village to open his own grocery store.

Hatice Koşan remembers her working mother and her father as sharing household tasks, and compares her husband unfavourably with her father. While she got married with some reluctance, he rushed into it in order to avoid an arranged marriage with his cousin. Marriage severed his ties with his mother. Now that he has a 'working' wife, his mother doesn't indulge him as she used to; she tells him: 'You two can take care of each other.' When he complains about his wife, she says, 'You found her yourself!' He feels that as the oldest of three brothers, there is nobody for him to confide in, nobody to give him advice. He wants someone older to restrain him from beating his wife, but such sanctions are not available.

Kadir Koşan had thought his wife would not be working, but found himself overwhelmed with responsibility and unable to ask her to stop. He compensates for her having to work by underestimating her contributions: 'Your money is barely enough to pay for childcare and my cigarettes', and by trying to bolster his masculinity with violence. Hatice Koşan's ambivalence about being a working mother is largely mediated by her husband's put-downs and lack of cooperation. Her frustration conflicts with his sexism and results in a tug of war over the allocation of family work and resources. Each refuses to help the other with their respective tasks: 'Repair work is not my responsibility if you won't go to the store!' she says. For fear that she might leave him, Kadir Koşan used to help with household tasks before their son was born; now he feels that the boy is old enough to stay with him, even if she leaves.

Knowing that her husband cannot afford to ask her to stop working, Hatice Koşan resorts to all the strategies in her power. One reason she changed from a day job to shift-work was so that her husband would have to take their son to daycare when she was at work. Finding it demeaning to serve his son 'as if he were an old man', when she works the evening shift, he wants her to change to a day job. When her husband challenges the amount of money she spends in the market-place, she tells him, 'You do it then.'

Knowing he will not want to be seen with a shopping bag and that he will not be able to stretch the money as she does, Kadir Koşan feels he has no choice but to let her do the shopping, knowing at the same time that she secretly saves from the money earmarked for household expenditures. They both attempt to secure control over resources and strive to maximize their spending money; in fact, he does not reveal the amount of his pay-cheque to her and retains a generous allowance before handing the rest to her for expenses. She also gets social rewards from her job and makes him even more insecure by keeping a tight network of friends. But ultimately, she lacks the support-system to risk divorcing her husband. She does not have her family nearby and as a result of losing seniority when she withdrew her compensation to pay for their house, her earnings are low.

This basic structure shows slight variations from other households', with women's strategies depending on the nature of extended-family relations and the relative earnings of the spouses. For example, Saray Sağlam's family is supportive of her decision to divorce her husband, which, combined with her strong economic position, makes it easier to go ahead with the divorce. Another woman, who practically runs the household on her income alone, decides to stop working as a way to invite her husband to use his earnings more responsibly.

Patriarchal accommodation
Under this second system, there is little *visible* contest of wills, encouraging us to look more closely at 'latent' or 'invisible power'. The wives are less challenging of the ground-rules and do not seem to aspire to a renegotiation of gendered prerogatives. They are careful not to override the implicit agreement against wives' use of their employment as a leverage for gaining power. Even as the only stable providers in their families, they see the breadwinning responsibility and the rights that go along with it as belonging to the husband. The men have latent power even when they do not use violence. As in the previous group, in those few households in which the wife is the secondary provider, the discourse is that she is *allowed* to work as long as the male prerogatives in the household are not challenged. Two cases will illustrate the different mechanisms

through which this system works.

Şimşir Doğar and Eyüp Doğar have been married for twelve years. In the first three years, they were both employed in the factory they are working in now. When one child became ill, the wife stayed at home for three years. About three years ago, she decided to make use of her past training to become a seamstress and found a well-paid job. Her upward mobility caused jealousy and violence on the part of her husband quite like that in the previous group, and led to a marital breakdown, triggered by her husband's family who 'were envious of our lifestyle'. Toying with the idea of divorce, and after several months of separation, she finally agreed to a reconciliation. After they made up, she returned to her first job at the confectionery factory. Having lost seniority, like Hatice Koşan, she started with the minimum wage. The status quo was stabilized with the husband consolidating his position as the primary breadwinner once again. The couples' interviews were similar, except for the husband's denial of her ever having been the primary breadwinner and the marital problems that it caused.

Şimşir Doğar's subjectivity about being a wage-earner needs to be understood in the context of her expectations and her husband's attitudes. Unlike Hatice Koşan, who witnessed her parents as sharing household tasks, Şimşir Doğar grew up with a mother who was at home and a father who did nothing around the house. Hence, she has no expectations of male participation; but even when she has occasional need for help, her husband responds, 'Quit if you can't manage both! After all, you only make 50 thousand liras.' Şimşir Doğar's small and thus 'humiliating' pay-cheque, and her perception that 'a woman should not work unless she has something creative or important to do, something which requires responsibility' (as in her previous well-paid job, from which she had to resign to save her marriage), collude with her husband's unaccommodating attitude and result in an unsettled stance that vacillates between modernity and traditionalism. She criticizes those women like Hatice Koşan above who save money without their husbands' knowing or others who 'order their husbands around'. Even when she was the primary breadwinner, she used to hand her pay-cheque over to her husband. Unlike Hatice Koşan, who sees herself as not too maternal, Şimşir Doğar invests all her passion in mothering her two boys.

Paternalism is one means through which patriarchal authority is maintained in the household without physical force. In the interview, Eyüp Doğar presents a 'Pygmalion' story of their marriage and sees himself as her 'educator and socializer', which accords with her story. Having married when very young to a man fifteen years her senior, she constructs the marriage as based on 'friendship and respect, not on love'. This age difference justifies his authority, even his extreme jealousy. His treatment of her as 'daddy's girl', and their consensus on child-centredness further compensate for his authoritarianism. Furthermore, his dissatisfaction with his family's role in their separation has somewhat tempered his arbitrary control over her behaviour.

Traditionalism is another means whereby authority is maintained. In the Onur household, the couple have been married for sixteen years. The wife has been employed in her current job for the last fifteen years; the husband had been working as a courier in a bank for thirteen years when he was fired – 'unjustly' they think – three years ago. After a short period of unemployment, he started to work in the neighbourhood coffee shop and his breadwinner status shifted from primary to secondary. Like Şimşir Doğar, Semiha Onur observes her husband's authority on traditional grounds, and sees him as basically a good family man who is not altogether irresponsible. She is protective of her husband while inwardly experiencing conflict. Though she questions the inequality in the proportion of their wages that go into the household budget, she overlooks it since 'he is not in good health and needs more pocket money to eat well at his job'; despite her fatigue, she tries to be accommodating to his sexual needs and tries to bolster his ego, in a manner typically associated with working-class women in the literature (Rubin, 1976). In the Onur household, the mesh between the gender ideologies of the husband and wife provides the cement that consolidates the patriarchal order in the household even when the husband is not securely employed. However, her internal conflict surfaces in such statements as 'If it weren't for me, he might have died somewhere, but he wouldn't appreciate what I did for him.' Women feel most conflicted psychologically if their gift of traditional deference is not appreciated by husbands whose agenda about marriage may have changed with their adoption of the urban lifestyle.

Traditional defiance
In the previous group, the men are not yet accused of being 'irresponsible', and hence are able to enjoy their wives' tolerant

and protective attitude towards them. The fact that conflict does not become violent is due to the women's accommodating stance. The characteristic pattern in a third group of households is neither an accommodation to male dominance, nor an active contestation for power, but a curious combination of ritualistic adherence to traditional norms in public on the one hand, and private mockery and manipulation of their husbands on the other, resulting from their feelings of betrayal and disillusionment. This group of women can be most aptly described as 'urban villagers' and best fit Kandiyoti's (1988) description of female conservatism in reaction to the breakdown of classic patriarchy: 'Despite the obstacles that classic patriarchy puts in women's way, which may far outweigh any actual economic and emotional security, women often resist the process of transition because they see the old order slipping away from them without any empowering alternatives' (p. 282).

These are women with more recent rural origins who experience the biggest gap between their expectations that they would not have to work after marriage, and their current situation. Although they are similar to those in the previous group in terms of their relative traditionalism, the manifestations of men's failure to fulfil their provider responsibilities are very different in the two groups. Women's dissatisfaction with their 'irresponsible' husbands and their conviction that, contrary to their expectations, they will continue to remain solely responsible for maintaining the household, leads them to challenge their husbands' authority, even if this questioning remains within traditional boundaries. This pattern resembles most closely the findings of Beneria and Roldan (1987) in Mexico City, and those of el-Messiri (1978) in Cairo, in that the man's provider role assumes centrality in women's depiction of manhood.

Hacer Itır is a hard-working woman who grew up witnessing her own mother in charge of the home and the farm and her father as a wanderer. Because of childcare problems, her daughter is with her husband's family in the village. They have both had different factory jobs, interrupted by plant closing or their temporary relocation to the village, neither lasting for long. The husband has not worked for a year-and-a-half. Hacer Itır sees herself as both the man and the woman of the house and says: 'Of course breadwinning is man's responsibility, otherwise why call him a man?' Although she does not mind working *per se*, it is hard for her to reconcile her image of womanhood with having to support her husband while her daughter has to grow up in the village. Yet, her employment poses no threat to male prerogatives in public. She still lets her husband do the actual transaction when they make a major purchase, as it is not in her interest to humiliate him in public – to that extent, they collude in maintaining the status quo.

The context within which these women operate facilitates the maintenance of the status quo. They are mostly insulated from the radicalizing influences to which more urbanized women are exposed. Hatice Itır is embedded in a tight kinship network and does not even look at men where she works, let alone talk with them. Her husband, whose brother owns a coffee-house in the neighbourhood, argues that he makes enough tips for his own, and even for household expenses, by just hanging around the coffee-house. While he cannot ask his wife to stop working, he protects his pride by denying his dependence on her. He has redefined the situation by seeing himself in control and her as deferential, and by projecting a self-sufficient image. The devaluation of their wives' contribution and overstatement of their own contribution are the symbolic ways by which these men maintain the balance of power in the household.

At home, Hacer Itır talks back to her husband, and even resorts to strategies like not sleeping with him and not paying attention when he is sick. In other similar households, women may mock their husbands, as when one woman responds to her husband's suggestion that he will get married again: 'Who would take you?' Another may refuse to cook or do her husband's laundry unless he brings home money. The women call their husbands to task not only for failing to be adequate providers, but for failing to take care of 'male tasks' such as shopping for food. While let down, they make frequent references to not wanting to 'lose their honour' by leaving their husbands; all invoke religion in their ambivalent responses to their situation. One woman says: 'Heaven is at the mercy of the husband', meaning that if she wants to go to heaven, she will have to be patient! In religious families female employment causes estrangement in the marital relationship, which reminds us of Mernissi's (1975) depiction of Muslim Morocco, where the increased economic participation of women comes to have an 'emasculating' effect on men, who are by law entitled to control their women.

Power renegotiated

There is another group of women whose primary breadwinner status, and personal resources such as self-confidence, responsibility, decisionmaking ability and perseverance, combined with their husbands' loss of social and economic status result in a more fluid situation with regard to power. In these households, women have gained an ascendancy with which they may or may not be comfortable, but which enables them to be assertive in the household with less challenge by their husbands than in the previous groups. Gündüz Bakır says, 'When I got married, I thought my husband was going to be authoritative and I was going to obey him, but things have not turned out that way.' She has gradually learned to enjoy her more forceful presence in the household. Her husband tries to bolster his masculinity by arguing that, 'the wife fits the home just as a flower fits a vase': quite ironic since she has always worked. But he feels respected by her despite his lack of stable employment.

The extent to which these women are able to enjoy their relative autonomy depends partly on their attitudes about gender. A comparison between the Türksan and Ceviz households will reveal the difference. Necmiye Türksan's expectations were initially very similar to those of the women in the previous group, but being a strong-willed woman and seeing that her husband is not the 'responsible man' she had hoped for, she does what she had to do when she was a single woman taking care of her mother – she takes the reins herself. She started working when she was 10 years old, and has been working ever since. She has been the household's primary and only steady breadwinner since marriage and her husband has been an irresponsible provider, until a year ago when they got back together after she separated from him for a year. Her decision to agree to a reconciliation has partly to do with her wanting to own a flat and knowing that she cannot take care of her daughters and pay for the flat at the same time. Now her entire pay-cheque goes towards the instalments for a flat, and her husband is responsible for maintaining the household.

Like Necmiye Türksan, Remziye Ceviz sees herself as 'like a man'. She arrived in Istanbul from Yugoslavia when she was 18 and declared herself the head of her parental household. Although both women are Yugoslavian immigrants, she has a more modern outlook than Necmiye Türksan. She never thought of stopping work; in fact, she told her husband, 'I might divorce you, but I would never leave my job!' She has been working in her present job without any interruption, while her husband has had a bumpy work history in the last five years and only recently got a steady though low-paying job upon his wife's insistence: 'She told me that from now on, I had to go to work at 8 a.m. and come home at 5 p.m. and that's what I'm doing.' He now hands over his pay-cheque to his wife. In both the Türksan and the Ceviz households, the men have assumed more parenting responsibilities since their 'rehabilitation'.

Both women have complete jurisdiction over household matters and enjoy full independence. To them their husbands appear 'childish and gullible'. Niyazi Türksan is alone in Istanbul and does not have any kin support. On the other hand, he is surrounded by his wife's mother and kin network. Like Niyazi Türksan, Özcan Ceviz has become disillusioned with kin, especially with his mother's role in trying to break up his marriage. His loss of economic power due to his alcohol habit brought about the loss of his support system as well, and he has taken refuge in his wife's support. Both men seem to have humbled over the years, and have had to come to terms with their wives' strengths. Like the Türksan couple, the Ceviz couple have been socializing mainly with the wife's network of friends and family, which is a significant indicator of the wife's relative advantage. Marital compatibility is higher in the Ceviz household, which makes it easier for the couple to define the wife's new role in maternal terms, whereas Necmiye Türksan is not willing to mother her husband and experiences the situation as more anomalous. There are other marriages in which women's maternalism is becoming an increasingly important resource for the men.

The patriarchal ideal of man as the primary provider is no longer viable for these women. If they are secretly harbouring a desire for more male authority/responsibility, and projecting their husbands as being a little more authoritative than they actually are, it is to match what they perceive to be the normative standard in society. But their lives and self-definitions appear to be quite independent of their husbands. They derive strength from their female networks, and those who live in close proximity to their mothers have a solid support system.

Resisting conflict

Lukes's concepts of 'latent' and 'invisible' power are most relevant to understanding the marital dynamics in two groups of households. In the group identified under 'patriarchal accommodation', paternalism or traditional attitudes deflect conflict. In yet another small group of households, conflict is again not the predominant reality. In these households, a compromise solution has stabilized which has the semblance of 'separate but equal' without implying equality in all domains of family life. A situation in which the interpersonal dynamics in the household cannot be adequately tapped by the concepts of domination or negotiation, it involves a relative lack of defensiveness on the part of men – which allows a definition of the situation in terms of, 'Two hands are better than one', and a comfortable sense of autonomy for women.

In this group, more than any other, the women insist that their husbands' failure to maintain their households did not have an adverse effect on their relationship. Like those in the previous group, women seek more initiative and resourcefulness on the part of their husbands, but they also enjoy the appreciation they receive for being providers and for the relative autonomy that comes with being the stronger spouse. The ethic of 'shared funds' is most characteristic of this group; similarly, it is in these households and in the previous group of households that the couples have the most satisfactory cooperation in childcare. The fact that the husbands are cooperating with them for the welfare of the household makes it difficult for women to use their employment status as a resource in marital negotiations, and buffers any further claims to power they might have had.

In the Mermer household, the husband is the traditional head of household, but the wife is the manager, the central figure. She makes the decisions about where she will go and on what she will spend money. There are areas in which she usually cannot go far when she first attempts to change his mind – he likes to make his own decisions about setting up partnerships, for example. But he is not an irresponsible provider, and manages to keep bringing in income, even if he is not securely employed. Nezaket Mermer is a resilient woman who holds her own and will not be dominated. She is also one of the women who likes to be in charge of housework, but has enjoyed her husband's cooperation in childcare when the children were younger. Although such women are again more resourceful than their husbands, the dynamics characterized by an ideology of 'mutuality' are different from those of households in which the marital history has empowered women in tandem with their husbands' behaviour as irresponsible provider, and loss of social supports.

Even when decisionmaking appears to be joint, a closer look sometimes reveals the husband's greater power of veto and asymmetries in the strategies of influence used by the couple. An example of a less visible power differential occurs in situations where the husband and wife have been working opposite shifts so as to take turns with childcare, and have by now come to a point where the man avoids being with his wife in order to stay out of conflict and to make sure he is not 'irritated'.

Conclusion

In the households of women breadwinners, conditions for the maintenance and transformation of the traditional patriarchal relationships are shaped by the interactive effects of the economic, cultural and emotional dynamics taking place. The women's dilemmas around using their employment as source of leverage for power point to the force of cultural constructions of gender, responsibility and male authority on the one hand; and to the limitations on women's choice posed by the threat of violence and lack of alternatives, on the other. Despite these barriers, employment forces the limits of traditionalism *in practice*. Whether or not the woman's position as breadwinner has a critical effect on her financial autonomy and on the allocation of household responsibilities, the traditional basis of male authority *is* ideologically challenged through a discourse that includes intra- as well as extra-household roles in the definition of 'male responsibility'. The scope of this challenge varies, depending on women's economic power, on the extent to which their expectations are affirmed in marriage, and on the characteristics of their cultural milieu. Nevertheless, the language of negotiation does seem to be changing, with such emotional factors as understanding and attention figuring more strongly in the equation.

Marital power is constructed through the complex interplay between male responsibility and female respect. The women's difficulties with subscribing to the norm of 'obedience' to male authority, and the men's uneasiness, need to be evaluated in this light. For many women, the traditional justification of male authority as 'might makes right' retains its validity often as a cultural script, without necessarily being internalized, suggesting a weakening of at least the 'invisible' dimension of male authority if not of the 'manifest' and 'latent' (Lukes, 1974). These dynamics are situated in the context of looser relations of support and control among different generations of men, which further contributes to the making of a more flexible basis for marital negotiations. Over time, women may encounter a paradoxical situation, characterized by their disproportionate burden resulting from male irresponsibility on the one hand, and their increased negotiating power on the other. It is clear that we need relational and process-oriented frameworks which are sensitive to the interaction of multiple levels of determination of power.

Notes

1. A 'one-dimensional' perspective compares the stated preferences of the parties involved to actual outcomes (manifest power); a 'two-dimensional' perspective attends to areas of non-decisionmaking to identify potential grievances and issues that one of the parties has been unable to place on the common agenda (invisible power); a 'three-dimensional' perspective carries the argument one step further by looking for interpretations of situations and relations that block alternatives from view and by identifying what seems 'inevitable' or 'unchangeable' to the parties in the relationship (latent power). Within this framework, a powerful position is one in which 'more stated preferences are realized, fewer grievances are harbored and fewer aspects of the relationship are interpreted as inevitable or unchangeable' (Meyer: 38).

2. While arguing on the one hand that negotiation of the terms of interaction and exchange between husbands and wives is a continuous process mediated by various factors, their analysis foregrounds the husband's loss of his role as breadwinner in facilitating such renegotiation.

3. Through a chain of contacts ranging from union leaders to company presidents, I gained access to five factories, each representing one of the five branches of the manufacturing subsector of the industry (tobacco, pharmaceuticals, garments, textiles and confectionery) with the highest concentration of women workers. These factories also displayed a wide variety in terms of wages and job security, type of ownership, availability of childcare facilities and location in the city.

4. The analysis revealed that an operationalization of women's breadwinner status based on their relative monetary contribution to the household budget alone was inadequate. An important component of this status resides in the stability of employment and the continuous nature of their contribution. The contribution of the stably employed women to the household made fluctuations in male income and employment possible, and their relative earnings during the last year was an imperfect measure of their relative contribution to the household. A more comprehensive assessment yielded the

following: (a) in 22 of the 41 households, the wives had made the major monetary contribution to their households, while in 11 households, men had made the major contribution, and the contributions of husbands and wives were about equal in the remaining 8 households; (b) in 27 households, women had been the only stable breadwinners in the recent past (and 20 of these women had also been the major providers), while in 10 households husbands and wives had both been stable breadwinners, and in 3 households, both had been unstable breadwinners.

References

Beneria, L. and Roldan, M. (1987). *The Crossroads of Class and Gender*, University of Chicago Press, Chicago.

Bolak, H. (1990). 'Women breadwinners and the construction of gender: urban working class households in Turkey', PhD Dissertation, University of California, Santa Cruz.

Bolak, H. (1992). 'He loves to show off even though he is poor!: Gender strategies in the working class household', Manuscript in preparation for submission.

Bolak, H. (1992a). 'When wives are major providers: Culture, gender and family work', Manuscript in revision for submission.

Duben, A. (1982). 'The significance of family and kinship in urban Turkey', in Ç. Kağıtçıbaşı (ed.), *Sex Roles, Family and Community in Turkey*, Indiana University Turkish Studies Press, Bloomington.

Ecevit, Y. (1986). 'Gender and wage work: A case study of Turkish women in manufacturing industry', unpublished PhD dissertation, University of Kent, Canterbury.

el-Messiri, S. (1978). 'Self-images of traditional urban women in Cairo', in L. Beck and N. Keddie, (eds.), *Women in the Muslim World*, Harvard University Press, Cambridge, Massachusetts.

Erkut, S. (1982). 'Dualism in values toward education of Turkish women', in Ç. Kağıtçıbaşı, (ed.), *Sex Roles, Family and Community in Turkey*, Indiana University Turkish Studies Press, Bloomington.

Glenn, E.N. (1987). 'Gender and the family', in B.B. Hess and M.M. Ferree, (eds.), *Analyzing Gender: A Handbook of Social Science Research*, Sage Publications, Newbury Park, CA.

Hochschild, A. (1989). *The Second Shift: Working Parents and the Revolution at Home*, Viking, New York.

Kağıtçıbaşı, Ç. (1984). 'Intra-family dynamics and relationships: a model of family change', in T. Erder (ed.), *Family in Turkish Society*, Social Science Association, Ankara.

Kandiyoti, D. (1984). 'Rural transformation in Turkey and its implications for women's status', in *Women on the Move: Contemporary Changes in Family and Society*, UNESCO, Paris.

Kandiyoti, D. (1984). 'Changes and continuities in the family structure: A comparative perspective', in T. Erder (ed.), *Family in Turkish Society*, Social Science Association, Ankara.

Kandiyoti, D. (1988). 'Bargaining with patriarchy', *Gender and Society*, vol. 2, no. 3, pp. 74–91.

Kıray, M. (1976). 'Changing roles of mothers: Changing intra-family relations in a Turkish town', in J. Peristiany (ed.), *Mediterranean Family Structures*, Cambridge University Press, London.

Kıray, M. (1982). 'The women of small towns', in N. Abadan-Unat (ed.), *Women in Turkish Society*, E.J. Brill, Leiden.

Kıray, M. (1984). 'Metropolitan city and the changing family', in T. Erder (ed.), *Family in Turkish Society*, Social Science Association, Ankara.

Komter, A. (1989). 'Hidden power in marriage', *Gender and Society*, vol. 3, no. 2, pp. 187–216.

Komter, A. (1991). 'Gender, power and feminist theory', in K. Davis, M. Leijenaar and J. Oldersma (eds.), *The Gender of Power*, Sage Publications, New York.

Kuyaş, N. (1982). 'The effects of female labor on power relations in the urban Turkish family', in Ç. Kağıtçıbaşı (ed.), *Sex Roles, Family and Community in Turkey*, Indiana University Turkish Studies Press, Bloomington.

Lukes, S. (1974). *Power: A Radical View*, Macmillan, New York.

McDonald, G.W. (1980). 'Family power: The assessment of a decade of theory and research, 1970–1979', *Journal of Marriage and the Family*, vol. 42, pp. 841–54.

Mernissi, F. (1975). *Beyond the Veil*, John Wiley, New York.

Meyer, J. (1991). 'Power and love: Conflicting conceptual schemata', in K. Davis, M. Leijenaar and J. Oldersma (eds.), *The Gender of Power*, Sage Publications, New York.

Özbay, F. (1994). See Chapter 5 above.

Rubin, L.B. (1976). *Worlds of Pain: Life in the Working-class Family*, Basic Books, New York.

Friend and Foe? Forging Alliances with Other Women in a Village of Western Turkey

Nükhet Sirman★

The issue of power has bedevilled attempts to analyse the exact nature of women's subordination in a variety of social and cultural contexts. The impossibility of attributing complete powerlessness to women has produced attempts to qualify the nature of the power that women may have in situations where they are obviously under the control of others. Concepts such as 'hidden' power or 'negative' power have recently been superseded by an increased interest in what Scott has called 'weapons of the weak' and by attempts to deploy Foucauldian ideas such as 'resistance', in the effort to seek out a more relational view of power that would to some extent allow the subordinated a greater role in defining their conditions of existence. On the other hand, all assertions of female power have met their own opposition from those who warn of the dangers of underestimating the structural obstacles posed by patriarchy to women's emancipation.

★ This is a revised version of a paper submitted to the symposium on 'Women in the 1980s and in Migration' organized by Kassel University. I would like to thank the participants, especially Gül Özyeğin and Ayşe Saktanber, for providing criticism and support. I would also like to thank Şirin Tekeli for her patience and trust in women.

It would be fair to say that assertions of female power have nowhere been more contentious than in the Middle East. With powerful symbols of powerlessness such as the veil and Islam, it has indeed been difficult to maintain that women are in any way able to determine their own lives. Attempts by various social scientists to discover a space for female power in segregation itself (Fallers and Fallers, 1976; Ahmed, 1982) have been criticized for ignoring the sphere in which power *really* lies. A justified concern for the rights of Middle Eastern women has, paradoxically, rendered them invisible and silent victims of essential traditions, and made writiing about difference indeed a peril (Lazreg, 1988).[1]

Writing about peasant women has a twist of its own. Their participation in production, the position of the household as a total unit of production and consumption, and the limited amount of power exercised by peasant men in relation to society at large, have raised questions regarding the applicability of well-known conceptual dichotomies such as production/ reproduction, private/public and power/influence, to the analysis of peasant society and culture (Rogers, 1978; Dubisch, 1986; Delaney, 1991). On the basis of the economic and political importance of marriage and family in rural societies, some anthropologists have even argued that the centrality of women in organizing in these domains allows them to gain a measure of power outside the 'domestic' sphere as well (Friedl, 1967; Harding, 1975; Dubisch, 1986).

These difficulties are echoed in discourses on peasant women generated by the elite in many modernizing Middle Eastern countries. In Turkey peasant women are perceived to be both stronger than urban women and yet more subordinated at the same time (Inan, 1968). This contradictory opinion stems in part from the republican ideology that entrusts the peasant woman with the job of bearing the imprint of a mythical pre-Islamic democratic order (Kandiyoti, 1988a). It also stems from both republican and Marxist analyses that, for rather different reasons, exalt the value of full participation in production. And yet both republicans and Marxists – until recently the two main ideologies shaping elite discourses in Turkey – also depict peasant women as victims, either because of a lack of education which hinders them from deriving the full benefits of republican reforms (Abadan-Unat, 1978: 135), or because peasant women are, like slaves, bought and sold like chattels as well as being worked to death (Altındal, 1977: 103, 113).

It seems that, rather than delivering judgements about which woman is more oppressed than the other (whether in the east or west; in cities or villages), we need to develop ways of understanding how womanhood is produced in specific contexts; the kind of pressures that shape women as well as the means available to women to resist oppression. This is particularly true in the case of Turkish village women, about whom there is indeed scant ethnographic research. Above all, we need to question received images of the 'typical' village woman and look at the specific conditions under which women in different villages live and work. Second, we need to allow more room for the experiences and and life-strategies followed by women themselves, rather than relying totally on structural determinants of household formation and production. Even studies which have attempted to incorporate change in their perspectives have identified the locus of change either in general social conditions or in familial status related to a woman's life-cycle (Kıray 1976; Kandiyoti 1988b). Thus women are seen as going through a cyclical process from victim to victimizer, whereby they begin as new brides at the lowest rung of the household hierarchy and gradually acquire power with age, children, and especially when they become mothers-in-law themselves.[2]

Another much abused concept, that of patriarchy, also needs to be questioned. Apart from recognizing that patriarchy has different forms (see Kandiyoti, 1988b), we need to be aware of the limitations of the concept itself. Too much emphasis on the systematic nature of the subordination of women not only removes any notion of agency from the concept; it also objectifies women by turning them into silent victims, as well as rendering relations of power static and unchangeable. More attention should be paid to the ways in which both women and men perceive and use social relations and cultural ideas regarding the nature of power and its operations. Bearing in mind that all social structures open up particular spaces of operation for socially positioned individuals, we should investigate what this space consists of for women and what women do within this space, as well as the means available to them for enlarging its boundaries. It is in the practice of everyday life, in the very process of negotiating these spaces, that notions of gender are redefined. This process of negotiation transcends the boundaries of the household and produces often contradictory ideas regarding what it means to be a man or a woman.

This chapter will attempt to describe the lived conditions of womanhood in a village in western Turkey by considering the relationships established by women in the family, in the neighbourhood and in the village as strategies for empowerment. The aim is to analyse the particular forms that the power relations generally called patriarchy take in a particular context, by looking at the ways in which women attempt to enlarge their space of operation. To this end, I will look at the relations of kinship, friendship and neighbourliness established by women as open-ended channels through which labour, goods and information flow. The network of exchange that emerges from these relations, I suggest, is the way in which women become more powerful vis-à-vis husbands, sisters-in-law, mothers-in-law or even neighbours with whom they compete. In other words, women have to depend on other women as well as on their own abilities in order to enlarge their effectiveness in social exchanges. In the process, I hope to show that womanhood is a changing concept, and that forms of gender subordination can only be grasped once the competitive and negotiable nature of gender identities is understood and analysed.

To study these gendered identities, I propose to look at the ways in which women are actively engaged in forming networks at the level of household, neighbourhood and village. Relations established at these three levels are intimately interconnected, as I shall try to show by focusing on two turning-points in household formation. The first is the process by which new households are formed during marriage negotiations. Next, I analyse the alliances entered into by a new bride in an effort to gain the respect of others and open up her own space of action within the novel web of relations into which she has to insert herself. These two processes feed into the general relations of inter-household competition for equality; relations, which ultimately define the social boundaries of the village itself. Women create these networks to enhance not only their own personal status but also that of the social unit (the household) of which they are a part. Thus these networks can be seen as forming the core of those inter-household ties that are constitutive of the village as a functioning social unit. It is in this sense that gender identity is centrally implicated in the formations of social units and identities much larger than the household itself.

Women's economic activities in the village of Tuz

Tuz, a relatively prosperous village composed of 170 households, is situated in the large Söke plain, south of the Aegean port of Izmir. It is a comparatively new settlement, established at the turn of the century by four or five Greek families, and containing as many shacks used temporarily by local nomads.[3] The history of the village's expansion bears the marks of republican Turkey's rural policies. Consequently, the village is made up of eighty-two households that were settled in the village by the state as part of its 1923 policy of population exchange with Greece and eighty *yörük* households that settled over the years in response to state policies encouraging agricultural production. More than half of the village (63 per cent of the households) earn their living only by producing cotton, largely on the basis of incentives provided by successive governments.[4] The state has not only made agricultural land available to peasants by reclaiming marshlands, distributing farm land and building dams and irrigation systems, but continues to subsidize cotton production by intervening in both input and output markets. The result has been a relatively protected financial environment that has encouraged the proliferation, and guaranteed the viability, of cotton production by small commodity-producers relying to a large extent on unpaid family labour.

In spite of the fact that cotton production has been one of the most highly mechanized agricultural activities in Turkey, using high levels of modern inputs such as chemical fertilizers and pesticides, it still contains manual tasks such as harvesting (and to a lesser extent, hoeing) whose completion in a short period of time is crucial for the success of the operation. Cotton has to be picked within a period of approximately sixty days, before the onset of autumn rains which would reduce substantially the market price of the product. Harvesting on the Söke plain is undertaken by migrant and local wage-labourers, as well as unpaid family workers. The majority of all the workers are women and children, unmarried girls over the age of 12 making up the bulk of the labour force. Mechanized tasks such as ploughing, planting, irrigation and the application of fertilizers and pesticides are undertaken by adolescent sons. The head of the household, by contrast, concerns himself with managerial aspects such as marketing, finding credit and decision-making. The growing importance in production decisions of institutions (such as banks and cooperatives) and individuals (traders, mechanics) outside the village have allowed men to expand their field of knowledge and social activity, upsetting the balance that existed between men and women with regard to access to the world outside village boundaries (Sirman, 1980).

Time and labour are the two critical factors in the process of cotton production in Söke. Cotton bolls in any one field mature at different times, requiring a relatively large labour-force for at least three different pickings. The labour available within one household often falls short of this requirement, as does the total labour available within the plain since most households produce cotton as well. Village households overcome this problem in two ways: by exchanging or hiring labour within the village (or with neighbouring villages) and by bringing seasonal migrant labourers from outside the Söke region. The first labour recruitment task falls basically on women's shoulders, while bringing migrant labour in is to a large extent (although not totally) a man's job. Thus, women are involved in the process of cotton production not simply as labourers, but also as labour recruiters and (in the field) labour supervisors. And yet this second form of involvement is often unacknowledged, and not only by the heads of households: developers and social scientists often pay scant attention to women's role in production as organizers of labour. One crucial reason for this stems from the way labour recruitment is intertwined with women's ties of kinship and neighbourliness, rendering recruitment a 'natural' extension of women's domestic duties.

The ability to secure an adequate labour-force is the product of the networks that women forge as part of their efforts to establish themselves in their households and their social milieux. Labour recruitment thus becomes an index of women's social standing in the village. It is through the channels opened up by these networks that women obtain a host of goods and services without which it would indeed be difficult to manage daily life.[5] These channels are the key to information; they are also the means through which a woman's reputation, or social identity, is built up and circulated. Judgements regarding a woman's character, reliability and trustworthiness depend perhaps more on women's comportment in these all-women networks than on women's accomplishment of domestic duties. The reputation a woman makes for herself through women's networks also affects her intra-household standing, affecting the weight her words will carry for her husband, children and in-laws.

Managing one's reputation in women's networks requires much skill and ingenuity. Relations between women, just like relations between households (and to a large extent, because of household relations), are characterized as much by competition as by cooperation. Just as a household that acquires a lot of wealth finds itself somewhat ostracized by co-villagers (Sirman, 1990), a woman who is on good terms with just about everyone in the village, easily going into a large number of houses, is viewed with suspicion. On the other hand, a woman who shuts herself too much away from the outside is equally suspect, accused of being unsociable. A woman on her own is above all bereft of the social ties necessary to function as a proper woman; ties that will allow her access to labourers, food, and even a bride for her son. To have a successful farming enterprise, as well as a good family reputation, a woman has to forge ties of cooperation with other women outside her immediate kin. Furthermore, it is these very ties that will allow her to exercise more power within the household as they will help her both to conform to her social role and question it. Let us now turn to two of the points in the life-cycle to see the social and personal effects of women's networking abilities.

The role of women in arranging marriages

Marriage can be defined as the constitution of a new production and consumption unit. It can also be seen as a complex unit of cooperation and competition which is the outcome of an arduous process of negotiation that establishes equality between two households. The first step to marriage is the constitution of a socially acceptable equivalence between different units. An ideology of equality constructed around notions of independence, autonomy and hence honour is a significant characteristic of small commodity-producers in Turkey, and households consider themselves to be more or less equal on the basis of both material and symbolic capital (Sirman, 1990). Marriage is the process that both verifies and produces this assumed equality. Since the measure of equality is as symbolic as it is material, it allows considerable variation in wealth and social standing between the two parties, variations which are then rendered insignificant by the successful completion of the marriage process, which acts in effect as a declaration of equality. To the extent that equality can only be produced through a dynamic process where claims for superiority are continuously and effectively negated, it can safely be assumed that equality necessarily entails competition. In short, marriage is a process through which social identity is established.

Thus, arranging a marriage is a dangerous and competitive process of negotiation requiring information, agility and courage. What is at stake is the reputation (and therefore the very viability) of households. Once the initial information-gathering is over, parties negotiate marriage payments and living arrangements informally. Only then do the groom's parents pay a visit to the bride's house, formally asking for her hand. An acceptance of the offer marks the period of betrothal. This initiates a period of reciprocal gift-giving that serves to produce equality between the two families. Inability to reciprocate proves either bad faith in the marriage or material inequality; in either case, the agreement is dissolved.[6] Since marriage in the Aegean is patrilocal, the groom's family is held responsible for providing the house for the new couple, and Tuz girls increasingly insist on living-arrangements that are separate from the groom's family. Furthermore, the groom's family is under the obligation to present the bride with gold jewellery, the amount of which serves simultaneously to reflect the social standing of both families and the value that the groom attaches to his bride. Responsibility for house furnishings is divided between the two parties according to general rules as well as particular arrangements. One of the parties may challenge the other with a 'surprise' gift, forcing the recipient to respond adequately.

As can be seen, marriage requires obtaining information about the most intimate aspects of another family's life. It also necessitates sustained contact between families in order to further negotiations. Both are available only to women, who can go into other houses much more easily than can men and who are able to obtain information and contacts over a wide-ranging social field through their networks. Men become involved only in the formalized activities at the end of the real process of negotiation. This is due not only to women's ability to obtain such personal information, but also to men's (at least public) contention that it is not manly to concern oneself with such personal details. Thus, arranging marriages is women's work.

The women who play an active role in these proceedings are the mothers of the prospective bride and groom, and mediators (dünürcü) who ensure smooth communications. All three parties expect to obtain certain advantages from the successful completion of the process. The mediator hopes to receive the same kind of help in the future, or may be paying back such a debt. She also hopes to enhance her reputation for having accomplished a pious deed (*sevap*), as such acts are considered in the village.[7] The groom's mother hopes to get a docile daughter-in-law worthy of her family's reputation, a bride who will serve her in her old age as well as provide male heirs to ensure the continuity of the patriline. Since the future bride and her mother strive to ensure living conditions that will give the bride as much autonomy as possible, the demands of the two parties are rather contradictory. This autonomy means a separate space, one to which women of the groom's family (namely his mother, sisters and brother's wife) will have minimum access. These demands are symbolized in the bride's wish for a separate front door. This would enable the bride to form her own independent network, since women would be able to visit without the mother-in-law's surveillance.

Negotiations over the marriage payment are also linked to the bride's desire for autonomy. The gold that the bride receives as part of her marriage settlement can be seen as a transformation of the Islamic *mehr*, but it also functions locally as a fund of capital with which the new couple can set up a farm for themselves.[8] Thus, the gold represents for the bride the future possibility of ensuring her own independence from her husband's female relatives, especially his mother, once the couple 'separate' from the groom's household. The groom, on his part, sees this as compensation for his work on his father's farm, of which he will inherit only a small portion, since he has to share it with his brothers and sisters. The groom's father is the person who ultimately pays for the gold and therefore considers it his own.[9] Although villagers maintain that the right to dispose of the gold lies successively first with the bride, then with her husband and only last with the groom's father, in reality the way this fund is to be used is the cause of serious disputes within the household. The bride usually tries to ensure that the gold is used to gain economic independence, rather than being squandered by her husband or father-in-law.[10] Once the couple is able to earn their own living, a woman's degree of autonomy will increase considerably. A bride's socially acceptable wish to control the marriage fund can, nevertheless, easily be frustrated by equally socially acceptable demands such as material difficulty or desires to remain within the parental economic fold (a desire which finds support in the idealization of the extended family) put forward by the groom or his father.

Cooperation between a bride and her mother in marriage arrangements nevertheless has limits of its own. The mother's main goals in her daughter's marriage are for her daughter to remain as geographically close to her as possible so as to maximize mutual aid and support; but also, and perhaps more important, a woman seeks to marry her daughter 'well' – that is, a marriage that will adequately reflect the family's social standing and will enhance its reputation. Although daughters share these desires, they are also seen as being easily duped by a few kind gestures packaged as love. Girls, on their part, have their own dreams, often influenced by the attractions of urban life as portrayed on television. Their desire to be different from their mothers often goes together with their wish (to some extent shared by mothers) for a life away from the dirt and grime of village life, especially the cotton field. Mothers, on their part, are apt to be suspicious of a daughter trying to be 'too' different.

But above all, it is the mother's efforts to establish family identity that produce conflict between mother and daughter. For one thing, the daughter is very much aware that her mother's demands for high-status gifts during the period of engagement might later lead to constant reproaches of rapaciousness by her mother-in-law. Moreover, a mother's attempts to support her daughter will also be construed as too much meddling in the affairs of another household. Thus the women in the husband's family will invariably hold a bride responsible for the actions of her parents, especially her mother, as this is part of the competitive process of establishing identity. The bride will have to prove her loyalty to her new family by keeping a minimum of ties to her own family. Ultimately, however, a daughter's claims to her inheritance (especially of land) will prove to be another important source of conflict between mother and daughter. A mother hopes, when she is a widow, to live with a son and his family, and to ensure their good will tries to make sure that he comes to own as much of the patrimony as possible. Daughters and their husbands, on the other hand, try to claim her rightful portion of the inheritance. But a mother has to remain on good terms with as many of her children as possible, regardless of gender, since the possibility of being looked after by a daughter and son-in-law in old age is equally quite strong. Thus each marriage reflects a particular balancing of all these contradictory requirements, and as such signifies a specific articulation of personal and family strategies for identity and power.

Marriage is thus both a private and familial as well as a public affair, defining an individual's identity at the level of village and household, as well as regulating participation within national networks of market and citizenship. By arranging marriages, women become involved in a complex set of relations that cannot be explained solely in terms of production or reproduction. In doing so, they take into account personal interests as well as those of the larger family unit, making it often difficult to distinguish between goals that are personal and those that are social (see Dimen, 1986). What the above attempts to highlight is the role played by women in the creation of identity through the process of marriage. To the extent that 'villageness' as a whole is defined in terms of the creation of a feeling of sameness (often articulated around notions of religion, occupation or way of life), I would argue that marriages are the means through which difference is minimized and identity (the feeling of being part of a larger 'we') created, asserted and verified. In Tuz, such identity is articulated around broad notions of religion (Sunni Islam as opposed to neighbouring Alevi) and autonomous farmer status (as opposed to labourer or civil servant), but is actually validated in marriage. Marriages made outside these broad notions are considered 'out' marriages, which obviate the necessity of entering into reciprocal exchanges and the establishment of equality. Women, by arranging marriages, not only create social identity for themselves and their families, but also are the regulators of group and class identity as villagers in contradistinction to urban dwellers.[11]

Brides and the formation of women's networks

As suggested above, serious conflicts of interest often mark relations between women involved in the constitution of marriages. The main conflict, that between the mother of the groom and the mother of the bride, is centred around control of the new bride. Where brides have to share domestic space with mothers-in-law, the latter's control over the bride's life is at its maximum. Not only is the mother-in-law able to make more decisions, but she also receives all the credit for a smoothly running household; one in which harmony marks both material and social relations. For a bride, this means that her labour is rendered socially invisible (since it is attributed to her mother-in-law); but it also means that she is deprived of a social identity.

But brides cause problems for mothers-in-law, too: a new bride heralds household fission, often presaged by an intensification of conflicts of interest. A woman's ultimate fear is the prospect of isolation from social networks, as well as a lack of security in old age.[12] A woman who is a mother-in-law will try to manage the inevitable process of household fission with the minimum of acrimony, so as not to alienate her children. One way of ensuring this is to ensure an obedient bride. This can, to some extent, be accomplished by finding a bride among one's own kin;[13] yet the number of old women living on their own while they have married children in the village attests to the fallibility of this strategy. But a more efficient strategy is to denigrate the bride's efforts towards independence, in the eyes of other women as well as her husband, by drawing on a fund of values extolling the virtues of respect and service towards elders. To the extent that the bride can also resort to the same means by reference to less righteous, but equally shared notions regarding the selfishness and childishness of the elderly, the struggle between a mother-in-law and bride takes the form of a public war of reputations. In short, the first years of marriage become a period of struggle, competition and negotiation that will in the end determine the conditions under which the new unit, and especially the bride, achieves autonomy and consequently social recognition.

Since the struggle between brides and their mothers-in-law is ultimately a struggle for social legitimacy, the word is the most effective weapon. Women need people within the family, in the neighbourhood, among relatives and in the village as a whole who will listen to them and disseminate their claims to legitimacy. This means that brides who move on marriage to a new village or a new neighbourhood will be at a disadvantage in the early years of their marriage. For the women in their immediate vicinity will be already part of a network of reciprocity involving visits and exchange of goods and labour, a network that will by definition include the mothers-in-law, thereby making it difficult for brides to insert themselves as independent agents. Brides will therefore have to try to establish their own networks, often among the other newcomers (that is, brides), as well as to exploit conflicts between mothers-in-law

and other women.[14] As the first, tentative, and often formal
visits evolve into communal work and exchange of labour in
domestic, gardening and agricultural work, women begin to get
to know one another, share information and finally talk about
problems within their households.

Much domestic work, such as gathering kindling or edible
wild plants, involves forays into the space outside the social
boundaries of the village. Since women cannot legitimately
transgress these boundaries on their own, finding another
woman to accompany them on such occasions becomes
imperative if they are to fulfil the expected gender role. To the
extent that a woman's identity is based on her ability to fulfil
this role, she needs other women just to get beyond the physical
boundaries of her home, if she is to be accepted as a woman. A
woman with adequate access to other women not only
functions as a proper woman, but she also has access to
information other than that provided to her by her husband or
his female relatives. Through such contacts and the information
exchanged, women are able to enlarge the sphere within which
they can move.[15] A woman with neighbours and acquaintances
can obtain the detergent she needs even if she is unable to go to
market herself, or can obtain an amulet from a *hoca* (religious
specialist) to protect her child from the evil eye. Neighbours
also enable a woman to participate in a social gathering such as a
wedding, visit relatives in neighbouring villages, and attend the
weekly market in the district centre, Söke. Without such ties,
women are limited to going to those places visited by their
mothers-in-law and sisters-in-law, and to their social world.

Women need other women to move independently. They
also need them to obtain information on topics such as family
planning; topics vital for a woman which cannot be discussed
with the husband's female relatives without incurring shame. A
woman who needs to see a doctor cannot directly confront her
mother-in-law wich such a request. Rather, she will get a
neighbour to imply the need for such a visit, thus not only
behaving in a 'respectful' way, but also making her plight
known so as to rally public support. To the extent that family
identity depends on reputation, both the husband and the
mother-in-law are quite sensitive to such opinion. In this way,
the bride will draw on inter-household relationships to get her
own way within the household and exercise more power.

A woman able to finish domestic work promptly thanks to
the mutual help obtained through women's networks not only

earns the respect due to the good woman, who carries out the role expected of her, but is also able to have the time to cultivate those extra-household relations that confer social identity. Women get to be known in the village for their special abilities and characteristics: some for speedy cotton picking, others for telling good stories. It is according to these specific abilities that women are sought out by other women in the village. For example, a good cook will be called on to undertake the cooking at a marriage or circumcision ceremony, a hard worker invited to wheat threshing or tomato-paste-making gatherings. The more a woman is sought out in this manner, the more powerful she becomes as an individual whose knowledge and capabilities have become socially validated. Women's gatherings are an important venue for the discussion of topics not generally broached in mixed company (so-called 'women's talk'). Proverbs relating to the 'strap-like tongue' of mothers-in-law (being both long and hard), or to the unavoidable misfortunes of marriage, are shared by these women amid laughter and jokes on sexuality and hence transmitted to the ever-present younger generation.

In short, economic cooperation takes place within the larger context of women's struggle to secure a place and a social identity both inside and outside the household, and they get defined in terms of both their deeds and their words. That is why women have to weigh carefully the way they expend both: to seem too zealous is as harmful as laziness; in the same way, and in the words of a well-known proverb (if words are silver, silence is golden), silence is just as strategic in the struggle for legitimacy as are words. A woman who constantly complains about her mother-in-law or daughter-in-law might at best be accused of divulging family secrets; at worst, slander. And yet sustained silence can also be interpreted as an admission of guilt. Conflicts among family, kin and neighbours are often influenced by the way in which public opinion assigns rights and wrongs to the parties involved. What guides public opinion in this process is the nature of existing alliances and networks as much as culturally set standards of acceptable behaviour.

Initially, contiguity, both spatial and social, determines the composition of these networks. The neighbourhood is a space which is considered to be 'inside', and thereby allows women free movement. A woman who can come and go in the neighbourhood without feeling the need to change her headscarf or *şalvar* (baggy trousers), or to be accompanied by other women, will have travelled a much greater social distance when she crosses the main square along which the men's coffee-houses are located, in spite of the fact that the physical distance involved is much shorter. Similarly, women will see boundaries demarcating neighbourhoods according to social rather than physical criteria,[16] and it is within these boundaries that networks are most intensive and effective.

The existence of kinship ties between women significantly affects the nature of the network which they establish. Women in any one neighbourhood are either affines (because of the patrilocal nature of marriage) or share no kinship bond. The increasingly higher incidence of neolocality means that in newly settled neighbourhoods, and more recently contracted marriages, women will have fewer kinswomen within their immediate vicinity. The hierarchical relations between agnates is often reflected in the relations established between women affines; relations between women with no kinship ties are rarely affected by the relationship that exists between their husbands. For example, a woman will be able to forge an egalitarian relationship with an unrelated woman in spite of an age difference; while her relations with her husband's elder brother's wife, to whom she owes service and respect, will be hierarchical. Thus women's networks are composed of two types of relationship: relatives one has the duty to service, and neighbours whom it is to one's advantage to service. While the first is based on obligation, the latter is based on choice and calculation; in the first, prestige and power are obtained through a proper performance of subservience, in the latter through a careful balance of cooperative exchanges.

Although the presence of a larger number of affines in a woman's network increases the amount of kin control over a bride, it should nevertheless not be assumed that relations between non-kin are free of conflict. To the extent that equality and competition are two sides of the same coin, cooperation with non-kin is also accompanied by intense competition. The more equivalent the structural position of women (in terms of age and marriage history), the fiercer the competition. Although this competition is about reputation (who is the more capable, the more visited), it is often verbalized in terms of trivial conflicts ('your child hit my child', 'your hens ruined my vegetable garden'). Such arguments may often lead to the complete breakdown of all relations (*dargınlık*), a situation which is the exact opposite of cooperation for mutual advantage, since women who are *dargın* will not refrain from belittling their opponents even when this may mean using the authority of affinal kinswomen (especially the mother-in-law) to restrict the options of the competitor. As a result of these complex relationships, a woman's network will be composed of a series of relations from full cooperation to complete antagonism, with a range of other options such as various degrees of avoidance lying in between. This often temporary and variable network is the product of women's active and carefully weighted participation in complex strategies to expand their sphere of activity and personal effectiveness.

The exchange of information that takes place during cooperation and competition is an important resource for forming a separate and autonomous identity. This information comprises details important in agricultural decisionmaking,[17] specific knowledge of significant events in the village, and knowledge of others, as well as being the forum for the relay of changing cultural conceptions of central issues such as gender relations. It is on the basis of such information that a woman is able to have her own opinion on a range of matters and construct, through discussion and comparison of her own experience with that of other women, her own world-view independent of her husband's or his mother's. This network also provides a woman with knowledge of her husband's actions outside the household; concrete information that will affect household decisions or limit the influence of her mother-in-law. A woman's position within the neighbourhood networks and the village at large is enhanced by the amount of information that she can wield, and this in turn positively affects her position within the household and among her affines in general. The more a woman's social identity helps to advance the status of the household as a whole, the more she will have power within the household and engage in more egalitarian relations with her husband, based on discussion and mutual agreement.

Conclusion

The social position of individuals in village society is intricately related to their struggle for identity. This is true for men as well as women. Both are considered adults eligible to occupy a recognized position in the shifting system of stratification only after marriage and participation in inter-household exchanges.[18] In this chapter I have tried to show that a woman's social identity cannot simply be reduced to that of her husband or her family, and that women play a crucial role in fashioning their own as well as their household's social standing. A woman has to struggle for social recognition and reputation just as much as a man does. Reputation and recognition are, as for men, contingent on the extent to which a woman is sought by others – that is, on the magnitude of social ties that she can establish within the village. Visits are the graphic presentation of a woman's social standing. In a village where the majority are small commodity-producers, a woman has to reproduce within the sphere of inter-household relations the equal yet autonomous identity around which farming is organized and conceptualized. To the extent that marriage can be seen as the process that constructs relations of equality between households, it can be said women produce the very structure of village society.

This chapter has also tried to emphasize the importance for a structural analysis considering women as socially significant actors who regulate intra-village relations. A woman engages in exchange-relations with others both as a means to enhance her own position within the household and as a way to obtain social identity for herself and her household as a unit. Other women are both competitors and allies, and a woman needs ultimately to fend for her own. The life-chances of her children as well as her personal wellbeing depend on the struggle for equality that the household engages in as a unit. To this extent, it is not possible to view women's networks as the means to subvert 'patriarchy'. But they are nevertheless the means through which women are able to create more egalitarian relations within the household – or, as they say, 'become the woman of her own house'.

What this chapter has tried to do is to show the social spaces that provide women with the possibility of changing the conditions under which they first enter marriage. I have argued that this comes in large measure from outside the household; from other women engaged in a network of cooperation and competition. Women need this outside network both to conform to and to redefine their gendered position within the household and community at large. To the extent that the network allows them to perform their womanly duties (secure agricultural labour, contract proper marriages, execute domestic tasks), it helps them conform; to the extent that it allows them to obtain knowledge of and respect from the community, it assists them in negotiating for greater equality vis-à-vis husband and mother-in-law. To gain power, a woman needs both to conform to gender definitions and to change them. It seems that power and identity are inseparable.

Notes

1. For exceptions see Fernea and Bezirgan (1977), Fernea (1985), Tabari and Yeganeh (1982) and the more recent collection of Arab feminist writing by Badran and Cooke (1990).

2. Kandiyoti (1988b) has depicted this process as a 'bargain with patriarchy', a bargain that allows women to endure subordination when young in return for the relatively expanded powers in store for them in old age.

3. These are ethnically Turkish transhumant pastoralists called yörük who have, over the last eighty years, settled down to a fully agricultural way of life.

4. All village households are linked to cotton production in one way or another. Some have economic activities aside from cotton growing, others are only wage workers in cotton planting and harvesting.

5. The goods and services women obtain through these networks range from help in childcare to the ability to purchase important items of consumption such as milk or olives. Not every household in the village produces all the items of daily consumption. And yet it is difficult to purchase such goods simply by offering to pay for them, as I found out for myself. Since consumption goods are produced only for immediate use, villagers are only prepared to sell their small surplus (when they have it) if they can expect to buy some other item in return.

6. The precariousness of this process is proven by high rate at which betrothals and engagements are dissolved in Tuz. In some cases, marriages between families of unequal wealth can be both possible and approved. Such was the case with the marriage of the physically handicapped daughter of the richest man in the village to a relatively poor tailor in Izmir. It should be pointed out that such (mis)marriages could only take place with partners from outside.

7. Marriage is seen as both a social and a religious duty in the village. This is why mediation in marriages is also regarded as a sacred duty. Yet men will often joke about mediation being a perfect task for women, who thereby satisfy their natural inclinations for curiosity and gossip.

8. Many farming families had in fact started out by selling the wife's gold to purchase farmland. In 1984, an average bride's gold could purchase about 5 hectares of cotton land.

9. Public opinion in the village agrees that the gold belongs to the couple. Thus, a father-in-law has to be very careful before he decides to appropriate his daughter-in-law's gold since this would lower his social standing significantly. See Sirman (1990).

10. Men have the possibility of spending money for personal pleasure such as gambling, hunting, travel, or even ill-advised business ventures, while women's personal activities are comparatively more circumscribed.

11. The rural–urban contrast still constitutes the most important social

distinction in Turkey; if not in actual class terms, at least in terms of social and cultural identity.

12. Studies of family structure in the Middle East have often underlined the close relations between mothers and sons as the source of security for women under conditions of patriarchy. See Mernissi (1975) for a general statement, and Delaney (1991) for the situation in Turkey. What these studies gloss over is the extent to which women will try to enlist their sons' as well as their daughters' loyalties, not only as security in old age, but also as part of their struggle for identity and social recognition.

13. See Delaney (1991) for a rather different explanation of this tendency.

14. Many new brides also forge close ties with the unmarried women in the neighbourhood, since they are closer to them in age and occupy a similar position in the gender-based division of labour. However this strategy is self-defeating since girls will ultimately marry and move out.

15. See Delaney (1991: 238) for an analysis of the restrictions to the movement of minors, especially women.

16. In spite of the fact that the village is composed of two major ethnic categories (migrants from the Balkans and indigenous *yörük*), broad categories such as ethnicity or primary occupation or even kinship do not on their own determine neighbourhood boundaries. Although these factors do account for some of the divisions, the main criterion is the history of women's networks.

17. During an agricultural survey I carried out in 1984, I found that women could provide me with specific and detailed information about cotton planting or current prices.

18. See Sirman (1990) for an analysis of stratification as perceived by villagers and the relation between marriage and male adulthood.

References

Abadan-Unat, Nermin (1978). 'Ekonomik ve Sosyal Değişmeler Karşısinda Türk Kadını', in Hamide Topçuoğlu, ed., *Türkiye Kadın Yılı Kongreşi*, Ayyıldız Matbaası, Ankara.

Afet, Inan (1968). *Ataturk ve Türk Kadın Haklarının Kazanılması*, Milli Eğitim Basimevi, Istanbul.

Ahmed, Leila (1982). 'Western ethnocentrism and perceptions of the harem', *Feminist Studies*, vol. 8, no. 3, pp. 521–34.

Altındal, Aytunç (1977). *Türkiye'de Kadın*, Havass Yayınları, Istanbul.

Badran, Margot and Miriam Cooke, eds. (1990). *Opening the Gates: A Century of Arab Feminist Writing*, Indiana University Press, Bloomington, Indiana.

Delaney, Carol (1991). *The Seed and The Soil: Gender and Cosmology in Turkish Village Society*, University of Carolina Press, Berkeley.

Dimen, Muriel (1986). 'Servants and sentries: women, power and social reproduction in Kriovisi', in Jill Dubisch, ed., *Gender and Power in Rural Greece*, Princeton University Press, Princeton.

Dubisch, Jill (1986). Introduction to Jill Dubisch, ed., *Gender and Power in Rural Greece*, Princeton University Press, Princeton.

Fallers, Lloyd and Margaret (1976). 'Sex roles in Edremit', in J.G. Peristiany, ed., *Mediterranean Family Structures*, Cambridge University Press, Cambridge.

Fernea, Elizabeth and Basima Bezirgan, eds. (1977). *Middle Eastern Muslim Women Speak*, University of Texas Press, Austin and London.

Fernea, Elizabeth, ed. (1985). *Women and The Family in the Middle East: New Voices of Change*, University of Texas Press, Austin.

Friedl, Ernestine (1967). 'The position of women: appearance and reality', *Anthropological Quarterly*, no. 40, pp. 98–105.

Harding, Susan (1975). 'Women and words in a Spanish village', in Rayna Reiter, ed., *Towards an Anthropology of Women*, Monthly Review Press, New York.

Kandiyoti, Deniz (1988a). 'Slave girls, temptresses, and comrades: images of women in the Turkish novel', *Feminist Issues*, no. 8, pp. 35–49.

Kandiyoti, Deniz (1988b). 'Bargaining with Patriarchy', *Gender and Society*, no. 2, pp. 274–90.

Kıray, Mübeccel (1976). 'The new role of mothers: changing intra-familial relationships in a small town in Turkey', in J.G. Peristiany, ed., *Mediterranean Family Structures*, Cambridge University Press, Cambridge.

Lazreg, Marnia (1988). 'Feminism and difference: the perils of writing as a woman on women in Algeria', *Feminist Studies*, vol. 14, no. 1.

Mernissi, Fatima (1975). *Beyond the Veil: Male–Female Dynamics in a Modern Muslim Society*, John Wiley, New York.

Rogers, Susan Carol (1978). 'Woman's place: a critical review of anthropological theory', *Comparative Studies in Society and History*, no. 20, pp. 123–62.

Sirman, Nükhet (1980). 'Women and development: the changing position of women in an agricultural valley of western Turkey', paper presented to the Conference on 'Social Movements in Southern Europe', University of London.

Sirman, Nükhet (1990). 'State, village and gender in western Turkey', in Andrew Finkel and Nükhet Sirman, eds., *Turkish State, Turkish Society*, Routledge, London.

Tabari, Azar and Nahid Yeganeh, eds. (1982). *In the Shadow of Islam*, Zed Press, London.

Gender Roles and Female Strategies among the Nomadic and Semi-nomadic Kurdish Tribes of Turkey

Lale Yalçın-Heckmann

Recent feminist debates on the specific nature and particularities of patriarchy have led social-scientific inquiries to focus on the power of women in different social systems; where this female power stems from and how it articulates itself. In this article I shall not deal with the definition(s) of patriarchy, nor with concepts such as oppression or male hegemony. My concern here is to present an example from the Kurdish tribal women, and hence contribute to the discussion on the power of women in a specific historical and sociocultural setting.

The social status of the women we are concerned with here is marked by two factors: the tribal setting and the semi-nomadic or nomadic mode of production.[1] Let me first outline the nomadic and tribal background. By 'tribe' and 'tribal structures' I am not referring to an evolutionist framework of society: the term 'tribe' is not to be understood as a 'primitive' form of social organization, nor the 'tribal system' as a historical survivor of some earlier political system.[2] I use the term tribe here in the sense that has been defined and used within the anthropology of the Middle East.[3] In this sense, a tribe consists of people who believe themselves to be kin to one another, who hold collective rights and duties with one another, and who share a moral code of tribal honour, righteousness and solidarity. In the Middle East almost all tribes share an ideology of patrilineal descent which influences inheritance and property relations, residence after marriage, extended families and household structure. For instance, as studies of tribes in Turkey by Bates (1974), Beşikçi (1969) and Yalçın–Heckmann (1991) show, women are denied the right to inherit land on the grounds of 'tribal custom'.[4] Immovable property like fields, houses and gardens, as well as movable property such as animals, are usually not inherited by women. Their rights, and the possibilities of controlling and managing these means of production, are limited indeed. When tribal rules and traditions are combined with semi–nomadic or nomadic modes of life, the exclusion of women from property rights seem to become stricter and more widespread.

Another particularity of Middle Eastern tribes is the existence of a tribal ideology which attributes historical significance to certain tribes, thus creating a hierarchy of status among them, and defines 'closeness' and 'distance' between the tribes.[5] Accordingly some tribes are classified as older, nobler, more heroic than others; similarly some tribes are classified as being 'closer' to others because of real or imagined historical and kinship ties. Furthermore, tribal ideology specifies the principles and lines of solidarity among men and the types of relationship which are created through women. For instance, when two tribal groups become affiliated through marriage, kinship terms such as 'son-in-law' or 'maternal uncle' could be extended in usage to refer to the men of the opposite groups, i.e. the men of the wife-taking group would be referred to as *zava* (son-in-law), and the men of the wife-giving group as *xal* (maternal uncle). Nevertheless, such tribal ideological signifiers are not only part and parcel of the symbolic discourse, as Bourdieu (1977) has pointed out, but also contain inconsistencies and contradictions. Because of these inconsistencies, meanings and symbols within the patriarchal ideology can be interpreted in various ways by men and women and individual strategies can be employed. Female strategies, which are the subject of this chapter and will be exemplified shortly, are especially important as a means to understand the limits and scope of tribal patriarchal ideology.

The characteristics of the nomadic and semi–nomadic mode of life could be summarized as follows: it is primarily marked by mobile residence. In Turkey purely nomadic groups – i.e.

groups who live only in tents and migrate between summer and winter camp sites – are rare, and are continuously declining in numbers. Bates (1974) and Beşikçi (1969) have shown the extent to which nomadic and non-nomadic modes of life are interdependent, and even interchangeable. The pastures of the nomads used to be traditionally 'owned' and used by tribal groups, but they are now becoming the private property of individuals, and the nomads are being constantly and increasingly forced into renting pastures from private owners or from village communities (see for example, Bates (1973), Beşikçi (1969) and Hütteroth (1961)). Hence it is not possible to consider nomadic society as having a closed economy or that nomads are marginal to a market economy. It is clear that the nomads are going through social changes comparable to those experienced by other rural groups in Turkey.

Nomadic and semi-nomadic modes of life affect the structure, homogeneity and composition of the household, as well as the use of space, time and labour by household members. Gender roles and the corresponding division of labour, the organization of production and patterns of consumption, like decision-making processes, are primarily influenced by nomadic and semi-nomadic modes of life. Let us look at some examples, showing how women cope with the constraints stemming from mobility in summer and winter residence, differentiated and complex usage of the environment, and the existing sexual division of labour.

The areas in which women's power becomes visible and where women employ different strategies are discussed under three sections. First, I discuss women's strategies in production and reproduction. Beşikçi, who carried out one of the first sociological studies of Kurdish nomads, stresses the link between women's status and their participation in production and reproduction (see Beşikçi, 1969: 172–3). He claimed that, although a woman's participation in production and reproduction approaches total exploitation, women are allowed a respectable position within the nomadic society and they have the right to take part in decisionmaking processes and in public life in general. I would like to question this link between the extensive participation in production and reproduction and the alleged higher social status of women: is it as automatic as Beşikçi has proposed, or are there other (or additional) mechanisms for giving social status to women? In other words, how far are women's planning, management, assignment and division of work activities related to their achievements in social status? As these productive and reproductive activities are sometimes excessive, are women able to decline work or carry out a chore inefficiently on purpose, and what happens in this case?

Let us look at women's chores. First, within the pastoral economy, they oversee milking sheep, goats and cows; preparing butter, cheese and yogurt; processing other animal products such as goats' hair, wool and skin; weaving the tent cloth and sacks; sewing skin bags and preparing other containers; taking care of and feeding the animals; cleaning the shed, sheep pen and stable; cutting hay and carrying fodder. In agricultural production: they look after tending, hoeing and watering the gardens and fields; preparing dung; picking, drying and storing fruit and vegetables; reaping, picking and beating corn cobs. In the area of production and reproduction directly concerning the household and its members, they can be seen taking care of the house; repairing and cleaning furniture; cooking food; doing the laundry; washing up the dishes; sewing and preparing the bedding; sewing and knitting clothes; weaving carpets and kilims; bearing children and nursing them; taking care of the elderly and sick; serving and hosting guests.

This list could, of course, be extended. The chores above are carried out mostly by women, without much help from men or children. How they are divided up among the women is dependent mainly on the degree and type of kinship and other relations between them, their kin link to the head of household, and the age and number of women within the household.

One could ask here to what extent the performance of these chores and activities is related to women's power relations in this society. After all, similar types and amounts of work are assigned to women in many settled agricultural and non-tribal societies, as well. The difference lies in the fact that the status and position of a woman in this case is additionally influenced by her position in the tribal hierarchy and the gender role defined by the tribal ideology. Apart from social class, age, wealth, profession, and urban-rural differences, which all determine women's social status, factors such as the place of her family within the tribe, whether it holds a leadership role, the type of marriage she has made and whom she married, are all relevant in determining her participation in production and reproduction.

In the region of Hakkari, where I carried out my anthropological fieldwork, whether a woman belonged to a prominent and leading tribal family was important in determining not only where she was to reside – i.e. in a mountain village, plains village or the city – but also what sorts of chores she would be expected to do. The jobs listed above are carried out throughout a village woman's adulthood. However, they are performed with changing frequency and intensity, and the jobs themselves are hierarchically arranged according to prestige. Moreover, qualities such as working hard and fast, or accomplishing a job with an aesthetic quality, are factors which add to a woman's personal prestige and fame.

Hence, women of the same household compete with one another and also with their contemporaries from the village for prestigious jobs such as baking bread, serving guests tea, weaving rugs or producing the milk products in the summer camp. A bride from a prestigious tribal family has an advantageous position in this competition from the beginning. Socially high-ranking families characteristically have many male members (sons and brothers) and are rich, led by respectable elderly men or women who are good speakers and politicians. Women from such families are able to take a special position in their affinal household: for instance, such a bride does not necessarily have to avoid her parents-in-law; if she is the eldest bride in the household (i.e. the first bride to be 'brought in' for a son in the extended household), she does not necessarily have to carry out the most arduous chores. Such a young bride could rely on the continuing protection of her parental family, which is reinforced through regular visits from family-members and close kinsmen to her affinal household. When a woman from a high-ranking tribal family is to be married, even as the second wife in a polygamous union,[6] she is able to bargain about the types of chores and work she will carry out within the household. She could, for instance, refuse to do the heavier and low-prestige chores such as carrying wood and hay on her back, or taking care of the children of her sisters-in-law or brothers-in-law. She can, furthermore, bargain with the other women of the household about which specific jobs she is to be assigned and which ones not.

Therefore, Beşikçi's assumption that women in a tribal nomadic society gain respect and status through hard work is not supported in the case of the semi-nomadic tribal Kurds in Hakkari. It is not so much the amount of work which affects the position of women in this society, but rather the quality and style of work. As Bourdieu (1977: 94) has suggested, the comportment and posture of a woman at work; if she carries out her chores with ease; if she makes time, whenever needed, for socializing and maintaining social networks; if she keeps an image of self-determination in organizing her relations and life – all are factors which account for her social status.

Let me now turn to another area of social relations, namely those of consumption, where women are able to implement their power in indirect ways. Similar to the differentiated and hierarchical symbolic value of production processes, consumption patterns also maintain complex meanings and symbolic values, which women manipulate to improve their status and prestige. On the whole, women's participation in consumption, especially of food, is secondary to men's. This secondary position corresponds to women's gender roles, which underline their modesty, obedience and self-sacrificing qualities. Even if the richness and glamour of women's clothes indicates their conspicuous consumption, this is the only consumption area where women are allowed to 'indulge'. Men claim to suffer from women's demands for new and expensive dresses; nevertheless, they see no contradiction in complaining about how expensive women's clothes are, and then boasting about them as a sign of their wealth and generosity. Personal clothes and jewellery are the only consumption items women privately own. Yet jewellery, which is given as a present to a woman at her engagement or wedding, is not totally free from being a communally disposable item. For instance, the male head of a woman's affinal household or her husband may claim the right to dispose of her jewellery, usually as a gift to a female member of kin, especially if this is demanded by social and kinship obligations.

The female consumption of prestige goods such as valuable clothes and jewellery therefore displays not only the status of women but also that of their immediate kin, parental and affinal. Similar to the extent and type of participation in production, taking part in consumption is a marker of social relations. If, for example, a woman does not dress up when she should, goes around in shabby clothes, and looks in general untidy and neglected, this appearance signifies not only the woman's personality or condition, but also her position within the household and her relations to other members of the household, particularly to her mother-in-law. To summarize, consumption patterns are equally open to the manipulation of symbolic meaning and the implementation of strategies through which women try to improve their status and prestige.

The last area of social relations in which female strategies and women's power struggles are observable is the area of marriage relations. Marriage relations in general, and in particular the choice of the marriage partner, and the negotiations for marriage exchanges and ceremonies, concern not only the marrying couple but also their family and kin, who have an interest in establishing, modifying or refreshing existing or new social relations between two groups. Here I shall deal with two particular marriage practices which are common in eastern Anatolian and tribal contexts.

The first of these is the practice of wife-kidnapping (in Turkish, *kız kaçırma*) and elopment (*kaçma* or *kaçışma*). Bates (1974) argued that the Yörük tribal nomads share a patrilineal tribal ideology which is strongly egalitarian and hence favours marriage between patrilineal parallel cousins (father's–brothers's–daughter or father's–brother's–son marriage) in order to maintain the homogeneity of the patrilineal kin group. On the other hand, the practice of bride-price payments from the family of the groom to the bride's family, and the fact that young men become 'socially adult' only after marriage, are restricting factors on the choice of marriage partner and marriage date for both young men and women. Therefore, marriage by elopement or wife-kidnapping, although contradicting the principle of solidarity with patrilineal kinsmen, prevents the patrilineal group from becoming endogamous and allows the young couple to determine the particular point at which they become socially recognized adults on their own. Moreover, through such a marriage by elopement, a woman could determine at which summer camp and with which group of kinsmen she would be together in production and reproduction. In other words, by choosing not to marry her patrilineal cousin (father's brother's son) and eloping with someone else from another group, she may not be directly influencing her productive activities in the short run, but in the long run she defines the patrilineal relationships and membership of her offspring – i.e. which patrilineal group her children would belong to and seek solidarity within.

Even if elopment and wife-kidnapping have the above-mentioned implications for the status of men and women as discussed by Bates, they are nevertheless part of the wider discourse on gender in which women are defined as the weaker sex, in need of protection and control. Both of these marriage practices among the semi-nomadic tribal Kurds of Hakkari, with whom I stayed, were seen and evaluated differently, according to context and persons involved. There were usually two sides, whose evaluations of the affair were diametrically opposed to each other. One side, that of the woman, almost always claimed that the woman was kidnapped. The other side, that of the man, claimed that she eloped with the man. Therefore, even if a woman who decides to elope may be implementing her own will and right to marry when she wants (as Bates claims), there is no unanimous agreement and recognition of her purpose, nor of her action. Furthermore, such a woman may be risking a total break of social relations with her parental group by eloping, and she may suffer from the lack of protection and hence have a lower status and recognition for many years to come.[7] The price of practising one's own will and implementing one's own choice could be very high indeed.

In any case, since a woman who elopes or is kidnapped is under suspicion concerning her role in the affair, she can hardly expect public support for her action. One could, of course, turn this assumption around and consider the ambiguty of interpretations (whether she eloped or was kidnapped) to be to her advantage: she would eventually benefit from divided opinions, and thus actually pursue her own interests. However, as I have already suggested, the possibility of interpreting these strategies in different and opposite ways leads to, or at least contributes to, restrictive practices and control over women. This control sometimes goes so far that women are withdrawn from the production process in order to be properly controlled and protected. Furthermore, such practices legitimize not only the total control and subordination of women, but also, if only partially, the use of violence against women, as often occurs in wife-kidnapping.

Finally I would like to turn to an equally significant marriage practice in eastern Turkey, that is, polygamy: the marriage of a man to more than one woman simultaneously. Patriarchal ideology is most clearly articulated with the practice of polygamy. Such marriages symbolically mythify and mystify the patriarchy; reproducing the image of men as being extraordinarily sexually potent while emphasizing their power to control women totally. Against such a myth and ideal, polygamous unions create a battlefield for emotions and for socially constructed gender concepts. Polygamy is not only categorically and ideally a clear proof of male supremacy; it is also the formal and religious right of men. In real life, however, the debate on polygamy is much more complex and controversial. Male and female opinions on the issue of when and how such a marriage might work differ considerably. On the whole, men favour such a marriage for themselves, but if their kinswomen (i.e. daughters, sisters, cousins or nieces) were to marry a man as his second or third wife, they would be against it. Men and women generally agree that under certain circumstances marrying polygamously might work. But such marriages (like all marriages) are not evaluated once and for all. How a man handles his affairs within the household and between his wives; how much real say he has in controlling relations between the household members; how his relations develop across time and space, are all factors which affect the overall success or failure of polygamous unions. In other words, successful or unsuccessful polygamous marriages are evaluated as a process.

As stated above, the areas of productive processes, consumption patterns and marriage relations provide a fair amount of ambiguity and social space for women to bargain, employ strategies and pursue their own interests. Relations of solidarity or rivalry within the tribe between patrilineal groups, or rights and duties within the solidarity group, could be used by women in plotting their strategies against other women and men.

Let me illustrate this point with a case from the semi-nomadic tribal mountain village of Sisin, where I stayed during my fieldwork. Hüseyin, my host in Sisin, was ten years younger than Esma, my hostess. Their marriage was a levirate one, in that Hüseyin had married the wife of his elder brother after he died. The primary reason for this marriage was the untimely death of the elder brother as a young man during his military service, leaving Esma widowed very young, as the second wife, without children. Further reasons were her beauty, the fact that she had been kidnapped to become the second wife,[8] and that she belonged to an influential family and lineage of the tribe, which had many influential male cousins and relatives. Hüseyin had waited ten years to become adult and marry her. During my stay in Sisin, Hüseyin was in his mid forties and Esma in her late fifties. Like all women in the village, she looked older than her real age. When Hüseyin wanted to warn or threaten his wife for some reason, the threat which he used most often was that he would 'bring in another wife'. Esma in return implied, even if indirectly, that in such a case she would make his life 'a hell'. Hers was clearly a serious threat to be reckoned with: men are expected to be in charge of their household's affairs and, at least in the opinion of most people, they should keep 'law and order' at home. If there is a threat to the publicly observable 'peace and quiet' at home, this affects the man's status as the head of household, and thus his status among other adult men. Moreover, in the case of Hüseyin and Esma, the latter had shown in former years how strongly she disagreed with him by leaving him for her parental home for brief periods several times. In Kurdish a woman, who leaves her husband and goes back to her parents' house, is considered to be *ziz bu*.[9] It is a public declaration of women's protest, and even if a woman who is *ziz bu* is often reprimanded for being 'unreasonable' or 'a bit crazy', nevertheless, her protest is publicly acknowledged. *Ziz bu* is, in a sense, an institutionalized form of protest for women, and even if it looks like a spontaneous and individual reaction, leaving one's husband temporarily because of a conflict, the procedures which follow have serious implications. For instance, when a woman is *ziz bu* and leaves her husband temporarily, she demands presents and payments to come back. Her family and relatives act as intermediaries.[10]

There are also different degrees of being *ziz bu*. If the woman leaves her husband for a few days and remains at a neighbour's house, or at some relative's within the village, this is less serious than leaving for a longer period and staying with her parents or kinsmen in another village. The closer the kinship relation between the woman and her host, the farther she goes away from her husband or the longer she stays, the harder and more expensive it is to bring her back. One then needs to employ many influential persons as intermediaries to negotiate the procedures for her return home. Against this background, it is possible to understand what Esma's threat meant for her husband. She comes from another village which is important for the tribe, she belongs to a family of influential men and women, and Hüseyin has multiple and intensive relations with the men of her lineage, which he would not want to risk so quickly.

Apart from the threat of becoming *ziz bu* if Hüseyin were to marry a second wife, Esma used additional and more indirect strategies to discourage him from such an action and to put pressure on him. She had opposed the choice of the bride for her eldest son, who was a close patrilineal cousin of Hüseyin. Esma could not resist strongly enough, and they married. She did not, however, get along with this eldest bride. The latter claimed that her mother-in-law was all to blame for the conflict: 'She does not give me any chores and does not let me do anything (especially baking bread or cooking meat); she buys me nothing new to wear', she complained. That was why she took hardly any part in consumption and production. She wore old clothes, scarcely ate together with the other women and children, and worked irregularly on the least prestigious chores. Esma was indeed formally in charge of the organization of household chores as the oldest woman and female household head (*kabani* in Kurdish). She was also responsible for the behaviour of the brides and other young women of the household. But she said her husband's choice had caused this situation: the daughter-in-law would not let her say anything. She knew anyway that it would turn out like this; that is why she had opposed Hüseyin's choice from the beginning. Thus, behind all the unfinished 'neglected' women's chores within the household (such as undone laundry, untidy children, unworthy food for honourable guests), and behind the petty fights between the men and women of the household, lay the unresolved conflict between Esma and Hüseyin.

In this illustrative case and in my discussion above I have argued that in semi-nomadic and nomadic Kurdish tribal society women have a heavy workload, but their direct participation in production does not lead to an immediate ascription of high status. Moreover, women do not accept the implementation of male dominance without any resistance. Through the employment of various strategies, they try to exploit the contradictory meanings and practices of the patriarchal system.

Notes

1. Not all tribal groups are nomadic or semi-nomadic. There are also tribal groups involved in agricultural production; some tribes are even divided between nomadic and peasant sections. The size and spread of a tribe is also problematic; there were about twenty-five groups defined as tribes in Hakkari. Nevertheless, whether these or others should be classified as tribe (*aşiret*), tribal section (*qabile*) or a lineage (*ocak/mal*) is disputable. There are also non-Kurdish nomadic and semi-nomadic tribes in Turkey such as the Yörük and Türkmen. For more on Kurdish semi-nomadic tribes in Turkey, see Yalçın-Heckmann (1991).

2. The question of whether 'tribe' is a primitive form of social organization, or a social structural form which could be observed at different historical periods is interesting not only for anthropologists but also for social scientists and historians. For a similar debate within the context of Turkish history, where the position of women is partly mythified and reified, see Hassan (1986: 76–96); Berktay (1983: 72–100).

3. See for example, Eickelman (1981: 85–104); Ahmed and Hart (1984); Bates and Rassam (1983: 241–68).

4. The exclusion of women from inheriting property is not only typical of Middle Eastern tribal societies, but is found also in other Middle Eastern, African and Asian societies.

5. For a discussion of the concept of 'closeness' in the Middle Eastern kinship and tribal context, see Eickelman (1981: 109–16).

6. I say 'even', because marrying polygamously is undesirable for women, but ideally proper and desirable for men in the tribal patriarchal ideology. Women say they have to tolerate it under certain circumstances, but on the whole, especially with such a marriage within the tribe, it is a conflict-ridden practice.

7. In one case of a woman who married after elopement, even her 18-year-old son was affected. She could never be reconciled with her kinsmen and her son feared meeting his uncles (mother's brothers) on the street, in case the latter recognized him and attacked him.

8. This was the generally held view; Esma said in private that she eloped.

9. In the Kurdish–Turkish dictionary of Yusuf Ziyaeddin Paşa, which was revised and republished by M.E. Bozarslan, *ziz* means 'heart which is full of compassion for others'. *Dilziz* is the word for 'touchy'. Within the colloquial usage here, *ziz bu* meant to have become 'touchy' or 'upset', even if this touchiness was interpreted by some as being excessive and unreasonable.

10. For similar politics and strategies of conflict management in marriages among Iranian peasants, see Friedl (1991: 111–39).

References

Ahmed, A.S., and D.M. Hart, eds. (1984). *Islam in Tribal Societies*, Routledge & Kegan Paul, London.

Bates, D.G. (1973). *Nomads and Farmers: A Study of the Yörük of Southeastern Turkey*, University of Michigan, Ann Arbor.

Bates, D.G. (1974). 'Normative and alternative systems of marriage among the Yörük of southeastern Turkey', *Anthopological Quarterly* no. 47, pp. 270–87.

Bates, D.G. and A. Rassam (1983). *Peoples and Cultures of the Middle East*, Prentice Hall, New Jersey.

Berktay, H. (1983). *Kabileden Feodalizme*, Kaynak Yayınları, Istanbul.

Beşikçi, İ. (1969). *Doğuda Değişim ve Yapısal Sorunlar: Göçebe Alikan Aşireti*, Doğan Yayınları, Ankara.

Bourdieu, P. (1977). *Outline of a Theory of Practice*, Cambridge University Press, Cambridge.

Eickelman, D.F. (1981). *The Middle East: An Anthropological Approach*, Prentice Hall, New Jersey.

Friedl, E. (1991). *Die Frauen von Deh Koh: Geschichten aus einem iranischen Dorf*, Knesebeck & Schuler, Munich.

Hassan, Ü. (1986). *Eski Türk Toplumu Üzerine İncelemeler*, V. Yayınları, Ankara.

Hütteroth, W.-D. (1961). 'Beobachtungen zur Sozialstruktur kurdischer Stämme im östlichen Taurus', *Zeitschrift für Ethnologie*, no. 86, pp. 23–42.

Yalçın-Heckmann, L. (1991). *Tribe and Kinship among the Kurds*, Peter Lang, Frankfurt.

Yusuf Ziyaeddin Paşa (1978). *Kürtçe-Türkçe Sözlük* (Translated and revised by M.E. Bozarslan), Çıra Yayınları, Istanbul.

Part V

Resistances

13

Women's Participation in Politics in Turkey

Ayşe Güneş-Ayata

The fact that the number of women members of parliament, considered to be the most manifest sign of women's participation in institutionalized politics, has decreased in Turkey has made women's place in politics a controversial issue. In this chapter, I try to analyse this problem, and discuss various ways in which women relate to politics, and the attitudes towards them within society. In the first part of the chapter I analyse women's voting behaviour, and in the second part I discuss the active participation of women in politics.

I will base my argument on a differentiation between two types of political participation: individual, and social. Individual political participation is usually listed amongst the duties of citizenship: it does not especially necessitate a two-way human relation and can be performed alone, of which the clearest example is voting. The principle of the secret ballot facilitates and protects the individuality of voting behaviour. Social political participation, on the contrary, necessitates human relations, group behaviour and social activity – for instance, being a member of a political party or a nominee for a certain position. The problems affecting these two different types of political participation are different, as are the roles undertaken by women in them.[1]

The first type of political behaviour – that is, individual political behaviour – is more prone to being influenced by 'objective' factors. For instance, it is determined by socioeconomic status, religion, racial and ethnic differences, education and age. Gender is also one of these determining factors, but its proportionate influence varies in different situations. The second type of behaviour is different by definition, as it implies interactions and group action.

Ever since women gained the franchise in 1934, they have been instigated, supported and directed to use their individual right to vote. However, this support has not extended to the right to be chosen, or to the second type of participation.

Individual political participation

In the analysis of voting behaviour, an individual political participation, public opinion holds up two hypotheses regarding women. The first is that women are uninterested in politics and therefore are not willing to participate. The second one is that women vote under the influence of men, i.e. they are not independent of men.

The most overt way of escaping from individual political participation for women would be not to use their right to vote. However, research on this issue shows that the number of women who do not vote is not significantly less than the number of men who do not vote. This indicates that women, far from showing a lack of interest, decisively use this right that has been given to them.

The second hypothesis regarding women's political behaviour is that women vote according to the directives of their husbands. It would be helpful to make the initial observation that both wives and husbands are influenced by the objective factors (income, education, etc.) I have already listed. That is to say, one of the important reasons that women might use their vote in line with their husbands is that they are influenced by the same factors existing in their common lives. Couples also influence one another reciprocally as a part of this common life. All in all, research indicates that a little more than half of women do not tell their husbands how they vote. Moreover, a significant portion of women say that they decide how they will vote without asking their husbands. Amongst the women who say that they ask their husbands before they vote, only half of them say they cast their votes always according to their husband's will. Of these women who ask their husbands, 25 per cent still vote independently; the remaining 25 per cent sometimes vote according to their husband's will.

This analysis entails a dual process. First, the woman votes without asking her husband, and more importantly she expresses this behaviour. This transforms individual behaviour to social behaviour. It is probable that the proportion of women who vote without consulting their husbands is actually greater than the number who have publicly admitted to this in the survey.

How is it possible for women to vote so independently in such a male-dominated society? I believe that the reason lies to a great extent in the fact that voting does not affect a woman's life outside the family or change her relation with the outside world; as I stated earlier, voting as an individual act does not entail extra-domestic relations. Because of this, it probably does not seem worthwhile for husbands to control the voting behaviour of their wives. Of course, this hypothesis needs further testing as a research topic. As it can be seen, women's individual political participation is not contentious in any social stratum nor in any political party – on the contrary, it is encouraged by even the most traditional social movements. Many parties use images of women to gain votes. The problems concerning women's participation in politics start with their active participation.

Social political participation

Women's social participation in politics is multi-dimensional. Even though all social political participation poses difficulties for women, research indicates that some forms of participation are easier than others. While the extent of the difficulty depends on various views and ideologies towards woman, it is also related to the types of relationship involved.

We can observe some political movements directed towards changing the position of woman in Turkey. Although it would not be comprehensive, we can list many of them ranging from Atatürkist women's organizations to women's sections in political parties. I will try to comment on one of these forms of social participation, women's participation in institutionalized politics, which underlines one point. In its general structure, the dominant view among women politicians in Turkey is the conformist view – namely the human-interest perspective (Hedlund, 1987) or humanist feminism (Odorisio, 1988) – which presents woman's interests as part and parcel of general human interests and perspectives, and which aims at working together with men. Even though there are some who aim at introducing the woman's point of view to a limited extent within the existing political system, those who perceive men's and women's interests as inherently conflicting, and thus oppose the system as a whole, do not exist.

The conditions that hamper women from active participation in politics are not very different from the conditions that deter women from taking part in, or from gaining promotion in other public activities. However, since this type of participation is very rare, it gathers a great deal of attention, increasing barriers and making conditions more difficult. In institutionalized politics, there are also additional factors – such as an inflexible working day, long and continuous hours, strong competition and night work – which makes women's participation more difficult. These factors conflict extensively with the demands on women in their private lives.

Of course, the distinction between public and private life – politics being the determinant element of the public sphere, and women's lives being trapped in the private – comes above all these, and is more important than any deterrent. While women are allowed to make politics among themselves, and a blind eye is turned to their such activities, those accidentally entering into institutionalized politics are pushed towards female-identified jobs such as social welfare, health, etc. Women are to a great extent excluded from political decisionmaking mechanisms, since they do not participate in certain behind-the-scenes processes. Even the women who work in political parties, sometimes holding high-level posts, cannot function as effectively as men.

It is not surprising that women do not become politicians; what is surprising is that some women, against all these difficult circumstances, do become politicians. Before looking at various role models of women participating in politics, I want to evaluate some of the attitudes in society at large towards women in politics.

In a large-scale public opinion survey, respondents were asked whether they would want their children (girl and boy separately) to become politicians. Neither men nor women think politics a fitting profession for their daughters and sons. The reasons behind this may be that politicians as a whole are looked down upon, and politics in Turkey takes place in an unstable environment. However, more women than men stated that they would say yes to their sons' political ambitions. This can be related to the male-dominated family structure that creates the conditions for the improvement of the mother's status when the son gains success. As for the daughters, the negative reaction towards daughters becoming politicians is much stronger than that shown for sons (43.6 per cent would say no to their sons; 67.4 per cent to their daughters. This proportion is even higher among fathers (70 per cent). Fathers' protection of their daughters from politics (which is regarded as an activity to a great extent outside the home and the family) must be analysed as a part of the male-dominated family structure. While 41 per cent of housewives do not want their sons to become politicians (in line with other women and with society in general), this rises to 78.5 per cent for daughters. In her research Kandiyoti points out that 45 per cent of mothers advise their daughters to keep away from positions that carry great weight by saying that women's competitive and masculine attitudes would diminish their chances of getting married (Kandiyoti, 1979). Housewives who believe that their daughters will lead a similar life to theirs do not want to decrease their daughters' chances of good marriages. According to the results of this research, no more than 15 per cent of the total sample group seemed to support their daughters' desire to become politicians.

Younger people were more positive than old people about both their daughters and sons becoming politicians; and educated people are more positive towards both politics and women's active participation in politics. When different professions are analysed, civil servants, managers in the private sector and the self-employed who have a higher education level are more likely to advocate that their daughters become politicians than professions with a lower education level, such as workers, artisans, farmers, or merchants.

The results indicate that great limitations are placed on women's (and daughters') social political participation, contrary to the assessment we have made about individual political participation. Politics now becomes an activity that directly affects the family, the home and the private sphere; rather than short-term behaviour that does not influence the private. Thus, women's involvement in public life and their participation in politics is prevented.

The same poll enables us to summarize the general trends in women's relationships with politics. Even though one person in ten is totally against women becoming politicians, approximately two-thirds do not have a negative attitude towards the idea of a woman mayor or prime minister. A woman mayor is approved of slightly more.[2]

In summary, according to the results of this research we can say that young rather than old; women rather than men; well-educated rather than poorly-educated; urban rather than rural population; and especially professional groups, students and housewives rather than entrepreneurs, approve women's appearance on the political scene.

When questioned, 66.3 per cent of the total sample and 68.3 per cent of the woman participants believe that a woman could be a politician; 68.6 per cent of the total participants and 73 per cent of the women believe that a woman could be a mayor, and 64.2 per cent of the latter think that a woman could be a prime minister. Moreover, compared with men women show a greater trust in themselves and their sisters, and believe that being a woman does not affect a person's success. Women indicate that they have their own problems and the great majority of them support the establishment of a Ministry of Women to solve these problems, but paradoxically would not support their daughters' participation in politics. And with minor variations, women do not differ very much from men on this issue. So although there is not a general reaction against women politicians in the abstract, it is not considered desirable for a member of one's family to participate in such a public behaviour.

Against all these barriers, there *are* women who actively participate in politics. We can basically divide these women into two groups. Those who make politics primarily among women; and those who are active not only among women. It should be mentioned that all of the women politicians whom I interviewed said that an important barrier against their participation in politics was created by the women, as much as by the men, in their families. That is to say, women try to protect their relatives and friends from politics as much as men do. Another point is that none of the women politicians has said that her husband is a barrier to her involvement. On the contrary, a majority of them said that their involvement was instigated by their husbands; few of them said that their husbands did not interfere. There are three reasons behind this. First of all, a significant portion of women participate in politics on behalf of their husbands and with their support. A second reason is that women who carried out independent political activity are well-educated professionals; their husbands are also well–educated and therefore perceive women politicians more positively. As a third reason I must instance the difficulty of any participation at all in politics when the husband poses strong opposition.

All of the men and women politicians that I interviewed for this research complain about the lack of women's participation in politics, and think that women should be encouraged. Even though a few people do complain about the male domination of politics, the most important part of this dissatisfaction is related to the mobilization of women's votes. I mentioned before that women vote very much independently from their husbands. Most of the male and female politicians know this as common sense, and so all political parties attach great importance to reaching women. That women are highly autonomous in individual political behaviour but do not participate in everyday public political life gives great importance to women politicians in this respect. Is it they who establish face-to-face relations with women voters; they are able to address housewives through 'feminine' speeches, to go into houses, and more importantly to use women's relationship networks. The most important way to reach women in the countryside in local politics, in small settlements and in communities is to use women. Women politicians are vote-gaining machines for all political parties. It should be pointed out that the basic relationship here is woman–to–woman, which sidesteps male relationships and rivalry. In basic terms, men are elected, and women help them to get elected.

Before 1980, women's sections within political parties were established for this purpose. Although women gained the vote as long ago as 1934, they started to work actively in groups in political parties only after the 1960s, with the establishment of women's sections. Although these were initiated by Republican People's Party (RPP) in Istanbul in 1954, the expansion of their activities did not take place until after the 1960s. A former deputy who was the leader of women's branches of this party for a long time, talks about two periods in the foundation phases of this organization. In the first period, she says, they met with strong opposition from provincial and district leaders, even though there were strict directives from the then party leader İsmet İnönü. She said that the provincial leaders evaded these in order to prevent the establishment of women's sections in their constituency. Their excuse was always the nature of the local culture; they never admitted they were personally not in favour, probably through personal difficulties of handling this novelty. While in the first period 'I would like it very much, but our local people are very traditional' was the typical excuse, in the second period the provincial leaders started to support and encourage the women's sections, as they realized that these both increased the votes of the party and raised funds through dances, tea parties, etc. But more importantly, women's sections had themselves started to form power centres, and province leaders realized that through women's divisions led either by their wives or by women relatives they had a power centre that could be more easily mobilized than could men. Women who made politics on behalf of the men in their families, very common in local politics, emerged at this point. However, we see that women, who were expected to support men both among the electorate and in inner party politics, were still excluded from decisionmaking mechanisms. The meetings continued to be held at hours and in places which made them difficult for women to participate in, and those women who were still able to attend were prevented by 'protective' behaviour which said 'don't tire yourself', or 'don't wear yourself out'. And those women who despite all these persisted in active participation, making speeches and expressing their views, were either regarded as 'ambitious' or 'uncontrolled'; men belittled them by saying that 'she does not know what she is doing', or 'women can say what they think, but we will do what we believe is right'.

It is necessary to indicate here that there is a parallel between the stated views of political parties and the way they perceive the role of women in politics. Women's activities within right-wing parties are more limited and more narrowly related to women. An understanding of the reasons behind this may be gained if one considers the negative reaction in conservative families towards women participating in politics and appearing in public. Moreover, to maintain a conservative image, it is not very good for women to be seen on the same platform as men. Thus, we see fewer women representatives in district, or provincial executive boards, or municipal councils of right-wing parties. However, even the right-wing parties had established women's sections by 1980. There were women's sections in the Justice Party (JP), which was the biggest party of the period. But there were structural differences between the women's divisions of the two main parties. The difference was most significant in their activities. The activities of the JP's women's sections were short-term, discontinuous and limited to election periods; although they existed on paper in non-election periods as well, their activities were restricted to fundraising, as they were not included in inner-party power struggles.

Among the right-wing parties, the Motherland Party is the only one which has established a women's section that functions efficiently and works in line with the party's central policies. The organization, called the Turkish Woman Promotion Foundation and established by the wife of the founding party leader Mr Özal, does not have any organic relation to the party, and functions exactly like a voluntary organization. This is related to the idea, central to the world-view of right-wing parties, that a woman's part in public life is limited to voluntary activities harmonious with her family life. The foundation's activities range from joining in women's lobbies in foreign countries to women's health issues. While bringing family-centred, male-dependent solutions to the problems confronted by women in their family and home life, it functions through face-to-face relations with a large number of women, making close contacts and providing services for them. It seems that these activities are very influential among lower-income groups and housewives.

Against the many negative circumstances which I have cited, women participated in politics in gradually increasing numbers in the period before 1980. For instance, the percentage of women in the municipal councils of big cities was rising.[3]

There were three factors influencing this rise. First of all, the routines of municipal politics fitted in better with the domestic duties of women politicians' daily lives than did national politics. The second reason is that the RPP was the ruling party, and women's activities were more common within RPP than in the other political parties (11 council members out of 14 were from the RPP). The third reason is that the women's sections, of which the importance was continuously rising, started to be influential in election primaries.

The activities of the women's sections were banned after 1980, and the most important channel to women in institutional politics (even though inadequate or limited) was shut down. After 1980, women's participation in politics has been possible only through direct competition with men. In order to compensate for this, the political parties have sought new solutions. Some parties instituted women's organizations under the name of women's commissions; others established voluntary organizations. Against all these unfavourable circumstances, some women are still active in politics, even though their roles and influence are still mainly determined by men. I shall go on now to discuss the varying roles of these women politicians.[4]

(i) Women involved in politics on behalf of or in support of the men in their families.

The majority of women in local politics, except those women involved in politics in big cities, carry out these activities on behalf of one or more men in their families (mostly their husbands) as a way of supporting them. Mostly these women are averagely or highly educated housewives. Among them are self-employed women, whose jobs can be reconciled with politics; some are retired. These women give priority to their homes and family lives: for them, political activity is secondary. The most important difference between these women and other women active in politics is that they behave in what is socially defined as a 'feminine' manner. Politics does not affect their clothing, their relations with men and women, or their family lives. For instance, these women do not frequent the headquarters of the political party; they do not talk to any men there that they do not personally know. They talk only to their relatives or family friends, and acknowledge in their conversations their difference from men. Such a woman is referred to as 'brother's wife' (*yenge*) by men. Although in male-dominated societies women's freedom of action in public life comes only with old age, these women may be quite young: according to my observations they are usually between 25 and 40 years of age. They do not make special efforts to hide their youth and femininity. For instance, if they are used to wearing make-up they continue to do so; they do not change their style of dress; they wear jewellery. Feminine topics such as childcare and family problems predominate among their concerns; politics, in a way, seems superfluous. However, they are frequently politically active. For example, they avidly debate political or semipolitical issues at women's tea-parties; they pursue politics as an important part of the competition among women; they know all the gossip in local political life; they have ideas about political forces and motivations. The basic driving force behind all this is to protect the men of their family. In a country like Turkey, where the most common way for women to climb the social ladder is alongside their menfolk, women try to prove their loyalty by pushing the men into politics and being so attached to politics themselves. However, direct political activities are very limited among these women. Sometimes they circulate propaganda among other women or raise funds for the political party, and in elections for the party's executive board and in preliminary district elections they vote for family members and for other candidates favoured by the men in their families. In a way, men encourage their wives and female relatives to participate in politics in order to increase their supporters, and thus their power, within the party. Women have communications networks within the community which are independent of men (Abadan-Unat, 1979), and by utilizing these women's networks men receive information and disseminate political propaganda. As her husband gains success in politics, a woman increases the status of her family, thus herself.

Kıray in her Ereğli research has shown that women who become publicly visible are not treated positively in Turkish society (Kıray, 1979), and as politics is a very public form of behaviour it must be expected that such activities for women would not be welcomed. In fact, women of the older generation within families (the mother-in-law or mother) may tacitly imply disapproval of such behaviour, as they regard politics as more of a 'male' job. They see women's stepping into the public arena in front of everybody's eyes as strange, and cannot reconcile this with the traditional roles of bride, mother and wife. However, the men, if they do not prevent it, as I have mentioned before, themselves register their wives with a political party and make them participate in these activities.

The point that should be underlined here is that these women's political activity is under the control of men, and is carried out on platforms which do not require relations with other men and which do not pave the way for women to act independently in the outside world. A woman in politics exists alongside her husband: she is neither independent of him, nor does she want to be so. Of course wives enter politics on behalf of their husbands at the national level, as well as at the local. From time to time women have taken up politics in order to circumvent a ban on their husbands and keep on the family name.[5]

(ii) Independent women

Naturally not all women politicians enter politics on behalf of their husbands: some of them have even entered into politics in face of their families' opposition and disapproval. These women who participate in politics independently talk about two different stages in their careers. First is the period in which there is the instigation and support of the party organization, but in which the family and non-political friends are not supportive. Second, then, is the period in which the family start to accept, and even encourage their involvement, but in which they start to face the barrier of competition with men within politics. There is a very clear split between women politicians when asked their views on the advantages and disadvantages of being a woman in politics. Whereas the very few women who have reached the positions they desired to attain say that men have helped them, or at least were supportive and did not hinder them, the women who have not succeeded claim that men have hindered them to a great extent, and that their gender has been a significant disadvantage. They complain that unless women's desired participation in politics is limited to selling ball tickets, they find very little support. It is important to note that the number of successful women is very low, and those who failed are numerous.

The women independently engaging in politics, both locally and nationally, have two initial similarities. First of all, they must have reached an age at when it is believed that they no longer need the protection of men;[6] that is, at least 45 years old. Second, these women are either married or at an age when marriage prospects are low: in such a male-dominated environment they need to show that they do not intend to enter into sexual relations with men. Neither the woman herself nor the men around her should think that she is unprotected, otherwise she will be excluded within politics: she will not be taken seriously, and may be mocked and face sexual harassment. For this reason women politicians try not to attract attention; they were dark-coloured tailor-made suits, and do not wear make-up or jewellery. They do not ask to be excused from a meeting or job because of family reasons.

According to my observations, independent women politicians are developing two models of behaviour. The first is the mother role, adopted more by local politicians, in which women pay attention to the problems of their men and women friends, give advice, share their troubles, show unselfishness, and try not to be perceived as very ambitious. They are especially friendly to those younger than themselves, and usually make others call them 'sister'. In this way they gain support and collect votes, especially for local positions.

The second model of behaviour is more common among politicians at a national level, and is usually adopted by women with high qualifications, that is, those who have higher education, and are influential in a profession other than politics – for instance they might have held a high position in the bureaucracy, or have been successful in their own business.[7] These women are eloquent, determined, and hardworking; they do not hesitate to go into public life, are in control over their lives and are trying to prove themselves. They argue and are outspoken, combative and competitive – attitudes which are considered masculine characteristics in Turkish culture. Women politicians behave as though they are asexual. They go to late-night meetings but do not drink; they work as enthusiastically as men politicians. They have to prove their importance at every opportunity, because they can guarantee their political existence and the positions they want only via their own effort. They have neither family men to protect them, nor sons to call on if necessary. The women who achieve success under these circumstances are proud of their achievements; their self-image is such that they consider themselves better than other women because they can succeed in a man's world. That is why they accept the under-representation of women in politics, and the problems of other women. They believe that most of the responsibility for their situation lies with the women, and take a negative attitude towards the women's movement and women's problems as they tend to identify themselves with male politicians.

Conclusion

Tekeli claims that women in politics depend mainly on their 'masculinization' (Tekeli, 1989). My findings show that a number of women politicians do effect such transformation, but that most work within male-defined 'feminine' roles. Nevertheless, both positions are ultimately determined by men. All of this shows how far politics is male-dominated. As a result of men's sovereignty, both in number and in power, men agree the ground-rules of competition and success in such a way that men's communication and consensus are facilitated, and women are excluded. Moreover, the clientelist structure of politics in Turkey and the developing networks among men exclude women from politics as well.[8] Women can only participate in politics under the domination of men. Of all the social activities of women, women's participation in politics is determined and controlled most clearly by men.

Here it is necessary to emphasize a point concerning the qualitative side of women's participation. Tekeli has said that, with the decrease of women's symbolic importance, the tendency to nominate women has fallen off, and thus the number of women candidates has diminished (Tekeli, 1982). Furthermore, Arat in her research has claimed that the women who were allowed to enter parliament tokenistically, hold back in the defence of their views; whereas the women who have entered parliament after 1960 not as symbols but as a result of competition with men, even though their number is low, behave more independently and are more active both on the issue of women's rights and on other issues (Arat, 1987). However, because of those features of women deputies I mentioned earlier, they keep a distance from women's movements and women's problems. Political parties tend to give priority to party identity over identity as a woman: whereas a quantitative increase in the participation of women in politics is of course desirable, it does not necessarily entail a closer understanding of or warmer attitude towards women's problems. Consequently, only a small proportion of women's votes are those of feminists, and almost none of the woman representatives in institutional politics are feminists. The participation of women in institutional politics should be seen as a means to this end.

Finally, it should be clearly recognized that the men who do not exercise direct control over women's individual political participation bring tight control to bear over their social participation. This situation emerges separately, and interdependently, through men's domination both in family and in politics.

Notes

1. The empirical findings of this research have two sources. Survey results refer to a survey of public opinion conducted among 2,000 respondents (Konda, unpublished survey 1988). As to the information regarding other types of participation, I have used the interviews that I held between 1978 and 1988 with men and women politicians who were active participants at various

levels in different political parties.

2. The reason behind this may be that municipalities deal with services that are closer to private life, and that being a mayor is less important than being a prime minister.

3. For instance, 10% of Istanbul municipal councillors were women (Tekeli, 1982).

4. These models are not comprehensive. The most dominant and common forms were taken as the models.

5. Tekeli calls this the 'widow's right' (Tekeli, 1982).

6. This is also true to a significant degree for other European countries (Walby, 1987).

7. Şirin Tekeli emphasizes these characteristics of most of these woman deputies, and underlines the importance of these high qualifications in their election (Tekeli, 1982).

8. This issue has been listed among the most important barriers to woman's participation in politics (Gillet, 1984; Papageorge, 1988; Chapman, 1987).

References

Abadan-Unat N. (1979). 'Toplumsal Değişme ve Türk Kadını', in N. Abadan Unat, ed., *Türk Toplumunda Kadın*, Türk Sosyal Bilimler Derneği Yayınları, Ankara.

Arat, Y. (1987). 'Türkiye'de Kadın Milletvekillerinin Değişen Siyasal Rolleri: 1934–1980', *Ekonomi ve İdari Bilimler Dergisi*, vol. 1, no. 1.

Chapman, J. (1987). 'Leaders and losers: a comparative study of competition, gender and the composition of local political leadership in Scotland, the Soviet Union and the U.S.A.' paper presented to the ECPR joint sessions, leadership and local politics workshop 10–15 April, Amsterdam.

Gillet, M. (1984). 'Strategies for power', paper presented to the Second International Interdisciplinary Congress on Woman, Gröningen, 17–21 April.

Hendlund, G. (1987). 'Women's interest in local politics', paper presented to the 'women and citizenship: rights and identities' workshop in the ECPR joint sessions, 10–15 April, Amsterdam.

Kandiyoti, D. (1979). 'Kadınlarda Psiko-Sosyal Değişim: Kuşaklar Arasında Bir Karşilaştırma', in N. Abadan-Unat, ed., *Türk Toplumunda Kadın*, Türk Sosyal Bilimler Derneği Yayınları, Ankara.

Kıray, M. (1979). 'Küçük Kasaba Kadınları', in N. Abadan-Unat, ed., *Türk Toplumunda Kadın*, Türk Sosyal Bilimler Derneği Yayınları, Ankara.

Odorisio, C. (1988). 'Women, men and political power', paper presented to the Council of Europe Workshop, June 30–July 3, Salzburg.

Papageorge, Y. (1988). 'Factors that inhibit or facilitate Greek women's involvement in politics', paper presented to the Council of Europe Workshop, June 30–July 3, Salzburg.

Tekeli, Ş. (1982). *Kadınlar ve Siyasal Toplumsal Hayat*, Birikim Yayınları, Istanbul.

Tekeli Ş. (1989) 'Kadınlar Politikada Neden Yoklar?' *Kaktüs* No. 5, January, pp. 18–26.

Walby, S. (1987). 'Gender Politics: an attack on malestream neglect', Lancaster Regionalism Group, working paper 26.

14

Has Anything Changed in the Outlook of the Turkish Left on Women?

Fatmagül Berktay

I believe it is meaningful, in reviewing the last twenty years of the Turkish Left from the women's side, to take 1980 as a dividing-line. Before 1980, a genuine 'women's question' was not really part of the Left's agenda: it was not taken seriously as a theoretical question, and neither were the specific dimensions of women's subjection considered worth dwelling upon. One would be willing, at most, to accept that 'feudal' relations and ideology had a more binding effect on women! But these were all, anyhow, problems subordinate to questions of class and revolution and, since they were going to be disappearing of their own accord in the future, burdening the agenda with such secondary issues could have only served to distract attention from the main tasks at hand. It is therefore difficult even to find adequate written documentation on the attitude of the Left to women before 1980, at least anything that goes beyond a simple collection of clichés. What I have to relate concerning that sub-period will therefore inevitably be in the nature of a 'personal history' that articulates into other 'histories' only through the interviews I have done since that time with various women who were also part of the Left, and on the basis of our common retrospective assessments.[1]

As long as we pretended we were men ...

The best way to begin is to state, simply and clearly, that what women actually lived through and experienced within the diverse parties, groups and organizations which made up the Turkish Left had little, if anything, to do with the much-vaunted slogan of 'equality between men and women'. Like the entire society of which it is a part, the Left – today as in the past – is a social organism or structure in which it is men who make and apply the rules. The norms and patterns of behaviour that women have to go by are determined by men in this male-dominated framework. As a result, women are excluded from virtually all decisionmaking, and even if some of them should occasionally come to be included in leading bodies, this is usually symbolic in purpose and function. In those few cases where women have emerged as leaders in their own right, they are so 'masculinized' mentally by the process of social elimination and selection to which they are subjected in rising to the top that it is quite rare for them to give any thought to questions specific to women, beyond problems of a general nature, let alone to using their authority to bring such questions on to the agenda of their organization.[2] However, it is a fact that, particularly since the mid 1980s, women belonging to various factions of the Left have increasingly been speaking up and even forming separate 'women's groups' under the umbrella of their respective organizations; this, indeed, is one of the major differences between the 1960s and 70s and the present.[3]

The Turkish Left has traditionally ascribed the oppression of women to the socioeconomic backwardness of a country said to be dominated by feudal relations, and this is also held responsible for the negative experience women have had with or in leftist organizations. But see how a leftist woman militant like Sheila Rowbotham describes her experience in a developed capitalist country very different from Turkey: 'We had a sense of not belonging. It was evident we were intruders. Those of us who ventured into their territory were most subtly taught our place. We were allowed to play with their words, their ideas, their culture as long as we pretended we were men. ... Either you played their game, or you didn't play at all.'[4] We women of a Third World country are no strangers to such feelings, and they point to the universal nature of discrimination against women.[5] At most, perhaps, there is a difference in degree:

Turkey's relative underdevelopment leads to less refined and more flagrant forms of subjection, and in a society where patriarchal domination is hardly ever questioned, the Left, too, feels freer to go along with and participate in such oppression. And certainly there is also a women's side to this, for women too regard it as 'natural' for men to make the rules and for themselves to obey, since that is the norm for the society into which they are born. Furthermore, in the case of the Left it is through appeals to 'revolutionary duty' that such acquiescence is additionally sanctioned, and as a result women find themselves submitting to constraints (such as being told by male leaders how to dress, behave and carry themselves in public; what to read and what not to read, etc.) which they might not accept in any other framework.

Woman as an element of discord capable of 'going off the rails' at any moment

One rather interesting argument utilized on the Left in Turkey to justify exercising control and supervision over women has been the idea that, precisely because they are women (purely on account of their gender, in other words), they have a greater tendency to 'go bourgeois'; it was therefore considered legitimate to exercise daily jurisdiction over their dress and behaviour. This is nothing more or less than a temporally and ideologically adjusted version of the ancient proposition, deeply ingrained in all monotheistic religions, according to which 'woman is closer to the devil' – or sometimes the devil himself. By the same token, women were considered 'an invitation to vice', along with drugs, gambling and alcohol; it was by way of defending itself against this danger that the Left came up with the 'sister' (*bacı*) stereotype. The rustic and folksy-sounding word *bacı*, drawn from provincial speech, denoted an unsexed, depersonalized kind of 'woman comrade'. Through the slogan 'The people are my only love, and all women are my sisters', male militants tried to protect themselves against women's potential for introducing discord (*fitna* in Islam) into revolutionary unity and solidarity. This entire notion was remarkably similar to Islamic ideology's exclusion and negation of personal erotic love for the sake of maintaining the inner cohesion of the community of believers, but nobody seems to have been struck by the parallels, then as now.[6] The Turkish Left is hindered from noticing such blatant connections by its notorious failure to question itself over the prevailing values and value-judgments, while its deeply ingrained conservatism regarding social relations acts as a further obstacle to efforts to change things in those infrequent cases where some kind of self-awareness does arise. And the transformations that have recently begun to manifest themselves have yet to provide any reason to modify this basic assessment.

In the name of 'cherishing the values of the people', the Turkish Left has steeped itself in feudal prejudice and behaviour, coming to embrace – partly under the influence of accusations of 'sexual collectivism' directed at communism over several decades – the family, monogamy and all else that goes by the name of 'the values of our people'. What is particularly interesting, of course, is that the people's values that are adopted in this way are invariably those having to do with sexuality and women. The Left has been of an exceedingly moralizing bent, regarding morality as a prerequisite for being a revolutionary. It has repeatedly declared itself against sexual freedom and homosexuality. These are, it has claimed, disgusting forms of deviant behaviour reflecting capitalist decadence. The image of virtue that it has exalted, on the other hand, has been essentially applied to women as a means of legitimizing male jurisdiction over them.

In the past – especially before 1980 – whenever 'the woman question' as such was brought up, and women were able to point to unequal practices (mostly in cases of extreme, very concrete and undeniable violations), leaders of Leftist organizations were generally prone to put the blame on the 'backwardness' of individual revolutionaries who, it was said, had not yet been able to shake off the influence of feudal culture. These, in other words, were interpreted as individual and isolated incidents which would gradually disappear over time. Women comrades should be patient, and in the mean time 'prove their worth' by throwing themselves wholeheartedly into the struggle. For some incomprehensible reason, it was always women who had to prove themselves, and who remained bourgeois until and unless they did so. What was glossed over was the fact that it was (and is) *the organization as a whole* that collectively kept (and keeps) oppressing and exercising jurisdiction over women. This was precisely why half-hearted warnings issued to this or that male militant regarding his 'errors' over 'the woman question' were never taken seriously. And this was as it should be, for male militants had no real reason to take themselves to task and to try to engage in self-correction over a form of behaviour which they saw as the organizational as well as the social norm. The organization exercised a certain degree of control and discipline over its entire male and female membership, of course. But vigilance was doubled when it came to women, and it shaded quite easily into outright oppression. For society at large, as well as for the revolutionary organization in particular, it was (and is) legitimate and more easily practicable for women to be tightly supervised: not only were they excluded from power and authority, their very sex put their revolutionary credentials into doubt.

The two extremes of the post-1980 spectrum

As I have already pointed out, the woman question was not really on the agenda of the Turkish Left before 1980. There were very few women who had developed a women's consciousness, and those who did kept their ideas to themselves for the most part. But ten years' experience had not gone for nothing, and it was not long before the ideas to which it gave rise began to rise to the surface, along with all the resentment and tension that had long been pent up.

Thus it has come to pass that we find the Turkish Left beginning to take a serious theoretical interest in 'the woman question' from the mid 1980s onward – in a very real sense it was compelled to do so. As manifested in various periodicals, from the most dogmatic and conservative to the most innovatory,[7] this interest has certain common features. For one thing, all fractions of the Left are now agreed on the existence of a certain 'woman question'. They also grant, grudgingly, that the present women's movement has evolved under feminist leadership; and it is in order to remedy this situation – 'scandalous' for some, 'not so very good' for others – that they recommend setting up independent women's organizations capable of establishing their own leadership. Attacks on feminism, meanwhile, also reveal a difference not of kind but of degree, ranging from the open hostility of 'a splinter group bearing a Septembrist stamp that is going nowhere'[8] to the condescension of 'a movement that is bourgeois-democratic in essence'. A lot of effort at self-questioning and introspection has nevertheless emerged between these two ends of the Left spectrum.

Once the fact of feminist influence over the women's movement is admitted, as already indicated, and it is further proposed to set up independent leftist women's organizations in order to wrest leadership away from the feminists, what follows next, interestingly enough, is the perception that such organizations could only be based on issues and demands *specific to women*. There could hardly be any clearer expression of the ambivalence of the Left regarding the women's question: on the one hand, they are positively influenced by feminism, which is also reflected in the revolt of militant women against gender hierarchies within the narrow framework of their own organizations. On the other hand, their ideological and field leaderships are worried and anxious to reassert their supremacy over 'women who have already gone off or could go off the right track' by repulsing the influence and example of feminism. It is important to add at this point that the new women's organizations in question are intended to be 'independent' only in the organizational, not in the ideological, sense. It has somehow come to be understood that mobilizing women depends on taking account of their specific demands; the overall intention, however, remains not women's liberation as such but 'to draw the rank and file of the women's organization, slowly but surely, into the arena of social struggle'.[9] This policy approach is no different from that of other political parties and movements, who persist in regarding women as ballot fodder for their own ends.

The periodical *Emeğin Bayrağı* (Labour's Banner), which has taken up a position on the most dogmatic end of the spectrum I have described puts its case in a nutshell with a citation from Ms Sibel Özbudun:

It is communists who really value and uphold the cause of the liberation of labouring women, and who are taking concrete steps to that end. The *task that devolves* on labouring women, meanwhile, is to organize not as women but as proletarians; not as the female rivals but as the comrades-in-arms of their labouring husbands.[10]

Mr Yalçın Gür, the author of this article, goes on to argue that drawing any lines of distinction between men and women is tantamount to splitting the ranks of workers by establishing scab unions. In contrast, Nedret Sena, writing in *Yeni Öncü* (New Vanguard), which in my view situates itself at the more self-critical end of the spectrum, elucidates a wholly different approach (one might think):

> Oppressed by the system as well as by men of all classes, it is necessary for women to realize, among themselves, an organization which is predicated on this form of oppression if they are to be able to move towards both equality and freedom. . . . Opposition to men's oppression of women is the basis for organizing in common by all women.[11]

But just when you are feeling somewhat relieved, the same Nedret Sena turns around to repeat that simile of union organization; simultaneously regarding feminism as positive and accusing it of being 'bourgeois' and 'not opposed to the system', going so far as to evoke the spectre of 'scab unions'.

It cannot be doubted that male domination and gender hierarchies have begun to be questioned and criticized, however hesitantly, within the Turkish Left. Such progress, however, is invariably accompanied by a lot of defensive posturing and the manning of crumbling ramparts. 'What, do you say "no" to men as such?' retort some; 'the failings of both men and women are all the failings of this deformed society', others philosophise; 'let women and men work shoulder to shoulder in order to solve all problems together: *this is the correct position*', still others presume to pontificate – value-laden propositions, every single one of them, whose currency reflects the latent anxiety and attempts at cooptation. Before 1980, men were not given to writing articles purporting to advise women on 'the correct line' and to remind them whose business it was to set the norms – they did not need to, for they did not yet feel their domination to be threatened. Now, however, their superiority has been shaken, and they are resorting to counter-measures: when man's failing becomes the failing of society as a whole, that specific man, Ahmet or Mehmet, need no longer feel so personally responsible! According to another bit of popular wisdom, we should learn to 'consider the problem as a whole' and 'establish the proper order of priorities', which is the prelude to establishing that 'the burning urgency of social problems of a general sort outweighs questions specific to women'. But since such 'social problems of a general sort' are never going to lose any of their urgency, it seems that we have ended up where we started, at a point where all the wonderful talk about women's oppression remains just talk.

By way of elaborating further on that verdict, I would once more like to call Nedret Sena to account. In another article in *Yeni Öncü*, Sena dwells at great length on the social and historical roots of women's oppression, and defends the idea of women uniting among themselves on the basis of sexual oppression in order to struggle against it; s/he[12] even accepts that the struggle in question would have to target men in general. 'As men and women, we are going to have to struggle among ourselves', Sena then concludes, 'but *the basic question* then becomes to uncover the proper forms for it that will not erode our *partnership* in the struggle against the system that is, after all, the mainstay of the ideology in question.'[13] Do we have to take it on Nedret Sena's authority that this, indeed, is 'the basic question'? And what can emphasising 'partnership' at this point signify, other than a move to suppress the 'struggle' that is actually beginning? Ms Deniz Eren has made the same point, and very neatly too, in her reply to Nedret Sena in the same periodical.

It is only superficially that an independent women's struggle appears to be unopposed to the system as a whole; in fact, however, even an egalitarian sort of women's struggle ultimately targets the existing hierarchy, and hence cannot be regarded as remaining purely within the bounds of the system,

says Ms Eren, and pursues her argument with the following words:

Today, it remains true that men and women are different in the sense that the former are on top while the latter are inferior, whether we want to call this an antagonism or not. This is also the case among socialists, between socialist men and women. Yet socialists of these two sexes are also partners in the struggle against the system. But what is behind this partnership? Certainly not 'forms that will not erode the partnership' in the struggle against the system. At present, this partnership hangs on women's self-sacrifice, even submission. . . . For it is impossible to talk of a genuine partnership in a relationship that is dominated by the man; that partnership, indeed, has ceased to exist the moment it is said to have come into being. It is illusory, sustained only by the woman's self-sacrifice.'[14]

Tender love – where have you gone?

There is yet another dimension of the defensive mood that has taken over leftist men which is particularly fascinating. In some unfathomable fashion, they have suddenly rediscovered 'love', which they had appeared to have forgotten all about long ago, and have taken to extolling its splendours: how it rises above all egoism and self-interest and requires responsibility and trust. 'The essence of genuine love has to do with sharing all aspects of life. . . . When love comes to be felt mutually and crystallizes into a relationship, it ceases to concern only a single individual, and evolves into an active partnership encompassing both people concerned.'[15] Note the recurring theme of partnership as the basic question. This author, moreover, is aware that a love relationship does not exist in a void: 'It is a fundamental truth that members of bourgeois society are not atoms divorced from their social contexts.'[16] But it would seem, to judge from his discourse, that members of socialist organizations somehow experience love in a vacuum, in a dream world where men and women are not hierarchically related to one another. This is not simply a lack of self-awareness, I fear, but an attempt to play on women's weaknesses by propagating the illusion that sexual oppression has ceased to exist, the objective being to promote that 'wonderful partnership of old' in which men were on top. To go back to the same article: 'But *responsibility* also requires that each partner should work on the other's "self". The sense of *responsibility* that is brought home by a love relationship resting on genuine affection depends on, and serves as an indicator of, the sincerity of the love and emotions in question. In such a relationship, *responsibility* and *trust* go hand in hand.'[17] (I have taken it upon myself to italicize all the trusts and responsibilities involved.) Ah, where are those gentle, affectionate, responsible, confidence-inspiring women of yesteryear? Is it the evil wind of feminism that has swept all of them away?

Faced with women who are increasingly critical of them, who take gender hierarchies to task, and who can no longer be cowed and subdued through traditional methods, men are now resorting to a tactic which they think is more sophisticated, but which is actually so transparent as to be almost comical. You are opposed to sharing and partnership, so you must hate all men as such; you want to lead a life of independence and freedom, so you must be unreliable and irresponsible; you want to develop your own individuality, so you must be after your selfish interests; you no longer behave in so docile and conciliatory a fashion, so you are cold and loveless. As Joanna Russ has put it:

> That's not an issue.
> That's not an issue *any more*.
> Then why do you keep on bringing it up?
> You keep on bringing it up because you are crazy.
> You keep on bringing it up because you are hostile.
> You keep on bringing it up because you are intellectually irresponsible.
> You keep on bringing it up because you are shrill, strident and self-indulgent.
> How can I possibly listen to anyone as crazy, hostile, intellectually irresponsible, shrill, strident, and self-indulgent as you are?
> Especially since what you are talking about is not an issue. (Any more.)[18]

A certain question of irresponsibility and unreliability has indeed come about not so much on the part of 'loveless and irresponsible women', however, as of leftist men who appear incapable of facing and coming to terms with themselves; it is their untrustworthiness that is the issue. And they cannot hope to inspire fresh confidence in women by penning high-handed theoretical articles from the outside, by evolving a meta-discourse, or by oh-so-graciously defining feminism as 'a democratic movement'. Statements such as: 'yes, women are oppressed, but we socialists are not oppressing them', or 'yes, we socialists also did similar things in the past, but no longer', or 'yes, men are given to oppressing women, but I don't; I even do the dishes', are ludicrous attempts to take refuge in an illusion which maintains the status quo. (There is a corresponding strain among socialist women who lack a woman's consciousness; statements of the type: 'yes, women are oppressed, but not I – for I am struggling shoulder to shoulder with men on an equal footing'.) In front of us there stands a woman question which can no longer be denied by anyone, but the fashion now is to pretend that it exists only in a distant realm far removed from socialist men and women;

certain revolutionaries, who of course (!) have nothing whatsoever to do with the said question as either oppressors or oppressed, are disinterestedly trying to evolve solutions on pages and pages of paper. This is, to say the least, not very credible.

In order to really persuade us, socialist men would have to start thinking about, publicly articulate, put in writing and document the ways in which they themselves, as individuals, both singly and collectively, have dominated and oppressed women; and simultaneously begin to do something about it in practice. It is easy enough to write theoretical articles from *the outside*, to preach about what is right and what is wrong, and to appear to extol love and affection; it is, however, rather irrelevant in the present context. Still, this remains the way in which the Turkish Left is in the habit of tackling such questions, as elsewhere. As Sheila Rowbotham observes, 'Their [men's] revolution has a symbolism for the outer shape of things, and the inner world goes along on the old tracks.'[19] The point, however, is precisely that the inner world should change. Hence, it is possible to conclude for the moment that, while things are no longer exactly the same in the Turkish Left's outlook on women, such change as there is continues to wander around in the sphere of outer shapes, not yet coming to be internalized. The only safeguard for sustaining change in that direction can be for feminism to continue to increase its role in pushing the entire Turkish women's movement forward; to evolve into a movement of truly broad scope; and to persist, as a genuinely oppositional locus, in shaking men's and women's inner worlds.

Notes

1. I am grateful to three close friends from very different factional backgrounds – Deniz Türkali, Muzaffer Kurşuncu and Neşe Erdilek – for such retrospective assessments; I have benefited immensely from sharing their life experiences, thoughts and emotions. This does not mean, of course, that they would necessarily agree with everything in this chapter. On the other hand, the attacks that I was subjected to at the 1989 Women's Convention in Istanbul after I read my paper criticizing the Left for its attitude to women, as well as an interview with Elif Tolon in the periodical *Defter* (or Notebook: no. 9, April–May 1989), would seem to indicate that my history is not so special after all. But others would have to speak up and write, too, for the common ground to be better elucidated.

2. Şirin Tekeli, 'Kadınlar Neden Politikada Yoklar' (Why women are absent from politics), *Kaktüs*, January 1989, passim. Kumari Jayawardena, too, in her

book *Feminism and Nationalism in the Third World*, Zed Press, London 1988, draws attention to the same problem in the concrete case of Vietnam.

3. At the time the Turkish version of this article was written, one example of the feminist circles that had arisen within existing organizational structures was the Feminist Women's Group, then part of the Socialist Party. At the First Enlarged Party Conference held by the SP, members of this group spoke up in criticism of the report prepared by the party's official Women's Commission (for the text of their intervention, see *Sosyalist Birlik* (Socialist Unity), March 1989). Since then, however, they have all resigned from the party in the face of the SP (now the Workers' Party) leadership's conservative reaction.

4. Sheila Rowbotham, *Woman's Consciousness, Man's World*, Harmondsworth 1973, p. 30.

5. It was also meaningful, in this context, to be told by many non-Turkish women after I had read this paper at the Kassel Symposium that they felt exactly the same way over this question.

6. Fatima Mernissi, *Beyond the Veil: Male–Female Dynamics in a Modern Muslim Society*, New York 1975, passim. On this point, also see two related articles by Aydın Uğur, 'Bir Kadın İçin Gözyaşları' (Tears for a woman); and Fatmagül Berktay, 'Günahtan Çok Aşktan Korkmak' (To be afraid not so much of sin as of love): both in *Gergedan* (Rhinoceros), October 1987.

7. The following periodicals were combed for this study until April 1989: *Bilim ve Sanat* (Science and Art), *Çağdaş Yol* (The Contemporary Path), *Demokrat Arkadaş* (Fellow Democrat), *Dünyaya Bakış* (View of the World), *Emeğin Bayrağı* (Labour's Banner), *Emek* (Labour), *Gelenek* (The Tradition), *Görüş* (Opinion), *Gün* (The Day), *İşçi Dünyası* (Workers' World), *Özgürlük* (Freedom), *Özgürlük Dünyası* (World of Freedom), *Saçak* (The Eave), *Sorun* (The Issue), *Sosyalist Birlik* (Socialist Unity), *Toplumsal Kurtuluş* (Social Liberation), *Yeni Açılım* (New Vistas), *Yeni Çözüm* (The New Solution), *Yeni Demokrasi* (New Democracy), *Yeni Öncü* (New Vanguard).

8. The 'Septembrist' epithet is a reference to the supposed favour done to feminism by the savagely repressive military coup of 12 September 1980. Since feminism went public at a time when (the rest of) the Left had been crushed, this is taken as proof of its bourgeois, counterrevolutionary, class-collaborationist nature (for how else could it have been permitted to develop?); alternatively, feminism itself is blamed for 'taking advantage' of the vacuum created by military terror.

9. Hikmet Beskisiz, writing in *Çağdaş Yol*, June 1988. What makes this all the more interesting is that Ms Hikmet Beskisiz is (was) the general secretary of DKD (Association of Democratic Women), an 'independent women's organization'.

10. Quoted by Yalçın Gür, *Emeğin Bayrağı*, March 1988, p. 26, my italics.

11. Nedret Sena, 'Ekonomik ve Demokratik Örgütlenmeler Bağlamında Kadın Örgütlenmesi' (Women's organizations in the general context of economic and democratic organizations), *Yeni Öncü*, September 1987.

12. To a Turkish ear familiar with the ways of the Turkish Left, 'Nedret Sena' sounds very much like a pseudonym deliberately chosen for its ambiguity; it could belong to a man as well as to a woman.

13. Nedret Sena, 'Sosyalizm mi, Feminizm mi?' (Socialism or feminism?), *Yeni Öncü*, July–August 1987, italics mine.

14. Deniz Eren, 'Bağımsız Kadın Örgütlenmesi Konusunda N. Sena'yı Okurken' (Reading N. Sena on independent women's organizations), *Yeni Öncü*, February–March 1988.

15. Osman Alkın, 'Asena, Kadın ve Sevgi' (Asena, woman and love), *Gelenek* (The Tradition), August 1987.

16. Ibid.

17. Ibid.

18. *Frontiers*, no. 4, 1979.

19. *Woman's Consciousness, Man's World*, p. 36.

Comparative Observations on Feminism and the Nation-building Process

Nilüfer Çağatay
and Yasemin Nuhoğlu-Soysal

Although feminism became an autonomous mass movement in Western societies in the 1960s, Third World countries did not live through such a process of change. In spite of the fact that in countries like Turkey and Egypt, the woman question and even feminism became an important item on the agenda from time to time, feminism never went beyond the status of an ideology defended by middle-class intellectuals. Towards the end of the 1970s in many Third World countries (Peru, Brazil, Turkey, Egypt, Pakistan, India, etc.), there was renewed interest in feminism and it came to occupy an important place in the political and ideological debates of these countries.[1] Nevertheless, it is difficult to say that feminism, both as an ideology and as a social movement, was accepted as a legitimate discourse, because it was considered by different sectors of public opinion as a Western-originated and divisive ideology foreign to the national culture; also, it was seen as an ideology promoting lesbian relationships among women.

In this chapter, we are proposing to examine the relationships between feminism and the process of nation-building (or nationalism) as well as exploring the conditions for its development as an autonomous movement, especially in the case of Turkey.[2] We examine both the obstacles to and the favourable circumstances for feminist organizing in the Third World, paying especial attention to the role of the state and the processes and ideologies of nation-building. Last, we focus on the role that nationalist ideology has played in the development of feminism as an autonomous movement in Turkey, in comparison to some other Middle Eastern countries.

Since the beginning of the twentieth century, women's issues and status have been a key aspect of political discourses and agendas in what now constitutes the Third World. In these countries – in which political regimes range from secularist to religious fundamentalist, from military dictatorship to civilian, and from capitalist to socialist (of whatever variety) – women have been the symbol of struggles over legitimacy, national identity, cultural authenticity, reform and development. Demands for women's legal and political rights have always been an integral part of struggles for national liberation and unity. Political agendas which emphasize women's rights have borne a special importance in instances of radical social transformation (Jayawardena, 1988).

This is for several reasons. First, reforms of women's rights tend to bring legitimacy to newly formed states or radical movements, within the international political system.[3] The changes these reforms bring about in the realm of gender relations are an important indicator of the break with the old regime. The emerging groups contending for power, and those who actually capture it, differentiate their ideologies from the old ones by proposing to restructure women's position in society. These changes, however, need not always be 'progressive' or 'modernist': they can equally aspire to revive conservative orthodoxies with regard to women's status, again in an attempt to sever ties with the old regime – as, for instance, in Iran during the Islamic Republic. Second, the nation-state building process usually requires the integration of women into the newly emerging economic and political system. This implies the mobilization of women in the public sphere, as supporters of the liberation movement or as reproducers and producers within the new regime.

The importance the gender question acquires in the social and political agendas of Third World states does not, however, imply a promotion of feminism as an autonomous movement or ideology. The contexts in which women's concerns are addressed often have contradictory implications for the possibility of autonomous feminist organizing. While at times state action might be in line with feminist politics and demands (especially of the liberal feminist type), such actions, by their reformist and state-initiated nature, may at the same time impede autonomous feminist organizing. Clearly the mobilization of women in the public sphere cannot be equated with the process of women's emancipation. What needs to be studied carefully is the framework and conditions within which women's mobilization takes place. Women's participation in the public sphere might simply be conjunctural and temporary, dictated by political expedience. And such participation might be shaped by 'indigenous' cultural forms and ideologies that are hostile to feminist and other non-traditional or anti-traditional forms of organizing. Finally, and perhaps most significantly, the role played by the state in the nation-building process in Third World countries might hinder autonomous feminist politics. Thus, our discussion in what is to follow concentrates on the implications of (i) the nation-building process and the role of the state, and (ii) the nature of the nationalist ideology for the women's movement and feminist organizing.

In many states, citizenship rights have been extended to women in the context of building the nation-state, in reforms which were often state-initiated and implemented in a top-down fashion. Even when women have organized themselves in national liberation movements, their demands have been primarily national liberationist: women's rights are defined within the framework of the national liberation struggle and their political participation often erodes after the seizure of state power. Subsequently, the discourse on 'the demands for women's rights' evolves into a consideration of 'the [legal] rights the state should grant women'. There is no doubt that this process of social and legal transformation undertaken by the state has been instrumental in the creation of a visible professional class of women, but at the same time state-led women's 'emancipation' often preserves the status quo for the majority of women in these societies. This is hardly surprising, since these reforms on women's rights are not predicated upon the need to abolish gender discrimination, but are perceived rather as a necessary component of economic development and the nation-building process (Çağatay and Hatem, 1987).

In the Third World, women's rights have generally not been seen as a part of the problematic of civil liberties and individual rights, but have been formulated within the framework of policies that aim to serve 'the social good'. Defined within a nationalist ideological framework, in which 'development' and industrialization (whether capitalist or socialist) are revered national goals, the concept of 'the social good' does not allow political breathing space for contradictions arising from class, ethnic and gender differences. Thus policies aimed at serving the social good usually fail to challenge patriarchal relations in any fundamental way.

It might more generally be remarked that in the nation-building process the interests of the individual are subjugated to 'the social good'. In terms of gender relations, this phenomenon manifests itself as the difficulty women face in their attempts to participate in the public realm as individuals. Even when women are extensively integrated into the public sphere, their identities are defined through the language and concept of the family. A case in point is men's frequent use in Turkey of the word *bacı* (sister) when they address women who are active in leftist as well as Islamist politics; a term which desexualizes women as a precondition of their acceptance in the public realm.

This phenomenon clashes with the basic principles of most varieties of feminist politics. For example, the initial project of liberal feminism in the West was to demand the extension of equal citizenship rights for women in the public realm. As women became more integrated within the public sphere, they organized to extend the limits of their 'patriarchal citizenship' which was predicated upon a gendered division of labour and a split between the public and the private spheres.[4]

In contrast, the incorporation of women into the public sphere in Third World countries can proceed without challenging the patriarchal structure of citizenship, and indeed at times may reinforce traditional forms of male dominance. Both the forms of address men use towards women (as mentioned above) and the revival of the Islamic code of dress among women in the Middle East might be seen as cases in point. Quite apart from ideological reasons, many middle-class women adopt the Islamic mode of dress as a means of preventing sexual harassment as they operate in public.

The lack of development of individualism poses obstacles not only for liberal feminism but also for radical feminist organizing. If we can see the principal ideas of radical feminism as being centred around women's control over their bodies as individuals, the difficulty of taking radical feminism as an organizing principle in the Third World becomes evident. While some of the issues that are principally associated with radical feminism, such as abortion rights, can be dealt with and gained as legal rights, other issues will meet with greater resistance unless proposed solutions are couched in innovative terms along with new forms of struggle and organizing.

One example of such a radical feminist struggle is the problem of domestic violence. The radical feminist solution in the advanced capitalist countries has been to open up shelters for battered women, thereby removing them from institutional structures such as the family and the church. Given the strength of these structures in Third World societies, such a solution may not be viable here. This is not to say that feminists in the Third World cannot organize around domestic violence or use the same means as feminists in advanced capitalist societies, but the conditions, the form and the meaning of such struggles might have to be different from those which have been used so far by radical feminism. Creative approaches to possibilities of trans-forming existing women's networks into more radical entities might open new venues for feminist struggle.

In Third World countries, the nation-building process itself must be considered as another factor for understanding the prospects for feminism. This process requires the economic, political and ideological mobilization of large sectors of society, and women constitute one such important target. Even though they are primarily perceived as reproducers within the family, the mobilization process necessitates a restructuring of women's presence in the public sphere as well – either as political supporters and legitimizers or as part of the labour-force.

The specific ideological framework within which this mobili-zation takes place shapes the future prospects for feminism. For instance, the ideological driving forces behind the nation-building processes in the Middle East have ranged from Islam, to Arab-socialism, to secularist Turkish nationalism, with each of these ideologies creating different conditions for women's mobilization. But the common trait in the movements/regimes backed by these different ideologies has been their need to monopolize political power in their effort to mobilize the masses, and their suppression of all separate and autonomous movements once a movement has acquired state power. This might perhaps be seen as a natural attribute of nationalism, which shuns class, gender and ethnic differences. Thus, the difficulty of organizing autonomous feminist movements under the political hegemony of nationalist ideologies is obvious.

The central element of the nation-building process is the construction of a national identity which is claimed to be 'authentic' and 'indigenous'. In the special case of the Middle East, the perception of the indigenous or authentic is conditioned by the East/West dichotomy. Feminism in any shape or form has generally been seen as a product of Western culture and is immediately suspect as a tool of Western imperialism, not only to Islamist nationalists but also to orthodox Marxists. This inevitably affects women's perception of the nature of their oppression, and to that extent hinders the independent development of feminism.

The framework developed so far in this chapter is a general analysis of observed trends in the Third World from the point of view of the women's movement. Within this framework the case of Turkey, though it is representative of other Third World countries, also contains a good deal that is unique to its historical and social development. These unique features can be better understood in the context of a comparative study of the Turkish women's movement in the context of other Middle Eastern countries. We now turn to such an evaluation of the feminist movement in Turkey, comparing it to the experiences of Middle Eastern countries which have had periods of strong women's movements, such as Egypt, Tunisia and Algeria.

The different types of nationalism in the Middle East (i.e. secular, Islamic nationalist and Arab-socialist) have borne a close relationship to the development of women's movement. Common to all these variants of nationalism is a political stand against Western hegemony with respect to women's emancipation and rights. However, despite their common point of departure, they contain important differences (Çağatay and Hatem, 1987). The defining characteristic of Islamic nationalism, which emerged in the early part of the twentieth century in Egypt (represented by Mustafa Kamil), was to oppose any change that might threaten the Islamic identity of the society. On the other hand the notion of an 'Islamic synthesis' expounded by other important twentieth-century thinkers, such as the Egyptian Qasim Amin and the Tunisian Tahir Haddad, was fiercely criticized by their contemporaries, including Mustafa Kamil. The eclectic views of Amin and Haddad were later to gain wider recognition in various Arab countries among the defenders of women's rights (Phillip, 1978).

Arab socialism, which had acquired considerable political power by the mid-twentieth century, has approached 'the woman question' from the vantage-point of national liberation. For instance, despite its potential for radical treatment, the notion of 'national culture' that was shaped by the Algerian national movement was based on the traditional Islamic/Arabic norms of gender relations and had an overall conservative attitude. On the one hand, women's participation in the national liberation movement was considered a precondition of achieving independence and creating a new society, and gender equality was stressed to secure the support of the French Left. On the other hand, a 'static' and traditional understanding of culture and nationalism was not abandoned (Minces, 1978). Consequently, the Algerian constitution upheld at the same time gender equality and the preservation of the traditional family based on Islamic and Arabic gender relations.

This ambivalent attitude at the level of the state is also reflected in the discourse of many feminists throughout the Middle East, who have tried to demonstrate their authenticity by arguing that their feminism does not conflict (for example) with Islam in its original historical form, or with pre-Islamic Arab culture. Much of the debate centres on whether feminism is in conflict with Middle Eastern culture, and more specifically with Islam, rather than on what social transformations it seeks.[5] In these debates the exploitation of women is seen to be mostly related to external forces, such as Ottoman colonialism, Western imperialism and capitalism.

By contrast, Turkish nationalism adopted a pro-Western and secular attitude at an ideological level, just as it was waging a struggle against Western imperialism. In the republican era, the main items in the agenda of Kemalist rule have been effecting a break with the Ottoman past and catapulting Turkey to the 'level of contemporary civilizations' (i.e. Western economies and societies). The Kemalist rule undertook its relatively radical reforms on women's rights as part and parcel of this agenda, seeing these as a gauge of its level of Westernization, and a means to break with the Ottoman heritage. In an effort to rewrite history, Kemalism tried to 'synthesize' new Western and secular forms with the presumably 'egalitarian' approach of pre-Islamic Turks towards women.

These types of synthesis brought about the legitimization of women's rights outside the scope of Islamic gender relations. In this context, Turkey provides an interesting contrast with these Arab Middle Eastern countries which had a stronger Islamic identity. By the 1980s, since women's rights were to a large extent recognized at the legal level and defended by the official republican ideology, much feminist debate in Turkey focused on questioning the meaning and the adequacy of the state's defence of these rights (Tekeli, 1982). Taking women's legal rights for granted, non-feminist and non-Islamist women's groups have not participated much in debates concerning gender equality and the indigenous roots of feminism in Turkey. By this period, the feminist movement itself had transcended the debates on 'divisiveness' and 'alienness' to produce a conceptually rich feminism that advocated an autonomous form of organization, opposing all patriarchal structures at the universal level. Taking as its point of departure universalist categories, feminism criticized not only 'state feminism', but also the Marxist approach to 'the woman question' (Tekeli, 1985). Furthermore, feminists also tried to develop these universalist categories by questioning their meaning in the particular case of Turkey.[6]

As a result, the transcendence of the debate on 'indigenousness/authenticity' and the focus on universalist categories have been the distinguishing characteristics of Turkish feminism, in comparison to other Middle Eastern countries. In large part, the cause of this difference can be ascribed to the difference exhibited by Turkish nationalism in relation to other nationalist ideologies in the Middle East. Even though Kemalism has opposed the development of an autonomous feminist movement, it nonetheless contributed to the development of conditions that eventually enabled the shift by women's groups in the eighties to universalist categories and themes. Likewise, despite its similar opposition to the autonomous organization of women's groups, leftist thought in Turkey with its own emphasis on universalist categories also helped feminists in transcending debates on indigenousness and authenticity.

In our analysis, we have discussed those factors that have contributed to the development of an autonomous women's movement in Turkey. In the period since the foundation of the republic, the women's movement has had certain achievements. At the legal level, although much needs to be done, many rights for women have nonetheless long been recognized; alongside more radical feminists, a significant female professional middle class committed to the ideals of liberal feminism has come into existence; there have been periods where women have widely participated in mass movements, acquiring individual political experience.

In this chapter, starting from the general conditions of the development of women's emancipation in the Third World, we have tried to give an account of the conditions particular to Turkey, considering the relative influences of the state, individualism, the nation-building process and nationalism. However, we see this study as but a part of a wider body of work that attempts a comparative analysis of the particular conditions of women within a number of individual Third World countries.

Notes

1. For an account of women's political struggles in Asia and the Middle East, see Jayawardena (1988).
2. We recognize the problematic nature of the concept 'the Third World', as there is a tremendous economic, political and cultural heterogeneity among Third World countries. However, we use it as an umbrella term to refer to countries with a colonial or semi-colonial history and underdeveloped capitalist structures with semi-feudal vestiges. We do not use it as a political category. In so far as we discuss the relevance of feminism for the Third World, and the prospects for autonomous feminist organizing, we have in mind the implications of those basic characteristics which, on the one hand, constitute the common denominator of the societies under discussion and, on the other, differentiate them from the post-industrial societies and countries commonly referred to as the Eastern Bloc.
3. The efforts of a radical movement to gain legitimacy obviously need not be directed at the totality of existing nation-states, by complying with widely upheld norms with regard to women's emancipation. Often these efforts are directed at those sharing the same ideological framework, such as the Islamic revolution in Iran.
4. For a discussion of the relationship between patriarchy and civil society see Yeatman (1984).
5. See Çağatay and Hatem (1987). For an example of such an approach see Saadawi (1982).
6. As an example, see Kandiyoti (1988).

References

Çağatay, Nilüfer and Mervat Hatem (1987). 'Feminism and nationalism in the Middle East', unpublished paper, University of Utah and Howard University.

Jayawardena, Kumari (1988). *Feminism and Nationalism in the Third World*, Zed Press, London.

Kandiyoti, Deniz (1988). 'Bargaining with patriarchy', *Gender and Society*, vol. 2, no. 3.

Minces, Juliet (1978). 'Women in Algeria', in *Women in the Muslim World*, ed. Nikkie Keddie and Lois Beck, Harvard University Press, Cambridge, Mass.

Phillip, Thomas (1978). 'Feminism and nationalist politics in Egypt', in *Women in the Muslim World*, ed. Nikkie Keddie and Lois Beck, Harvard University Press, Cambridge, Mass.

Saadawi, Nawal el (1982). 'Women and Islam', in *Women's Studies International Forum*, no. 2.

Tekeli, Şirin (1982). *Kadınlar ve Siyasal Toplumsal Hayat*, Birikim, Istanbul.

Tekeli, Şirin (1985). 'Türkiye' de Feminist İdeolojinin Anlamı ve Sınırları Üzerine', *Yapıt*, Şubat-Mart.

Yeatman, A. (1984). 'Despotism and civil society: the limits of patriarchal citizenship', in *Women's Views of the Political World of Men*, ed. Judith H. Stiehm, New York, Transnational, pp. 153–176.

Part IV

Pragmatic Forms of Resistance

A Comparison of Violent and Non-violent Families

Şahika Yüksel

Violence against women by their husbands or other male members of their family has existed in almost every human society throughout history. The concept of 'violence in the family' is generally used in the context of child abuse; indeed, most of our knowledge about family violence comes from research on child abuse. In this study, our primary concern is the silent female victim of family violence, who has so far been selectively ignored in Turkey. This selective inattention on the part of researchers and clinicians reinforces cultural barriers against women identifying battering as a reason for seeking help. It is, therefore, essential for psychiatric teams to differentiate and recognize the battered women reluctant to disclose this intrafamilial violence among their referrals from quite different complaints (Rounsailler and Weisman 1986). We designed a study to see whether any of the particular factors linked with violence could reliably distinguish couples with a history of domestic violence: (1) individual (or psychiatric); (2) social-psychological; or (3) socio-cultural. The hypotheses we wanted to test in this study fell into these three frameworks.

According to the first model, the male offender's personality characteristics are the main determinant of violence. We tested to see if alcohol consumption, jealousy or other psychological problems in the male offender could on their own explain wife abuse. Second, we wanted to see whether the transmission of violence from one generation to the next was a significant precursor to violence, as the social–psychological model predicts. According to this view, men who are wife abusers have witnessed such behaviour in their own families as children. Finally, a macrolevel analysis would suggest an association between socioeconomic status and violence towards women. We tested the assumption that battering is a phenomenon that exists only in families with low socioeconomic status in society.

Underlying these assumptions is the common myth of the inevitability of conjugal violence by men, given the right circumstances. Questions such as why a loss of self-control due to alcohol abuse should result in selective violence towards the wife; why wife-beating due to jealousy is often interpreted in a highly segregated society like Turkey as an expression of masculine commitment, and not as an illegitimate means of controlling female sexuality; and why only husbands are justified in suffering from the effects of economic hardship, never get asked.

The survey

The subjects for this study were 140 married women between the ages of 18 and 58. The women were selected randomly among the clients admitted to the psychiatric clinic at the Faculty of Medicine, University of Istanbul. The first group of participants (VG) consisted of 80 women with a story of repeated violence,[1] as well as several psychological problems. The second group (NVDG) included 30 women who sought help for their psychological and psychosomatic problems, as well as marital difficulties, but did not have a story of conjugal violence. The last group (NVNDG) was composed of 30 women who did not express any marital problems, but suffered from different psychological and psychosomatic problems.

Subjects in the study first individually filled in a questionnaire of seventy-six questions. This questionnaire yielded data on sociodemographic characteristics; the frequency and degree of violence, if it existed, as well as factors leading to violence; the attitudes of family members, social network, and medical personnel to the incidence of violence; and other aspects of marriage. After the subject finished answering the questionnaire, she was interviewed by one of the authors of the survey. The husbands of the women were asked to cooperate, but only a few accepted, and even fewer participated in and successfully completed the joint therapy. Therefore the interpretation of our findings is limited to data from our women subjects.

The survey yielded the following results. The age of marriage for women ranged between 13 and 51, with the majority marrying at the age of 25 or younger. The abused group were the youngest married in the sample. In all cases but three, it was the woman's first marriage. The percentage of those who had married through mutual consent and those whose marriages had been arranged by their families were similar in both groups. All the women (12) who married without their families' consent were in VG, and half of them had married under 17.

The results indicate that although 39 per cent of the battered women witnessed violence as children, only husbands' experiences (65 per cent) were significantly related to the present occurrence of violence. Furthermore, in 28 per cent of marriages, both husband and wife reported encountering violence in childhood. Alcohol consumption was significantly most problematic in VG families; however, men's excessive jealousy and psychological problems were not found to be significantly related to violence. The educational and occupational backgrounds of women subjects and their husbands varied over a wide spectrum. The findings indicate that 41 per cent of women in VG and 44 per cent of their husbands were educated at high-school level or above. Only men's educational level was found to have a statistically significant relationship to violence. Although the distribution of occupations was not significant, all of the unemployed men were in VG. In the same group, 14 per cent of women and 20 per cent of their husbands had a stable business life.[2]

When and under which conditions do mental health professionals have a chance to see battered women? With the exception of 6 cases who came with the direct purpose of avoiding physical assault, the majority of women reached us with psychological and psychosomatic complaints. If we attempt to list the syndromes observed in the women in the order of frequency of appearance, the most common was depression. There was a history of attempted suicide in a quarter of the women, half of which were recurrent attempts. The second most common cause was bodily disorders. Common problems observed were headache, insomnia, gastro-intestinal problems, fainting, pain and/or paraesthesia in legs and arms; and other bodily sensations such as palpitations, tremors, anxiety, feelings of despondency or hopelessness. Generally, women believed that their problems had a physical cause. This perception, which was exaggerated in some instances, could be a source of difficulty and anxiety by itself. The referral cases were mostly drug-resistant and had several symptoms that showed recurrence.

The question of why women do not terminate an abusive relationship has stimulated much controversy. A simplistic explanation has been that women stay because of their masochism. In order to explore the validity of this ideology, we questioned them on their marital sex lives. Findings suggest that only a limited number of battered women were satisfied with their sex lives, and the situation of women whose husbands forced them to submit to sexual intercourse should not be ignored. A quarter of the women in VG tried to leave the house on one or more occasions, although these attempts had only a temporary effect. Only 6 women (8 per cent) actually tried divorce, which had a permanent effect on the situation. The number of children, and lack of perceived alternatives after divorce, were other constraints in battered women's lives which influenced their decision to continue their relationships. Although relative differences in the number of children between the three groups were not significant, it is noteworthy that 61 per cent of women in the VG had at least two children, and 20 per cent had four or more. One quarter had no expectation of an income or of receiving support from the family in terms of money or shelter. However, the number of women who thought they could sustain their lives by working in jobs for which they were qualified did not differ among the three groups.

The origins of domestic violence

Our results confirm the earlier findings of a relationship between younger marital age and conjugal violence (Gelles, 1976). All of the women who had married against the will of their families, and most of those under 20, were in the violence group. When the battering started these women had more difficulty in disclosing their problems and seeking help from their families. Our results provide partial support for the notion that 'violence begets violence'; that if violence was the model of resolving conflict in the man's parental home, he has little prospect of learning new skills when adult (Gayford, 1975; Coleman and Weisman, 1980; Schumacher, 1985).

According to the psychiatric model, we would expect to find a significant relationship between wife-battering and alcohol abuse, as well as jealousy and psychological disorders in the husband. However, we did not study enough factors to explain this phenomenon. The need for future research, to determine the psychological factors differentiating abusive from non-abusive husbands, is apparent. The abuse of alcohol by husbands involved in conjugal violence is a consistent finding (Gelles, 1976; Pizzey, 1974). In our study, husbands of the abused wives were reported to use significantly more alcohol than did the nonviolent husbands. This does not necessarily indicate that alcoholism causes battering. It is possible that alcohol provides a temporary escape from other problems, and functions as a trigger, rather than a cause, for the expression of violence in an individual who is already prone to it. However, it must be remembered that this violence under the effect of alcohol is selectively limited to the wife, while control is maintained towards other people (Davidson, 1978). It was understood from our abused subjects that their husbands did not engage in violence towards other people in the community.

Data on socioeconomic status provide cross-cultural evidence against the hypothesis that violence is more prevalent in families with low socioeconomic status (Gelles, 1980). Our findings support the fact that wife abuse can be found in families across the whole socioeconomic spectrum. There was a significant number of economically and occupationally stable men among the wife-abusers in our sample.

Our previous research has pointed to a reluctance on the part of violent husbands to participate in therapy (Yüksel and Kayır, 1986). In this study also, violent men were mostly indifferent to their wives' therapy. The husbands' noncooperation had a disruptive effect on the treatment, and on any attempts to change the situation (Szinovacz, 1983; Telch, 1984). It was observed that many of the abused women made unsuccessful attempts to leave the house, and a few of them attempted a divorce. These findings challenge the hypothesis that battered women do not try to leave the abusive relationship. Further research is needed to uncover the factors enabling a woman to pursue and obtain a divorce (Boegard, 1984; Waites, 1977).

Violent couples were observed to be different from nonviolent couples in many respects. It seems that any model for the eruption of conjugal violence must integrate social, economic, cultural, familial, and psychological factors. We can conclude that none of the above-mentioned factors could alone explain a violent situation. The vitally important problems experienced by this group of women at mortal risk should not be considered without getting rid of the predominant myths and prejudices surrounding them (Boegard, 1984; Hilberman, 1980; Martin, 1981). Professionals interviewing these women should help them to understand that the situation is not normal or common; and that violence cannot be rationalized by alcohol consumption, unemployment and other economic problems. The interviewer should be especially careful not to imply by any means that women provoke such situations by being neurotic and naggy; or that they are expected to avoid violence by remaining patient and keeping quiet. If we want to elicit the real situation, we should also keep in mind that women will often try to mislead the interviewer by using the mechanism of denial, and making different excuses.

It could be argued that, beyond recognizing the syndrome, one cannot go very far in such cases. However true this may be, we must remember that recognizing and expressing a problem are the first steps toward its resolution. Our proposition is that this issue, which we know for sure to be widespread, should not be neglected and ignored but recognized and discussed as a major problem calling for urgent action. In our culture and other cultures with similar characteristics, in which attributes of leadership and dominance are reinforced in men while the virtues of patience and servitude are expected of women, the inevitable outcome is that men have a great deal of control over women's lives. It should not be surprising that this mechanism of control should find expression in physical violence. Domestic violence is not merely an infliction of bodily injury but also a form of control embodying contempt and insult, which limits a woman's rights over her own body and her life.[3]

Conclusion

So far I have been reporting the results derived from an experimental group of women who have experienced violence, and the differences between these results and those of other groups of women whose problems did not include marital violence. But my relations with these 80 women were not restricted to the survey. Women were provided with counselling, and some were taken into short- or long-term therapy, while interviews were conducted with their children and husbands. The framework was much wider than that of a psychiatric clinic or psychotherapy. The research team gained an intimate knowledge of interfamilial violence, and this knowledge was shared with other colleagues.

It was emphasized to the subjects that what they had suffered was not their fault; we tried to enable them to form the link between being a woman and being exposed to violence. We aimed at improving their coping mechanisms through raising their self-esteem. They kept on visiting us whenever in trouble, bringing their children and neighbours along with them. Perhaps they felt less guilty about their problem, which came and went. But the basic long term violence to which they were exposed persisted. Of course, there is much more that needs to be done about violence against women, including outside of the psychiatric clinics and hospitals. In the next section I would like to discuss an important campaign, led by feminists from Ankara and Istanbul, against violence against women and violence in the family.

The campaign against battering

On 17 May 1987 a march was organized by feminists from various groups. This was the first time that women were voicing a demand related exclusively to themselves and their bodies. The occasion was a court decision to the effect that the husband's battering was not grounds for divorce in a court case in which a woman had had a miscarriage as a result of her husband's abuse. After the march, which caused quite a stir among women, a decision was taken to start a special campaign about this issue. The Campaign Against Battering was led by a flexible and informal organization. *The Feminist Journal*, The Association of Women Against Discrimination, socialist feminists and women who did not belong to any particular group were among those who initiated and led the campaign. In short, the campaign was open to all women who were sensitive to this issue.

The second major step in the campaign was the publication of the jointly authored book *Cry, Let Everyone Hear* (1988), which contained the first-person accounts of twenty-three battered women. The taboo on talking about violence against women had been broken. The book and the topic were being discussed not only by feminists but in all kinds of settings. In the meanwhile, battered women were asking the campaign for help to improve their lives. Women from the campaign were giving counselling over the phone, and showing their solidarity with battered women by keeping up a guard in their homes.

The Turkish version of this paper originally came to an end at this point. But important new developments have since occurred, which I will summarize in the next section.

Epilogue: Purple Roof

The women participating in the campaign thought it was the preliminary step to founding a shelter. However, at that time it was extremely difficult to get organized, to obtain an official identity and to carry out the type of work done in associations. After long deliberations it was decided that the most convenient way of being structured would be by means of a foundation.

The first obstacle, the guarantee money required to initiate a foundation, was received from an institution in Germany. Thus 'Purple Roof – Women's Shelter Foundation' was founded in 1990 as an independent and non-governmental organization. It did not have a continuous source of income, and neither did it receive any critical support. Purple Roof was expected to survive through the efforts of volunteers and donations. Apart from trained volunteers who were to be on duty once a week, there was only one paid member of staff, who fulfilled the role of administrator, secretary, and every other required person when the shelter started. Under these circumstances and being aware of our inexperience in this field it was decided that what should be established in this first stage was a counselling centre, not a shelter.

As a part of the preliminary preparations the first volunteer group was trained under the supervision of a psychologist who had had experience in shelters. In the training sessions, interview methods suitable to the women who had applied to the centre because of the violence to which they were exposed in their families, as well as the content of our suggestions, were discussed. The first goal was to provide legal and psychological counselling and to finding suitable jobs and nurseries for women with children. The centre aimed to create conditions which would bring women together, so that people in need could communicate and share their problems, as well as help them develop their initiative, social abilities and autonomy. In order to help the women's self-confidence, long-term group meetings were suggested. On first applying to the centre, a woman would have a preliminary talk with a volunteer, in which her needs and demands were to be determined. Her further contacts were to be made with the same volunteer, and psychological or legal counselling would be provided according to her needs. Assistance would also be given with problems on accommodation and job placement.

In this framework in the first eighteen months, between November 1990 and May 1992, 350 women applied to Purple Roof because of domestic violence. The majority of these women were legally married, with two or more children. Many of them were between the ages of 20 and 35, the youngest being 17 and the oldest 61. Of all these women, 90 per cent had attended only primary school, were primary school drop-outs or illiterates with no schooling. More than half had never worked, and a considerable number were unemployed at the time of their application. Almost all working women were without qualifications and received low wages. Among the employed applicants, the number of women whose incomes were sufficient to keep themselves and their children was very low. Their husbands also frequently had limited financial resources, and many of them lacked qualifications. The number from traditional families was huge, and violence in their childhood was very common.

In most of the marriages violence became apparent in the first years of the relationship, and women generally attempted to conceal this situation from their own families for a very long period. Cooperative families who try to help their daughters with new opportunities or support such endeavours were very rare, even in cases of serious injuries. The husbands and families of women taking refuge in the shelter were at first full of promises, but similar problems would recur shortly upon the wife's return home. Except for a couple of teenagers trying to escape the sexual assault of their fathers, the rest of the women were seeking help in freeing themselves from the physical, emotional and sexual tyranny of their husbands.

If we compare the battered women who form the survey earlier in the chapter who came to the hospital, and those who applied directly to Purple Roof as a result of violence, similarities in their ages, in the number of children, and their complaints about their husbands are apparent. In both groups similar problems were frequently observed. The causes of violent behaviour and its distribution were about the same. However, in the hospital group, the level of education was higher (middle to high), and there was a higher percentage of working women, especially in jobs requiring qualifications – in short, the number of middle-class women was higher. Nevertheless, in both groups violence started with marriage, and women's families were not in favour of a change in their lifestyles. Women in both groups shared the same feelings of helplessness about escaping this vicious circle: not knowing how to solve the problems, and possessing unrealistic expectations from Purple Roof or from hospital staff; denying or only partly realizing that they were in a difficult situation, their efforts proved to be inadequate. The women had common goals of fleeing from husbands' violence, but their expectations with regard to the realization of their demands varied. These expectations could be listed as follows:

- 'I don't know what to do. I'm confused. You direct me. You decide what I should do.'
- 'My husband told me that he would shoot me if I divorced him. Hide me. I would be willing to work at any job you get for me.'
- 'I need psychological counselling. My husband is ill. That's why he behaves this way. Treat him. Help him to give up alcohol and abusive behaviour' (where the husband has no desire to cooperate).
- 'I need legal counselling. I want to get a divorce. He should hand over the property to me. He should go to the courts, for he has attacked me.'
- A demand for employment for which the applicant is not qualified.

Not having a shelter or the ability to put the applicants on welfare, to provide free legal aid, or to find them jobs that would enable them to live independently, were significant problems. A large number of the applicants needed a shelter. We were able to send only a very limited number of women (10 per cent) and their children to municipal shelters. We suggested that it would be possible for the women to share homes having met each other, and such set-ups took place in emergency situations. Purple Roof volunteers sharing their homes with the women who had run away from their own homes in helpless situations proved an inconvenient solution.

At the time of the establishment of Purple Roof, two other women's shelters were founded by the social-democratic municipalities. However, these shelters reflected the general political outlook of the municipalities, not the outlook of women, and they were run with an authoritarian attitude, resembling that of a traditional girls' dormitory. Moreover, with the election of new mayors, the employees' styles changed. Women from the lowest socioeconomic group, women with no alternatives, applied to Purple Roof when they really felt themselves in an impasse. This was an indication that the women coming to Purple Roof did not accurately represent the number of women battered by their husbands. Some difficulties arose from working in an independent and non-profit making feminist organization. If these had been problematic only in material terms, struggle against violence would perhaps have been less complicated, but the most serious problems arose because our feminist outlook and expectations, and our concept of family, were not compatible with those of the applicants. We had no security forces, and every now and then needed to quiet down wrathful husbands and relatives who were ready to resort to violence at our door. Our principle of giving the individual responsibility for making her own decisions was considered strange and alien by the women, who were not used to deciding for themselves. There was another inner obstacle which was more difficult to break: women brought up with the expectation that the nuclear family was the only route to happiness found it very hard to accept alternative lifestyles, and did not enjoy the prospect of sharing a residence with other women, even to escape their husbands' brutality. Foreseeing these problems we had planned to form self-help groups to foster greater self-confidence and develop new outlooks on life, but the women did not wish to take part in this process and only three or four turned up to 'open door' group meetings.

As there was no shelter we were obliged to supply women with common houses. But serious quarrels took place among the women in the common housing project, and Purple Roof had to pick up the unpaid bills. Every day, we were obliged to solve practical problems for which we were not ready, and this too created confusion and problems among us, as we attempted to evaluate the situation and discussed new suggestions.

To summarize, Purple Roof, the first independent non-governmental women's shelter, was founded in 1990. It received a significant amount of attention from the mass media and women's circles. Violence against women in the family has kept its place on the agenda ever since. Since then, three municipal shelters and a few counselling centres have been opened, and Purple Roof has purchased a building for a shelter.

However, due to financial problems the necessary restoration has not taken place, and the shelter has not been opened to service. Eighteen months after its foundation Purple Roof is still the only non-governmental shelter administered by a women's initiative.[4]

It is my belief that for a long-term solution, feminist endeavours should not be limited to the work at shelters. The struggle should continue on many fronts against the hitherto unexamined male-dominated ideas which are responsible for physical, emotional and sexual violence. The campaign against wife-battering and the Purple Roof project have been a significant experience for the feminists, as the first public feminist campaign and cause, which opened up their methods to new debate. The project became means by which problems about hierarchy, division of labour and many other critical issues were explored for the first time. As I write this in June 1992, the feminists are carrying out intensive discussions about working within a structure, about working methods and especially about their style of address.

Notes

1. There is considerable confusion about the definition of conjugal violence. Women in our sample were subjected to serious and repeated physical injuries as a result of deliberate assaults by their husbands (Yüksel and Kayır 1985).

2. Among women in the violence group there were 5 teachers, 2 nurses, a pharmacist, an architect and an economist. Among their husbands there were 7 businessmen, 3 teachers, 2 doctors, 1 lawyer, and 1 architect.

3. This control is economic as well as physical, as Turkey does not have a system of welfare or unemployment benefit which would enable a woman to leave a violent partner on whom she is economically dependent.

4. A report has now been prepared by Purple Roof on the first year and a half of its existence.

References

Boegard, M. (1984). 'Family systems approaches to wife battering: a feminist critique', in *American Journal of Ortopsychiatry*, no. 54, p. 558.

Davidson, T. (1987). *Conjugal violence*. Ballantine Books, New York.

Gayford, J.J. (1975). 'Wife battering: a preliminary survey of 100 cases', *British Medical Journal*, no. 1, 194–7.

Gelles, R.J.J. (1976). 'Abused wives: why do they stay?' in *Journal of Marriage and the Family*, no. 38, pp. 659–668.

Martin, D. (1981). *Battered Wives*. Volcano Press Inc., San Francisco.

Roussauille, B., and M.M. Weissman (1986). 'Battered women: a medical problem requiring detection', in *International Journal of Psychiatry in*

Medicine, 8, pp. 191–202.

Telch, C.H. (1984). 'Violent versus nonviolent couples: a comparison of patterns', *Psychiatry*, no. 27, pp. 242–248.

Yüksel, Ş. (1985). 'Özel' bir Şiddet, Düşün, 6, pp. 78–82.

Yüksel, Ş., A. Kayır (1985). 'Identification of wife battering in psychiatric practice' Paper presented in World Psychiatry Association Regional Symposium, 11–18 October 1985, Athens.

Yüksel, Ş., A. Kayır (1986), 'Comparison of violent and non-violent families'. Psychiatry Congress, Regional Meeting, August. Copenhagen.

Women and their Sexual Problems in Turkey

Arşalus Kayır

In this chapter, I aim to discuss the questions arising from the cases of women referred to hospital in order to seek solutions to their sexual problems. This research was carried out in the psychoneurosis outpatients' clinic in the psychiatry department at the Faculty of Medicine of Istanbul University. In 1979 a modern unit was established which used the approach of 'milieu therapy', in which a team consisting of psychiatrist, psychologist and nurse began to apply psychotherapy to neurotic female patients. In the treatment of the sexual problems we adopted the 'sex therapy' method of Masters and Johnson, which began to be applied in the West in the 1970s. As word got round inside and outside the hospital that sexual problems were being treated, the number of referrals, especially of women, began to grow; and since the mid 1980s, there has been a considerable increase in the number of applicants. Drawing on the experience of fourteen years I can now say that a certain system has been developed in our approach to the types and treatment of the sexual problems in this society.

A few years ago a 'unit for studying sexual functions' was established in the Cerrahpaşa Medical Faculty of Istanbul University. In this centre, a multidisciplinary team worked on the research and treatment of male sexual dysfunctions exclusively. The First National Congress of Sexual Functions and Dysfunctions in Turkey was held in 1988, and research papers were presented on the subject. The fact that two prominent medical faculties had begun to investigate sexual problems, and that these studies were made available to the public, encouraged people to refer themselves to hospitals without hesitation. On the one hand this was a positive improvement; on the other, however, it led to the idea that each sexual problem is an 'illness' that can be treated by doctors. For instance, it became harder to make a woman with an obvious marriage conflict to understand that her low sexual desire originated from the marriage. Still, direct complaints about sexual problems should be regarded as an improvement in this direction.

We live in a society where it is commonly believed that sex is a physiological necessity for men, whereas a woman is entitled to sexual experience only after marriage. Thus, men have the right to get to know their sexuality and to make sexual explorations, but women can express their sexuality only after their future husbands appear. This age for women may be as low as 12 in rural areas, against the young girl's wishes; it may, however, be as late as 35, depending on when the spouse appears. Before marriage, it is not common for young boys and girls to establish relationships, or to date. This type of relationship is usually carried out secretly, without the knowledge of the parents and always with the fear of being caught. Under this pressure, it is only natural that the first relationship established inevitably ends up in marriage. When sexuality starts in secret experiences, with accompanying fears of damaging the family's sense of honour and feelings of guilt, the foundations are prepared for future sexual problems even before the marriage has been realized. In many cases the woman does not have the right to choose the man she is going to marry, and if she is in love with one man, it is highly probable that she will be forced to marry another who is preferred by her family.

The woman's feelings are disregarded first by her father and then by her husband; for her, there is no such thing as being sexually attracted. Even if she had had a choice, it would not be possible for her to be aware of this sexual attraction before marriage, i.e. without sexual experience. In the young girl's imagination, sexual intercourse is identified either with extraordinary pleasure or as an activity to be feared and avoided. Sexual relations with inexperienced partners inevitably end in disappointment.

Asking for professional help for psychological disorders is generally postponed in Turkish society. And when sexual problems, especially problems related with female sexuality, are in question, we are faced with over-delayed cases, which are therefore difficult to cure. When a sexual problem makes itself felt and continues as it is, does the responsibility lie only with the person suffering from the problem? It is seldom possible to be referred to a suitable place of treatment. What kind of a person the therapist is and the form of treatment are also very important. Being knowledgeable and experienced may be enough for other types of medical services, but this is not the case for the treatment of sexual problems. An ideal therapist must be expert at tackling sexual matters with a relaxed and direct attitude, sensitive to the erotic feelings of both sexes, and also flexible. We do not consider sex therapy that focuses only on sexual behaviour to be adequate. The method we have chosen employs the general principles of psychotherapy in a multidimensional approach geared towards the couple's relationship rather than the individuals involved.

The different types of therapy we have been applying include individual therapy, couple therapy, marriage therapy, and sex therapy groups for men and women sharing similar problems. Sexual disorders are the expressions of sexual conflicts, anxieties, frustrations and also of erroneous or incomplete education in these subjects, and each person receiving therapy is at the same time undergoing a process of learning. The educating role of the therapist becomes all the more important and necessary, the less basic sexual knowledge the patient possesses (Kayır, Tükel, et al., 1986).

The main sexual problems we have observed in the women who referred to us are lack of arousal, low sexual desire, vaginismus, lack of orgasm, sexual aversion (especially in cases of incest and rape), homosexuality and transsexuality. Our experience is largely based on vaginismus, as a greater number of cases have been referred to us, and to a lesser degree on cases of low sexual desire and lack of orgasm. In the following section of the chapter, the results obtained from the research carried out by our team in the Faculty of Psychiatry on female sexual dysfunctions will be summarized.

The incidence of vaginismus

Women coming to us with complaints of vaginismus, together with their husbands, were included in the first two study groups. Vaginismus consists of an involuntary spasm of the muscles surrounding the vaginal entrance whenever penetration is attempted. The treatment was generally applied by two different therapists, one female and the other male. Forty-four couples were evaluated altogether; they were all referred to us with vaginismus and, although they had been living together for a minimum of six months, they had not yet been able to accomplish sexual intercourse in spite of their willingness to do so. The 40 of these couples who did not have marital conflicts were taken into the treatment.

Some of the findings in the evaluation of these women and their spouses were as follows. The women who were not able to accomplish sexual intercourse had first applied to a gynaecologist. However, 8 women said that they had been humiliated and reprimanded because of their problems, and thus their fears were reinforced. It is a sad fact that this attitude, of which we encountered more examples in the following years, mostly pertained to female gynaecologists. The majority of the group consisted of women 20 to 29 years old. The duration of their marriages ranged from six months to twelve years. Of these women 3 were unmarried. A great majority of them (32 couples) told us that they had married of their own free will. It was significant for us that the proportion of university graduates and professionals was high among these couples (Tables 17.1, 17.2).

Table 17.1 Duration of marriage

Years	Number of couples
less than 1	7
1–2	11
3–4	14
5–7	7
8–12	5
m=3.79	sd=3.31

Table 17.2 Level of education

	Men	Women
No education	1	–
Primary school	7	4
High school	18	17
University	18	23

Most of the women (26) were born in big cities, and 12 of them had to move to another city after their marriage, 6 against their wishes. Twelve of the couples stated that their main problem was the inability to have children. Twelve of the women said that they masturbated, while 18 others confessed that they were shy of and repulsed by touching their genital organs. The limited knowledge of sex observed in both sexes was striking. It was established that both males and females in this group mostly came from families in which traditional values dominated; 30 of the women and 23 of the men had traditional and/or religious families.

The relationship between the vaginismic women and their husbands was examined in two parts: the relationship before and after marriage. It was found that in terms of their relationship with spouses, in 8 out of 44 couples there was no sexual closeness and the relationship was limited to emotional closeness only; in the others foreplay (petting and cuddling) was attempted, and that in 4 couples sexual intercourse had been attempted but was not finalized. Only 2 of the women had had limited love-making experience with a man other than their husband. No women in this group had tried sexual intercourse with a man other than their husbands. Of the men, 33 had had sexual intercourse limited only to prostitutes, and 8 of the men had had no sexual intercourse at all. When sexual intercourse after marriage was investigated, it was seen that, faced with vaginismus, 13 men were intolerant and threatened to divorce their wives, while the rest were defined as 'understanding' by their wives.

In terms of sexual activities, although the attitudes of the women were conflicting, 35 women had no arousal problem.

Of the women 36 were orgasmic with clitoral stimulation: the high orgasm rate in the vaginismus cases were parallel to Kaplan's findings (Kayır, Yüksel, et al., 1987). The fact that 23 of the women gradually shied away from sex on account of their fear of sexual intercourse was evaluated as low sexual desire by their spouses, even by the women themselves. Thus, men were kept in the position of constantly suggesting sex but always being refused. As a result, both partners defined the men as having 'excessively high sexual desire'. During the treatment, the difference between men's suggestions and their practice became more apparent as women's desire increased. The party who brought up the suggestion of lovemaking and the one who refused it thus changed places. It was seen that 13 men had various sexual dysfunctions, which they had previously suffered from, and 9 men had fear of sexual intercourse. On the first night of their marriage, 6 men had tried sexual intercourse without any foreplay and 7 men had preferred to postpone intercourse without even attempting it. And 7 of the men who were unable to have full experience of sex had begun to beat their wives within the first month.

The origins of sexual dysfunction

In our next study, women with sexual dysfunction were compared with a group of neurotic women Yüksel Tükel et al., 1988. A total number of 90 married women were included in the research, 60 of whom had come to us with complaints of sexual problems and the remaining 30 with neurotic complaints. In both groups, the history of sexual development, acquisition of sexual information, sexual attitude, sexual practice, marital relationship and sociodemographic characteristics were examined, and the similarities and differences were established. Some of the results obtained were as follows. The length of marriage of the women, whose ages ranged between 18 and 25, was 6.35 in the sexual dysfunction group and 10.56 in the control group. In terms of educational level, the SD (sexual dysfunction) group had a high proportion of university graduates (38 per cent) and 48 per cent of the control group were graduates of high school. In both groups, more than half of the women worked outside the home, and only one-third were housewives. In the sexual dysfunction group, 21 per cent had strict religious upbringing; but this rate was only 1 per cent in the control group. In the SD group the family was the source of sexual information in 31.6

per cent of cases, whereas in the control group the percentage was 16.6. The duration of the sexual problems varied from 6 months to 20 years, with an average of 5.35 years. While all the vaginismus cases had first referred to a gynaecologist, the low sexual desire and non-orgasmic cases had applied to psychiatrists first. In terms of diagnosis, the SD group had the highest rate of vaginismus or painful sexual intercourse, at 65 per cent; in the control group lack of orgasm was the case for 33 per cent.

When the quality of the relationship between the couples in both groups was examined, it was seen that both groups had marital problems. Some 38 per cent of the couples in the SD group and 23 per cent of the couples in the control group suffered from sexual dysfunctions of which the main problem was premature ejaculation. Seventy-seven per cent of the women in the SD group and 63 per cent of those in the control group said they found their husbands attractive. Before their marriage, 20 per cent of the women had had no sexual closeness with the opposite sex, and 13 per cent had had full sexual intercourse (Table 17.3). One woman in 4 of the SD group, and one woman in 6 of the control group said they had feelings of aversion, shame and guilt after sexual intercourse (Motovallı, Yücel, et al., 1991).

Table 17.3 Distribution of women's sexual contact with men before marriage

	SD group no.	SD group %	Control group no.	Control group %
No contact	12	20	6	20
Emotional closeness only	6	10	3	10
Kissing–caressing	12	20	7	23.3
Petting	20	33.3	10	33.3
Sexual intercourse	10	16.6	4	13.3
Total	60	100	30	100

Group therapy

The common approach for sexual problems is to apply individual or couple therapy. Group therapies focusing on the sexual dysfunction of one gender, without the participation of the partner, have been experimented on in recent years. Studies concerning women are more frequently conducted in the case of anorgasmic disorders. Taking into consideration the predominance of social factors in the generation of vaginismus, and the frequency of referrals, in 1989 we applied group therapy for the first time in cases with this disorder, presuming that the group dynamics would be therapeutically more beneficial for them (Sarımurat and Kayır, 1989).

During the research period two groups were treated, one consisting of 6 and the other of 8 married women (14 in total) whose ages varied between 16 and 30 and the duration of whose marriages varied from three months to eleven years. Five of these women had married with the help of intermediaries, and 9 had met their spouses and chosen them freely. In the group, there was one women who had had a child; she had had a normal birth but had still not been able to accomplish sexual intercourse.

In sex therapy conducted in groups emphasis was placed on the following themes, as they were found to be particularly pertinent to this society: style of upbringing; family attitude; the necessity of protecting virginity until marriage; a woman's unwillingness to give up her virginity, as required by the conventional behaviour and beliefs; unrealistic expectations, either positive or negative, regarding the marriage night or marriage in general; the concept of honour in women; avoidance of intercourse for phobic reasons; the attitude of the partners towards vaginismus; the universality of sexual difficulties; to what extent the subject is ready to pass from maidenhood into womanhood, etc. Ten women out of 14 accomplished sexual intercourse as a result of the therapy (71 per cent). The subjects in the group often received more useful and effective advice and information from the other participants in the group than from the suggestions of the therapists themselves. We observed that women in couple therapy worried about hurting their husbands, and this prevented progress in therapy. Groups consisting only of women did away with these types of worries. In a therapy program of this kind, the woman's spouse is not paid much attention, and so the possibility of building up defences is lessened. The woman, who has been suffering from a sense of inadequacy, takes on responsibility and gives up her attitude of postponing the problem; as she gets more self-confident she decides the direction of therapy herself.

In conclusion, we can say that we consider sex therapy groups to be a good field for sexual education, as they relax sexual taboos and offer women the possibility of evaluating themselves and others. For this reason, we can suggest that group therapy is a suitable model in our society, where there is no sex education.

The partner's role in sexual dysfunction

In 1990 we aimed to obtain detailed data over a period of one year about both men and women coming to us with sexual dysfunctions (Kayır, Geyran, et al., 1990). The total number referred to us with sexual problems was 161 (of whom 82 were women and 79 men). We want here to indicate some of the results regarding mainly women.

Of the sexual dysfunctions in women 52 per cent were cases of vaginismus; 25 per cent cases of low sexual desire; 15 per cent of anorgasmy, and 2 per cent of dyspareunia. A total of 96 per cent of the women and 56 per cent of the men were married. Twenty-six of the married women had marital problems; 35 of the men had complaints regarding the sexual attitude of their partners; 42 of the women had sexual complaints related with their partners, which were: premature ejaculation (20 subjects), undesirable sexual attitude (14 subjects), and erectile dysfunction (8 subjects). More than half of the 76 women experienced clitoral orgasm.

Arousal problem in two married women was thought to be related to homosexuality and so no treatment was suggested. The duration of foreplay was found to be more than ten minutes in 60 of the women applying with complaints of vaginismus and less than ten minutes in 70 per cent of those complaining of low sexual desire. This duration was over fifteen minutes in 50 per cent of the anorgasmic women. The duration of marriage in those applying for treatment for sexual problems ranged from under one year to over ten years (Table 17.4).

Sex therapy groups has been applied to 18 women with complaints of vaginismus, and of those undergoing therapy 61 per cent were cured. Out of a total number of 15 women with complaints of low sexual desire and lack of orgasm, 3 have

Table 17.4 Sexual problems of men and women

Woman's sexual problem	Referral form		Marriage problem		Sexual problem concerning the partner			Orgasm	
	Individual	Couple	Yes	No	Premature ejaculation	Erectile dysfunction	Sexual attitude	Clitoral	Coital
Vaginismus	19	21	12	27	9	5	9	38	–
Lack of sexual desire	14	5	8	10	5	1	2	3	2
Anorgasmy	13	2	4	10	6	2	1	3	–
Dyspareunia	2	–	2	–	–	–	2	2	–
Total	48	28	26	47	20	8	14	46	2

improved. And in the therapies of individuals or couples, 68 per cent of the women with complaints of vaginismus, 2 of the 11 women with low sexual desire, and 1 out of the 8 women with problems of anorgasmy have been cured.

It was interesting for us to notice that women and men applied for treatment in the same proportion. However, the fact that vaginismus referrals were greater in number raised the proportion of the female applicants. Among the applicants, one woman and 17 men were single, a proportion which suggests that women are not generally aware of their sexuality until they get married. Again, the fact that there were no women over 44 among the applicants may lead us to think that women disregard sexuality after a certain age, just as they do before marriage. The high rate of complaints about partners, among both women and men, shows that, to a large extent, sexual problems cannot be considered independently of the partners. Possibly, the fact that a large number of women do experience orgasm is related to the frequency of cases of vaginismus, in so far as, in many such cases, foreplay is not a prelude to sexual intercourse. There seems to be no relationship between lengthy foreplay and orgasm as, for those women who fail to attain orgasm the duration of foreplay is reportedly the longest; a fact that is apparently in conflict with the relationship between short foreplay and anorgasmy. This, however, may be explained by the fact that the majority of anorgasmic women – and in many cases their husbands, too – used the term 'trying', that is, endeavouring to enable the woman to attain orgasm through prolonged foreplay. But this fixation on orgasm militates against the woman experiencing pleasure and thus, the longer the foreplay continues with the salient aim of inducing orgasm, the less likely it is to occur.

Women's sexual beliefs

Another research study carried out in 1991 looked at three groups of women with the aim of observing the extent to which sexual experience was influenced by consolidated sexual beliefs (Motovallı, Yücel, et al., 1991). The first two groups consisted of those referred to the hospital for sexual dysfunction (30 subjects) and those who had various neurotic complaints (30); another group of 30 was formed of women who had never referred to any psychiatric clinics before. Thirty out of the 40 women applying with sexual problems turned out to be cases of vaginismus as usual; 6 were cases of low sexual desire and 4 of anorgasmy. The mean age was 30 and the level of education was generally high-school or university. We gave all of these 90 women, the 'Sexual Myths Scale' and the 'Sexual History Form'. Our findings were as follows. The statement, 'If sex is really good then partners have orgasms simultaneously' was considered correct by all three groups and received the highest score; this was followed by the statements, 'Sex should always be natural and spontaneous: thinking or talking about it spoils it' and 'A man always wants sex and is always ready to have sex'. The items that received low scores and were considered incorrect by all of the three groups were the following: 'Any woman who initiates sex is immoral'; 'Men should not express their feelings'; 'A man cannot say no to sex/a women cannot say no to sex'.

When we had compiled the results of this study, we thought it significant that, compared to the other groups of women, those who suffered sexual dysfunctions were least prone to accept conventional beliefs. Twenty out of the 30 women in this group had had vaginismus, and throughout their marriage (seven-and-a-half years on average) sexual problems were a constant difficulty in their lives, for which solutions were being sought. One could speculate that these women's husbands might often have adopted the role of the 'understanding spouse', and that this might have helped undo the adverse effects of conventional beliefs. In women among the normal population, belief in sexual myths seems to be much more prevalent. Among this group, an inability to discuss sexual problems with their partners or others, and a belief that these types of problems do not deserve to be considered at length, have been effective factors in consolidating erroneous beliefs.

Husbands' attitudes to treatment

In our last study, which took place in 1992, we studied the roles of partners in delaying treatment for vaginismus (Kayır and Şahin, 1992). Positive results can generally be obtained in the treatment of vaginismus. However, at that stage of the treatment in which sexual intercourse is approached, common symptoms may emerge, such as a weakening of the motivation for therapy in the couples undergoing treatment. In this study, we wanted to look into the roles played by the partners in the extension of the problem throughout the treatment period.

Seven women who had been diagnosed as having vaginismus and their husbands were included in the research programme.

The duration of their marriages ranged from six months to eight years, while the ages of the men ranged from 24 to 40. Throughout the therapy period, these couples were seen at regular intervals, and their relations and attitudes evaluated.

In men, traits such as lack of sexual self-confidence, limited sexual experience, fear of injuring their sexual partners, confusing sexual activity with sexual aggression, and taking pleasure in not being an aggressive man, were observed. It could be said that, in a sense, they were enjoying themselves as the 'understanding' husbands who deserved to be loved by their wives. As was indicated in our earlier studies, when women and couples are referred to us with complaints of vaginismus, women are generally introduced as the party who avoids sexual intercourse and is suffering from the problem, while men are usually introduced as having no sexual problems and being the 'understanding' and patient partner. However, our reserach showed that men had adopted a delaying attitude towards sexual intercourse as much as, and sometimes even more than, their wives did. In fact, at the end of the therapy period, the improvement did not bring them the pleasure and happiness in the degree that they had expected, nor was there an increase in the frequency of sex.

Conclusion

In the light of fourteen years of clinical practice and research, I would like to discuss how women in Turkey experience their sexuality. My ideas on this subject stem from the fact that I have had the chance of witnessing each woman discovering her sexuality step by step throughout the treatment process. It was a remarkable point for us that the vaginismus cases, which are said to be rare and 100 per cent treatable in Western culture, have no parallel in the findings in Turkey. The proportion of vaginismus cases is not only high in Turkey, but they are also rather difficult to treat. In 1986, 32 vaginismus cases were referred to us within eight months; in 1987 the 23 vaginismus cases made up 38 per cent of referrals for sexual dysfunctions within a period of ten months; in 1990 the rate was 52 per cent. However Arentewicz and Schmidt found this proportion to be only 12 per cent in research carried out in Hamburg in 1983.

Taking into consideration how important virginity is still considered to be in Turkey, the frequency of vaginismus cases should be seen as alarming rather than surprising. Most young girls when they have been constantly warned to protect their hymens experience difficulties in their first sexual intercourse. In 44 cases of vaginismus, 24 subjects were afraid of the nuptial act. Sexual fears of experiencing a lot of physical pain, or that their vagina would be torn or constantly bleeding consolidated these fears. To some women, the idea of accomplishing marriage seemed almost a miracle, which shows the extent to which they were exaggerating the importance of sexual intercourse. Young people raised under these circumstances cannot be expected to behave in a relaxed and experienced way the moment they get married.

The vaginismic women's husbands' participation in treatment is much higher than in the treatment of other types of sexual problems, as not only is the husband's sexual pleasure limited, but also the possibility of having a child is decreased. This problem, which is generally kept as a secret between the couple, is sometimes found out by the family, who then get involved. They are concerned as to the possibility of treatment, almost bargaining with the therapist; their first reaction to failure in treatment is to push for a divorce. This treatment of the vaginismic woman as if she were defective makes her feel deficient; newly married or pregnant women give vaginismic women the feeling that they themselves are not female enough. When vaginismic women and their husbands are over-fond of and over-dependent on their families or have to live together with the family, the problem is made even worse.

Vaginismic women refer themselves to us relatively readily because they need to seek a solution to their problems; the number of referrals for low sexual desire and anorgasmy is relatively smaller, as these women are shy of 'seeking after pleasure'. Most of them came to us without their husband's knowledge, hiding behind other types of psychological problems. And in such cases, a lack of cooperation on the part of the husband has a negative effect on the results of the treatment. Husbands have a strong tendency to blame their wives exclusively for the problem, and the number of husbands who look at their wives' low sexual desire with a slight satisfaction, as if they do not want them to change, is far from negligible. Sometimes the husband who engages in an extra-marital affair justifies this illegal relationship by the 'coldness' of his wife, and thus consolidates the ideology of female 'frigidity'. Sex therapy naturally brings no relief in such cases. Men have a strong and widespread tendency to regard their wives as having low sexual desire. However, it is interesting to find that only 2 out of 60 of the sexual dysfunction group of women, and 1 out of 30 of the neurotic women, found the sex to be more frequent than their desire. In spite of some sexual difficulties, women generally complained of insufficient sex and of the lack of physical closeness. They also said that when they felt estranged from their husbands emotionally, they refused their husbands' offers of sexual intercourse in astonishment and anger.

Although the number of referrals for anorgasmy is not high, many women confuse low sexual desire and arousal problems with anorgasmy. A woman who cannot be sexually aroused usually comes to us with the complaint 'I am not satisfied', that is, 'I don't experience orgasm.' She only states the result, skipping over the process of lovemaking. A significant number of the women who had been orgasmic when petting and cuddling without actual sexual intercourse during engagement or dating said that they gradually became anorgasmic after they had got married. To a large extent, this stems from the fact that sexual intercourse and coital orgasm are adopted as goals after marriage. The reason why three-quarters of vaginismic women are orgasmic is that sexual intercourse cannot be accomplished. In the sexual dysfunction group 29 out of 60 complained of coital anorgasmy and 10 out of 30 in the control group did so. In most cases, it is not surprising that the women could not experience orgasm with the type of lovemaking described. In fact women can find sex satisfactory in spite of irregular orgasms as long as orgasm is not considered a problem.

At the beginning of the therapy, women stated that they often experienced extended foreplay as an extraordinary emotional closeness, expressing it with joy. During treatment, the biggest change is effected by the couple providing feedback to each other without fearing criticism. This leads to the couple getting even more pleasure out of this joint experience, and after they have established a certain dialogue they both have the desire to add to their discoveries. It was observed that women benefitted more than men from sexual treatment. Indeed, women believed in the importance of the communication established between partners, and also grasped the importance of this type of communication earlier and more easily; whereas men did not seem to believe that psychological reasons could cause sexual problems, and were also non-committal and felt vulnerable when they were expected to learn new things about their sexuality. Training the couples to notice and emphasize the positive aspects of each other had a lasting effect, although it took a considerable time. Sometimes, a single word heard from the mouth of the partner has the magic power of accomplishing what several special techniques cannot.

Men may sometimes emphasize the needs of their wives while simultaneously not considering them to be important. In such cases it is very useful to point out the differences between women and men in terms of thinking, feeling, perceptions, behaviour and needs, and also in terms of expectations. During the treatment, when an increase is observed in the sexual desire of the woman, the husband's desire may be lessened or he may start creating problems. This is a sign that the harmony and balance in the marriage actually rests on a specific sexual problem. It is not so easy to shake off the power relationship in such cases and to finish the treatment.

Sexuality should be a matter of education, but the initial stage of that education is in the family. However, what is being preached and what is being experienced at home are two different things. Parents give their children the impression that they are less interested in sexuality than they really are. In general, fathers are regarded as having more sexual desire than mothers. Mothers usually submit to their husbands' desire, and daughters grow up with the example of women who appear to be 'without any sexual desire'. Mothers repress their sexuality feeling that they would raise their children more healthily that way, but in the meantime they forget that they are women, and as a result, girls' sexuality is repressed. Little girls who are 'caught' masturbating are immediately rushed to the doctor, while boys courting girls are admired and encouraged. In our research, only 43 out of the 90 women said they had masturbated, and some of this experience occurred after marriage, whereas almost 100 per cent of men had masturbated.

A woman's beliefs about her body and sexuality, as relayed through her husband's evaluation, are usually far from being correct. For instance, a women who has fear of sexual intercourse and therefore shies away from it is often regarded by her husband as having low sexual desire. Unfortunately the woman herself is eventually convinced that this is really the case. I believe that our main task is to show how wrong it is for women to get to know their bodies through the evaluations of their husbands. The sexual experience of most of the men usually depends on a few instances of sexual intercourse with prostitutes, and so sexual difficulties can be tied to both partners' lack of skill and experience.

Last but not least, we should try to find an answer to the question, 'What is the role of the sex therapist in helping women enjoy their sexuality better?' Relying on my experience with a group of women whose treatment I followed carefully, I can say with confidence that there is every reason to be optimistic about sexual therapy given to women. It is essential that teams concerned with women's problems should be understanding, patient, sensitive, and reliable. Although we cannot accommodate large groups because of the limited possibilities in hospitals, I still consider it important to cater to individuals. I do not think it is a negligible accomplishment that 100 women have been enlightened within a period of one year, for we should also take into consideration the children they will be raising and the other women and men with whom they will be in contact. I usually emphasize that they should share what they have learned with those who might need this type of information. Whatever her cultural level may be, when a woman is with a cooperative partner she learns to express her sexuality and gets to know her body very quickly. And then, she is willing to put into practice what she has learned, which raises our hopes for this type of therapy. What accelerates this process is not only supplying women with correct information, but also the follow-up on their experiences in the process of psychotherapy. We see striking changes taking place when they begin to experience sexual arousal. The fact that women can start experiencing sexual pleasure, in spite of all the sexual repressions and taboos, makes us therapists feel as much excitement and happiness as do the women who come to us with sexual problems.

In sexual therapy groups that consist exclusively of women, those common female problems stemming from the way society raises its children are raised, and we feel hopeful because women's ingrained sense of insufficiency is transformed into self-confidence in a relatively short time. Here again, group solidarity, adopting others as examples, seeing that one is not unique, the universality of the problems and experience – all of these contribute to lighten the problem and speed up the process of change. Supplying information, discussing sexual taboos and repressions, and tackling marital relationship make up the content of most of our psychotherapy sessions. Even if the reasons for referral are not completely transcended, it can be observed that the individuals have learned new things about their womanhood. More often than not, the women themselves follow their own development with interest, get to know their bodies better and learn how to inhabit them with ease.

In conclusion, we can say that the most important job we accomplish is to give back to women the sexuality that had been taken away from them before and after marriage, and to make them aware of the right and responsibility of using it as they please.

References

Arentewicz, G., and G. Schmidt (1983). *The Treatment of Sexual Disorders*, Basic Books, New York.

Hawton, K. (1985). *Sex Therapy: A Practical Guide*, New York.

Kaplan, H.S. (1974). *The New Sex Therapy*, Brunner/Mazel, New York.

Kayır, A. (1988). 'Attitudes and interactions in sex therapy', *Proceedings* of 24th National Congress of Psychiatric and Neurological Sciences, 19–23 September, Ankara.

Kayır, A. (1989). 'Sexuality and sexual treatment in women', *Sendrom* (Syndrome Monthly Medical Journal), vol. 1, no. 2, pp. 14–30. Istanbul.

Kayır, A., P. Geyran, M.R. Tükel and A. Kızıltuğ (1990). 'Referral characteristics of sexual problems and choice of treatment', *Proceedings* of 24th National Congress of Psychiatric and Neurology Sciences, vol. 2, 1–4 November, İzmir.

Kayır, A. and D. Şahin (1992). 'Roles of the partners in delaying the treatment of vaginismus', presented at the 28th National Congress of Psychiatry, September 27–30, Ankara.

Kayır, A., M.R. Tükel and Ş. Yüksel (1986a). 'Treatment of vaginismus and its difficulties', paper presented at the 18th European Congress of Behavior Therapy, Lausanne.

Kayır, A., M.R. Tükel and Ş. Yüksel (1986b). 'Vaginismus and treatment', *Proceedings* of National Congress of Psychiatric and Neurological Sciences, October 29–November 1, Marmaris.

Kayır, A., Ş. Yüksel and M.R. Tükel (1987). 'Discussion on the causes of vaginismus', *Psychology Monthly*, Special Issue on National Congress of Psychology, vol. 6, no. 21, Ankara.

Motovallı, N., B. Yücel, A. Kayır and A. Üçok (1991). 'Evaluation of sexual beliefs and experiences in women', *Archives of Neuropsychiatry*, vol. 28, nos. 2–4.

O'Sullivan, K., and J. Barnes (1978). 'Vaginismus: a report on 46 couples', *Journal of the Irish Medical Association* March 31, vol. 71, no. 5.

Sarımurat, N., and A. Kayır (1989). 'Group psychotherapy in vaginismus', *Proceedings* of 25th National Congress of Psychiatric and Neurological Sciences, October 15–21, Mersin.

Yüksel, Ş., M.R. Tükel, A. Kayır and N. Sarımurat (1988). 'A socio-demographic comparison of women with sexual dysfunctions to the control group of neurotic female patients and an evaluation of marital relationships'. Paper presented at the 1st National Congress of Sexual Functions and Dysfunctions, Istanbul.

Patterns of Patriarchy: Notes for an Analysis of Male Dominance in Turkish Society

Deniz Kandiyoti

The aim of this chapter is to propose a tentative agenda for an exploration of changing forms of male dominance in Turkish society. Although patriarchy is a problematic concept which is the subject of an ongoing critique,[1] I retain it here to refer to a range of institutional and cultural practices resulting in the subordination of women.

I am adopting the position that neither universalistic assumptions about gender oppression nor the reduction of such oppression to particularism and difference can further our understanding of specific patternings of power and dominance and their changes through time.[2] In that spirit I have argued elsewhere[3] that the operations of different kinship systems also define distinct systems of male dominance which circumscribe women's life options, inform their survival strategies and influence their forms of resistance and struggle. Using a broad comparative perspective, I situated Turkey, together with most of the Middle East, South and East Asia, in the historical region of 'classic patriarchy' where senior males hold authority in patrilocally extended households. Among the structural features of this form of patriarchy are patterns of deference based on age, distinct male and female hierarchies and a relative separation of their spheres of activity (which may be institutionalized in practices of spatial segregation), and an appropriation of women's labour and reproductive capacities by the patrilineage into which they marry. Since the actual incidence of this form of householding is quite variable even in the areas designated classically patriarchal,[4] I used it primarily as an ideal-type to explore the ways in which women at different points in their life-cycle may accommodate or attempt to subvert a particular form of male dominance in the family. I also considered the various ways in which this system may be eroded under the impact of a wide range of socioeconomic changes, ranging from the forced sedentarization and loss of autonomy of nomadic tribes to the commoditization of peasant agriculture to the various processes of urbanization and migration of labour.[5] I attempted to show how changes in the material conditions of production and reproduction created new areas of uncertainty and a renegotiation of relationships based on age and gender which are reflected in new processes of household-formation and family dynamics. This analysis thus inscribes itself among approaches which privilege the institutions of marriage and the family as the most important site of patriarchal relations.

In this chapter I would like to argue that whilst this level of analysis is undoubtedly important it can yield only partial and limited insights into the mechanisms of male dominance. Gender asymmetry in Turkish society is produced, represented and reproduced through a wide variety of cultural practices that extend beyond household, class and labour market. It is therefore important that we broaden our agenda to include the whole range of social institutions which are implicated structurally, relationally and symbolically in the reproduction of gender. However, in doing so, we can no longer pursue the woman-centred 'checklist' approach which has gained considerable currency in women's studies in Turkey (such as women and the law, work, education, politics, the media, etc.). First, because this deflects us from extending our analyses to institutions which specifically exclude or marginalize women, like the Turkish army, but are centrally responsible for the production of masculinity and masculine identities. It is difficult to account for the fact that questions pertaining to masculine identities in Turkey, which are central to an understanding of patriarchy, have so far escaped any form of systematic scrutiny. Second, because there is no possibility of achieving some cumulative model or understanding of the different facets of gender subordination by enumerating the contexts in which they occur. Social institutions do not merely reflect some unitary patriarchal logic but are the site of power relations and political processes through which gender hierarchies are both created and contested.

In this case, a potentially fruitful avenue for feminist research in Turkey would be to explore the tensions and contradictions between gender practices and ideologies implicit in different institutional spheres.[6] For instance, the Turkish state has moved to curtail the legitimacy of domestic patriarchy: directly, through family legislation, and indirectly, through the inclusion of women in the definition of full 'citizenship'. It has on the other hand continued to endorse discriminatory practices in employment, education and social welfare. The absence or weakness of public welfare provisions has acted to perpetuate women's caretaker roles with relation to children, the sick and the elderly. Meanwhile in an economic climate aggravated by the economic policies of the eighties and nineties, women's monetary contributions have become increasingly crucial to the survival of households. This has expanded the pool of potential female workers who can be utilized in the low-waged sectors of the economy in part-time or intermittent jobs, in non-unionized small workshop production or in other forms of home-based or so-called 'informal sector' activities. Despite the fact that women's entry into the labour market often takes place under unfavourable terms, it may still be instrumental towards a partial renegotiation of their marital contracts and may force some redefinition of the sexual division of labour in the household (see Bolak, this volume).

However, this occurs against an ideological background of growing conservatism concerning the appropriate place and conduct of women. It is noteworthy, for instance, that the endemic political debate about secularism and Westernization in Turkey is yet again targeting women as the prime bearers of either Islamic authenticity or secular emancipation.[7] This was evidenced recently in the 'headscarf debate' and the legislative skirmishes that accompanied it.[8] It is also reflected in the growing output of the Islamist media (see Acar and Arat, this volume). We are witnessing an extensive 'politicization' of gender. All major contenders for state power are formulating relatively explicit platforms on a whole range of women's rights issues and attempting to co-opt women into their party apparatus. Conversely, a seemingly gender-neutral phenomenon such as inflation is having gender-specific effects on voting preferences, since more women than men mention it as their most important grievance against the government, a fact that reflects their growing role in the daily management of the family budget. There is little doubt that an active and growing female political constituency is having some effect, especially in view of the strong evidence that women voters do act independently of their male kin (see Güneş-Ayata, this volume). However, Turkish women as social actors bear the full set of contradictions implied by their class and geographical locations, and have no unified conception of their gender interests, as evidenced by a plurality of movements ranging from Islamist tendencies to varieties of secular feminist platforms.

Turkish society is thus riven by powerful cross-currents producing complex and often contradictory effects, acting both to reinforce and to mitigate the manifestations of male dominance in different institutional contexts. The language and models we have used as social scientists have served to reveal certain aspects of these contradictions and to mask or ignore others. An extensive reevaluation of our working assumptions is therefore in order, alongside an attempt to deepen our understanding of the specificities of the institutionalization of gender in Turkey. Since such a broad agenda is impossible to address in a short chapter, I will limit myself to a brief illustration by analysing the evolution of discourses on women and the family. This discussion aims to reflect both the changing patterns of male dominance in Turkish society and the shifts in the language used to express such changes. I will conclude with possible directions for future research.

Women, the family and the discourse of modernity

At the turn of the 19th century and the beginning of the 20th a wave of vocal protest erupted against Ottoman marriage customs and more generally the plight of Turkish women. Most of these protesters were upper- and middle-class men who were allowed by *sharia* law to marry up to four wives, supplement them by an unspecified number of concubines, repudiate them at will and exercise strict control over their mobility outside the household. Since this phenomenon of apparent male feminism extended to other parts of the Middle East as well as to the Third World generally, it naturally attracted a lot of scholarly attention.

Jayawardena,[9] for instance, links the emergence of such feminist movements to anti-imperialist and nationalist struggles, a general move towards secularism, a concern with social reform and modernity and the rise of an 'enlightened' indigenous middle class. Cole,[10] in his analysis of turn-of-the-century Egypt, also points to the importance of emerging class cleavages between upper-middle-class reformers like Qasim Amin who championed the emancipation of women, and lower-middle-class intellectuals like Talat Harb who felt threatened by it. At the heart of this conflict lay their different orientations to and links with European powers: the former was integrated both economically and culturally into their sphere of influence; the latter, marginalized and threatened by it. Thus women's emancipation became closely identified and confused with a modernism that in fact consisted of 'Westernism', a fact that is regularly invoked as the 'original sin' of feminism in the Middle East.[11]

However, this justifiable preoccupation with the tensions between Westernism, modernity and cultural authenticity (mainly expressed as an attachment to Islamic values and practices) has deflected our attention from a crucial issue: What exactly did these male reformers want for *themselves*? Which aspects of their domestic existence did they find so intolerable? This is where the work of Ottoman male novelists proves extremely enlightening;[12] they apparently no longer wanted arranged marriages, controlled and manoeuvred by their older female relatives; they desired romantic involvement and love, educated wives with whom they could have intellectual communication, a social life where the sexes could mingle freely without fear of scandal or gossip – in short, freedom from the oppressive conventions of traditional Ottoman life. This was neither a superficial emulation of the West, nor quite the rise of what Stone[13] calls 'affective individualism' in the nuclear family. It undoubtedly was a form of male rebellion against Ottoman patriarchy in the family, and one that could only succeed if they carried the women of their generation along with them. Most of the same men no longer wished to be the subjects of an absolutist monarch, the Absolute Patriarch, but hankered for citizenship under constitutional rule, an ambition that was to be realized by the Young Turks after the 1908 takeover by the Committee for Union and Progress.

It is after this period that ideologies concerning women and the family took a decisive and truly original turn. Turkish nationalism, finding its ideological expression in the Turkist currents of the Second Constitutional Period, introduced new elements into the debate which had so far remained caught between the terms of Westernism and Islam. Cultural nationalism started appropriating for itself as indigenous Turkish patterns many of the features of what could have passed for modernity. The leading ideologue of this current, Ziya Gökalp, asserted for instance that ancient Central Asiatic patterns involved total equality between conjugal partners in a monogamous and democratic family. More importantly, the CUP made an attempt to incorporate this vision into their family policies. Toprak's analysis of the National Family (*Milli Aile*) and of the social policies of the CUP is extremely pertinent in this respect.[14] The 1917 Family Code was an expression of these policies and represents the first incursion of the central state into the realm of the family, which had previously been under the exclusive purview of the religious authorities of the various Ottoman *millets* (who vigorously resisted such incursion).

It is however with Kemalism and the transition to the republic that we encounter a major break. Mustafa Kemal Atatürk went further than any Young Turk (many of whom still had imperial pretensions) could have anticipated, in dismantling the central institutions of Ottoman Islam. Not only did he abolish the caliphate and secularized every sphere of life but he took measures to heighten Turkey's 'Turkish' national consciousness at the expense of a wider Islamic identification; the compulsory romanization of the alphabet, the new dress code and an elaborate rereading of Turkish history stressing its pre-Islamic cultural heritage were important elements of the cultural mobilization in the service of the new state. The secularization of the family code and the enfranchisement of women were, as Tekeli[15] quite correctly points out, part of a broader struggle to liquidate the theocratic remnants of the Ottoman state and create a new legitimizing state ideology.

Meanwhile, the 'new woman' of the Turkish republic became a prominent figure in the iconography of the regime; parading in shorts and bearing the flag, in school or military uniform, or in Western evening dress in ballroom-dancing scenes. Atatürk himself significantly adopted daughters in this male-oriented society in which boy preference was the rule. A whole generation of highly trained women professionals started swelling the ranks of republican cadres.[16] The new regime seemed to signal the beginning of a different era for the women of Turkey.

Initially, these changes affected only a small urban layer. Much of the Anatolian hinterland remained weakly integrated to markets, and agriculture was unevenly commoditized. The penetration of society by the central state and its apparatus was variable, remaining confined in many areas to conscription and the extraction of taxes. The spread of schooling and health services proceeded gradually. Little had taken place to erode the material basis of classic patriarchy, as indicated by anthropological studies carried out as late as the 1950s.[17] As far as women and marriage alliances were concerned, these remained firmly under the control of local communities and followed customary practices, which were now denounced as 'traditional' or even 'backward' by the enlightened technocrats of the republic. The discourse on tradition and modernity acquired a new dimension, and the civilizing gaze turned inwards. 'Tradition' was no longer used to designate Ottoman mores versus the West, but those of the urban elite versus villagers and tribesmen.

Capital penetration into rural areas after the 1950s is excellently documented. All we need to note from it for our purposes is that two seasons of agricultural mechanization succeeded where the republican reforms had failed. Domestic patriarchy was threatened and patriarchal authority in the family challenged by new processes of stratification and avenues for mobility. The erosion of status experienced by one category of men – generally older, less literate and politically marginal – in no way implied a loss of status for men as a category; instead, the bases of male dominance were being redefined and renegotiated. Authority could no longer be derived from status in the domestic sphere, the village or the lineage. New material and symbolic resources such as capital, education, access to patronage and political clientship assumed crucial importance. Men's continued ability to act as patriarchs in their own households was increasingly mediated by access to extra-domestic resources.[18] Furthermore, the pace and content of these changes were regionally uneven and diverse.

Turkey had become more than ever a country where a myriad of different gender regimes in the family coexisted historically. However, the language adopted to describe this variety and diversity was, for a long time, that of modernization theory. Turkey was assumed to be embarked upon a trajectory leading from tradition to modernity, with corresponding structures for the family and conjugal relations. Sociological and demographic studies described the extended family as rural and traditional, and the nuclear family as modern and urban. Household compositions defying this classification were assumed to be 'transitional'. The idealized model of the 'modern' nuclear family involved companionate marriage, role-sharing between spouses and child-orientation. Ironically, at a time when this type of conjugal family was being denounced as the site of women's oppression in the West, it was held out as a more liberated state of being in Turkey, as well as in other parts of the Middle East. This vision was by no means totally misguided; it celebrated the greater autonomy of the young heterosexual couple from interference and control by older kin. If we take Mernissi's[19] arguments seriously concerning the cultural pressures against exclusive forms of heterosexual intimacy in Muslim societies, the ideology of the modern nuclear family may have appeared a fresh and radical departure.

One of the major shortcomings of the language of modernization was undoubtedly its conceptually impoverishing effect. The demographic emphasis on household compositions and typologies, and the use of role theory to describe sexual divisions of labour, prevented us from recognizing distinct gender regimes for what they were: genuinely different expressions of power and authority in the family – or to use Poster's[20] terminology, different patterns of love and authority. We ended up with relatively little information about the emotional interior of family lives in different social strata, or on the dynamics of gender in each context.

There were of course notable exceptions to this trend. Kıray,[21] who was the first to spot the tensions occasioned by the crisis of legitimacy of fathers' authority over sons, commented on how mothers acted to mediate such conflicts and noted the changing value placed on daughters, who now often replaced sons as the 'dependable' child. Olson[22] suggested that the Turkish nuclear family, despite the structural similarities to its Western counterpart, allowed for a much greater extent of separation of the spheres of activity and involvement of spouses. Kağıtçıbaşı[23] argued that the 'modern' Turkish family did not exhibit the pattern of separateness and autonomy of members from one another and their wider kin which modernization theory implied, but one of continued emotional interdependence. In a sensitive analysis, Ayata[24] commented on the joint reproduction of class status and the role of the housewife through an examination of the patterns of use of the guest room, which is a feature of urban middle-class 'apartment' living. This study reveals that the tensions between images of tradition and modernity are being lived concretely in Turkish households as a literal 'split': between the styles of consumption, formal dress and conduct displayed in the guest room; and those adopted in the intimate inner space of the rest of the house, which is a place of informality and closeness. Bolak's study in this volume provides a fine-grained analysis of the negotiation of conjugal rights and responsibilities among working-class couples. There is a growing trend towards micro-analyses which will undoubtedly enrich our understanding of the operations of gender and class in Turkish family life.

However, there has been a gradual but definite shift from acknowledging the role and agency of the state in shaping gender relations and their ideological representations, to marginalizing or ignoring it. This may have stemmed in part from a reaction against first-generation Kemalist feminists' propagandistic emphasis on republican reforms and their assumed efficacy in changing the condition of women. Social scientists (this author included) could more readily relate the transformations in the family and gender relations to the changing material conditions of production and reproduction and to new patterns of social stratification. The state often figured as a remote agent whose social and economic policies had indirect and possibly unintended consequences on patriarchy in the family. The ways in which forms of male domination were created and reproduced by the state itself through a whole range of social institutions and practices received only partial and unsystematic attention. Nor were the connections between earlier state-sponsored 'feminism' and the authoritarian nature of the single-party state's attempts to harness women to the creation of a uniform citizenry ever made fully explicit.[25] Moreover, the earlier emphasis on legal reforms as a major transformative tool had obscured equally important but less tangible ideological interventions in the realm of gender, such as the production of new male and female identities. It could be argued that the terms of modernity and tradition also came to represent important but unacknowledged differences in patterns of masculinity and femininity. These patterns nonetheless informed the lifestyles and gendered subjectivities of consecutive generations of men and women in the late Ottoman and republican era.[26]

I argued elsewhere[27] that women's entry into public life in Turkey was partly legitimated through the projection of an 'asexual' or even slightly masculinized identity. As members of a strictly segregated society, in which male honour is dependent on the behaviour of their womenfolk, women could only enter the public arena by emitting very powerful signals of their respectability and non-availability as sexual objects. The unveiled 'new woman' of the republic embodied a whole code and language to delimit new boundaries: severe two-piece suits, simple short hairstyles and a lack of make-up were not simply the predilection of dedicated working women who had no time for frivolity, but could also act as a powerful symbolic armour. Even Arat's[28] relatively recent study of women politicians conveys the continuing pressure on women in public roles to act as 'honorary men' and to de-emphasize their gender identity. That such pressures also exist in other societies does not diminish the urgency of analysing specific cultural codes and their effects on the patterning of masculinity and femininity. At present, we do not seem to have found an adequate language to articulate such concerns as social scientists. Indeed, our women fiction writers, unencumbered by the models of the various social science disciplines, have already ventured into this difficult terrain with courage, sensitivity and often with humour.

In summary, I am proposing that we broaden our agenda to include the whole range of social institutions and practices which are implicated in the creation and reproduction of gender hierarchies, that we pay particular attention to the tensions and contradictions implicit in different institutional spheres, and that we probe into the production of specific forms of masculinity and femininity in the Turkish context. An exploration of these areas would force us to consider a host of important questions. What are the key contexts and social practices instrumental in the patterning of gender? What are the possible relationships between class and gender codes? What contending forms of masculinity and femininity does Turkish society display? What sorts of ideologies are mobilized to articulate these differences? What role do forms of power and domination among men play in the reproduction of patriarchy? What are the relationships between institutionalized modes of coercion and violence and the production of specific male identities? These questions at present enter almost uncharted territory. We may well discover that concentrating on men and masculinity in relation only to the subordination of women, rather than in the broader context of the institutionalization of forms of power and domination in Turkish society, ultimately detracts from our understanding of the workings of patriarchy. I conclude with a keen awareness that this chapter has raised more questions than it has answered, and of the tentative nature of its proposals. However, if it makes a contribution to stimulating debate it will have fulfilled its purpose.

Notes

1. For relatively recent examples see: M. Walters, 'Patriarchy and viriarchy: an exploration and reconstruction of concepts of masculine domination', *Sociology*, vol. 23, no. 3, 1989, pp. 193–211; S. Walby, 'Theorising patriarchy', *Sociology*, vol. 23, no. 2, 1989, pp. 213–34; J. Acker, 'The problem with patriarchy', *Sociology*, vol. 23, no. 2, 1989, pp. 235–40. Also, M. Mann, 'A crisis in stratification theory: persons, households/families/lineages, genders, classes and nations', in *Gender and Stratification*, ed. R. Compton and M. Mann, Polity Press, Cambridge 1986. Arguments range from the inappropriateness of the term patriarchy to describe the domination of men in post-industrial societies to the necessity of theorizing gender (which is implicated in the constitution of all social life) rather than patriarchy, which smacks of the sorts of totalizing categories which post-structuralist feminists did so much to combat. I am sympathetic to the latter position, provided that it treats gender not only as sexual difference but as sexual hierarchy, keeping power as a central term in understanding gender. Since some confusion still exists on this issue, I will use the term patriarchy despite its shortcomings because it conveys inequality and hierarchy in a way that gender does not.
2. For a useful discussion of such questions see L. Alcoff, 'Cultural feminism versus post-structuralism: the identity crisis in feminist theory', *Signs*, vol. 13, no. 3, 1988, pp. 405–36. Also, M. Barrett and A. Phillips, eds. *Destabilizing Theory: Contemporary Feminist Debates*, Polity Press, Oxford 1992.
3. D. Kandiyoti, 'Bargaining with patriarchy', *Gender and Society*, vol. 2, no. 3, 1988, pp. 274–90. The different forms of male dominance alluded to in this work are not meant to convey monolithic and homogenous systems of patriarchy but 'family resemblances'.
4. For an analysis of demographic factors curtailing this pattern in Ottoman-Turkish households see A. Duben, 'Nineteenth and twentieth century Ottoman-Turkish family and household structures', in *Family in Turkish Society*, ed. T. Erder, Turkish Social Science Association, Ankara 1985.
5. D. Kandiyoti, 'Sex roles and social change: a comparative appraisal of Turkey's women', in *Women and National Development*, ed. Wellesley Editorial Committee, University of Chicago Press, Chicago 1977; D. Kandiyoti, 'Rural transformation in Turkey and its implications for women's status', in *Women on the Move*, Unesco, Paris 1984.
6. I also find R. W. Connell's use of the term 'gender regimes' to denote the state of play of sexual politics in different institutions extremely useful, and

refer to it in this text. See R.W. Connell, *Gender and Power*, Stanford University Press, Stanford 1987.

7. For the historical precedents to this tendency, see D. Kandiyoti, 'End of empire: Islam, nationalism and women in Turkey', in D. Kandiyoti, ed., *Women, Islam and the State*, Macmillan, London 1991.

8. This debate was provoked by the deletion of a stipulation from the dress code for university students requiring them to attend class in 'contemporary forms of costume'. This amendment, which was interpreted as legal permission to wear the Islamic headdress, was annulled by the Supreme Court through the direct intervention of the president, and triggered protests and demonstrations from students demanding the right to wear headscarves.

9. K. Jayawardena, *Feminism and Nationalism in the Third World*, Zed Press, London 1988.

10. J.R. Cole, 'Feminism, class and Islam in turn-of-the century Egypt', *International Journal of Middle East Studies*, no. 13, 1981, pp. 387–407.

11. See, for instance, L. Ahmed, *Women and Gender in Islam*, Yale University Press, New Haven 1992.

12. D. Kandiyoti, 'Slave girls, temptresses and comrades: images of women in the Turkish novel', *Feminist Issues*, vol. 8, no. 1, 1988, pp. 35–50. For a detailed and rewarding discussion of the polemics around Ottoman domestic mores at the turn of the century, see A. Duben and C. Behar, *Istanbul Households: Marriage, Family and Fertility, 1880–1940*, Cambridge University Press, Cambridge 1991.

13. L. Stone, *The Family, Sex and Marriage in England, 1500–1800*, Weidenfeld & Nicolson, London 1977.

14. Z. Toprak, 'The family, feminism and the state during the Young Turk period, 1908–1918', paper presented at the Workshop on Turkish Family and Domestic Organization, New York, 23–25 April 1986.

15. Ş. Tekeli, 'Women in Turkish politics', in *Women in Turkish Society*, ed. N. Abadan-Unat, E.J. Brill, Leiden 1981.

16. A. Oncu, 'Turkish women in the professions: why so many?', in *Women in Turkish Society*.

17. See, for example, P. Stirling, *Turkish Village*, John Wiley, New York 1965.

18. D. Kandiyoti, 'Social change and social stratification in a Turkish village', *Journal of Peasant Studies*, no. 2, 1974, pp. 206–19.

19. F. Mernissi, *Beyond the Veil*, Al Saqi Books, London 1985.

20. M. Poster, *Critical Theory of the Family*, Pluto Press, London 1982.

21. M. Kıray, 'Changing roles of mothers: changing intra-family relations in a Turkish town', in *Mediterranean Family Structure*, ed. J. Peristiany, Cambridge University Press, Cambridge 1976.

22. E. Olson, 'Duofocal family and an alternative model of husband–wife relationships', in *Sex Roles, Family and Community in Turkey*, ed. C. Kağıtçıbaşı, Indiana Turkish Studies, Bloomington 1982.

23. C. Kağıtçıbaşı, 'Intra-family interaction and a model of change', in *Family in Turkish Society*.

24. S. Ayata, 'Statü Yarışması ve Salon Kullanımı', *Toplum ve Bilim*, no. 42, 1988, pp. 5–25.

25. For a discussion of this issue see D. Kandiyoti, 'End of empire: Islam,

nationalism and women in Turkey', Nora Şeni further argues that there is a continuity between the imperial edicts of the sixteenth century making women's attire and movements the object of direct legislation, and later more modernist attempts on women's behalf, including republican reforms, since they emanate from the same authoritarian state tradition. N. Şeni, 'Ville Ottomane et représentation du corps féminin', Les Temps Modernes, no. 456–7, 1984, pp. 66–95.

26. Surprisingly little has been written on the question of gendered subjectivities. A useful beginning on the question of female identity may be found in A. Durakbaşa, 'Cumhurıyet Döneminde Kemalist Kadın Kinliginin Oluşumu', Tarih ve Toplum, vol. 9, no. 52, 1988, pp. 167–71. On masculine identities see D. Kandiyoti, 'The paradoxes of masculinity: some thoughts on segregated societies', in A. Cornwall and N. Lindisfarne, eds., Dislocating Masculinity: Comparative Ethnographies, Routledge, London forthcoming.

27. D. Kandiyoti, 'Slave girls, temptresses and comrades', and 'Women and the Turkish State: Political Actors or Symbolic Pawns?', pp. 45–6.

28. Y. Arat, 'Obstacles to political careers: perceptions of Turkish women', International Political Science Review, vol. 6, no. 3, 1985, pp. 355–6.

Index